Louise Cooper began writing stories when she was at school to entertain her friends. She continued to write and her first full-length novel was published when she was only twenty years old. Since then she has become a prolific writer of fantasy, renowned for her bestselling *Time Master* trilogy. Her other interests include music, folklore, mythology and comparative religion. She lives in Worcestershire. Her latest novel, THE KING'S DEMON, is also available from Headline Feature.

'One of fantasy's finest talents ... Ms Cooper melds rich, imaginative concepts, superlative language skills and intense emotional colouring into a stunning reading experience' *R*A*V*E Reviews Magazine*

'Never has the battle of order and chaos been better recorded than in Louise Cooper's magnificent trilogy. She has a sharp understanding of human ambiguity, a gift for narrative and a wonderfully original imagination' Michael Moorcock

Sacrament of Night

Louise Cooper

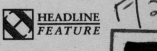

HEADLINE
FEATURE

First published in 1997
by HEADLINE BOOK PUBLISHING

First published in paperback in 1998
by HEADLINE BOOK PUBLISHING

A HEADLINE FEATURE paperback

10 9 8 7 6 5 4 3 2 1

ISBN 0 7472 5372 2

Printed and bound in Great Britain by
Mackays of Chatham PLC, Chatham, Kent

HEADLINE BOOK PUBLISHING
A division of Hodder Headline PLC
338 Euston Road
London NW1 3BH

Remembering the Charn of another name and nature . . . and remembering, too, that though the moon's light may be eclipsed from time to time by shadow, it is merely hidden, and not truly extinguished.

You meaner beauties of the night
Which poorly satisfy men's eyes
More with your number than your light;
You common people of the skies,
What are you when moon doth rise?

(Michael East, c. 1580–1648)

Prologue

Calling to the stars. Not with words, for she could no longer find the words, not now, not after so many years. But something within her was calling, crying still.

Each evening as the daylight fled she would move to her window and gaze out and up, waiting for darkness to come, watching for the first faint pinpoints to show against the sky's velvet. When that first tiny light appeared, she wept. It was an old, familiar ritual with her now, and in a strange way it brought a little comfort, though she no longer understood why. As more stars began to follow the first harbinger, her tears faded and her vision cleared once more, and she simply gazed, silent, rapt, alone with the thoughts that drifted like ghosts through her damaged mind.

There was never enough time for watching. Never enough *time*, before the other lights, the cruel lights, took the stars away. The lamplighters, moving through the town streets to kindle their small, harsh fires. The hospice angels, crisp and rustling in white linen, bringing lanterns that she didn't want but had no words to refuse. And the moon. She hated the moon's light above all others; when it shone, there was room for nothing else in the sky, and each evening as she saw its bland face rising she would clench her fists and beat them against her own upper arms, railing in silent fury. The lamps; the lanterns; the moon. All to drive the night back, keep it at bay, hold it fast lest *they* should come: the twilight ones, strange and cold and fragile as the stars, who moved in darkness and could not bear the blaze of day. So afraid. Everyone was so *afraid*, and they would not see, and would not learn, and would not give her the darkness that allowed the door to open.

Yet she had closed the door with her own hand. That much she knew, with a terrible certainty that lodged like iron in her and, unlike the stars, did not diminish. She had closed it, turned

1

her face away and tried to return to the light. But light had nothing to give her, and so she had come to this place and would remain here, where people cared for her and were kind to her and took such pains to ensure that she would never, ever be alone in the dark again. She did not speak to them; there was nothing she could say that they would understand, and she had passed so much time in silence now that they thought she had no voice. But she had a voice. She knew it in . . . ah no; not in her heart, for that was withered, long withered, like the hearts of the willow trees in the garden. She could see the willows from her window, away beyond the lawns which she would not walk on, beyond the beds of flowers which she would not look at; abandoned and forgotten in their own small, overgrown wilderness. By day the willows were like flowing green water under the sun, but by night, if the wind blew, their leaves trembled and shimmered with faint silver. Like the stars. And when the lamps and the lanterns and the moon had dimmed the stars and snuffed them out, then sometimes she would remember that she had a voice, and would whisper the words of the old song that her mother had sung to her, a world and a life ago. *Sad is the willow tree; the willow stands apart: for when life is done, the willow wan must perish from the heart* . . . The willows alone knew her secrets, so she sang the song for them, to let them know that she had not forgotten the debt she owed. It was the only tribute she could give now. But if they, and what they guarded, heard her, they sent her no sign.

So at last she would yield to the light, to the lamps and the lanterns and the moon, and would retreat from her window and return to the wooden table and the wooden stool and the work which was never finished. The angels let her have as much clay as she wanted, and water to soften it, and little wooden spatulas to shape and carve it, and they spoke softly and encouragingly to her, urging her to let them see, let them admire. She acquiesced, because the sculptures she made were never right. They were skilled, they were beautiful, but they were never *right*. When the angels had admired and exclaimed and gone away hoping to leave her contented, she would take the sculpture they had praised and twist it, mutilate it, working it with the heel of her hand until it was nothing again. Once, just once, it had been *right*. But never since then. Never.

For twilight was fragile and darkness elusive, and without the dark, the memories could not truly return. *Drive the night back, keep it at bay, hold it fast lest they should come* . . . All she could do was call.

But still there was no answer.

Chapter I

Foss Agate had not wanted to make the visit. These occasions had been an unhappy ordeal from the beginning, and in the last year or two he had begun, privately, to feel that they served only to upset all concerned to no good purpose. But tomorrow was Calliope's birthday, and she had taken the notion into her head that it would somehow be fitting for the whole family – that was, Griette's whole family – to go to the hospice together. Foss thought it a futile exercise, but Calliope had pleaded and Philome, his second wife, said that it was surely not asking too much of him to indulge his eldest daughter on the eve of her special day. So Foss had given way, and as the bell in the hospice's central tower rang to announce the afternoon visiting hour he and his three eldest children duly joined the sad little procession of relatives and friends making their way through the iron gates and along the gravel drive towards the imposing building.

The weather was fine and the spring breeze warm, and some of the inmates – those the Hospice Master tactfully termed the 'less troubled' of his flock – had been allowed into the gardens to walk on the lawns or sit by the ornamental pond where they could enjoy the intricate play of the fountains. Not Griette, though. She was not 'troubled' in the way that some were; she was never violent and could have had many freedoms if she had chosen to take them. But she did not choose, and efforts to persuade her met only with a sad, blank look and a turning away of her face. So, as always, an angel, crisp and rustling in her white gown, led the family through the corridors with soothing blue walls, to the little room, one among so many other little rooms, in the east wing.

The door was not locked, for Griette never tried to leave. She

3

was working at a sculpture when they went in, and although she looked up as the door opened, her face expressed no recognition and she did not acknowledge them, only turned back to the tiny clay shape taking form beneath her hands.

Calliope, who in fifteen years had never become inured to the effect of these first moments, said softly, 'Hello, Mother.' Tears sparkled on her dark lashes; she blinked them away, not wanting the others to see. Her sister Celesta and brother Luthe were already stepping forward to tentatively lay the gifts they had brought on the table where Griette sat. A pot of spring flowers. A shawl, the embroidery kindly and beautifully finished by Philome when Celesta had found it beyond her abilities. Rose and violet sweets – once Griette's favourites – in a box tied with silver ribbon. Griette stared at them all for a few moments, then looked away.

The angel moved soft-footed to the table. 'I'm sorry,' she said and smiled sympathetically at Calliope, at the same time deftly untying the ribbon on the box of sweets. 'She shouldn't have this. We must take the greatest care . . . I'm sure you understand.'

Calliope nodded, taking the ribbon and folding it. Of course. no scarves, no sashes, no belts, no ribbons. Just in case. She had forgotten the rule and the reason for it.

It was time now to enact the familiar ritual once more; to sit on chairs, drink tisane and pretend for a little while that all was as it had been fifteen years ago, before the calamity struck. Calliope alone among Foss's children was old enough to recall that time clearly. She remembered how strange and quiet her mother had become in the moon before the irrevocable blow had fallen. She still dreamed, horribly, of the final two days; Griette in an upstairs room, screaming and screaming and screaming, while her father brought all his medical and alchemical skills to bear and could do nothing for her. Then very early on the third morning the screaming had stopped, and in the shocking aftermath of silence two strangers had come to the house with a litter, and Calliope had stood, with Celesta gripping her hand and Luthe clinging to her skirt, as they put Griette into the litter and closed the doors and bore her away. The expression on her mother's face then was the expression on her face now; a strange, serene yet hopeless emptiness from which all animation had gone. The face of someone who had found a kind of death, but no peace.

4

Griette's mind, the physicians said, was shattered, and no skill known to mankind could repair such damage. But her body was healthy and there was no reason why she shouldn't live out her natural span. So Foss had placed her in the hospice's care, where she would have kindness and attention and protection. He could afford the best of everything; the best she should have. And since the day she was confined he had never, ever spoken abut her madness or its cause.

Now he sat awkwardly holding her hand and trying to make a pretence at conversation, telling her about his patients, the newest town gossip, the progress of his latest ideas for the garden. He even talked of Philome and her two young children, for it did not seem to upset Griette to hear of the woman who, as the law allowed in such cases as these, had taken her former place. Griette appeared to listen and made no effort to pull her hand away, but her eyes looked through Foss and focused somewhere far beyond him, and when she smiled, as she occasionally did, the smiles had no meaning. No matter what was said or who was addressing her, she uttered not a single word.

Even Calliope couldn't help but feel relief when at last the tower bell tolled again. The Hospice Master was flexible about his rules and there would be no hurry to chivvy the visitors out, but Foss grasped at the reprieve and rose quickly to his feet.

'Well, my dear, it seems we must go.' He hesitated, looking down at Griette with an expression of helpless bafflement in which just a faint trace of irritation showed. 'The children will come to see you again next quartermoon, as always, and I shall be back in another moon or so.' It was a lie but he always said it as a matter of habit; in the early days his visits had been much more frequent than they were now. He bent to kiss her brow. 'Goodbye, Griette.'

Calliope, Celesta and Luthe all kissed her in turn, Calliope's lips lingering on her cheek as she whispered, 'Goodbye, dear Mother . . . perhaps next time you'll be able to remember me.'

Griette suffered the kisses and farewells impassively and, as her family moved towards the door, turned back to her sculpture and began to work the clay with steady concentration.

The Hospice Master was at the main doors, with an appropriately sympathetic word or two for each visitor as they left. Knowing what was expected of them, Foss's three children went outside first and waited at a discreet distance while a little conversation ensued and a purse of money changed hands; Foss's regular gift to the hospice to ensure that Griette continued to receive nothing but the best of treatment.

No one had anything to say as they started back down the gravel drive. Foss was frowning uncomfortably; Celesta's face had closed in as she defended herself from her own thoughts, and Luthe simply looked solemn and a little bereft.

Outside the gates a number of carriages were waiting, but as the weather was good and the distance to their home not great, the Agates had elected to walk. The sun was westering now and shadows vastly exaggerated, but although twilight fell quickly at this time of year they would be safely home before dark. They turned down the long, tree-lined slope of Charity Hill and fell into step two by two, Foss and Luthe leading while the girls followed. The spell of silence slowly faded as the hospice and its atmosphere of well-meant but contrived pleasantness fell further behind them, and Foss started to talk about a new piece of scientific equipment that a neighbour had recently acquired and of which he was greatly envious. He was still talking as the hill levelled out and they turned into a broad street that curved round towards the town's main square. Dominating the skyline, the great dome of the Institute of Natural Sciences rose elegant and gleaming against a sky now turning gold and smeared with crimson as the sun touched the horizon. Foss paused in his discourse to squint upwards with a small burst of civic pride – then suddenly Luthe's hand closed on his arm.

'Father. Along Postulants Row – something's to do, by the sound of it.'

Foss turned, blinking in the red afterglare, and looked along the narrow lane leading off the street on the opposite side. There was a noise in the distance, he realised now, faint but distinct; the clamour and shouting of a sizeable crowd. And something else . . . just a flicker at rooftop level, but he would have taken any odds it was more than a trick of the light.

Then a figure appeared at the far end of the lane. A scrawny boy, running fast and banging two metal pots together as he approached them. He was shouting something, but the din of his makeshift alarm drowned out the words.

'*Boy!*' Foss's bellow eclipsed the clangour and he stepped into the way as the child shot out of the lane. 'What is it, what's afoot?'

The boy's face was flushed with excitement. 'It's another one, sir!' he cried. 'Another one's broken through, and they're after it! It's a big one, sir, and it can fly, so I've to go and rouse everyone I can find!'

Foss's eyes lit eagerly. 'Where, boy? Where's the chase on?'

'Down Verity Street and towards the Public Garden, sir!' The boy wriggled past him. 'Your pardon – got to go!' He was away down the street like a bolting cat.

Foss swung round and saw his family looking at him wide-eyed. 'You heard the child? Come – we'll go and see for ourselves!'

They started to run, the girls picking up their skirts with no thought for dignity in the excitement of the moment. As they hastened down Postulants Row Celesta called out breathlessly, 'Father, how long has it been? One hasn't been caught for moons, surely?'

'Three moons or more,' Foss shouted back.

'The child said it's a big one – what could that mean?'

'Doubtless he's exaggerating, as children do, but we'll see. Hurry, now!'

Word was spreading fast, and as they ran they were joined by other townspeople who spilled from houses, shops, workrooms, swelling the tide now converging on the Public Garden. The Garden was in a smaller square behind the town's main market, flanked on three sides by tall, gracious houses and on the fourth by a parade of small but exclusive shops. It was only two streets from the Agate family home, and as the first of the Garden's clipped specimen trees came into view ahead, so did the vanguard of the crowd – and their quarry.

It burst out of a side lane almost too narrow to contain it, and in the light of the setting sun the silver-grey nacre of its body, twice the length of a man's, had turned to blood-red. The huge head, like a grim marriage of toothless reptile and beakless bird, gaped wide, and a high, thin screaming issued from its throat. There was something piteous in the screams, and as Foss slid to a halt at the square's entrance, spreading his arms to stop the others from rushing on past him, Calliope realised that the creature was in pain; terrible pain, which it could only express with this whistling cry.

7

Now she could see it clearly. Its body was slender, almost scrawny, and the featherless, membranous wings that beat frantically above it looked no more substantial than cobwebs. One wing was broken, the area around the break scorched and blackened, and the creature could no longer fly; yet still it was struggling to get airborne, lurching and hopping with a clumsy gait as it careered towards the garden.

Behind it came the mob. There were some seventy pursuers and more were joining them with every moment. Some brandished weapons, others blazing flamboys; one individual in the crowd's midst was even carrying a ceremonial flag, which swayed bizarrely on its pole above the bobbing heads. Sober citizens every one, they were yelling and cheering and whooping, throwing stones that flew through the air and ricocheted from walls. Somewhere the sharp music of a window shattering was audible above the cacophony, and Foss swung round and shouted to his children.

'Stay back! They won't be content until they've finished what they've begun, and it's too riotous for safety! Go under that portico' – he pointed – 'and we'll watch from there; we don't want any broken heads!'

They all ran for the shelter of the pillared arcade that fronted a group of shops. Other spectators had already gathered there, people who wanted to see the affray but were reluctant to take part; as the Agates joined them there was a warning cry and several men dodged as another stone thrown at the quarry went dangerously wide of its mark. Then a tearing sound snatched their attention back to the heart of the tumult.

The wounded creature had reached the Garden and crashed through the low ornamental hedge that surrounded it. It lost its footing and stumbled; a tree snapped in half and the damaged wing ripped, causing the monster to shriek anew as it slewed sideways. Its neck twisted into a mad, agonised contortion; for a moment the great head was facing them directly and Calliope saw that its eyes were white, blind, as if the light of the sun had burned them out. The thing struggled to regain its balance, but one thin leg had tangled in the curlicues of a wrought-iron seat and was inextricably trapped. The intact wing flapped desperately but without co-ordination; then the body began to keel over—

And the crowd were on it.

The shrieking rose to such a pitch that Calliope had to block her ears against the frequencies that knifed through her brain. She saw the mob beating, stabbing, hacking, sticks and swords and even a meat-cleaver rising and falling as they launched a concerted onslaught on their prey. Borne down under the tide of attackers the creature threshed wildly, but the second wing was shattering and the writhing body losing strength as a clear, glistening fluid bled from multiple wounds. Calliope had one more glimpse of it as it raised its head and uttered its wailing deathcry, a despairing sound which the crowd answered with a howl of triumph. Then the great head fell back for the last time, the wings crumpled, and the mangled form was finally still.

Shouting fell away to chatter, to mumbling, to a peculiar silence as the crowd lowered their weapons and stood gazing down at what they had accomplished. For all its size there was nothing formidable about the creature, and in death it looked fragile, almost wraithlike, as if the smallest breeze would scatter it to smoke and blow the smoke away.

But its enemies were not done yet and, breaking the hiatus, a lone voice rang out.

'Burn it, then! Burn it to ash! Make sure!'

The demand was taken up. 'Yes, burn it!' 'Bring a flamboy!' 'Make sure nothing remains!' The excitement which had briefly ebbed was flowing again; a flaring torch was passed from the back to the front of the crowd, hand to hand over ducking heads, and there was a general shuffling backwards and outwards, clearing a circle around the creature's corpse.

The frail wings caught with a *whoof* of fire as the flamboy was thrust at them, and those closest jumped quickly back. Flames leaped, rivalling the gory afterglow in the sky overhead, and the cheering began again as the body burned. The blaze drove back the gathering dusk, lighting the ring of faces; the crowd had the rapt, eager looks of celebrants at a festive bonfire, and a younger, rowdier element were even starting to sing.

But the fun was soon over. There was, it seemed, little substance in the creature for the fire to consume, and within a few minutes the flames were dying down. As the last golden tongues flickered and went out and the fierce heat faded, the strange hush fell again. The creature was ashes. Someone trod out an ember that threatened to set light to a specimen bush; a few others trampled

9

and kicked at the ash to ensure that no other sparks remained. A charred remnant, fine as a cobweb and feebly glowing, fluttered on an updraught and disintegrated. Suddenly the exhilaration that had animated the mob was gone, and a creeping shadow of sobriety took its place. Tension ebbed, breathless zeal gave way to calm, and the calm took on a timbre of self-consciousness, almost of shame. Abashed looks were exchanged; one or two groups near the edge of the square began quietly to move away. Close to where Foss and his family stood, a woman was shaking her head censoriously, while the keepers of the shops in the arcade withdrew discreetly through their open doors. A bolt clanked and keys rattled as the first of the emporiums closed to the world for another night.

The main body of the crowd had also started to disperse. It was almost dark, and when the dark fell it was better to be indoors until the lamplighters came at their appointed hour to make the streets safe again. Many stayed close to the flamboy-bearers, though a few carried pocket-tapers which they lit and held before them like charms as they hastened into the lanes.

Foss carried no such tapers, for he despised superstition as the crutch of fools who were either too ignorant or too idle to learn the error of their beliefs. Darkness held no terrors other than those conjured by a rioting imagination, and even when the shops and houses had all closed their shutters against the night, the sky was clear enough for the stars to show their way without risking a turned ankle in the gloom.

He made to gather his family and start for home, but before he could speak a voice called out of the heavy dusk.

'Foss! Foss, is that you?'

A spare, middle-aged man with a small, neat beard was approaching them along the now otherwise deserted arcade. He nodded courteously though perfunctorily to the others, then took hold of Foss's arm and drew him a little way off to be out of earshot.

'Well, Nempson.' Foss looked towards the dishevelled Public Garden. 'The townsfolk have been as thorough as ever.'

There was a wry note in his voice, and Nempson Trinity pursed his small mouth. 'Indeed; and with as little thought as ever for the waste and foolishness. Two of my colleagues are collecting some of the ash, but I have small hope that it will

10

yield anything of value. Ash never does; it's the *undamaged* corporeal matter we want. Or better still, a live specimen of a size worth the trouble.'

Foss watched the two shadowy figures busy among the creature's burned remains. 'We've little hope of that. One word of a breakthrough and it seems the entire town loses its reason.'

'Quite; and no amount of logical argument will change matters. But there is another possible option.'

Foss looked at him keenly and raised interrogative eyebrows.

'This isn't the time or place for further discussion,' Nempson went on, 'but we – by which I mean a few of the more sober and responsible members of our Society – would like to raise the matter with you in detail.' He paused, and his expression grew just a little sly. 'We have no wish to impose on a family occasion, of course, but I understand that tomorrow is Calliope's twenty-fifth birthday.'

'Ah.' Foss understood and returned a dry smile. 'Yes. Tomorrow, Calliope will come of age.'

'Then I wonder if I, and two or possibly three others from the inner group, might have your permission to call at the house and express our felicitations . . . and perhaps, as the saying runs, to wear two gloves on the one hand?'

'Or,' Foss said, quite gently, 'perhaps three?'

Nempson made a self-deprecating gesture. 'That, my friend, is a matter entirely for your discretion, and any thought of influencing you couldn't be further from my mind. However . . .' He smiled frankly and disarmingly. 'In the matter of the third glove, as it were, I'd be a liar if I tried to pretend that I'm not intensely curious – and more than a little excited.'

Under the portico, the children were growing impatient. Foss could hear Luthe complaining to Celesta; then Calliope's voice broke in, calming both before the complaint could become an argument.

He nodded once, but emphatically. 'Yes,' he said. 'Yes, Nempson. Come in the evening. There's to be a small gathering to celebrate the occasion – Philome's idea, of course; I wouldn't trouble with it myself and Calliope's much of the same mind. But with the others distracted I'll be able to speak privately with Calliope and give her the legacy. Your presence will be welcome. In fact I think it will be for the best all round.'

Nempson eyed him shrewdly. 'You've not told her about it, then?'

'No. That was a condition of the undertaking.'

'So you can't yet judge how she might react. Mmm, yes; I quite see. But Calliope's a sensible girl. And dedicated. If the legacy is what we suspect it to be—'

'*If* it is.'

'Quite so. But on that assumption . . . well, I believe she'll be ready to share our own view of the matter.'

Foss smiled. 'And, we hope, to share a good deal more than that. But the decision must be her own. Legally, we have no other choice.'

'Of course. Our role will be simply to advise.' Nempson clasped his hands together. 'Well then, Foss, until tomorrow evening. I thank you, and wish you goodnight. Please give Calliope my congratulations for her auspicious day.'

His two colleagues were waiting for him; they exchanged a few brief words, then Nempson raised a hand to Foss in a farewell salute and all three walked away across the square.

As Foss turned back to the portico, Celesta's face and pale hair loomed out of the gathering night. 'Are you done, Father? My hands are cold, and Luthe's complaining that he's hungry.'

Luthe was always hungry, but Foss considered that a healthy appetite was a positive virtue in a man, young or old. Philome would have waited dinner for them, and he felt a sudden urge to be comfortable in his favourite chair with the meal set before him and nothing beyond a choice of relishes to trouble his mind.

'Very well.' He clapped his hands to call their attention, an old habit that had persisted since Calliope was small and the other two barely toddling. 'Give Celesta your arm, Luthe. And mind for the broken paving on the other side of the square.'

He held out his own arm to Calliope and they set off, heading towards their home. As they passed the Public Garden, Calliope tried to peer in and see the remains of the burnt creature where they lay scattered, but shops and houses alike had closed their shutters now and the shadows were all one. Then the multiple sounds of their footsteps faded, and the square was left deserted.

Or so it seemed.

He knew the moment when they vanished entirely from view, for in the dark his eyes saw much that theirs could not. But his eyes hurt, and the slow, throbbing pain behind his temples had barely abated even with the coming of night.

At last, when they were gone, he dared to move. Not into the Garden, not that far, lest one shutter should open and someone look out; the danger was too great for him even to give the dead creature the simple courtesy of his last respects. But he stepped a little way from the shadows that had hidden him, and stood gazing towards the Garden, knowing what was there, picturing it in his strange mind and enshrining a little of what he felt, though it could make no difference to the dead soul now.

A minute passed, then the reverie was done. He was shivering, not with cold but with the bitter ague that had been on him for two days past. He couldn't stay any longer; he knew that. If he stayed, then he would have to feed, and to feed would be to draw too close to them, the denizens of the bright world. That had been the dead creature's great mistake; the terrible temptation to break free from the dark that had shrouded her and take what she needed, what she craved. She had been of too low an order fully to understand the perils of such a choice; hunger had driven her blindly, unthinkingly to reveal herself, and they had killed her, as they always killed her kind.

A gloved hand, grey and phantasmic in the night, caught at the heavy cloak that wrapped him, drawing its folds more closely around his body as he tried to stem the trembling. Every muscle ached, every bone hurt; for a moment he closed his pewter-coloured eyes, seeking the relief of absolute darkness, but it was an illusion and after a few moments he let the illusion go and looked again. His hair was damp with the fever, clinging to face and neck, and when he pushed it back he could feel the brittleness of the strands and the frail, desiccated quality of his skin beneath. He *must* not stay, or he would become as the dead one was. Burned to ash or falling to dust; there was little to choose between them, and no third way. He must return, and report yet another sorrow and another failure.

He looked up to the sky. The sun was far below the horizon now, even the afterglow gone, and stars were showing their faint, tiny faces against blackness. He had no fear of the stars, for their light was dim and quiet and redolent of the light of his own world; they could do him no harm. But soon they would be eclipsed by the rising moon, and then the lamplighters would come to kindle the small, ferocious fires that were too hard and too hot and too colourful for his eyes. They and the moon would banish the true dark until the sun rose again. He could not afford to wait through another day.

Behind him, where the shop walls joined the last pillar of the arcade, there was a sliver of absolute blackness, untouched by the meagre starlight. A sliver was enough, and he moved silently back, his form merging with the shadows' intensity. The dark felt cool, a balm that eased the shivering a little, but although it comforted his body it did not comfort his mind. Another sorrow, another failure. Another of their own dying to no purpose because the lure had been too great to resist. And he had found nothing of the key, and nothing of Malorn.

In the clocktower of the market square, only four rooftops away, a bell began to chime with a silver note, announcing the hour for lamplighting; a fixed hour that took no account of the true fall of night. The respite was ending, and he moved once more, further into the utter dark. It embraced him; he reached out with senses that no human could have comprehended, and felt the door between worlds sliding open.

The clocktower bell fell silent, and the square was truly empty.

Chapter II

The queen had had word of her emissary's return, and anxiety was like smoke in the air of the great hall as the denizens of her court waited for him to arrive. Thinking to do a kindness, one attendant had summoned musicians to play and sing for her, but it seemed that even music hadn't the power to lighten the atmosphere, and the airs that shimmered through the hall sounded wistful and melancholy.

Selethe sat, as she did through almost every hour of every day, on the black throne atop its black dais. Earlier she had slept for a little while, but now the cobweb-like curtains were drawn back once more and her huge silver eyes, framed in heavy coils of charcoal-dark hair, pensively watched the courtiers who

14

moved quietly about or stood talking together in low voices. Now and then one would pass close by the throne and bow to her in the appropriate fashion, but although she acknowledged each gesture with a grave nod, Selethe had no word to say to anyone.

At last, he arrived. There was a sudden stillness in the hall, a turning of heads in the dim, shifting light. Then the great black doors opened, and with a whispering rustle the company of attendants parted as Selethe's emissary entered the hall.

He had come directly to the court on his return, and was still swathed in the heavy cloak he had worn on his sojourn. It lent a hardness to his tall, gaunt frame, and as he approached the throne the queen saw many of her courtiers shrink back, as though he had brought with him the dangerous taint of the human world. But then a stray, drifting shaft of light caught him, illuminating his stark expression, and she realised what the others had already seen in his face.

Her hands clenched on the throne's carved arms and she tried to rise, only to find that the strength wasn't in her. Shapes, wraithlike, moved quickly to support her as she swayed, and she was helped gently back into the cushioned chair. But her gaze didn't leave the emissary's face for one moment. She was aware that all attention in the chamber was focused tensely on her now; even those beings who were too simple or of too low an order to understand nonetheless sensed the undercurrent and were watching.

The emissary reached the dais and stopped. He was half a head taller than most in the hall, and even with the dais between them his eyes were almost on a level with the queen's. Then he bowed his head. The light struck cold silver on his hair and Selethe said softly, 'Charn?'

He looked up and met her gaze. 'I am so sorry, my lady.' His voice was quiet but clearly audible in the hush, and a cascade of sighs echoed through the hall as all present heard him.

Selethe's face became immobile, masking the mental pain that went through her. 'Then again there was nothing?'

'Nothing, madam. Not even the smallest sign.'

The queen nodded, dignified, composed. 'And my other emissary.' She paused, forced herself to ask the question. 'Dead?'

'Yes, madam.'

'I see. Yes; I see.' She looked up. 'The poor creature tried to feed?'

'And was seen, and hunted down.' Charn's mouth hardened a little. 'They burned her.'

From the throng a new voice spoke softly. 'Another one lost to us . . . did you try to stop them, Charn? This time, did you try?'

Charn's head snapped round sharply, and his high-boned face was suddenly ferocious. 'There was nothing I could do!'

Selethe raked the interloper with an equally angry look. 'Nor would I have wished him to do anything, or have permitted it! The danger is too great, and to lose Charn would be unendurable for us all!' She raised one hand, an imperious gesture, long ingrained. 'No more music.' The players, shadows among shadows, fell silent, though she sensed them watching her uncertainly. Then abruptly her anger turned to dust, as it always did, and she continued more quietly. 'Leave us, please, all of you. Leave the hall. I wish to speak with Charn alone.'

The courtiers withdrew, black and grey and silver figures making their obeisances before flowing towards the doors. A starker silence fell on the hall as the last departed, then was broken by the very soft sound of the doors closing. Empty but for the two figures at the throne, the great chamber felt suddenly hollow and desolate, and Selethe turned and reached out frail grey hands. 'Come here to me, Charn. Sit beside me and tell me all you can. It's better that I should know.'

He stepped up onto the dais and took his familiar place, cross-legged at her feet. As their hands touched, the queen felt the feverish heat in Charn's skin, and she pushed aside the cloak he still wore so that she could see his face more clearly. His hair was clammy where it lay on his neck and shoulders, and beads of moisture gleamed on his forehead. She said, 'You're unwell. You were away too long – their world has harmed you.'

He caught her fingers and kissed them. 'I'll recover soon enough, madam. A few days' rest and I'll be ready to return and continue the search.'

'No.' Selethe pulled her hand away. 'No, Charn, you will not.' She leaned against the throne's towering back, her eyes unhappy. 'It's time I acknowledged the truth, my dear; the truth that many of my people have been trying to tell me for a long time now. This undertaking of ours, this pursuit, is futile. We both know that if we are to have any hope of finding what we seek, we must have help from the world of humans. Yet in fifteen years of trying to make them understand, we have achieved nothing. They refuse to listen; they refuse to *understand*. Their minds are closed, and all they do is destroy without thought.' She sat forward once more, gazing into his face with painful intensity. 'You were my last hope, for you are of the highest order of our kind; you look much as they do and you understand their tongue and many of their ways. But I can't let you go on taking the risk. This newest foray – you were gone only two days, yet their world has already damaged you. I won't have that. I *can't*, for I can't afford to take the risk of losing you.'

Silver-grey lashes came down over Charn's eyes as they narrowed. 'There are others who could take my place,' he said.

'That was not what I meant, and you know it was not. I could find another successor, yes. But I couldn't replace my son's dearest friend and my only comfort since his loss.'

For a few moments Charn didn't reply. Then at last he did speak, and immediately Selethe recognised the change in his tone. He would not argue with her; she was his queen, his liege and the one living soul whom he was bound to obey. But Charn had a persuasive power which few could stand against for long – and in this, he meant to use it.

'Madam,' he said, 'you pay me a compliment to which I have no answer. But if you fear the risk of losing me, think of the other and greater risk. The risk of failure.'

Selethe made a small, unhappy sound and looked away. She knew this argument of old, and her defences against it were weak. But they were defences of a kind, and she said, 'There's no certainty that failure would bring disaster on us. The chances that any human will find the key are slender, and even if they did—'

Her words died away as Charn's right hand closed over hers where it lay on the throne arm. 'Slender,' he repeated quietly, 'but not impossible. If it were to happen, if humans were to find the way into our world, they would do to all of us what they have already done to so many of your emissaries. They would kill and maim and destroy, until there was nothing left. *That*, my lady, is the risk we dare not take.'

She refused to meet his gaze. 'Many others disagree. They say

17

the doorway should be sealed now. They are pressing me to act.'

'They have no right to do so, madam, and I'll teach a very sharp lesson to any who think otherwise!'

'No, my dear, you won't, for I can hardly be angry with them when so much of me sympathises with what they say. I know you're right, and that we can't be truly safe unless the key is found, but if that task is beyond us – as I am beginning to believe it is – then it would be better to close the doorway now, before any more of us perish in the humans' world.'

'Only to have those humans open it again one day in the future?'

'It might not come to that.'

'But it could, madam.' He paused. 'Forgive me, but this must be said. If you seal the doorway now, as you are being urged to do, then you'll die unhappy and unfulfilled, for you will never know what became of Malorn.'

Selethe shrank back as though she had been stung. 'That is a despicable thing to say . . .' Pain flared in her face and she turned away. 'To use that weapon against me – it is despicable and cruel!'

'No, madam, it is *honest*,' Charn said, then uncurled and rose to a kneeling position beside her. 'The words are your own, not mine. You've said them to me many times; that you have no hope of contentment, in life or in death, unless the enigma is solved.'

For some moments there was silence. Selethe did not seem to be breathing; she was gazing across the hall at something invisible to Charn yet clear and tangible in her own mind's eye. Eventually, softly, she exhaled, and the exhalation became a sigh.

'I can't argue with you. What you say – what *I* said – is true.' One hand clenched and unclenched, as though groping in darkness. 'But I have a duty to protect my realm as best I can.'

'You also have a duty to yourself,' Charn told her gently.

She shook her head. 'In the past, perhaps, but not now. I'm old, and I have little time left; in a year or two what will it matter to me? I shall be gone.'

'I don't like to hear you say such things.'

'Dislike it or not as you please, it makes no difference to the truth – and when I *am* gone, the burden of protecting this realm will lie on your shoulders. It won't be easy for you, and I have no wish to make it harder.'

He smiled, a smile she knew well and which had always disarmed her. 'My lady, I know that. But if you have a duty, so have I. To you and to Malorn, who was my friend and mentor.'

She shook her head. 'Malorn wouldn't want you to risk your life for his sake.'

'He would have risked his for me.'

Yes, Selethe thought, *so he would. And he did risk his life – perhaps even forfeit it – for someone.* A terrible emotion moved in her and in its wake came surrender. *It's no use; I can't fight this. Charn is right. I need to find the truth. We both need to find it, or there will be no peace for either of us.*

Charn saw her expression change and knew that she had capitulated. It gave him no pleasure but only a sense of bleak relief, and he rose to his feet. 'I'm sorry,' he said very quietly.

She made a negating gesture. 'Don't be. You're right, and I can't deny it. You have my permission to return to their world and try again.' She attempted to smile but it didn't convince. 'I only ask that you take care.'

'I shall.'

'Then leave me now. Change your clothing, eat and rest. At least I may have the pleasure of your company for a day or two before you depart.'

He kissed her hand again and she watched him leave the hall. The shadows seemed to close in when he had gone, and for a while Selethe sat motionless, gazing down at the floor beneath her feet. Then a small shimmer of light impinged; she looked up and saw the fragile, spectral form of one of her personal servants hovering at the foot of the dais. The being – which might have been a human child but for its alien eyes and the strange, old wisdom in its face – offered a gentle, empathic query, and the queen smiled.

'No, I want nothing now, and I would prefer to be alone. Tell my courtiers that I will send for them when I wish them to return.'

The servant had no voice and so could not answer directly, but she sensed its compliance. As it glided from the hall, Selethe leaned back against her cushions, closing her eyes and willing her body to relax. Charn had had his way, as he always did. When the time came he would rule this world more forcefully than she had done, and that could only be to the good. She could no longer remember how many years had passed since she had been crowned in solemn ceremony in this very hall, but she believed it must be more than a hundred. High time, then, for a breath of fresher air to blow through the realm; though Charn's influence was such that many of the changes his rule would bring about had already begun. He had been at her side for fifteen years, taking the place that had once been Malorn's; he was her eyes, her ears, her right hand, and not one of her subjects dared defy his authority now. Perhaps he was not loved as she loved him; perhaps he was not even entirely liked. But he was strong, and this fragile world needed his strength. As she had said, and he had known, he was also her last hope. For if the events that had taken her son to an unknown fate in the world of humankind were not resolved, then one day in the future her realm's safety – and even its existence – might be in jeopardy.

She could not hold Malorn to blame. She knew how powerful a snare love could be, for when she was young she had loved Malorn's father, her consort, with a captivating power; and though he was dust now and had long been so, she could still close her eyes and recall his face, his voice, his touch, as though he had stepped quietly out of the mirror of her memories to stand beside her again. But he had been of her own kind; of her own *nature*. For Malorn, events had taken a different and far crueller course; for he had fallen in love with a human woman.

Though whether that woman had returned his love was a question that had never been answered.

Selethe closed her eyes and put a hand to her face in sudden distress, silently railing against her own foolishness and weakness. As well that her courtiers were not here; they would have sensed what was in her mind and flocked anxiously round her, offering comfort, trying to soothe. Though they might have known the outward reason for her sorrow, they could not understand the confusion and uncertainty that lay deeper within her. Or, deepest of all, her fear. The old fear, never resolved, of the world of men, and of the unquenchable yearning that it drew from the depths of all their souls. The yearning that lured so many of them to a hard, blazing death . . . and that had taken her son from her.

They had all known the longing; the fascination of a bright and vibrant existence that seemed to promise so much more than this twilight. To them, the world of humankind burned like a vivid flame; so colourful, so tangible, so *alive*. For ages past they had known and used the doorway that allowed them to move between dimensions. It was a simple way, needing only true darkness to dissolve the barrier, and many had been tempted to step through and see and taste the human world's wonders for themselves.

But there was danger hidden in the pleasure. Those who made the journey dared not linger on the other side, for their nature was such that the bright vibrancy which lured them also inflicted harm. The human world was too intense, its substance too strong, for their more fragile bodies to tolerate for long. Its light seared their eyes; its noise wounded their ears; its elements weakened and blighted them. Only one thing could hold the blight at bay, but it was a desperate resort and carried a terrible risk. To stay and survive, they must feed. And to feed, they must draw perilously close to the humans whose life-essence would give them succour.

Selethe did not know how many had died over the years. But in recent times there had been a mysterious and alarming increase in the numbers of those who did not return from the human world. That was why Malorn himself had made his first foray there. She had never permitted it before, for inasmuch as her duty could not allow her to make the journey, so duty also demanded that her heir should not put his life at risk. But Malorn had urged and cajoled her, insisting, as Charn insisted now, that the mystery must be solved, and at last, reluctantly, Selethe had given way.

Malorn had returned with grim news. The twilight-dwellers had believed in their naivety that humans knew nothing of their existence, let alone of their presence in the bright world; but they were wrong. Malorn had seen one of their kind taken captive. A tiny creature, of very limited intelligence but quite harmless. It had been crying out piteously, Malorn said, for the hands of its captors were inflicting dreadful wounds on its frail body. But the humans either could not hear its voice or cared nothing for its suffering. It was carried away; Malorn dared not follow and so could not tell what became of it. But it had never returned.

Then there were the higher beings, larger in form and with greater sentience. They were not captured but hunted down and destroyed, and even those who could speak the human tongue were unable to make their tormenters understand that they were not hostile and intended no harm. Beaten, torn and burned, like the winged one whom Charn had been unable to save tonight.

Why? Selethe asked herself. It was a question to which there seemed to be no sane answer. So Malorn had asked her to let him go to the bright world again. Perhaps, he had said, the humans destroyed the greater creatures because they feared their strangeness. But he would not seem strange to them, for his form was much like theirs. He could speak with them. He could reason with them. And she, not dreaming of the consequences, gave her permission.

She had known as soon as her son returned that something was troubling him, but at first Malorn refused to speak of it. Then, without a word to anyone, he had begun to go to the bright world again; brief visits but frequent, and with each return his distress seemed more acute. Eventually he told Selethe the truth – that he had met a woman of the human race, and that he loved her.

Selethe was not easily moved to hatred, but at first she had hated that human woman with all the passion her heart could muster. Who she was, how they had first encountered one another, she didn't know and didn't want to know; when Malorn tried to speak of her, Selethe had angrily ordered him to be silent. But Malorn quietly and gently persevered, and at last Selethe's anger began to crumble. She saw that his devotion was real, not an illusion that would fade as she had thought and hoped. Without his human love, her son would never be happy.

But even as she relented, she had also realised the bitterness of Malorn's plight. He and his love could not be one in her world, for he would be unable to survive there; and no human had ever crossed the threshold from the bright dimension into the twilight that was Malorn's true home. Malorn, she knew, clung to a hope that his woman would not be blighted by his world as he was by hers. Selethe felt such a hope was unfounded, but she couldn't bring herself to voice her doubts; it seemed too cruel. So when Malorn asked her if he might create for his beloved a key that would allow her to open the dark doorway and enter their realm, she had granted his wish.

That was the last time she had ever seen him.

A small sound impinged suddenly on Selethe's reverie, and she raised her head, looking quickly and instinctively towards the tall black doors of the court hall. A zephyr of air was moving there, disturbing the shadows a little; as she watched, it flitted

22

towards the dais and stirred the filmy curtains around the throne, and the small, irrational hope that had caught at Selethe's mind faded and died. How many times had she sensed such movement and looked towards the doors, thinking to see them open and Malorn appear? More times, she thought, than she had years to count; and each time it had been just another fond dream. Her son was gone. He had made the key, and he had never returned.

And because of what he had done, her world was in danger.

The zephyr had evaporated to nothing, as such ephemeral things did. The curtains were still again, the hall silent. Long shadows moved slowly, inscrutably across the floor, shifting and transmuting their form in the dim and constantly changing light. Selethe felt sadness welling up within her; a sadness that seemed too vast and too potent for her to contain. Yet there was hope. There must be hope. *Must.*

She turned on the throne's cushioned seat and gazed around the hall. Her courtiers would be troubled, worrying for her well-being, so it was not kind to banish them from her presence for too long. Her gentle old physician would prescribe music to lift her melancholy, and perhaps he was right. Perhaps tonight her court would dance for her and she would step down from the throne and find solace in the stately round. If nothing else, it would please those who loved her.

She raised one hand and made a calm, beckoning gesture. Light shimmered at the dais foot; the ethereal figure of her servant appeared. Selethe smiled.

'Let them return,' she said. 'Let there be music. Tonight, we shall be happy.'

For tonight, she added silently, *we shall pretend that all is well.*

Charn had burned the cloak. There was no real need, for any influence from the human world that still clung to its fabric would fade in a little time. But he wanted it gone from him. It had the heat of the fever about it; it felt unclean. So he had thrust it into the fire that blazed in his private rooms, and had watched the cold silver flames destroy and devour it until only ash was left.

The fever was still on him; less obvious to any observer now that he had bathed and put on fresh clothes, but lingering achingly in his bones. For a little while after the cloak was burned he continued to sit before the fire, letting the flames cool him and seeing pictures in the patterns they made; then, with a slight stiffness that pride had not allowed him to reveal to his queen, he rose and moved towards the door.

Strains of music drifted from the court hall and the black doors were open, welcoming all. Not wanting to be drawn into the pretence of a celebration, Charn retraced his steps and took another route to his destination. He passed other beings; some lower creatures who moved respectfully out of his path, some of a higher order who acknowledged him with grave nods. But he had nothing to say to them, and at last he came to the staircase that wound down, into the depth and the heart of the court, into darkness, into absolute silence.

The gallery that lay at the end of the spiral was long and narrow, and filled with sombre, tenebrous gloom. Charn closed the door softly at his back and listened to the echoes that sighed away. Then he moved forward.

He had taken only a few paces before the sense of other presences began to gather around him. Faces, one after another, looming from the dimness then ebbing away. Voices, whispering and murmuring as though a great throng had gathered just beyond the borders of perception. And memories. Charn felt the memories brush his mind, sweet or sad, joyful or bitter; the memories that the dead left behind them when they passed on to whatever awaited them beyond life. Countless thousands whom he had never known; others who had been friends or enemies or whose existence he had simply been aware of. All here. All of them, in this gallery, small remnants of what they had been preserved and enshrined for all time.

But not the one he was seeking.

The darkly shimmering walls to either side of him reflected back shadow-images of his own figure, moving and blending with other, less tangible forms. Charn stopped walking; his shadows lost their substance and faded into the dark. For a moment the faces and the sounds drew back, and the glimmer of others' recollections slid away from his mind as his senses probed the hall of remembrance. Then he said, quietly, 'Malorn?'

The echoes flowed again, like water, like the surging and sighing of the wind. A woman's face, sorrowing, skimmed past him; an old, old man laughed joyfully; a lovely being with the face of a cat conveyed artless puzzlement. Something tiny, winged, delicate, piped its simple song three times and faded to nothing. But Malorn's memories were not here.

Where, then? Charn didn't voice the question, for mere images could not answer. Did his old friend still live, or had his death been such that nothing of his being had returned, at the last, to his home? The queen clung to hope: for her sake, and for his own, Charn tried to share that hope and believe in it.

And for her sake and his own, he would not rest until the riddle was solved.

A voice had begun to sing, sweetly but hopelessly, and the memories the voice carried made him angry for reasons that he knew better than to try to understand. Other lives, other griefs; they were not his and he could not be burdened with them. For his liege, though, for Selethe, he would suffer anything and risk anything.

The fever had not abated yet. Charn's bones ached still; his eyes were hurting again and he could feel the ague coming on him. No matter: it would pass. A little rest, a little recuperation, and he would be ready to return to the bright world. To continue the search. To find the key that Malorn had given to his human love; the key that, if ever it should fall into the wrong hands, would imperil them all.

Or, if that task proved hopeless, to ensure that the way between worlds was sealed forever.

He looked back, once, as he retraced his steps to the door. The faces swam, the memories crowded; his departure would make no difference to their endless pavane. Charn inclined his head in a silent gesture that conveyed respect and thanks. Then he left the hall of remembrance to its ageless solitude.

Chapter III

The Agate home was a genteelly impressive house of four storeys, on the south-eastern side of a smaller square not far from the Public Garden. This was a well-to-do area, populated by small gentry and practitioners of the better-regarded professions, and at present it boasted among its residents scholars, masters-at-law and at least three physicians including Foss himself. The house had been bought with Griette's money when she and Foss first married, but even since his second marriage Foss had felt no desire to move elsewhere, for it was large enough to accommodate Philome's two young additions to the family, and its proximity to the Institute of Natural Sciences was a convenience which he valued highly. In the early days Philome had not been easy with the idea of inheriting Griette's home – it felt, to her, a little like wearing a dead woman's shoes, with the added discomfort that the woman in question was in fact still alive. But Foss dismissed her qualms as female caprice. There were no ghosts here, he had told her firmly. He had put his first wife aside, as the law allowed in sad cases such as Griette's, and taken a new one to be his comfort and his companion. Philome's place in his affections was assured; his home was now also hers, without caveats, and as it had *been* his home for over twenty years, he had no intention of leaving it. And, as he always did in major matters, Foss had had his way.

Calliope's birthday celebration was in full flow when Nempson Trinity and three of his colleagues arrived. The house's portico was swathed with red and yellow celebration garlands, and two great etherea lamps glowed beside the front door, their green globes shining spectrally and the tiny, fierce nucleus in each (which might or might not be sentient; the truth had yet to be established beyond doubt) performing complex spiral dances as they fed on the energy within their glass prisons. The interior of the house had also been decorated. Though she might be no match for Foss in areas of greater importance, Philome had learned how to cajole him in lesser things, and as he was now a wealthy man in his own right she could easily persuade him to let her spend money as she pleased. So tonight she had stinted nothing, given her natural enthusiasm free rein, and ribbons and leafage and good-luck mirrors festooned the entrance hall and the staircase that led up to the large reception room. The adornments weren't in the most elegant or subtle taste but they were undeniably cheerful, and if they pleased Philome then Foss was content to indulge her.

The reception room was ablaze with light and colour. Most of the lavish spread of food was gone, and now with felicitations and gifts presented, bellies full and moods mellowed by wine, the guests were mingling genially and indulging in gossip and general small-talk. Foss, immaculate and formidable in a new suit of clothes chosen by Philome, and with his fair hair dressed and pomaded by her hand, was engrossed in conversation with an archivist from the Institute of Natural Sciences, seemingly oblivious to the tide of colour and noise around him. Luthe was whispering in a corner with two of his friends, and Celesta, overdressed in lilac and gold, and hampered by her small half-brother and -sister whom she had been delegated to shepherd, was trying to catch the eye of a neighbour's handsome young son and becoming increasingly flustered and annoyed by her failure.

Calliope was amid a small group of women dominated by her stepmother. Though she smiled and talked animatedly enough, she felt distracted and a little weary. The room was overheated, the talk loud enough to make individual speech hard to distinguish, and Philome, vivacious and resplendent in red satin and with her abundant dark hair elaborately piled, was pursuing the subject of prospective husbands whom Calliope's eye might potentially fall on now that she was of age and could choose for herself. The talk made Calliope uncomfortable, as did Philome's blithe assumption that she would naturally marry and settle in her own household before much longer; for she knew that the prospect was unlikely and growing more so with each year. Not that she was becoming too old for marriage, or losing her looks, or any of the considerations that beleaguered Celesta's every waking hour. It was simply that as time went by the idea of ever leaving her father's house and her involvement in her father's work seemed to become less and less tenable. Oh, there had been suitors, plenty of them, since she was sixteen. But somehow events had always conspired to bring the courtships to nothing. While Foss had never actively discouraged Calliope's romances, neither had he ever taken steps to encourage them. Calliope loved her work, as he had reminded her on many occasions, and for a girl of her intelligence and acumen there was surely more reward to be found in earning scientific respect than merely as a wife.

Philome, however, didn't share Foss's view, and now with her husband occupied in another part of the room she was making the most of the opportunity to air the subject. Only when a hand

27

on her arm stayed her did she abruptly stop in mid-sentence and look up to see Foss at her elbow.

'Philome.' Foss's dense eyebrows knitted together and there was a faint warning in his eyes. 'Not tonight, my dear, if you please. Not now.'

Philome's cheeks pinkened and she flustered. 'Foss, I was merely pointing out—'

'We'll consider the matter at another time. Some new guests have arrived, and we have business to discuss with Calliope.'

Philome's mouth pursed. 'Foss, this is her *birthday* celebration, not a meeting of your Society! I really think that just for *one* evening you might forget your scientific research and allow the poor child to do the same!'

Foss smiled. 'But she's not a child any longer, my dear; she's of age now, so the choice is hers to make.' He looked up from his diminutive wife and focused on his daughter's face. 'Calli? Nempson Trinity and three more of our colleagues are here and wish to speak to us both.' His look became faintly conspiratorial. 'I think you might already have some idea of the subject they want to air.'

Calliope did, for she had seen Nempson and her father talking in the square the previous night, and though Foss hadn't related any details it was obvious that they had been discussing the creature from the elemental world. Her expression quickened with interest and she said, 'Yes, Father, of course I'll come.'

Philome protested helplessly, 'Calli—' but Calliope only turned and smiled fondly at her. 'I'm sure I shan't be gone for long, Philome.'

Foss, magnanimous in victory, kissed his wife's cheek then bowed a gracious apology to the three other women in the group. 'Ladies, if you will forgive us . . . ?'

Nempson and the others were waiting by the doors. The men stood back to let Calliope precede them out of the room, and in the comparative quiet and cool of the landing Foss said, 'The library, I think. No one will interrupt us there.'

As they descended the stairs back towards the ground floor, Calliope watched her father's face obliquely. She had a growing suspicion that there was more to this encounter than met the eye; logically, yesterday's incident in the Public Garden didn't warrant the interruption of her party, and logic was reinforced by a growing intuition that something portentous was in the wind. Foss seemed tense, Nempson and the others gripped by an eagerness which they were trying not to show too overtly. Something was afoot.

The library was dark and quiet, the shutters closed against the night outside. Foss lit the ornate pressure-lamp that stood on the central table, pumped the handle until the flame burned brightly enough to push the shadows into corners, then asked his companions to sit. Chairs scraped on the polished floor; taking her own seat, Calliope watched curiously as her father crossed to one of the ranks of bookshelves. She heard a click, then a small section of the shelving swung aside to reveal a panelled compartment behind. The library had many such caches, but she had not known about this one.

Foss took something from the compartment and turned back to the table.

'Calliope.' He used her full name, as though to emphasise the formality – or significance – of the moment. 'I have another birthday gift to give you.'

Well-trained in polite convention, Calliope began to say, 'But Father, you've already been more than generous—' but was interrupted.

'No, daughter. This is not from me. It is from your mother.'

Calliope was suddenly very still. On a peripheral level she was aware that the visitors were all watching her intently, but their probing gazes meant nothing as all her preconceptions about this enigmatic meeting crumbled away. She stared at Foss, then touched her tongue to lips that were abruptly, unexpectedly dry. 'From Mother . . . ?'

The object that Foss held registered on her mind at last. It was a carved wooden box, some three hands long by two wide, with brass clasps and a brass lock. Unbidden, the thought came to Calliope: *I've never seen that box before. Why have I never seen it before?* and with it she felt a peculiar frisson.

Foss set the box down on the table, then settled heavily onto a vacant chair. 'Fifteen years ago,' he said, 'shortly before she was admitted to the hospice, your mother wrote her will.'

'Her *will*?' Then Calliope's hazel eyes narrowed as though with some private and painful memory. 'But at that time she was . . . ?'

29

'Mad?' Foss uttered the word for her when it seemed she couldn't bring herself to do so. 'Oh, no. Not then. The madness hadn't come upon her then. But I think she knew that it was coming.' He paused, heaved a difficult breath. 'You were only nine and your brother and sister younger still; there's a great deal that you won't remember, or have never known, about the events of that time.'

Calliope remembered a great deal more than anyone realised, but she said nothing, only waited for him to continue.

'As I said, your mother wrote her will. She was of sound mind when she did so, as two independent physicians attested, and the document was witnessed and properly sealed by a master-at-law, so there can be no doubt as to its validity.' Foss looked up and attempted a smile, though the result was pallid. 'You will understand why I stress this fact if I should be proved right in my suspicion as to what the box contains.'

'You don't know, Father?'

'No. Or at least, not with certainty. Your mother never told me. She locked the box and bequeathed both it and the key into my keeping, with the strictest instruction that you and no one else should open it. She also stipulated that you were not to do so, or even to know of its existence, until you should come of age.' He hesitated a second time. 'So, Calli, this is your legacy from her. And I— we—' he glanced quickly at Nempson and the others 'think that it might be of great significance to us all.'

Calliope also looked at the visitors but her gaze lingered for several seconds. Their eyes gave them away; that tiny touch of guilt mingled with self-consciousness and more than a hint of impatience. It was likely that they had known about the box since the day her mother's will was signed and witnessed; Foss had confided to them the secret which he had kept from Calliope for fifteen years, and for all those years they had been waiting eagerly for the day when the legacy would at last be revealed.

'I had no choice, my dear.' Foss's voice broke into her thoughts. 'Your mother's instructions were explicit, and to break them would have been—'

'No.' Normally Calliope wouldn't have dreamed to interrupt him, but suddenly normal circumstances didn't seem to apply any more. 'No, Father. I understand.' As she looked at him she could see the same hunger in his eyes as in the other men's; only, knowing him better, she also glimpsed the underlying resentment which he had suppressed for so long. Resentment that his quietly obedient Griette should have withheld some knowledge from him and taken care, before the madness claimed her, that he could not gainsay the terms she had set. Witnessed and sealed by a master-at-law: Foss wouldn't have dared under any circumstances to defy such a sanction. For all this time he had seethed, *ached*, to know what the box contained. Even now, with the elusive prize so close, he resented the fact that his compliant daughter must give her permission before he could at last discover the truth.

She let her gaze drop. 'Do you wish me to open the box in your presence?'

The acute silence gave her her answer, and Calliope was a little shocked to find herself amused by it. Philome often proffered conspiratorial advice on the subject of manipulating men; not for any reasons of malice but simply, as she put it, to 'add a little helpful oil to the cog-wheels of daily life'. Calliope paid small heed to the advice, for such games had never appealed to her. But now, suddenly, she understood Philome's meaning. For the first time she had power over her father; her father knew it, and he didn't like it, and the fact that he didn't like it stirred a small thrill in a dark corner of Calliope's mind.

But the thrill didn't last. Certain habits were too ingrained and too long-established to be set aside; obedience to Foss, deference to his will, respect for his wishes – and, of course, affection. Games of power had no place. He was her father; it was natural for his wishes to take precedence.

The hiatus broke in a fond smile from Foss and a sigh of relief from Nempson Trinity as the men all realised that Calliope didn't intend to be difficult. They had feared that feminine vagary might affect even this level-headed and practical girl, and that for some convoluted and illogical reason she might want to examine the box's contents alone before revealing them – possibly selectively – to their scrutiny. If Foss's theory was right, that would not have suited their purpose at all.

Foss's chair creaked as he leaned back and reached to a side pocket of his brocade waistcoat. He drew out a key, handed it to

Calliope, then slowly pushed the box across the table towards her.

'If your mother were able to give you her blessing at this moment,' he said gravely, 'it is my earnest belief that she would do so. It gladdens me greatly to think that I am carrying out her wish at last.'

For one sharp moment Calliope wished that he hadn't thought it necessary to mark the formal moment with such a sentimental embellishment, for something about it didn't ring true. But she rejected her reaction as unworthy, took the key and inserted it into the lock of the box. The lock was a little stiff but engaged after a few seconds' experimentation; the key turned, she felt the lid yield, and lifted it.

The box was filled – crammed – with papers. Each one was neatly aligned and carefully folded so that no space inside the box was wasted or unused. Calliope's heart gave a strange, queasy little lurch as she saw the familiar but half forgotten curlicues of her mother's handwriting.

The five men leaned forward and stared. Nempson Trinity said, 'Ah . . .'

Calliope reached into the nest of papers and took the topmost sheet out. No one spoke while she read what the paper contained. Then she put it down.

'I didn't know,' she said quietly, and lifted her eyes to meet Foss's. 'I didn't know Mother was involved in that.'

Foss stared back at her and she sensed his excitement. 'In what, daughter?'

'The creatures from the other world. The experiments, the research. Trying to break through.' Suddenly she felt an irrational desire to laugh, and did, though it was a slightly uneasy sound. 'I suppose I was too young to understand at the time, wasn't I? You've never told me much about the nature of the work you and she did together. But . . .' She picked up the paper again and held it out to him, feeling an answering excitement beginning to rise in herself. 'Is it what you hoped for, Father?'

Foss took the paper and studied it. Then he swore, very softly, under his breath, and looked at Calliope again. 'May our guests see this?'

'Of course.'

The paper was passed round from one man to another.

Nempson said, 'Living spirits . . . you were right, Foss. You were *right!*' and the rest added their own comments. Calliope watched them all, watched their faces and their eyes and the way their hands clenched with a kind of eager passion as turn by turn they saw for themselves what Griette had written. It was in fact no more than a simple statement listing and describing the rest of the box's contents. But its implications were giddying. For Griette claimed that she had fathomed the secret of the doorway between this world and what was known as the 'twilight dimension' – the elusive, unknown home of the creature killed in the Public Garden, and so many others before it.

The last man read the document, and Foss spoke. 'Her own notes.' His voice was very quiet, almost awed. 'I've always known she must have chronicled all she did . . . but if what this first page claims is true, there's far more here than any of us had dreamed!' He looked at Calliope again. 'You understand your mother's meaning? What this document implies? Yes, I see you do. Well then, I think it's time to be done with equivocation.' He glanced succinctly around the table. 'You're an intelligent girl, Calliope, and I don't believe I need to specify to you the true reason why Nempson and our other colleagues have come here tonight.'

Calliope noted the change of reference; in the past Foss had always referred to Nempson as 'Master Trinity' in her hearing. Not tonight, though. Tonight she had come of age, and now she was their equal.

'Your mother and I carried out a great deal of scientific and arcane work together, and like many of our colleagues in the Society we were greatly interested in the twilight dimension. Our ambition was to discover how the beings of that dimension are able to enter our world; over the years we experimented with all manner of theories and possibilities, but none bore any worthwhile fruit. But then your mother embarked on a private experiment of her own. She told me a little of the direction she was taking, but insisted that she must test her hypothesis more thoroughly before revealing its nature. She became . . well, I don't wish to speak ill of her, but she became *secretive* about her work. Sitting up late into the night, spurning all offers of help, working herself to a shadow . . . I became greatly concerned for her health—'

'As did we all,' Nempson put in firmly.

'Yes. Yes, indeed. But she refused to heed our warnings, or

even the warnings that her own constitution began to signal. She became ill; a weakness of the body that quickly grew chronic.' Foss sighed. 'I tried to persuade her then to confide the results of her work to me, so that I might carry it on for her while she recovered her strength. But she would not. Then . . .' A frown; earlier he had referred to Griette's insanity for the first time in Calliope's presence and now found that he couldn't bring himself to do so again. 'Well, the first signs of that great trouble began to manifest. That was when she prepared the box and gave her instructions regarding its disposal.'

Calliope took the document back, moved to lay it carefully in the box, then changed her mind. Fingering the paper, she looked levelly at her father. 'Why did she choose to entrust it to my care?'

Foss lifted his shoulders in a faintly uneasy shrug. 'I've no more idea than you, Calliope. Your mother had a sound belief in your talents, and felt that you would follow where she and I had led. But why she should have wished her notes to remain unread for fifteen years is a question that I've never been able to fathom.' That little flicker of resentment was in his eyes again; Calliope saw and recognised it but said nothing, and Foss continued, 'Now, however, they *are* exposed to the light once more. So the question which we – which you – must consider is, what's to be done with them?'

Silence fell, and the visitors all looked at Calliope again. Their gaze made the back of her neck prickle and she suppressed an impulse to twitch her shoulders in an effort to shake the sensation off. She had noted Foss's small slip when he said *we* and changed it hurriedly to *you*, and knew what it meant. The group had already decided in their own minds what they wished to do, and although there would be no attempt made to coerce her into agreeing with them, there would be pressure. It might be subtle and gentle, it might be very carefully disguised, but there would be pressure.

She said, a little tentatively, 'You're wondering, Father, if there might be enough in these notes to enable you to continue Mother's experiments?'

Foss smiled thinly. 'For *all* of us to continue them, Calliope. And I think' – he glanced at Nempson for confirmation and received a surreptitious nod – 'that you know what that would mean.'

Calliope did, and it took her by surprise. She hadn't dreamed for one moment that the persuasion would take this form: far from applying pressure to her, the men were offering her a lure in the form of full admission into their Society, with all the privileges that such admission entailed. The greatest privilege of all would be the prospect, one day in the future, of election to the Inner Arcana of the Institute of Natural Sciences; a prospect open only to those who had been properly initiated into the Institute's recognised and affiliated groups. That, as Foss knew well, was a private ambition of Calliope's, a great and incalculably valuable step along the road to knowledge, and the fact that very few women had ever achieved such a step added its own spice. Griette had been one of the exceptions; now though, only one other female carried the title of an Arcane. Calliope very much wanted to follow where her mother had led.

She stared down at the papers again, aware of new excitement quickening within her. Was this, she wondered, what Griette had intended all along? Had she made this gift to ensure that Foss would sponsor their daughter to the Society when the appropriate time came? Calliope couldn't answer that question with any certainty, but it seemed likely. The price for the fulfilment of her ambition was, simply, to make Foss and the other men privy to the secrets of her mother's legacy.

Hardly daring to believe that the bargain could be so simple, she looked up again and said tentatively, 'It might be possible to revive and recreate Mother's experiments. If all the notes are here, as the list implies, the secret could be unravelled.'

Foss nodded. 'I believe that's what your mother wanted, Calli.'

'Yes, I believe so, too. But . . .'

'But?' A faint edge to Foss's voice now, and suddenly Calliope decided to set discretion aside and stop pretending that this was anything other than a clear and pragmatic negotiation.

'But,' she said, 'I can't conduct those experiments alone. I haven't the skill or the experience or any of the proper facilities.' She gave a quick, wry smile. 'You know as well as I do, Father, that I need the Society's help. If, as I think is the case, the Society would also benefit from the . . .' She faltered as she realised that she didn't quite have the courage to be as blunt as she wished. She might be wrong; might be presuming too much.

Nempson Trinity cleared his throat. 'Foss.' There was dry

amusement in his voice. 'I believe the word Calliope was about to use is *exchange*. She clearly understands our position, so I suggest that we stop equivocating and come to the point. With your permission . . . ?' Foss nodded quickly and Nempson turned to Calliope. 'Will you stand, please?'

Calliope rose and he followed suit, pushing back his chair. Then, to her surprise, he made a bow to her. 'Madam.' His voice took on a ritualistic note. 'It has been proposed that you, Calliope Agate, daughter of Arcane Foss Agate and former Arcane Griette Agate, should be admitted to membership of our Society.' He pivoted. 'Who sponsors the candidate?'

Foss stood up. 'I sponsor the candidate.'

Nempson raised one hand and made a ceremonial sign over the table. 'It is recorded that the candidate is sponsored by Associate Foss Agate. As senior Associate I declare his sponsorship to be valid, and I call upon those others here present, who are three in number and thus constitute a quorum, to signify objection or agreement.' He pivoted again and made lesser but equally punctilious bows to all the others in turn. 'The vote will be cast in the traditional manner.'

Bemused, Calliope watched as one after another the three men stretched their hands out, palms upwards, over the table. It was the sign of agreement, and when it was done Nempson turned to her again with a smile. 'Madam,' he said, 'it is both my duty and my privilege to issue to you a formal invitation of initiation into our Society. Do you accept, or do you decline?'

Calliope's heart had begun to pound. Eagerly, though striving for propriety's sake to keep the emotion from her voice, she said, 'I accept, sir.'

Though she did her best to make a show of enjoyment, Calliope's frustration as the birthday party continued into the small hours was hard for her to bear. She was keyed-up with excitement of an entirely different kind and found it impossible to concentrate on anything other than the events that had taken place in the library. The presentation of her mother's legacy, and the small ceremony which had followed it, had in the space of a mere few minutes opened up a new, vast and giddily exciting horizon. In the wake of such a thing the trappings of ordinary life seemed suddenly very trivial.

With their business concluded, Nempson and his companions had made their excuses to Philome and left. Within the next few days a second ceremony would take place in which Calliope would be officially initiated to full membership of the Society, and until that day the matter of Griette's box would remain in abeyance, at least for them. For Calliope herself, however, it was a different matter.

At last the first guests began to leave, and within another hour even the diehards were making their noisy farewells as their carriages rumbled to the front door. Calliope stood in the hall with Foss and Philome, smiling and thanking everyone, then as the front door closed for the last time she cut short something Celesta was trying to say to her, gave her own goodnight to the family and fled up to the top floor.

She had carried Griette's gift to the sanctuary of her room on leaving the library, and now, by the light of her new and highly decorative scented oil lamp – one of Philome's gifts – she sat down on her bed, set the box on her lap and lifted the lid once more. So *many* papers – it was impossible to know where to begin, and realistically she knew that there wasn't enough time now to examine them all. So, then; she would glance through quickly, and see if anything especially caught her eye. Tomorrow, when she had helped Philome to oversee the clearing up of the party's debris, she could begin to read in earnest.

The first documents she took from the box comprised mathematical equations, closely written in Griette's hand. Next came a series of sketches which, without studying their accompanying notes, would be impossible to decipher. Then the notes themselves, many of them, each page carefully numbered. Then . . .

Calliope paused as she lifted out the next handful of papers. There was something different about these. The careful and meticulous script was showing signs of deterioration; the letters were less well-formed and in places the ink was smudged, as though Griette had written these words in great haste – or great distress. Many of the sentences were incomplete or even incoherent; phrases thrown in like random thoughts and apparently with nothing to connect them. There were other strange references: several times Griette wrote of 'utter darkness; there can be no light' and, once, 'the elusive border between dream and reality which is so hard to capture and hold'.

Then came the first real shock, for suddenly, half-way down the last page she held, the handwriting collapsed altogether. In a scrawl which splayed right across the paper and in places had torn through it, Griette had scribbled a desperate sentence: '*Impossible – it is impossible!*' The rest of the sheet was blank, and quickly Calliope delved into the box again. Only a few documents remained now, but as soon as she drew out the last handful she saw that these told a very different story. With a sense of creeping chill that seemed to form in her marrow and eat its way outwards to her skin, she realised that she was witnessing the clear signs of her mother's impending madness.

There was little to read, and less that made any lucid sense. One page contained only the words *white flowers*, repeated over and again; another referred to *the Sacrament*, but the rest of what Griette had written was completely illegible, as though her hand had been shaking too violently to control the pen. Then, as Calliope picked up the last page but one, suddenly her mother's writing returned to something like its old clarity. Steadily and carefully, she had written: '*I cannot do this. I fear it too much, for I fear what it might mean and what might become of us if I dare to take this chance. The risk is too great, and even knowing what I know, I do not have the courage to take it. I am sorry. I am so sorry. But I must fail this last test. And in failing, I will end all.*'

So neat, so controlled: and yet underlying the calm in the words Calliope felt, like a psychic shock reaching to her across the years, the depth of her mother's emotion and fear. Foss believed that Griette had known of her own impending fate. Now Calliope believed it too, for she held the stark evidence in her hand. Her mother had felt the pull of insanity, and had made the conscious decision to yield to it. For her only hope – the 'risk' of which she wrote – had been an alternative that she couldn't find the courage to face.

The risk. White flowers. The Sacrament. Slowly, Calliope let her hand sag to her lap as she stared at the page. It was possible that the sheaf of records, when she read them, would shed light on what truly lay behind this sad, cryptic message; but in her heart she doubted it. This, she sensed, was something else entirely. Something a world away from science and alchemy and the pursuit of knowledge. Something very, very personal, which neither she nor Foss nor the Society nor, perhaps, any living soul in the world, had the ability to understand.

She let the paper fall at last and turned to the one sheet that still remained at the bottom of the box. It had been neatly folded and then folded again, presenting a blank face to her, and she lifted it out and opened it.

Griette's hand again, but this time the word – a single word, in the centre of the page – was printed in capital letters. No smudging, no scrawling. Just the word.

DEATH.

Calliope re-folded the paper along its knife-edge creases and laid it back in the box. Then she stood up, turned down the lamp and moved to the window. The night was warm, and on warm nights she preferred not to close the shutters, so as she lifted the curtain back a thin flood of moonlight washed into the room from the cloudless sky. Calliope stared up at the moon's bland face. It was near the full, so bright tonight that it almost eclipsed the small golden flames of the street lamps in the square below, and it cast an ethereal patina over the scene, draining it of colour. Calliope stood motionless, gazing, for perhaps five minutes or a little more. Then she let the curtain fall, turned back to her bed and began, carefully and methodically, to tidy the papers and put them away. When all were safe inside the box again she lowered the lid, turned the key and set the box on the small table beside her bed. When she woke in the morning, it would be the first thing she saw as she opened her eyes.

The heavy curtains had excluded the moonlight, but a light breeze blew in where she had earlier opened the window a crack. It smelled of trees and warm paving, and just a little – though that might have been her imagination – of something burned. Calliope slipped off her gown but didn't trouble to undress any further. Morning would be here soon, and in the morning she would have a very great deal to think about.

She turned down the wick in the oil-lamp until the last reflection died from the glass prisms and the room sank into darkness. Then she laid her head on her pillow, and hoped that she would sleep.

Chapter IV

Calliope's official induction into the Society took place at the Institute three days later. Fifteen of the group's twenty-eight members were present, and the small but intricate ceremony was conducted with grave formality. Kneeling on a velvet-covered footstool before an Arcane of the Institute, Calliope solemnly pledged to obey the Society's rules, preserve its secrets, honour its principles and uphold and advance the furtherance of knowledge through diligent study and application of the natural sciences. With great dignity the Arcane placed the Scroll of Indenture on her outstretched palm; with equal earnestness Calliope closed her fingers around it and touched her forehead five times to the proffered Institute Seal, while behind her Foss, Nempson and the other Associates chanted the Inauguration Salute that welcomed her to their midst.

Calliope felt a little giddy when the formalities were over; due less to the nature of the ceremony itself than to the sense of elation, almost of power, that elevation to the Society's ranks had brought. Yesterday she had been nothing more than an amateur seeker after knowledge; today an emphatic seal had been set on her ambitions and doors had been opened through which it would otherwise have been impossible for her to pass.

But for all her euphoria her mind was still earthbound enough to recall the price she must pay for her good fortune, and when the small party gathered in a crimson-furnished anteroom to celebrate less formally with wine and biscuits, it wasn't long before her father reminded her of her new duty. The news of her legacy had spread swiftly, and the Society's members were very eager to have sight of Griette's notes as soon as possible. Foss's suggestion, carefully couched, was that Calliope might care to consider giving the box into his care; as a senior Associate he was – no slight to her, but age and experience had relevance in these matters – better placed to know how best to disseminate the information they contained. Calliope sipped her wine and nodded and agreed, thinking of the copies she had carefully made over the past three days and which were now placed between two linen shawls in her bedroom closet. It wasn't that she didn't trust her father or

Nempson; she simply wanted to have her mother's legacy to hand at any time she might choose, without the need to refer to anyone else. She didn't care to examine her reasons too deeply; perhaps it was simply a feeling that if Griette had intended the notes for her eyes, that wish should be respected. Or perhaps there was another motive . . . but if so, it wasn't something she wanted to think about too deeply.

She had, in fact, brought the box with her, and it clearly pleased her father when she handed it and its contents into the Society's keeping without any demur. Or almost all its contents; for she had kept a few pages back, said nothing of their existence to anyone. The last scrawlings, the agonised, cryptic messages which Griette had penned as the desperation of madness finally overcame her will. If there was truly a key to the secrets locked in her mother's damaged mind – and Calliope believed that there was – then these pitiful remnants were, she felt, the ultimate clue. As yet, she did not wish to share it.

She and Foss walked home under a vivid sunset, buoyed and exuberant from the wine's effects. Crossing the square where the winged creature had been cornered and killed gave Calliope a brief but sharp frisson, and she found herself, a little morbidly, looking for traces of its remains. But the town officers had been thorough; already the broken trees and hedges and gates had been repaired or replaced, and there was no sign that any disturbance had ever taken place.

Philome had prepared a celebratory meal for Calliope, and to mark the occasion Foss produced two bottles of a vintage effusive wine from his well-stocked cellar. Philome's children, four-year-old Diona and three-year-old Tobery, were allowed a mouthful each in honour of the occasion, and the dinner turned into a lively affair which cheered even Celesta, who had been sulking sporadically since the birthday party because of her failure to snare the interest of the neighbour's son.

Foss, however, did not consider the day's work over by any means, and as the meal was drawing to a close he told Calliope that he would like to speak to her in the workroom. Not an urgent matter, he added, but one which he believed would interest her. Intrigued, Calliope excused herself – Philome was a little put out but only smiled stoically – and followed her father downstairs.

Foss's workroom was on the ground floor at the back of the house, reached by a dark, narrow passage beyond a door under the stairs. With the exception of Calliope, the family were strictly forbidden to enter it; not that Foss had any secrets to hide from his wife and children, but the idea of anyone meddling with and possibly damaging his equipment was something he dreaded. It was a slight bone of contention between him and Philome, who hated the idea of any room being denied the civilising influence of a thorough cleaning now and then, but Foss was adamant. The workroom was his own province and would remain so.

He and Calliope walked in silence along the passage to the door at the far end. The workroom was large and had a south-east aspect; daylight levels were excellent, and at night if the shutters were left open the moon added strength and emphasis to the huge etherea lamp that stood on the central table and dominated the room.

The leather-covered door closed at their backs with a soft sound, and Foss moved to the lamp. The moon was strong enough tonight to illuminate the room reasonably well, but nonetheless he spun the wheel that allowed the vapour to pass from the silver reservoir to the globe, and as nutrition flowed into its prison the nucleus stirred, rose from the bottom of the sphere and began to glow. Slowly the shadows receded; rows of crammed shelves lifted into visible relief, and Calliope sat down on the stool her father indicated.

'Calli.' Foss glanced over the table, satisfying himself, as he always did, that nothing had been disturbed since he was last here. 'There's no real need for us to be in this room, but I want to speak to you without any possibility of interruption. It's better, I think, that your stepmother isn't privy to what I have to say.' His blue eyes flicked to her face briefly, then he moved to the window and stared out at the dark garden. 'This concerns your poor mother's records.' A pause. 'I doubt you'll be surprised to learn that Nempson and I have already begun to consider how we might put them to the best use.'

Calliope watched him thoughtfully. 'I'm not surprised, Father. It's what I'd expected.'

'Good.' Foss realigned something on the table that wasn't exactly to his liking; an indication that he was faintly uneasy – or excited. 'Well, we've agreed on what our first priority should be, and it strikes us as a logical and simple strategy. If we're to gain the maximum benefit from your mother's notes, we need to have a specimen of the twilight creatures, and not simply the few ashes that the townsfolk were content to leave us after that incident the other day. I mean a *live* specimen.'

Calliope considered that with quickening interest. 'But you've had such specimens before, Father. I remember seeing some of them; and they yielded little—'

'No, no; you misunderstand. I'm not speaking of the ephemeral things we've succeeded in capturing in the past. They're of no real value; their substance is small and they never survive long enough for any worthwhile experiments to be carried out. I am – we are – thinking of a greater prize.' He met her gaze. 'Something of the magnitude of the creature in the Public Garden.'

There was silence for some moments. Then, quietly, Calliope said, 'How would you capture it?'

Foss was a little taken aback. He had expected her to be astonished, possibly shocked, and certainly impressed. But she behaved as if the idea had come as no surprise to her. For an irrational moment he felt piqued, until memory jogged his mind and he recalled other instances of that strangely phlegmatic quality that Calliope so often exhibited. It was a characteristic of his daughter's which he had never quite understood, and sometimes in the past he had wondered if it sprang from some lack of attention, lack of understanding. But it didn't. It was simply her way; to accept facts as facts and ideas as ideas, without making a great fuss about either.

'Well,' he said again, 'that of course, is something we'll need to work out in detail. But Nempson has made a suggestion with which I'm inclined to agree. As you know, these twilight beings are weakened and possibly frightened by daylight; we saw clear evidence of that in the Public Garden and it bears out a suspicion we've long held. Logically, it would be a great deal easier to hunt them down during the day; but there is an attendant difficulty, for at the first rumour of such a being's discovery the ordinary people do precisely what they did a few days ago – they go into a ferment of fear and rage that isn't slaked until the creature is killed and burned.' His lips twitched. 'Their civic zeal might be commendable, but from a scientific point of view it's a wanton waste. So we propose a night hunt.'

Calliope's eyes widened keenly. 'A *night* hunt? Do you think it might be successful?'

'Oh, yes. For the most part the ordinary folk are too afraid of what the dark might contain to venture out even when the lamps are lit. We, however, are not hampered by their superstitious terrors. We propose to patrol the streets after sunset. That, we know, is when these twilight beings are at their most active. If we persevere, I firmly believe that we'll succeed in capturing a greater prize than our Society, or any other for that matter, has ever snared before.'

Calliope stared at the shelves, but her imagination was ranging far beyond their crammed contents. One of the great twilight creatures, captured alive ... It would be *fascinating*. Some Institute members, she knew, held the view that the larger beings from that dimension were intelligent; possibly even capable of communicating. To put that theory to the test, and prove it one way or the other, would be a spectacular achievement.

It might even cast some light among the shadows of her mother's last, desperate notes ...

Foss uttered a small, contrived cough designed to catch her attention. 'I would prefer, of course,' he said, 'to keep this enterprise strictly within the province of our own Society. However, that could create one small problem – the question of where such a creature, if we do succeed in capturing it, should be housed.'

Calliope understood. If the prize should be taken to the Institute, it would immediately become, in effect, the Institute's property. Foss didn't want that, and she was inclined to agree with him. This was their own Society's enterprise, and to involve the Institute would make for a lot of unwanted complications. But then, as Foss said, that raised the question of where such a creature could alternatively be held.

She saw abruptly where he was leading, and her eyebrows went up a little. 'Philome would be horrified. And frightened.'

Foss returned a knowing look. 'Indeed. But if the arrangements were to be made and carried out before she knew of them ...' He smiled thinly. 'Your stepmother is very adaptable.'

In truth Calliope herself wasn't entirely happy with the idea of keeping such a captive here in the house, and Philome's reaction if she were to be consulted didn't bear thinking of. But the temptation . . . to have free and constant access to their prize; to be able to work, examine, experiment, without any form of hindrance . . .

Without realising it she had begun to flick her eyes about the workroom, instinctively calculating the practicalities of the idea. Foss saw and understood the reaction, and smiled a thin, dry smile.

'It's a logical solution, Calli. We have better facilities here than Nempson or any of the other members can provide.' He paused. 'As a woman, I think you will know how best to persuade your stepmother to accept our way of thinking once the deed is accomplished.'

There was a brief silence. Then Calliope met her father's gaze, and in her look was tacit conspiracy.

She said, quietly, 'When do you propose to begin the hunt, Father?'

The men's refusal to allow her to go with them angered Calliope, but despite her protests Foss was adamant. He would not, he said, permit his daughter to endanger herself in such an undertaking. She was a woman and this was not woman's work. Furious and disappointed, Calliope wanted to argue that as a Society member she was surely entitled to take a full part in all the Society's activities, and she was also sorely tempted to point out that, now she was of age, her father no longer had the right to dictate what she should or should not do. But at the last her courage failed. She didn't have the confidence to express her feelings honestly and bluntly, nor the courage to put her supposed independence to the test in the face of Foss's opposition. Perhaps in time she would claim that freedom. But not yet.

So Foss, Nempson and three other men of the Society began their patrol. Philome was mildly put out by her husband's planned night absences, but innocently believed his story that he was to be occupied in some astronomical experiment at the Institute which could only be conducted after sunset. Calliope pretended ignorance, held her tongue, and waited with uneasy impatience for news of success.

The first two nights of the patrol yielded nothing of any value. On the second night the men did see one of the twilight entities, but it was a tiny, flittering thing, like a skeletal bird, and at their first attempt to approach it, it skimmed away into the shielding dark of a side-street and was lost from view. There was a brief debate over whether it was worth pursuing, but the consensus was that it had nothing worthwhile to offer. So the group went on their way and again returned home empty-handed.

But the third night was a different matter.

During that day clouds had swept in from the west, and shortly before dusk rain began to fall in a steady, saturating drizzle. For all its discomfort the weather was a boon to the hunters, for it blotted out the moon and gave the town an extra and welcome edge of darkness. The street-lamps burning in their high brackets were an inconvenience, but the gloom and wet dimmed their glow to a chill, remote nacre unable to penetrate beyond its own dim nimbus into the night's veil. Conditions were ideal.

It was well past midnight when the breakthrough came. Finding nothing in the squares and broader thoroughfares, they had made their way into a less populous part of the town where the streets were narrow and the quiet acute. The clocktower bell, muffled by the rain's susurrus, had announced the first hour of morning, and the last note was fading away when Nempson's keen eyes caught an untoward flicker of movement in an alley a little way off. A gesture stilled his comrades; they watched in motionless silence, their gazes following the direction he indicated. There was a small sound, as of a door being surreptitiously closed; then the movement showed again and this time they all saw it. A shape, almost but not quite blending with the dark. Moving as a human form might move. Charcoal black of a cloak, rain-shimmer on hair that looked silver. And, for one moment only, the glimpse of a face. A *grey* face.

Glances were exchanged; expressions, in the shadows, tensed with cautious hope. Slowly, they began to advance towards the alley.

It was a fundamental mistake and one which, had matters not gone awry, Charn would never have made. But his preoccupation had eclipsed the caution which otherwise would have alerted him, and he was unaware of the humans' approach. Two days in this world, and the effect it was having on his body and mind had blinded him to anything but the need to replenish himself. He had intended to feed last night, but by a chain of circumstances it had proved impossible, and throughout the day he had felt himself weakening rapidly despite the cloud that lessened the sun's savage influence. Now that darkness had fallen again, he had a straightforward choice; to return to his own world, and quickly, or to find the sustenance that would allow him to stay. He wanted to stay; wanted to fulfil his promise to Selethe. And the woman who emerged from a narrow door in one of the alley's shabby houses had provided the opportunity he needed.

Charn had learned enough of this world to have an idea of what the woman was. Human men, it seemed, sought sexual pleasure not only with their chosen consorts but often, also, in other and more clandestine ways; and there were females of their kind whose sole function and purpose was to fulfil that desire. Charn made no attempt to comprehend the logic of it; it simply seemed, to him, a form of hypocrisy that men should trouble to pretend loyalty to one woman whilst practising another code entirely. But tonight the human aberration had played into his hands.

She had seen him, as he intended, only moments after she emerged from the house. Whether she had had a destination in mind, or whether she had simply meant to walk the streets in the hope of finding another buyer for what she had to offer, he didn't know, and it was irrelevant. She was quite young; probably, he thought, inexperienced and naive. Very unsure of herself. So when her uneasy gaze lit on him in the darkness she didn't notice – or chose not to notice – the fact that he had no colour but was a figure of grey and black and silver monochrome, and saw only a quiet, serenely compassionate face and a figure that was not gross or repulsive like so many who courted her service. She hesitated; hope and indecision clashed briefly in her eyes. Then, slowly, she approached him.

He did nothing then, not overtly. He only spoke to her in the gentle way that was second nature to him when he chose. His voice and his words reassured her; even, at one point, made her laugh, albeit nervously. She thought he had money; from his clothes and manner there was no reason for her to assume otherwise. When with a gauche attempt at coquetry she indicated the house's door, Charn went with her up the steep stairs and into the shabby lodging-room where a single lamp burned beside her drab bed. He watched her as she took off her dress and began to unfasten the strangely complex undergarments beneath. Then he touched her, at the same moment switching his mental focus with a quick, confident and unerring skill. Her mind was trapped instantly; her body was suddenly very still, caught in the thrall of his control. Charn smiled, with an undertone of regret that he knew he couldn't afford to acknowledge, and prepared to take from her the life-energy that he needed.

He left her lying motionless in the bed's disorder and emerged from the house as silently as a shadow. The door closed behind him and he paused, allowing himself to relax and savour the sense of relief as he felt strength returning to him. He was sated, and, by feeding in the way he had, he would be sustained for a good while; time enough to intensify his search.

It was then, as he enjoyed the new tranquillity in his mind, that the first psychic stirrings of alarm sounded. It caught him unawares; swift as a cat he turned – and sensed, in the moment before he saw, five dark figures closing in on him. Suddenly, violently, he was alert, and shock mingled with a sense of horror and fury at his own lapse. But recrimination came too late; they had seen him clearly now and were coming at him.

Charn turned and darted towards the alley's far end. *Darkness* – in the last doorway there was dark enough for him to elude them, slip through the gate between worlds and be gone. But as he neared it, almost reached it, a flare blazed suddenly in one of his pursuer's hands, and the wedge of blackness that had promised sanctuary shattered.

'*There it is!*' Nempson Trinity's voice cut through the rush of booted feet. '*Take the creature – take it!*'

They lunged as one; five solid, powerful forms, and against such a force even Charn's newly replenished strength wasn't enough. The flare blinded him; he felt the onrush of its heat and the heat of the men themselves, and it was like a hammer-blow to his mind and body; reason collapsed and, driven by sheer instinct, he turned like a cornered animal to face them. One thought, one alone, ricocheted through him – *no sound, no voice! Don't betray that secret—*

Foss neither knew nor cared whether the quarry was silent or screaming. He was aware only of his own voice joining with those of Nempson and the others, as they bore down on their prey. Grey and black and silver, and though it looked human it had no humanity; it was a prize beyond price.

He saw a gloved fist fly, heard one of the other men grunt in agony as Charn's first, ferocious blow hit its target. The creature was wild, demented, fighting them with unnatural speed and skill and energy. Foss glimpsed whipping hair, the cloak it wore flailing like a black wing; another strike found its mark and a second man reeled back—

'*Nempson!*' Foss's stentorian shout set echoes clashing down the alley. 'Hit it! Hit it, before—'

But Nempson had already drawn the truncheon that hung at his belt. It was a last resort, a measure they had hoped to avoid for none of them knew what physical damage such a weapon might inflict on alien flesh. Now, though, reason had no relevance. The creature had a madman's strength; caution must be thrown to the winds or it would escape and leave half their number maimed in its wake.

The truncheon was a short, dense length of solid wood, tipped with iron, and Nempson had perfected the art of using it. It swung, a brief but emphatic blur in the darkness, and Foss heard the dull sound as it connected with their quarry's skull. He had a momentary glimpse of the being's face above the cloak, its expression one of astonishment, shock, disbelieving outrage. Then, like a weighted sack dropped from a small but significant height, Charn collapsed senseless to the pavement.

They knew nothing of the prostitute or the part she had unwittingly played in their triumph. Their sole preoccupation was with their prize and, now it was captured, ensuring that it could not escape. The captive's strength had shocked them; remembering the winged creature in the Public Garden they had expected this being to be as frail and insubstantial. Instead, they had encountered something with a strength to match any two of their number, and the ferocity of a rabid dog. But for Nempson's timely strike the creature could have inflicted untold damage and might well have escaped. The question of security, therefore, was paramount. Their original plan simply to tether the creature in Foss's workroom was clearly out of the question; a far better safeguard would be needed, and one of the party had a suggestion. At the Institute was a particular chair which might solve their problem. It had been constructed some years ago, during an experiment designed to find a cure for the Dancing Disease, but the experiment had proved inconclusive, and with no better use suggesting itself the chair had joined other redundant exhibits in the Curiosities Hall. But the fundamental principle of its design was security. If anything could hold their prize immobile, the chair would be the answer.

The idea was accepted wholeheartedly, and it was agreed that as soon as the curator arrived at his post in the morning, arrangements would be made for the chair to be borrowed. The Institute loaned all manner of objects to its affiliates, and it would be easy enough to invent a plausible reason for the request that wouldn't arouse unwanted interest.

Taking turns to carry their spoils two by two, they continued on their way to Foss's house. The captive was a dead weight and none of them was overly fit; Foss, sweating despite the rain, was thankful when at last they reached their goal and hauled the unconscious Charn – wrapped and hidden for prudence's sake in his own cloak – up the steps to the front door. Two of the party murmured their goodnights and hurried quietly away; the house might be dark and silent but there was no point risking disturbance, and the fewer their numbers from now on, the less likely they were to wake Philome. Gesturing for his two remaining companions to stay back, Foss opened the door and went inside. In the hall he paused, listening. No sound from upstairs; no flicker of a light. The household was asleep, and he turned and beckoned to his colleagues to bring their burden inside.

They had almost reached the understairs door and the passage that led to the workroom, when there was a footfall overhead and someone appeared on the stairs. Foss looked up – and his heart almost stopped as he saw what looked like the figure of Griette gazing down at him. Dark hair unbound, nightgown pale as a shroud, a living ghost gliding out of a past he had tried for so long to forget—

Then the figure said, softly but urgently, '*Father?*'

'Calli . . .' Illusion and Griette's phantom vanished, and Foss breathed a sigh of painful relief as his pulse began to function again. 'Living spirits, for a moment I thought—' He caught himself. 'I thought you were Philome!'

Calliope skimmed down to the hall. 'I was watching for your return.' Her eyes flickered quickly towards Nempson and the other man, and she added eagerly, 'You've succeeded?'

'Yes. And it's a far greater success than any of us anticipated. You'd best not come with us now, but in the morning—'

Above them, on the upstairs landing, a sleepy voice said, 'Foss?'

Foss swore in shock, and Calliope spun round. Philome was on the landing, wrapped in a crimson robe, her hair awry and a frown creasing her features.

'Foss, do you have any idea of the *hour*? And Calli, whatever are you doing downstairs in only your night shift with the weather so cold? I really don't understand what—' Abruptly she stopped as she saw her husband's consternation, and the guilt that had made a mask of Calliope's face. Her gaze wavered, then travelled across the hall to where Nempson and his colleague had frozen with their burden held awkwardly between them.

Philome said, in an ominously tight little voice, 'What is *that*?'

Foss interposed himself in her line of sight, hoping to block any closer view of the shrouded captive. 'My dear.' His tone was unctuous, soothing, but Calliope was well aware of the alarm underlying it even if Philome was not. 'It's nothing to worry about; nothing you need concern yourself with. We've merely brought back something from the Institute. For an experiment.'

Philome continued to stare past him at the other two men. 'Wrapped in that way?' she said. 'It looks like a . . . *body*.'

'It's no such thing, my dear, of course it isn't,' Foss reassured. 'We simply covered it to keep the rain from damaging it. A filthy night; quite unseasonable for the time of—'

He was interrupted by a startled oath from Nempson, and at the same time Philome uttered a small, thin shriek and clutched at the banister rail. '*It moved! I saw it move!*'

Foss swung round and saw that his colleagues had almost dropped the captive. The wrapped bundle was stirring; feebly and slightly, but enough to warn him that the creature was on the verge of regaining consciousness.

'Living spirits!' He was across the hall in three strides, reaching out to the understairs door. 'Get it to the workroom and deal with it, *quickly*!'

'Foss, what *is* it?' Philome shrilled. But he didn't answer; he was fumbling at the door's latch, opening it, hustling the other two men through. 'I'll join you within the minute – *hurry!*' They vanished into darkness, and Foss turned to face his wife again.

51

Philome was staring at him, fear and horror and anger mingling on her face. 'Foss, I *must* have an explanation! That thing is *alive!*' She put a clenched fist to her mouth. 'It's some animal, some monstrous wild beast, I *know* it is! What have you *done?* Oh, Foss, the danger – the children, their safety – *what have you brought into our home?*'

Foss tried to cut through the tirade and calm her, but Philome wouldn't be reasoned with. She burst into tears, and impatience, guilt and the fading but still potent after-shock of the twilight creature's violent attack combined to trigger Foss's temper.

'In the name of all the powers, woman, stop your noise!' he snapped at her, 'I have *work* to do – urgent work, and no time for your hysterics!'

'But I want to know what you've done!' Philome wailed.

'Then Calli shall tell you.' He gestured irritably towards his daughter. 'She knows what we're about, and she's perfectly able to explain.'

Calliope's jaw dropped. 'Father, what should I say?' She hadn't begun to think how Philome might be persuaded to accept this, and she was at a complete loss. Foss, however, was past caring; thought of the havoc that might even now be taking place in the workroom eclipsed all else.

'Tell her everything! She'll simply have to abide by my decision, like it or no!' Then before either of the two women could make any response at all, he disappeared through the understairs door.

Calliope turned slowly, reluctantly, and looked at her stepmother. Philome's tears had stopped but her lower lip was trembling, and when she spoke her voice was extremely strained.

'Calliope.' She used her full name, as though to emphasise the gravity of what she intended to say. 'Come upstairs to my bedchamber, if you please. I wish to speak with you. And I expect . . .' Her mouth quivered more violently; she brought it under control. 'I expect, as your father said, to be told *everything*.'

Peace of a kind was eventually restored to the household. There had been no mayhem in the workroom, and with the captive secured Nempson and his colleague departed, while Foss reluctantly steeled himself to face the inevitable fray upstairs. Calliope had done her best to pacify Philome and explain matters as far as she could with no preparation, but Philome was still verging on hysteria and it took Foss's authority and dominance eventually to persuade her that there was little to be gained from protesting against what had already been accomplished. The captive was under their roof; the damage – as Philome saw it – was done. Foss gave his absolute assurance that the creature could not break free and thus presented no possible danger to any man, woman or child in the house. As a last resort, he reminded his wife pointedly that he was master of his own home, and inasmuch as he did not interfere in her domestic arrangements, he considered it only the merest courtesy if she would kindly refrain from interfering in his. As always he won the argument; Philome's small rebellion gave way before his forcefulness, and eventually she accepted that she had no choice in the matter. The creature was here. It would stay. Though she might not like it, she must learn to live with it.

With a truce called at last and everyone wanting nothing more than to sleep, Calliope, who had been an unwilling and embarrassed witness to the wrangling between her father and stepmother, was able to excuse herself and return to her room. Foss accompanied her to the foot of the upper staircase, ostensibly to light the way for her but in actuality to exchange a few low-pitched words. The prize, he said, was tied up in the workroom and would be safe enough until better arrangements could be made. There was no time to tell her the whole tale now; Nempson and the others would return in the morning and then they would all find out in greater detail exactly what they had snared.

'Speaking of morning,' Foss glanced towards the tall landing window with its coloured glass panes, 'it will be on us before we know it; the street-lamps have gone out and the dawn's almost breaking. Best go to bed, Calli. I wish you a good night.'

Calliope was disappointed not to learn more, but obediently kissed his cheek, wished him goodnight in return and climbed up the stairs to the top floor. From the room below she heard Philome's voice, half petulant and half cajoling, and her father's deeper, louder tones. Then silence fell, and with a sigh she went to her own bedchamber, wondering fleetingly, and not for the first time, what strange chemistry had caused Foss to choose Philome for a second wife, and she to accept him. They were like fire and water in so many ways; nearly twenty years between them and utter opposites in their tastes, their attitudes, their interests. Yet perhaps, she thought, that was a part of the attraction. As for the rest: well, Philome was bright-natured and pretty, and Foss had wealth and standing and had offered her security and a fine home. Calliope smiled a little sadly and acknowledged wryly that she, of all people, was hardly qualified to sit in judgement on questions of love, or what passed for it.

The shutters of her window were open and the pre-dawn glimmer was strong enough now to make a lamp unnecessary. Calliope sat down on her bed and gazed for a few moments at the linen-chest where the copies of her mother's papers were safely shut away.

White flowers. The Sacrament. I do not have the courage. For some reason those strange, wild words had come back to haunt her. *I do not have the courage . . .* Courage for what? She didn't know. But she felt – and feelings, Calliope had learned over the years, could all too often catch one unawares by being proven valid – that there had been love, real love, in Griette's helpless confession.

White flowers. For a wreath? A funeral? *DEATH . . .* Calliope shivered, and slipped under the bedcovers. She thought of her mother, perhaps sleeping now or perhaps awake through the night, as the hospice angels said sadly was her habit. Gazing from her window at the growing light. The rain had stopped now and the sky had begun to clear, though Calliope didn't remember noticing when the change in the weather had come. The sun would rise soon. She thought of the captive, the prize, bound and helpless in the workroom; a creature of darkness who shunned the light. What clues might it hold? Could those clues ever be unravelled?

In the distance a horse's hooves sounded brisk and staccato. The town was coming to life as the perilous dark was pushed back by another day, and Calliope hugged her pillow like an old and comforting friend, closing her eyes and letting her thoughts pass into weary oblivion.

Chapter V

As Calliope laid her hand on the door-latch Celesta said, 'You are sure, Calli? Sure that it's safe?'

'It's safe.' Calliope's voice was a little impatient. 'The creature can't harm you. Father and the other men took every precaution.' She paused. 'I'll go alone, if you'd prefer not to see it.'

In truth, deep curiosity and morbid fascination were fighting a war with fear in Celesta's mind. She had seen some of the other entities which Foss had captured in the past, but they had been tiny things, often no larger than butterflies; and as fragile, for they had never survived for longer than a day. But this . . . 'A higher order of being,' her father had said this morning. She didn't know what to expect, but her imagination was in full spate.

She shook her head. 'No. I *want* to see it.' Her gaze slid sidelong to her elder sister. 'Besides, you can't go alone. You know what Philome said.'

Calliope sighed, and silently railed against Philome and her injunctions. However well-meaning the motive, Celesta's company – or that of anyone other than Foss for that matter – was a nuisance. But with Foss away and Philome adamant that she should not venture into this room alone, there had been little choice.

The day had not gone according to plan. Calliope had slept almost until noon, to her great annoyance, and by the time she woke, Nempson and the two other Society members had already been to the house, completed the work of securing the prisoner more thoroughly and left again. Shortly after their departure Foss himself had been called away to a confinement; Philome, taking advantage of his absence, had ordered lunch to be served early and, as soon as the meal was over, pounced on Calliope and coerced her into a shopping expedition. To placate and divert Philome in the wake of last night's upset, Foss had given her a generous amount of money over and above her usual allowance and had told her to spend it entirely on herself. Philome, benevolent as ever, wanted to share the bounty, so Calliope and a far more willing Celesta spent the afternoon in her wake as she visited sempstresses, milliners and shoemakers and ordered new items for all their wardrobes. Calliope emerged from the expedition with one new gown, two pairs of shoes and a hat with a triangular, feather-trimmed brim which was the latest fashion, and did her best not to seem ungrateful. But she was distracted, and seething with frustrated impatience.

Foss was still away when they returned, but a note from him had been delivered by messenger. The birth was proving difficult and protracted, and even if there were no further complications Foss doubted that he would be home before midnight. In a brief, separate message to Calliope he asked her to 'take steps to ensure that all is well in the workroom'. Calliope understood. The captive had been left unattended since morning, and Foss's agitation was obvious; he feared either that the creature might have escaped, or, worse, that it had died. He relied on her to make certain all was well.

Philome, however, had insisted that any visit to the workroom must wait until after the ritual of dinner was over, saying that their own sustenance was more important than that of whatever unearthly monstrosity Foss had chosen to confine in his sanctum. Then, as they ate, she stated flatly that she would not permit Calliope to face the creature alone. Philome would have preferred Luthe to accompany his sister, but Luthe planned to meet a group of his friends at the theatre – or so he said – and wouldn't co-operate. So when Celesta, agog with fascinated interest, asked that she might be allowed to go, Philome agreed.

Celesta was staring at the door-latch as though it were something alive and not entirely pleasant. Again Calliope pushed down a faint feeling of resentment, and said, 'Very well, then. You haven't forgotten your gloves?'

'No.' That, too, was strange and frightening, Celesta thought; that the creature must not be touched, under any circumstances, with uncovered hands. No one had explained the reason to her; it had simply been stated as a rule not to be broken, and it was enough to set her lively mind racing.

Calliope opened the door. The workroom was very quiet, very still. The great etherea lamp burned in its mounting on the central table, the green nucleus darting and quivering and casting restless shadows, and outside the moon was high, its light refracting coldly in through the half-open inner shutters. Celesta had only entered this room two or three times in her life, and then under

Foss's close supervision, and her eyes widened with a mingling of suspicion and faint distaste as she took in the clutter.

'It's so *cold* in here.' She spoke softly, turning towards Calliope as she did so. But Calliope was paying her no heed. She was staring across to the far side of the room and the corner opposite the window.

The etherea lamp's radiance barely reached to the corner, but the moonlight did. All Calliope's expectations, all her thoughts and imaginings and preconceptions, shattered as she saw the captive.

He was confined in the experiment-chair, which Nempson Trinity had borrowed from the Institute and which had been delivered to the house that morning. Tall, narrow, constructed of wood and iron with a hinged copper cowl rising above the high back, the chair had a deep seat, high, hard arms, and iron restraints carefully placed to hold the wrists, ankles and waist of an occupant and keep him helpless.

Charn had regain consciousness twice since his capture. The first recovery, soon after his arrival, had been swiftly and efficiently dealt with by another and harder blow from Nempson's truncheon, and he had remained oblivious for the rest of the night. But on the second occasion he had come to while the restraints were being bolted around his wrists and ankles, and he had tried to fight. Again the resistance was wild and soundless – but it was short-lived. As Foss had remarked, either the creature had recognised their greater numbers and greater strength, in which case the likelihood was that it did possess intelligence, or it was simply too exhausted to continue the struggle. Whichever the case, it was decided that no risks should be taken, and a third strike of the truncheon, at a carefully calculated point on the skull, had rendered their captive unconscious again without inflicting serious damage. A day or two to recover and contemplate its situation, Foss added, should bring it to its senses, if senses it had.

Charn was slumped now in the chair, arms outstretched at an awkward angle where the clamps held them and his head turned aside, resting against the chair's back. He was either asleep or still senseless and, taking courage from his immobility, Celesta moved slowly closer in an effort to see him better in the dim light.

'Not too near.' Calliope touched her arm, voice pitched low.

Celesta halted and looked uncertainly at the two tall brass stems with fat candles, half burned down but now extinguished, set in front of the chair as though to mark off the corner of the room. Then her gaze returned to the recumbent figure and she gave a little shiver.

'He's grey,' she whispered wonderingly. 'Look, Calli, he's all grey and silver . . . he has no colour at all.'

'I know.' Calliope, too, was gazing at Charn, and in a small, dark crevice of her mind she felt a creeping sense of uncertainty. She hadn't expected this. Foss had not had the chance to tell her that the entity from the other world looked human, and emotions and reactions tangled together in her: chagrin, a sudden sapping of confidence, a half-recognised feeling that its – no, *his*; Celesta was right – his form made this captivity somehow wrong.

Disquieted by the feelings, and wanting to earth them as the copper net on the house roof earthed lightning, she took refuge in mundanity and spoke to her sister. 'He has nothing to drink; he'll need water when he wakes. See if there's a flask and beaker on the table.'

Celesta gave her a slantwise glance, a little surprised by her sudden brisk tone, but obeyed. She found the items, filled the glass and carried it carefully back. 'If he won't take it—' she started to say.

'I'll just have to try. Otherwise—' Calliope stopped with a jolt of shock as she saw that the prisoner was looking straight at her.

Celesta turned her head. Then she gave a high-pitched squeal, and the glass in her hand dropped like a stone to shatter on the floor. '*Oh, Calli! His eyes—*'

The illusion of humanity was smashed, for those eyes were like hard, polished pewter, alien and flaring and filled with a flood of rage, hatred and scorn that hit Calliope as violently as if he had physically struck her. She jerked back, heard Celesta's feet scuffing, running, the slam of the door as she fled. Suddenly, in a silence that seemed to clamp suffocatingly around her, she was alone with the captive.

Forcing her gaze to move was hard, for she could sense that the terrible stare was still fixed unwaveringly on her, and the thought of facing it again shot a wave of prickling cold through her. But she made her courage rally; made herself look.

Great powers, but there was danger in him! And terrifying intelligence . . . With a tremendous effort Calliope pivoted until she was facing him directly. His silver-grey hair was damp, she saw now, and perspiration formed faintly shining patterns on his face and neck. His features weren't delicate, as her first, brief impression had suggested. The bones were fine and narrow, but there was a stark strength about his face, an angularity that bordered almost on heaviness. His mouth, wide and full-lipped, was turned down and looked lethal, his jaw was set with ruthless anger, yet the anger was under fearsome control. And his eyes burned with a fire that was arctically cold. Oh no, Calliope thought; this was no half-sensate being such as the winged creature the mob had destroyed in the Public Garden. He had a power of reason to match or outstrip any human mind. He was sentient . . . and dangerous.

For one chaotic moment she thought that she couldn't face this being alone, and she almost turned and ran out of the workroom in her sister's wake. But then rationality and a measure of indignation came to her rescue. Sentient and dangerous he might be, but the creature was no threat to her, for the chair held him fast. Was she a silly girl like Celesta, Calliope asked herself angrily, or a grown woman, a scientist and a seeker of knowledge? She was equal with the men of the Society, a partner in their venture: what would they think of her if she let fear overcome her at her very first test?

The combative thought pushed her terrors out and shut her mind's doors on them, and very slowly Calliope took a step towards the captive. Smiling was not easy in the face of his ferocious glare, but she did her best, striving to add a measure of reassurance in the look she returned.

'Please,' she spoke softly. 'Don't be afraid. I— we— mean you no harm.' Glass crunched beneath her shoes, making her start and silently curse Celesta's foolishness. Recovering her poise, she added, 'Can you speak? Do you understand me?'

The prisoner turned his head away and his eyes closed. He made no sound, and Calliope couldn't tell whether he had comprehended or even heard her.

She persevered. 'Do you want food? Or water? You must be thirsty.' Was there another beaker on the table? She looked swiftly, saw there was and went to fill it.

59

'Water.' She repeated the word slowly, pointed to the glass and then drank a little of its contents herself to show what should be done and that it was not harmful. But although his eyes had opened again, he ignored her.

'You must have sustenance,' Calliope said. 'Please, if you can understand, speak to me and tell me your needs. We can provide them for you. I *promise* that we wish you no harm.'

She could hear him breathing, rapidly, shallowly, and his hands clenched under the restraints. No further reaction though, no unbending, and she sighed. 'Well, if you won't drink, what must I do to persuade you?' She bent to set the cup down on the floor, then looked up at the squat candles in their brass stands. These creatures were afraid of fire. Perhaps that was the way to cure him of his stubbornness?

He paid no heed as she took her firebox from her apron pocket, but at the scratch of the flame-strip on flint his head turned with a quick, wary movement. The bright yellow tongue flared with a whiff of sulphur, and Calliope touched the strip first to one candle and then to the other. Ah, yes; *that* provoked a reaction. The creature's hands gripped the chair-arms with a sudden, convulsive movement and he tried to strain his body back, away from the flames. Sweat broke out anew on his face and neck and Calliope heard the tenor of his breathing change and become swifter, labouring. Then she looked at his eyes again, and what she saw in them made her stomach lurch. He was in pain. The candles' light, small and insignificant though it was to a human, was burning and blinding him, and though he was trying to bear it, not to show weakness to one he considered an enemy, the effort was costing him dearly.

Her earlier doubts returned suddenly and flowered into a sharp pang of conscience. This *was* wrong. To keep him confined like this, unable to move, deprived of the smallest modicum of comfort or dignity – it was an uncivilised and unworthy act. Even if he was dangerous, surely a more humane means of securing him could have been found with little extra effort? Nempson Trinity and his partiality for gadgetry and complication . . . doubtless the chair had been his idea and Foss had agreed for the sake of convenience. Well, Calliope thought, it would not do. She wasn't in the habit of standing up to her father – few people did – but for once she intended to make an exception. And before speaking to

Foss, she would try to make some small amends of her own.

She snuffed the candles out with two small movements. The captive relaxed instantly; he tried to conceal his reaction from her but she saw and noted it. Well, then; one kindness was accomplished. What else could be done?

Cautiously, hoping that she was not making a dire mistake, she moved past the candle stands and stood before the captive's chair.

'I'm sorry.' She looked down at him. 'I didn't know that the candles would cause you pain. We know very little about you, you see; and unless you can tell us how to avoid harming you, we must learn by trial and error.' She paused. 'I would like to release you from the chair, but I can't do so without my father's agreement. However, I will speak to him. And if he . . .'

She stopped as she noticed his hands where they lay limp on the chair-arms. The skin on both his wrists was darkened almost to black where the restraints had chafed. It was hard to tell when he had no colour, but the marks looked like scalds, or scorches; as if contact with iron had burned him in the same way that the candlelight burned his eyes.

Calliope uttered a soft, shocked oath under her breath. 'Your *arms* . . .' she said, and looked quickly, dismayed, at his face again. 'Is it the metal? Does it hurt you?'

No reply, no reaction; his face was coldly immobile. But she couldn't leave him to suffer, Calliope thought. The fetters at his waist and ankles would be enough to hold him, and though the possible risk she would run in freeing his hands unnerved her, he would surely understand that it was meant as an act of compassion and wouldn't try to—

She quashed that thought before it could take hold, and reached out towards the chair's left arm. He had a strong hand, far less frail than she might have expected, and though the wrist and forearm were narrow they had a powerful look. Fine, silver hair gave the skin a faint sheen, and the veins beneath the skin looked like streaks of charcoal in an artist's half-finished sketch.

'Now,' she said, aware that her voice was unsteady, and angry with herself for letting her cowardice show, 'I'm going to unfasten the clamps and release your arms. Don't try to hurt me. I have fire – you saw that I have fire – and if you try to hurt me I will strike it again.' A pause, but it was impossible to tell whether he understood. 'Very well, then. I shall—' *Living spirits, the gloves! She had almost forgotten the gloves!* A wave of heat followed by a wave of cold prickled down Calliope's spine as she hastily took the gloves from her pocket and pulled them onto her hands. Such an *elementary* mistake; the creature had upset her composure, flustered her. She took two deep breaths, flexing her fingers, wishing she didn't feel quite so tense. 'There. Now, keep still.'

Though pretending to stare across the room, Charn watched obliquely and uneasily as her hands moved slowly to the restraints. Her body's heat radiated from her and hurt him, and the fact that it did hurt him made him realise how seriously weakened he had become. He felt as if the blood in his veins was burning, and the truncheon blows he had sustained were still echoing in slow and powerful waves of pain that pulsed through his skull. The hours of daylight during which he had been confined here had drained him further; now even the moonlight pained his eyes, though not as savagely as the bright candles had done, and his mind was dazed, making everything around him seem very unreal.

Except for the girl.

How old was she? Charn found it impossible to judge human ages with any certainty but thought she must be young, though an adult rather than a child. Her face was pleasing and her body oddly delicate for a human, hands slim, arms not fleshy or muscular. The other – younger? – one, who had been in the room with her when he woke but had then run away in fear, she had been different; to his eyes she seemed gross, like the men who had attacked him. This one was less alien . . . but for her hair. So much *colour*. Warm brown, the hint of red, falling over her shoulders in a wave. It fascinated him. Her eyes were a lighter brown flecked with green; that was strange, too. And her mouth. A small mouth but well shaped. Colourful. *Strange.*

A sharp click roused him suddenly from his meandering reverie and he saw that the shackle had fallen away from his left arm. For one instant he thought to reach out and grasp the girl by the neck – his speed would surprise her, as would his strength. But the impulse died as quickly as it had come. If he caught her, even if he killed her, what good would it do him? He couldn't free himself without further help, because the restraint at his waist had been locked with a key. Besides, at present he didn't have the strength that he might otherwise have used on her; he was badly debilitated and wouldn't recover without sustenance.

Calliope's fingers were working at the second manacle. Her confidence had grown when Charn did not attempt to attack her as the first restraint came free, and he sensed that she was doing her best not to hurt him. He flexed his left hand, and suppressed a sharp sound of pain as he felt the skin tear where the iron had seared it. The girl glanced at him anxiously but he affected not to be aware of it, and as she turned back to her work he moved his fingers more carefully. There was no serious damage, but he could feel blood oozing cold onto his wrist and knew that in his weak condition the wounds would take an unpleasantly long time to heal. He needed to feed. Needed to gain strength. Though it was dangerous, the danger had to be risked if he was to survive with any hope of release.

He looked again, sidelong through half-lidded and stinging eyes, at Calliope. She was absorbed; the second restraint was stiff and recalcitrant, and with her attention closely focused on it and thus diverted from him, Charn decided to gamble. If she sensed what he was doing and was alerted to the truth, he would lose his one potential advantage. But if he took only a small amount of energy, just enough to begin the healing, it seemed likely that she would never know.

He closed his eyes, focused his mind. So *much* life within her. Warmth and colour and brightness . . . she could spare what he needed. And if she came again, she or the pale girl or others, any others, as they surely would, then soon there would be more. Much more.

With a squeak of metal and another click, the second manacle fell away. Calliope immediately darted back out of Charn's reach, and as she looked at him again he quickly broke the spell he had been exerting on her. He had gained a little of her essence; not as much as he had wanted but enough to see him through another day. It would have to suffice for the present.

He sighed and withdrew his hands from the arms of the chair, pressing them against his ribs and trying to cool the searing pain. Calliope heard the sigh, but she didn't try again to persuade him to speak. Instead she stepped back, then drew the gloves from her hands and stood still, gazing at him with a solemn and pensive

63

expression. She could see the depth of his relief now that his hands were free, but there was still pain in his look and it disquieted her.

'What is it?' Her voice broke the silence at last, softly. 'Something still hurts you, I know. Can you not tell me?' Charn said nothing, and she continued to watch his face for a few moments more. The beads of sweat on his face, the damp hair. The shaft of moonlight falling directly on the chair . . .

'Is it the moon?' Understanding dawned suddenly, and Calliope moved aside so that her figure blocked the slanting silver beam. Her shadow fell over the captive and she saw his relief, the sudden easing of tension. 'I didn't know,' she said, her voice gentle. 'I'll close the shutters.'

He heard her cross the floor, then the moonlight vanished and blessed dark closed down on the room as she folded the shutters and fastened their catch. The only light now shone from the etherea lamp, but its glow was weak and did no harm. Her face spectral as she stood beside the dim green globe, Calliope smiled tentatively. 'It will at least be a reprieve until morning,' she said. Then she moved away from the lamp and became a silhouette in the gloom as she walked to the door. Opening it, she paused and looked back.

'My name,' she told him, 'is Calliope. I hope that one day you'll tell me yours.'

The door closed quietly behind her.

'I'll allow that it's given us a piece of information which we weren't privy to before,' Foss said irritably, 'but that doesn't change the fact that I would have preferred to be consulted – even *informed* – before you took matters into your own hands!' His blue eyes were focused on Calliope, then abruptly he frowned. 'And it is impolite to yawn at the breakfast table, daughter. What's amiss with you?'

Calliope shook her head. 'Nothing's amiss, Father. I simply feel tired this morning.' She paused. 'I'm sorry. I didn't mean to put you out; it simply seemed a kindness to—'

'Yes, yes, so you've already said. But kindness is a misplaced virtue with these beings, Calliope. Whatever the creature's appearance might suggest, it's no more human than a dog, and probably considerably less intelligent or tameable. This really isn't responsible conduct for a member of the Society, and I trust it won't be repeated.'

Philome, who sat at the opposite end of the table from her husband, sighed pointedly and said, 'My dear, *must* we discuss the Society's business at this hour? Breakfast is a family occasion and should be enjoyed by the *whole* family. If Calliope has done wrong, I'm sure she'll apologise properly and make amends; but, please, not *now*.'

Foss's brows knitted more deeply and he would have turned on her, but a sudden howl from Tobery diverted his attention. The little boy had upset his cup of weak tisane over the table and into his lap, and no one else could speak until his indignant yells had been soothed. Foss watched the mopping-up with bemusement that gradually became laced with amusement at his small son's antics, and by the time peace was restored his irritation had faded. He helped himself to more roasted kidneys and continued to Calliope, 'We'll say no more of it this time. But if such an impulse takes hold of you again, kindly *tell* me before you take any rash steps. Living spirits, who knows what the creature could have done to you once his hands were freed? We could have found you lying strangled, or with every bone—'

'Foss!' Philome interrupted. 'If you *please* – my blood is already hectic enough from the thought of it, without you to insist on reminding me again!' She gave Calliope a look that promised a lecture of her own as soon as a suitable opportunity arose; then as Calliope yawned once more the look modulated into a frown. 'Really, Calli, you *do* look tired. Foss, don't you think she looks tired? And pale. In fact, Calli, I'd say you look unhealthily pale. Perhaps you need a tonic; or more probably a few days' rest. All these experiments and the spirits alone know what other falderal; it really isn't *suitable* for a young woman.'

Philome went on to explain in detail why such 'falderal' was unsuitable, but Calliope let the words wash over her like summer rain. She had heard Philome's views on this subject too often to pay them a great deal of attention, and she felt too indolent to get involved in yet another debate. In fact, though nothing would have induced her to admit it to her stepmother, all she really wanted was to go back to bed and sleep for a few more hours, and she didn't know why. Waking this morning had been a great effort, despite the fact that she had retired at her usual time and, to the best of her knowledge, had slept as soundly as normal.

But for the dream.

That, though, was something she didn't want to dwell on, and she thrust it firmly away into a deep-buried compartment of her mind. Her mother, weeping and then screaming, while she could only stand by and watch. White flowers; a snowstorm of them, getting into her throat and choking her. The creature confined in the chair in the workroom, with his skin peeling away to reveal raw flesh and sinew beneath as the moonlight burned him like fire . . . A quick, ferocious shudder went through Calliope and she made a show of turning her attention to the breakfast she must force herself to eat.

She made her voice maintain its composure as she asked, 'How is the creature this morning, Father? Have you persuaded him – it – to take any nourishment?'

Foss shook his head. 'Not as yet; though whether it's stubbornness or an inability to ingest what is palatable to our species has yet to be established.' He glanced more keenly at her. 'We might need to put that to the test before much longer. Have you read the treatise I recommended, on the etheric humours common to physical and spiritual nutrition?'

'Yes, I have,' Calliope said. 'I was greatly interested by the methods Arcane Toller uses to create an artificial—'

'Calli.' Philome interrupted with a sweet but strained smile. 'Perhaps later, my dear . . . ? I really *do* think that you should show some concern for your own humours before you tire yourself further by worrying about those of creatures which by all rational standards shouldn't be in this world at all, let alone under our roof.'

Silence fell. Calliope looked at Foss, and Foss raised his fair eyebrows in a clear signal that implied, *later, we will discuss this without unwanted interruption*. Calliope inclined her head just enough to convey agreement, feeling yet again the small thrill of pleasure at the thought that her father viewed her as a peer rather than a subordinate. But at the same time something else stirred in her. Something she couldn't analyse, nor even quite assimilate. A small, inward and unexpected voice that said: *No. I shall make experiments of my own. I shall break down the barriers between me and our captive . . . and I shall do it in my own way.*

* * *

66

No one had come near him since Foss's brief foray shortly after dawn, and Charn was well aware that he was weakening. His latest encounter with the heavy, fair-haired man had been a very uneasy one, and although he had managed to maintain his silence in the face of Foss's intimidation he hadn't dared feed from him to even the smallest degree. The girl called Calliope – his jailer's daughter, he surmised – had been a relatively easy target; Foss, though, was far more likely to sense anything amiss, and the risk simply couldn't be taken.

His wrists still hurt, for the blisters and burns hadn't yet begun to heal, but at least the bleeding had stopped and the clamps had not been replaced on his arms. He had thought at first that Foss was going to negate that small kindness the girl had done for him, and fear of the pain had been enough to make him swallow his pride and make a show of docility. It had worked, but Charn was under no illusion that the respite would last for long. His unhuman mind had detected a resolve about his jailer, an aura of purpose and determination that had an extremely cold core, and coldness in the inhabitants of this world was something that he intuitively associated with cruelty. Foss wanted knowledge: knowledge of what Charn was, of where he had come from, of what powers he might or might not possess. And he would use any means necessary to achieve it.

Charn turned his head and cautiously looked towards the window at the far side of the room. Foss had opened the shutters, but only a crack; just enough to allow the early sunlight to cast a narrow, hard-edged shaft across the floor. The angle of the shaft was changing as the morning wore on, and before much longer it would reach the chair and cut across him where he sat. Foss had stated quite bluntly that he knew the sunlight would hurt his captive, and had added that the degree to which he was subjected to its touch would depend on his willingness, or otherwise, to co-operate in what would be asked of him later in the day. The words had been accompanied by a long, assessing stare which told Charn that the man didn't yet know whether he could understand human speech, and he had affected not to comprehend, only returned the stare with steady indifference. But he wasn't looking forward to the test. Unless he could find a source of nourishment, he wasn't even sure that he would be able to withstand it.

His eyes had begun to sting from looking at the gap in the shutters, and he let the lids droop again, turning his attention instead to the sounds that had been filtering to him from other parts of the house since dawn broke. Thus far they had registered only as a vague background disturbance, but now he concentrated on them more intently. Earlier there had been a lot of hurried footfalls, suggesting that a number of humans were engaged in some energetic activity. That had ceased, to be replaced a little later by a faint, steady drone of several voices from somewhere above, accompanied by a muted clattering and clinking. He had recognised the fair man's rumbling tones and, counterpointing those, several others which had the lighter, higher pitch that implied the presence of females or the very young; among them, he thought, the voice of Calliope. It seemed likely, though he couldn't yet be certain, that this place must be their family home, and it surprised him that he should have been brought to a human household rather than confined somewhere more secure. Was it ignorance or confidence that had persuaded them to be so incautious? Impossible to be sure, but it was a question worth bearing in mind, for the answer might contain the seeds of his own salvation.

For a while he continued to listen to the sounds, but they gave him no further information of any value. At last, with nothing better available, he lapsed into a light, uneasy and unpleasant inertia that hovered on the borders of sleep. When something impinged suddenly and sharply, he was awake in an instant, eyes wide, body tense under the restraints, scanning the room with a quick, suspicious stare. Nothing untoward; but the shaft of sunlight had moved across the floor and was now only two paces from him.

The sounds overhead had ceased, but there was a new noise somewhere outside the door. A shuffling, as of small feet. Charn looked at the door, and saw that the latch was moving. Twice it jerked and bounced and failed to unfasten; then at the third attempt it joggled free and the door swung open.

Someone entered, hesitated on the threshold. It was a small child. Charn couldn't judge its sex, for the creature was too young, but it bore a very distinct resemblance to the fair man. It blinked in apparent surprise at the gloom, then advanced slowly towards the chair. When it saw him more clearly it stopped again, but if it feared him its fear was eclipsed by curiosity, and it stared openly at him, taking in every detail with wide, solemn eyes.

Charn's tenseness took on a new dimension. This human was very young – but what youth lacked in substance it often made up for in vitality, and he could sense the sheer life within the child, a force which could provide him with far more than he had been able to take from Calliope last night. If he could only persuade the little creature to come close enough . . .

As the thought went through his mind, the child abruptly turned away, wandered to the table in the centre of the room and began to touch some of the implements and objects set there. Charn's jaw clenched with frustration and he tried to will the child's interest back in his direction. But, perversely, it took no notice. There was only one thing he could do.

Tobery knew he wasn't allowed into his father's workroom, but the very fact that it was forbidden territory gave it an allure impossible to resist. To a little boy this was a treasure-trove. So many things to look at; strange things, bright things, which in his small but active imagination had the enticement of magic about them. He had heard about the new thing that his father had brought here, and had been determined to sneak in and see it for himself, but now that he had seen it he was disappointed, because it was only a grey man and there was nothing wonderful about that. Far more interesting were the jars and bottles and instruments on the table, and the coils of wire, and the big bowl, far too big for him to lift, made out of nine different metals, and—

Behind him, a voice said, 'Child.'

Tobery looked over his shoulder. The grey man in the chair was watching him, and he wondered uneasily if the man was going to scold him for being here; perhaps even tell his father. Alarmed by that prospect, Tobery said defensively, 'Didn't mean to . . .'

The statement made no sense to Charn and he ignored it. He held out his left hand, the hand nearer to the table. 'Child,' he said again. 'Come here. Come here to me.'

A frown creased Tobery's small features. 'Come here' might mean a number of things. Sometimes, when he had done something he shouldn't and his father said it, it meant a punishment; or from his mother a spoonful of something he

69

didn't like but was 'good for him'. Yet on the other hand it sometimes meant a game or a happy surprise, or even a present.

The grey hand was still extended. Tobery saw that there were stains on the wrist, and he pointed at them. 'Blood,' he said. 'Hurt yourself.'

Charn smiled faintly. 'It doesn't hurt now.' The lie was glib, but such a young child hadn't the subtlety to judge that. 'Come and look.'

To Philome's squeamish despair Tobery was fascinated by wounds of any kind, and the chance to examine one at close quarters was an irresistible enticement. He started to move towards the chair, then hesitated.

'You mustn't tell I come.' Wariness mingled with eagerness. 'I'm not supposed.'

Charn smiled again. 'I won't tell anyone.'

'Promise . . . ?'

'I promise. No one will know.'

It was reassurance enough. Tobery went towards the chair and touched Charn's wrist with a tentative finger.

'*Cold.*' He withdrew the finger quickly, rubbed it on his sleeve as if the contact had stung him, then stared up into the captive's face with new interest. Charn's mind was already focused and ready; with a quick mental manoeuvre he snared the little boy's gaze, held it, felt his own will take hold of Tobery's and eclipse it. The risk he had taken in revealing his ability to understand and use human speech had paid off, for the child's own anxiety not to court discovery would ensure his silence. Charn wouldn't take too much energy, not a draining that would do serious harm, for that might alert others. Just enough to sustain him, and to bring back a measure of the strength he had lost.

It took less than a minute. Tobery stood motionless, his eyes still regarding Charn's face across the distance between them. When it was done he recalled nothing of it, only left the room with an untroubled mind, pleased by his secret foray and certain that his new friend would not give his disobedience away. After all, he had promised. Tobery was confident that the promise would be kept.

Chapter VI

Nempson Trinity and one of his colleagues arrived shortly after noon, and the first experiments on the captive began. Today's priority was to learn all they could of the creature's anatomy, preferably without doing irreparable damage, and thus discover how he could be kept alive and healthy. For propriety's sake Calliope was asked not to join them in the workroom, and the three men began their tests.

The first experiment lasted for four hours, and by the end of it they had added some very useful items to their store of information. To begin with, apart from his strange lack of colour the creature appeared to be physically human in every respect. His skeletal structure seemed much the same as their own, and judicious pressing and prodding – with gloved hands – suggested that his major organs were in the same locations as a man's. He had a tongue, his teeth and nails were firmly rooted, and when they opened one of his veins the blood that flowed from it, though black, was of similar consistency to their own. Nempson wanted to open an artery as well, to measure the speed and intensity of the blood-flow from rather than to the heart, but it was decided that the weakening effect might be too great until they could determine how to feed the creature and maintain his stamina. Instead, they drew off enough of the venal fluid to be distributed, together with cuttings of his hair, among interested associates for further analysis, then bandaged the wounds they had made in his arms – both arms, in case there might be some notable difference between the left and right sides of his body – and turned their attention to other matters.

Contact with iron was definitely harmful to him, as Calliope had discovered, and so was the direct touch of any base metal against his skin. Even cold, it seemed to have much the same effect as boiling water on human flesh, and when heated the effect produced was still more spectacular and elicited the first sounds they had ever heard their captive utter, though they were inchoate and no indication of his capacity for lucid speech.

But for all their new knowledge, still the most valuable fact in their catalogue to date was the creature's response to light. It was

71

already well known that the denizens of his world found any bright light inimical, and a few further experiments on Charn added more detail. Light, it seemed, did not physically injure these creatures as metal did, but it drained their vigour and made them (though as a physician Foss hesitated to apply such a term to an unhuman being) ill. That, the men decided, would be a great asset in their efforts to persuade the prisoner to speak, if he could. To use metal against him might produce the desired effect, but at the price of risking unwanted and possibly permanent damage to the body. Subjecting him to light, in carefully planned and controlled doses, would be likely to produce the same result, but with less injury to repair once the end had been achieved.

The three of them pondered that possibility as they surveyed the results of their afternoon's work. Charn, naked and with the waist and ankle restraints burning dark scars on his skin, seemed to be unconscious. A pity in one sense but, as Foss remarked, to attempt too much on the first day was probably unwise. Provided the problem of sustenance could be solved, time was not of the essence, and as the creature's strength clearly had limits it was as well to allow him a respite. They had achieved enough for the present, and they cast Charn's cloak over him – his other clothes were to be taken to the Institute, where their alien fabric could be studied – and left the room, savouring the prospect of a leisurely meal and an evening's discussion of what they had gleaned.

Neither the meal nor the discussion materialised, for as they emerged into the house's entrance hall Philome came down the stairs in a flurry of agitation. Tobery was ill. It had begun, she said, two hours ago, with fretfulness and tantrums, and thinking that perhaps the child had caught some mild spring fever she had put him to bed and dosed him with a febrifuge. But his temper had worsened and now he was fluctuating between bouts of tearful rage and alarming listlessness. And there was something wrong with his hand.

Foss hurried upstairs to Tobery's room. Calliope was sitting with the little boy, stroking his brow, and Tobery had sunk into a fitful sleep in which he whimpered wordlessly. His cheeks were flushed as though with great heat, but when Foss touched his face the skin felt abnormally cold.

'It is a fever.' Foss frowned, not adding that for all his experience he had never seen symptoms quite like these before. He looked over his shoulder at his wife, who hovered anxiously behind him. 'Find my medical pack, my dear, and fetch the magnet-box, the silver-backed reflecting glass and two sulphur candles.'

Philome blinked rapidly. 'Foss, you don't think he's—'

'I don't think anything but that it's a fever!' Concern made Foss's tone waspish. 'Do as I ask, please, Philome, and don't question my judgement!'

Philome fled, and Foss examined Tobery's hand. The skin of one finger was badly puckered; its normally healthy colour had a grey tinge and the nail felt brittle. The hand was icy. Baffled, he looked up and saw Calliope watching him.

'What has the boy been doing this afternoon?' Foss demanded. 'Was he properly supervised during my absence?'

'Yes, Father. Celesta and I both had charge of him, and he was always within sight of one of us.'

Foss's expression betrayed his opinion of Celesta's reliability, but he didn't comment, only shook his head. 'Well, though I'd not say this in front of your stepmother, I confess myself puzzled by it. I think' – he lifted one of Tobery's eyelids; the child mumbled a protest, batting feebly at his hand – 'that it's unlikely to prove serious, but we must take precautions nonetheless. Ah,' as Philome returned with the items he had asked for. 'Good, very good.' He opened the magnet-box and took out two of the magnets inside. 'Now you see, Philome, I shall put these inside Tobery's slippers – yes, yes, of course put the slippers on his feet – then attach them by this light chain to the rail of the bed; that too is metal and so will conduct the energies. Then this third magnet is to be set against his forehead – use this strip of cloth to hold it in place. There. Now; the magnets will draw down the ill humours in the brain, through the body to the feet and out via the chain to dissipate in the air. With the sulphur candles lit, we can be sure the air is strengthened enough to cleanse the taint.'

Philome nodded. Medical science was a closed book to her, but she trusted Foss's skills implicitly. 'What of the reflecting-glass?' she asked.

'Simply an additional precaution. If there should be a spiritual dimension to the fever, the glass, properly angled in front of Tobery's face, will reflect away any etheric contamination in his breath.' He sat back. 'Beyond that, my dear, all we can do is wait for the condition to abate. It would also be a good idea to have a

73

fortifying and nutritional broth ready for him when he begins to recover.'

Philome grasped at the chance of practical action. 'I'll prepare it myself, immediately,' she said and, with a last, helpless glance at her small son, left the room.

As the door closed at her back Calliope looked at Foss again. 'What about his hand, Father?'

Foss frowned. 'I'll put a salve on the finger. Beyond that, there's little to be done.'

'If it wasn't for the colour and the coldness,' Calliope said, 'I'd believe he had burned himself.'

'Mmm. So would I. But he obviously hasn't, for there's no reddening. Some poison I expect, probably from the garden. But by drawing out the fever we'll also draw out the physical impurity, so there's no cause for concern.'

Tobery's sickness effectively put an end to the Society members' plans for the evening. Nempson and his colleague went home, and with the small crisis occupying their minds neither Foss nor Calliope had any desire to discuss the day's experiments. Foss briefly outlined the results they had achieved to his daughter, but beyond that the captive was entirely forgotten.

Soon after sunset Tobery woke from his uneasy sleep and seemed a good deal better. Philome persuaded him to take some broth, together with a herbal dose prescribed by Foss, and the two elder girls took turns to sit with him throughout the evening. But the little boy was still very fretful, and at last insisted that he wanted only Calliope to stay with him; in fact, he said, he would not go to sleep at all tonight unless she did. He had developed a habit of latching on to one particular member of the family for a time; last moon it had been Luthe who was the centre of his attention, but now that phase had passed and Calliope was the favoured one. Calliope still felt tired, but assured Philome that she could as easily sleep in a chair as in her own bed, and so settled herself as comfortably as she could to keep vigil with Tobery.

They both slept for a while, but shortly after midnight Calliope stirred and woke. The room was filled with moonlight – she had opened the shutters to banish the stink of the sulphur candles – and by its glow she could see Tobery moving restlessly in his

74

small bed. The house was silent. Then suddenly, uneasily, Tobery said, 'All *cold* . . .'

Calliope sat up and leaned over the bed. 'What is it, lamb? Did you say you feel cold?'

She reached out to pull up the blankets, but in the dimness Tobery's eyes sleepily opened and he gave her a very earnest look. 'No-o,' he said, drawing the word out into a yawn. 'Not *me*. All cold. All grey.'

A shock went through Calliope. *All grey* . . . 'Tobery.' She took hold of his shoulder, shook him gently. 'What's all grey? What do you mean, lamb?'

Tobery yawned again. 'Grey man,' he said, then abruptly his eyes widened with apprehension. 'But he promised not to tell. I said I'm not s'posed, so he mustn't tell, and he said promise.'

The pieces of the jigsaw fell abruptly into place in Calliope's mind. Tobery must have been to the workroom, the room he was strictly forbidden to enter. He had seen their prisoner, the 'grey man'. The creature had *spoken* to him.

'Tobery, listen to me.' She tried to keep the excitement she felt from her voice, not wanting to alarm him. 'Are you *sure* the grey man talked to you? You didn't just think he did?'

A shake of the small, fair head. 'No. He said. He said promise, 'cause I said he mustn't tell I been.' He blinked uneasily. '*You* won't tell, will you, Calli? Won't tell Papa? You promise, too?'

'Yes, of course I promise.' She stroked his cheek. 'It'll be our little secret. Go back to sleep, now. Happy dreams.'

She watched him settle with one thumb firmly lodged in his mouth, and waited, counting the slow minutes until she was sure that he was soundly away and unlikely to wake again. Then, very quietly, she rose from the chair and left the room.

He said promise. By a sheer caprice of fate, Tobery had been the first and most unlikely witness to the fact that their prisoner could speak. Rationally, Calliope knew, she should have left the matter until morning, but if she was to preserve Tobery's secret that wasn't possible. Foss would be furious if he discovered the little boy's disobedience; besides, she had given her word not to tell him. If this was to be put to the test she must carry the test out herself, alone and in secret and at an hour when there was no danger of discovery.

The ground-floor shutters were closed and the hall pitch dark, but Calliope was familiar enough with every part of the house to have no need of light. She slipped through the door under the stairs, hastened along the short, narrow passage beyond, reached the workroom. For a moment as her hand touched the latch she almost changed her mind; but then courage returned and she eased the door quietly back on its hinges.

Foss had left the shutter half open, so that moonlight illuminated the chair. The captive was slumped at an angle, head drooping, and for a moment Calliope thought that all was as it had been on the previous night, when she had last visited him. But then she saw his face, and the fact that, beneath the folds of his dark cloak, his legs were bare.

'*Great powers . . .*' She whispered the oath, but he heard it. His head jerked up sharply – then he flinched back with a violent, hissing sound of pain.

'What have they *done*?' Calliope started forward, then belatedly remembered the stricture about gloves. Did that answer the mystery of Tobery's finger? Had he touched the creature, and been injured by the contact? She didn't know and at this moment it didn't matter; she must have gloves now, urgently. On the table she found a pair. They were Foss's and too big for her, but that couldn't be helped; they might make her clumsy but they would be better than nothing. She dragged them onto her hands then ran across the room.

'Why this? *Why?*' She didn't know whether she was talking to herself or to him, for anger and indignation and alarm were boiling up in her mind and obscuring all else as she bent to lift aside the cloak's folds.

They had taken every stitch of clothing from him and replaced the restraints, so that the metal was in direct contact with his skin. Calliope had never seen a living adult male body before, though she had viewed corpses during her studies and experiments, but any embarrassment she might have felt was eclipsed by the urgency of Charn's plight. The lacerations and blisters at his waist were raw and bleeding; she started instinctively to reach out, wanting to examine them more closely, then withdrew hastily for fear of causing him more pain. *Why* had her father and Nempson done this? They must have seen for themselves the harm it caused. Did they want him to *die*?

Charn moved suddenly, convulsively, and she heard his teeth

clamp together with a sharp sound as he bit back another gasp. Calliope laid her hands on his shoulders, trying to calm him as she might have gentled a frightened horse.

'No,' she said. 'Keep still. I'll try to get it loose, ease the hurt.' *Rot every nerve in her, where was the key to the waist-clamp?* But she didn't know, and couldn't waste time in finding it—

'Wait.' Her hands slid down his arms, which were still free; for a moment, reflexively, he seemed about to grip her gloved fingers as though clutching for relief, but checked the reaction. He was breathing rapidly, sweat soaking and shining on him like oil, and furious pity rose in Calliope. This was *barbaric*. It was nothing less than deliberate torture, and she simply wouldn't countenance it.

'I can't release the restraint.' She knew now that he understood what she was saying but could only hope that he was in a condition to take in her words. 'It needs a key, and I don't know where Father has put it. But I think I can stop it from touching you. If I slide the cloak between your body and the metal—' Her hands worked fervently, without any thought for the modesty which had so concerned Foss. Standing, the creature would be very tall, she realised; he was long-limbed and his body had a sharp, tensile vitality, slender yet strong. Her father had told her that he put up a ferocious fight when he was captured and had almost got away from them despite their numbers; now, she could believe it.

'There.' She had done the best she could; thankfully his waist was narrow, and there was room under the restraint for the cloak to be interposed. 'I don't know if it will ease you, but I hope it will.' She paused. 'I don't understand why the men did this, but I think they were wrong, for it was cruel and I don't condone cruelty.' Would he believe her? She doubted it. Why should he, after what he had experienced? Inwardly Calliope railed against her father – how could they possibly learn about this creature unless they succeeded in winning at least a measure of his trust? This treatment would only alienate him further. He was alive, he was sentient, he was *intelligent*. Wanton brutality was no answer at all.

She stepped back and looked at him. The ankle clamps were wounding him too, but there was nothing she could do about them, for the cloak wasn't long enough to protect his legs and she dared not release the shackles. Her gaze travelled upwards again. He was shivering violently now, as though in shock. Then she saw the bandages on his arms, and the black stain seeping through them.

Blood. They must have opened his veins. Another experiment . . . Calliope said a foul word under her breath and moved closer again.

'Please, listen to me.' She dropped to a crouch before him and, greatly daring, reached out to take his hands in her own. He didn't resist – perhaps didn't have the will to resist – and the touch of the gloves didn't seem to hurt him. Calliope's fingers closed round his.

'I know you can speak,' she continued. 'I know that you spoke to Tobery today – the little boy, my brother. He told me. He said you promised him you wouldn't tell anyone that he'd been here. I'm not asking you to break that promise, because Tobery confided in me, too. It's our secret, between the three of us. But I ask you, please, speak to *me* now. Because if you don't—' oh, but how could she say it without deepening his mistrust? Calliope racked her mind and knew she must at least try. 'If you don't, then the experiments will continue. My father and the other men won't stop until they have what they want. Or until they kill you. They don't want to do that, they don't mean you harm. But we know so little about you, and the others don't *realise* that you're more than just a – a creature.' She drew breath. 'If I had the power, I would stop them. But if the others find out I've been here in secret, then they'll forbid me to come again; they'll rescind my membership of the Society and I won't be able—'

She stopped abruptly as she realised that he neither knew nor cared anything about the Society or her dilemmas. This wasn't the way to convince him. She had to find another.

'*Please.*' She gave the word desperate emphasis now. 'I won't give you away. I won't tell the others anything unless you should ask me to do so. But *try* to believe that I want to help you. Try to trust me. Tell me what I can do for you.'

As she spoke, her grip on his fingers intensified, and with a sudden, violent movement Charn snatched his hands free as a wave of sick agony flowed over him and seemed to stab him to the core. Her *heat* – he couldn't bear it, not with the moonlight already searing him and draining away the little strength that his ordeal hadn't already torn out of him. His mind was giddy with pain and confusion, his body felt as if it was on fire. He *hurt*, to the core of his soul.

But though his body was weak, his will wasn't yet broken. He would not speak. He would not answer.

Calliope watched his face, the closed eyes, the taut muscles, and saw something of the battle going on in his mind. A mixture of pity, frustration and despair filled her, and with it a small stab of anger at his stubbornness. At last, she sighed and rose to her feet.

'Very well.' She spoke more quietly. 'I can't force you to talk to me, and I don't want to try.' She couldn't stay much longer; if Tobery should wake and find her gone he might rouse Philome, and that would put paid to Calliope's embryonic plan. Time and patience were the keys. She couldn't demand this being's trust; she must win it.

'Let me at least look at your arms.' For all her father's skills she could see that the bandages had been put on carelessly, and she approached him once more, cautiously reaching out. Charn didn't resist, but let his hands lie passively in his lap as she unfastened the linen strips. The cuts had been made with a scalpel and had bled profusely; black fluid still welled sluggishly in one and nothing had been done to staunch the flow.

'I'll give you a salve.' One side of the workroom was lined with shelves on which Foss kept a stock of herbs and tinctures, and Calliope went quickly to fetch an ointment that she knew aided the healing of lacerations, together with a small wooden spatula. His skin, she judged, was much like any human's, and if the ointment soothed his arms then she might also use it on his wrists and ankles.

She returned to the chair and dipped the spatula into the pot she held. 'Keep your arm still,' she told him. 'This will help the bleeding to stop, and assuage—'

Suddenly, shockingly, Charn's voice snapped from his throat. '*No!*'

Calliope froze, the spatula only an inch from his arm. Slowly, his head turned and he met her gaze.

'It will burn,' he said hoarsely. For he could feel the aura of it, as devastating as fire. She meant kindly, he didn't doubt that now, but the substance she had been about to use on him was so alien that one touch, one contact, would bring an agony that made mockery of all the men had done. It was a final straw that he simply couldn't face.

He looked away from her again, feeling the bitter impotence of defeat but unable to conjure the fury that should have augmented it. Cowardice and weakness had had the better of him. He *should* have withstood . . . but this final, small onslaught had taken him over the brink, and the last of his resistance was gone.

Calliope had set the pot and spatula aside and was staring at him as her mind sought frantically for words that would stop this contact between them from slipping away. At last, haltingly, she said, 'Forgive me. I didn't know.'

Charn nodded once, fractionally.

'Shall I . . .' Her mouth was dry; she swallowed. 'Shall I replace the bandages, or do they hurt you, too?'

'They . . . help. A little.'

She tied them again, carefully, tentatively. Now that his tongue had betrayed him Charn saw no point in maintaining a charade, and courtesy was inbred in his kind, so as she finished he said quietly, 'Thank you.'

Calliope masked a small, sad smile. 'Is there anything else I can do for you? Anything that will bring you relief?' She hesitated. 'You've had no sustenance since you arrived here. What can you eat?'

A shake of the head was her only answer.

'Drink, then? Water – can you take water?'

'No.'

She frowned, thinking about that. 'Can't you eat or drink at all?'

'No.'

'What would happen if you tried?' *Or*, Calliope thought, imagining the nature of her father's and Nempson's plans, *were forced to*.

His eyes, which had closed again, opened. Behind the silvery lashes they looked very cold and alien. 'I would choke,' he said.

'Then how can we sustain you?'

Charn could have told her; but that was one secret which, even in this extremity, he was not about to reveal.

His eyelids drooped again. 'I need nothing. I can survive.'

80

Was that true? Calliope wondered. The idea that any creature could exist without nourishment went against every established law of nature and science; yet at the back of her mind was the uneasy thought that, in the case of this being and his kind, established laws might not apply.

The captive's head was slumped back against the chair once more, and his breathing had abated to a slow, irregular hiss. Sweat still seeped from his skin, and his hair was wet with it, fine drops forming at the end of each strand. Thinking of Tobery alone in his room, and aware that time was against her, Calliope said distraughtly, 'I can't stay. I must go back upstairs, in case anyone should come looking for me. But before I leave you here, there must be *something* more I can do?'

He didn't respond at first and she thought uneasily that his consciousness had slipped away. But then, with a great effort, his eyes opened again.

'Shut out the moon.' He spoke very softly. 'As you did last night. That will be . . . a great kindness.'

Angry with herself for not having thought of it before, Calliope went quickly to the window. She dared not close the shutters entirely, lest suspicions should be aroused in the morning, but she altered their angle so that the moonlight no longer touched him, and heard him give a small sigh of relief as the cold silver light dimmed.

'I must go now.' She walked slowly back to the chair and looked down at him. 'I know it's little enough to say, but . . . I'm sorry. For what has been done to you.' His mouth twitched with silent cynicism at that and she felt ashamed. 'I'll tell no one of this,' she added gravely. 'If you want to keep your secret, I won't betray it. I promise.' Another pause. 'Do you believe me?'

At first he didn't respond. Then, faintly, he smiled.

'I believe you, Calliope.'

Just for one moment the smile transformed his face, and something deep within Calliope's psyche stirred with a strange, disturbing sensation.

'You remember my name.'

'Yes.'

'Will you not tell me yours?'

Charn's mind was beginning to wander and he knew that he was slipping between the harshness of reality and a half-dream

81

of something kinder; a delusion which was comforting yet dangerous. But what did it matter? What was a name? A name had no power, for it imparted no knowledge that could be of any value. A name was just a sound, without meaning.

He said, so quietly that Calliope could barely catch the words, 'I am Charn.'

'Charn . . .' She repeated it to herself, trying the single syllable on her tongue. Not so strange. In some indefinable way, it seemed to forge the first stirrings of trust between them.

She moved away, towards the door. When she looked back she thought he was watching her, though in the semi-darkness that now enclosed the room it was impossible to be sure. A question came to her mind and she almost asked it, almost said, 'Did you harm my little brother?' But she didn't believe he would answer.

Calliope lifted the door-latch. She couldn't say goodnight; for him, it would hardly be appropriate. So she said nothing at all, only left the room and hurried quickly, quietly back to the upper floor and the seclusion of her own thoughts.

Chapter VII

There was an argument when the Society members met at the Agate house the following day, but to her own surprise Calliope won it, thanks in part to the unexpected support of Nempson Trinity. It was perfectly reasonable, Nempson pointed out, to allow the captive a modicum of comfort, provided it could be done without risking the chance of escape. To return the creature's clothes would be a small courtesy (Foss snorted at the choice of words) and might, as Calliope said, be a step on the way to winning its trust, thus making the task of assessing its intelligence a great deal easier.

Foss gave way in the end, though not with an entirely good grace. Charn's clothing would be restored to him; the fabrics they had examined seemed no different in essence from familiar materials, simply a little finer, so there was probably nothing to be gained from further study. With other experiments in plenty to be made, one less would be no hardship.

Calliope also won another compromise when she urged against tormenting the prisoner by leaving the shutters open at night. Moonlight might not harm him as the sun did but it still had a weakening effect, and as they didn't yet know how to nourish him, any further decline could put his life at risk. Foss saw the logic of that, and it turned him to the subject of sustenance and how best to discover what the creature needed. Calliope, telling a white lie, reported that she had tried the captive with both water and food but he seemed unable to take either, so Foss was eager to begin as soon as possible on a new experiment to discover what would sustain him and keep him fit.

The work began, but two days later they had learned nothing of any use. Attempts to force-feed Charn with various substances – some edible to humans, others not – had met with violent resistance which left two men with wrenched arms before the prisoner could be subdued again. Foss, after a further study of Arcane Toller's treatise on etheric humours, tried a number of other methods. He burned various substances under Charn's nose in the hope that smoke would be a suitable medium for the nourishment he obviously needed, but that only brought Charn into a feverish sweat and made the skin of his face turn pale and papery. Other elements were equally useless as vehicles; even when the creature, rendered unconscious again for safety's sake, was immersed in a bath of water in which an assortment of metaphysically replenishing ingredients had been dissolved, it seemed to make no difference. They did discover, at least, that contact with water didn't damage his body; though he was as capable as any human of drowning and, thanks to a small oversight, almost did.

Calliope took part in many of the experiments, but privately she was growing more and more uneasy. Thus far Charn had managed to preserve his secrets from the men. They didn't know he could understand and speak their language, they hadn't been able to assess the extent of his intelligence, and they were certainly no closer than they had ever been to learning anything about his world or its nature. Until now the Society members had been relatively patient, but Calliope knew that wouldn't last for much longer. To gain the information they wanted, the first walls had to be breached. If gentle methods failed to work, harsher ones must be tried.

She had managed to pay three more clandestine visits to the workroom. Charn seemed to be bearing up surprisingly well; in fact if anything he seemed to have regained some strength during the past few days, and the injuries inflicted by the chair and Foss's scalpel were healing well. Calliope wondered if perhaps some of the attempts to feed him had worked in ways which the Society members didn't understand, but when she asked Charn about it he refused to answer. He would talk to her – he saw no point in maintaining his silence when there was no one but her to hear – but he told her nothing. Least of all did he have any intention of revealing what he did, and would continue to do, to survive.

Calliope was completely unaware of the subtle psychic manipulation that, on each visit, drained her of a little of her life and energy. All she knew was that she seemed to be waking up more and more tired each morning, and that Philome was now constantly berating her for not taking proper care of herself and working too hard. It was only a mild debilitation, for Charn kept his predations under extremely careful control. He had three reasons: firstly, he didn't want to alert Calliope or her father; secondly, he had an instinct that Calliope might prove useful to him in other ways. She was clearly fascinated by him, and not, he suspected, solely out of scientific curiosity. The first signs of a more personal interest were beginning to show. Charn had every intention of playing on that. And the third reason for his moderation with her was the fact that he now had other sources from which he could feed.

Luthe was the first. Charn had taken an immediate and intuitive dislike to the youth when he first entered the room in a show of bravado to see the curiosity for himself. What Charn did, what he took, brought Luthe to a state of vomiting collapse late that evening; but as he had spent the previous two hours drinking with his friends, nothing had been suspected; Foss simply dosed him with a purge, lectured him on his shortcomings and warned him not to make such a disgraceful exhibition of himself again. After Luthe there were two more men from the Society, who came to examine Charn and take more clippings of his hair, and who, Charn sensed quickly, had no psychic awareness whatever.

84

They were easy targets, the mild fevers that both suffered over the next few days put down to another bout of wet weather. Then came a valuable bounty when Philome, finally overcoming her terrors, ventured to the workroom for a glimpse of the strange being, and brought Celesta, Tobery and Diona with her. Though she found the captive frightening and his lack of colouring repulsive, Philome's heart was moved to a squeamish kind of pity. Charn felt her thoughts, scorned them and ruthlessly took what he needed. It gave him comfort and added considerably to his growing strength; that was all that mattered.

Foss was baffled and more than a little put out by the fact that more than half his family, plus two servants who, unbeknown to anyone, had taken a furtive look at the 'monster' in their master's workroom, went down with a mysterious ailment the following day. The sickness, however, was short-lived, except for Diona's affliction, which the little girl seemed to have trouble shaking off. But with Calliope and the recovering Philome to nurse her, Foss felt he could return his full attention to the prisoner once more. His patience was wearing thin; he had waited long enough. It was time to put Charn to a more stringent trial.

On the eighth day after his capture, they finally broke him. Calliope was with Diona, who was still weak and confined to bed, and was reading her a story from her favourite chapbook when the peace of the house was shattered by a scream that rang from foundations to roof. Diona squealed in terror and Calliope sprang to her feet, the book falling to the floor and a word breaking involuntarily from her.

'*Charn*—' Ignoring Diona, who had started to sob, she flew from the room, down the first flight of stairs, along the landing to the second. She had almost reached the hall when the understairs door opened and Nempson emerged from the passage. His face wore a satisfied smile, and there were scorch-marks and smears of dark fluid on his gloves.

'Nempson!' Calliope's voice went up the scale harshly. 'What's happened?'

Nempson raised his stained hands in a calming gesture. 'Nothing to fear, Calliope; no one has come to any harm. I'm delighted to say that our newest experiment has borne fruit. The creature *can* speak after all, and it understands our tongue.'

85

'But that scream—'

'Oh, not conclusive proof in itself, I quite agree. But rather than be tested again it now seems willing to talk lucidly. Your father is just about to—'

He was interrupted then as Philome came hurrying from another part of the house. 'Calli! Nempson! What by all the powers was that *dreadful* noise?'

Nempson made a contrite bow to her. 'I do apologise, Philome; we didn't mean to disturb you. There's nothing amiss, rest assured.'

Philome frowned. 'Was it that creature in the workroom? My dear life, what are you *doing* to it?'

'Philome.' Calliope turned quickly to her stepmother before Nempson could reply. 'Diona's crying; she was frightened by the sound.'

Philome said something under her breath and gave Nempson a glare. 'I'll see to her. Really, you men – disrupting the house and upsetting the children; you're little better than savages, any of you!' And she was gone, skimming up the stairs towards her daughter's bedroom.

Calliope turned back to Nempson. 'What's that on your hands?'

'Eh?' Nempson looked at them. 'Oh, nothing for concern, my dear. I was a little clumsy with one of the torches; burned through the glove and scorched my own fingers.'

Calliope's mouth set into a hard, angry line. 'I meant the stains.' At this moment she wouldn't have cared if Nempson had immolated himself, though she didn't have the courage to say so. 'It's Ch— the creature's blood, isn't it?'

'Oh, yes; yes, it is. I'd better clean myself. If I may use the scullery?' He glanced up, saw her expression and gave her a flicker of a smile. 'Don't worry, we won't lose it. In fact I think it's a good deal stronger than we'd assumed.'

The door behind him opened again at that moment and Foss appeared. He was pulling off his gloves and he, too, looked pleased.

'Ah, Calli. Has Nempson told you of our breakthrough?'

'I have,' Nempson said. 'A splendid achievement, don't you agree?'

'Most certainly.' There were dark stains on Foss's gloves, too, Calliope saw. 'Well, we've done enough for the day.' He looked at his daughter. 'How is Diona?'

'Philome's with her.' Calliope didn't elaborate.

'Mmm, well, I'll take a look at her this evening before dinner. You'll eat with us, Nempson? Good, good. Best get ourselves cleaned up, then we might take a glass or two of wine in the library and discuss our findings. Join us there, Calli. You'll be most interested by what we've learned.'

'But the captive—'

'Oh, the creature's unconscious now. Annoying, as I would have liked to persuade it to talk further, but it can't be helped. There'll be no need to check on it again before morning.'

'Yes,' Calliope said. 'Of course. I— I can't join you just at the moment, Father. I have a task to do for Philome.'

'Well, we'll speak after dinner.' Foss smiled at her, then gestured in the direction of the scullery. 'Nempson?'

Calliope watched the two men disappear into the nether regions of the house. Her heart was pounding, pulse thick, and she was shaking with a mixture of fury and fear that made breathing hard. What had they *done*? What torture had they inflicted on Charn to force him, finally, into betraying his secret?

From the scullery came Foss's booming laugh; it was a catalyst which snapped her thrall and she ran towards the understairs door. *Gloves, gloves* – thank the powers, they were still in her apron pocket after last time – she wrenched the door open, darted into the passage, raced to the workroom. In her hurry to enter she barked her knuckles on the latch but didn't care, didn't even notice. The door swung back . . .

The shutters were wide open, daylight streaming in and illuminating the workroom with hard, appalling clarity. Calliope uttered a shocked sound and ran to the window, slamming the shutters together, bringing down the gloom that Charn needed – and which she needed, too, to lessen the hideous impact of what she had seen. Then, shutting her eyes briefly and taking a deep breath to calm herself, she turned to face the chair.

'Charn?' She whispered his name, not knowing whether she was more terrified of receiving no answer or of finding that he was conscious. But he didn't respond in any way; the dark shape in the chair was still.

Calliope's footsteps sounded obscenely loud to her own ears as she crossed the floor. Reflexively she had pulled the gloves on, and as she reached the chair her hands stretched out unsteadily towards Charn.

He was wet; saturated with sweat that was still oozing from every pore of his skin. Though he was senseless, muscles in his shoulders and arms were twitching in violent and rapid spasms, as though he was in the grip of a lethal fever. Down his left side – face, neck, arms, like the stigmata of a terrible disease – his skin was seared and blistered, its smoothness ripped apart and the grey turned to black ruin.

They had burned him. 'Clumsy with one of the torches,' Nempson had said. Calliope could see the instruments they had used; a larger and more sophisticated variant of pocket-tapers. The flames at their tips could be adjusted to give anything from a pinpoint glow to a tiny, roaring and almost white-hot inferno, and Calliope felt sickness and suffocating rage clutch under her ribs as she took in the full extent of what the torches had wrought on Charn. Blood was trickling from the sides of his mouth; he must have bitten his tongue savagely, ready to mutilate himself rather than utter a sound. But in the end, he hadn't been able to bear any more. He had screamed; a scream of such abominable pain that the echoes of it still seemed to reverberate in Calliope's head.

Suddenly she found herself crying. The tears welled like a cataract and fell, splashing onto Charn's cloak and hair and damaged face, and Calliope couldn't make them stop. Her hands clutched at his shoulders; she wanted to do something, *anything*, yet she was helpless, for there was nothing within her power that could bring him any relief.

Beneath her hands there was an abrupt, convulsive movement, and a sound quivered in Charn's throat. He seemed to be trying to speak – or to moan – but there was blood in his mouth and he choked, retching. Calliope tore off her apron; if the touch of gloves didn't hurt him then surely linen, too, should be safe, and she held the apron for him as he spat dark bile, then gently dabbed at his mouth, trying to wipe away the stains. Charn's entire body had started to shake uncontrollably. His hands moved blindly, unco-ordinated; suddenly he found and touched her, and to Calliope's shock his fingers clamped on her waist.

'Charn—' She spoke his name again, then started to say words; anything, however meaningless, that might soothe or ease or reassure. His grip tightened and she swayed as he almost pulled her off balance; bracing one knee on the seat of the chair she leaned towards him, and suddenly he was clinging to her as if she were sanity's last refuge in a world gone mad. His forehead pressed against her breast and she put one arm around him, her other hand stroking the tangled, sweat-soaked mane of his hair. His body felt ice-cold, chilling her, and his breathing was fast and alarmingly laboured.

'What have they done to you – what have they *done*?' But she knew what they had done, she had seen it. Tortured him, maimed him, nearly *killed* him. She hadn't known. She hadn't tried to stop it. Calliope's tears were splashing on Charn's hair and running down his forehead and cheeks, and suddenly he raised his head and looked up at her. His strange eyes were filled with shock and pain, but amid the confusion in his look there was a glimmer of wonder.

'Your eyes . . . are wet . . .' His voice was barely recognisable; the quiet, oddly warm timbre that she had come to know was reduced to a fractured whisper. He raised one hand, made as if to touch her cheek, then drew back. Another tear fell on his face; he closed his eyes and the edges of his mouth quivered. 'It . . . soothes.'

Tears, a balm? 'Take all you need,' Calliope said, her own voice breaking. 'If my crying can help you— Charn, Charn, this is barbaric! To inflict such suffering—'

He either didn't hear or couldn't take in the sense of what she said, for he whispered, 'Crying . . .?' in a vague, distracted way, as if the word was quite alien to him. Then he murmured again, 'It soothes. Cools. Like the flames of my own world . . .' A shudder went through him. 'Put your face close to mine. *Please* . . .'

She did, not quite touching him for she didn't dare; though their hair mingled, the warm dark of hers and the alien silver-grey of his. Charn's eyes had closed again and he turned his head so that her tears touched the seared scars where the torches had mutilated his skin. A hiss escaped between his lips but it was a sound of relief, not pain, and after a few moments Calliope felt a tiny easing of the tension in her shoulders. But her tears were beginning to abate, and though she inwardly cursed her own perversity she could no more control their cessation than their onset. Not even for him.

His lashes flickered and the pewter-dark eyes focused on her once more. With a great effort, Charn's mouth curved in a sad smile. 'Can there be no more?' he asked.

'I can't.' One stray drop fell, but it was the last, she knew. 'When we cry, there is no control . . .'

'Why do you cry? What does it mean?'

'It means that we are . . . in the hold of an emotion. Sorrow. Grief. Joy, sometimes . . .'

'And now?'

Calliope's lower lip trembled. 'Grief, Charn. And anger. Such *anger.*'

'For me?'

'Yes.'

He sighed. 'You have shown kindness. Alone of them all, you have shown such kindness.' His hands slid away from her waist suddenly and he leaned back in the chair, weariness washing over him so profoundly that even Calliope's human psyche sensed the wave of it.

She said, 'What more can I do? There must be something.'

He shook his head. 'No. Just let me sleep. Sleep will help me.'

'But the pain— what the men did—'

Another negating gesture, though weaker this time. Charn wanted oblivion. Above all else he needed that now, to escape from the burning agony that had rooted in his skull and spread through his entire being. 'I will heal. In time.' But how much time did he have? *Couldn't think of that, couldn't concentrate on it.* More torment; it would come. Now that the greatest secret had been wrenched from him, the human men wouldn't be content but would increase their efforts to take all he had to give.

'I can bear the pain.' A simple statement but true, at least for now. She had helped far more than she knew; given him her tears – such a strange, strange thing, utterly new to him – and, without knowing it, just a little of her life's power. Something else, too. Charn had no word for it, not yet, not one he could be sure of. But the first stirrings were there in her. Her kindness, her crying, the hurt he had felt in her that was hurt for his own distress. *We cry when we are in the hold of an emotion.* He believed he was beginning to understand.

She had drawn back from him, standing upright now, her face unhappy and uncertain. He raised his right arm and held it

90

towards her, a surviving vestige of pride in him despising the way the muscles shuddered and made the gesture unsteady. 'Calliope.'

Her face tautened eagerly. His eyes grew intense. 'I know you didn't betray me. The betrayal was entirely my own.'

She shut her eyes briefly with painful relief. Though the knowledge made her ashamed, she had feared he might believe that she had given Foss and the others some hint of the secret she knew. So small and petty of her, to care about her own standing in his eyes under circumstances such as these. But she did care. It mattered.

She looked down at the floor, unable to meet his gaze. 'Thank you.'

'No. *I* thank *you*.' Charn turned his hand, palm upward, wordlessly inviting her to respond, and abruptly a rash impulse flared in Calliope. She snatched off her right glove, reached out, took hold of his fingers. So *cold* – but the shock of the contact was eclipsed by the eerie enchantment of his touch, flesh to flesh for the very first time. In that brief moment the barrier between their worlds seemed to break down; he was real, alive, *tangible*. Not a creature, no longer alien. Simply a man, a friend, holding her hand.

Emotion lurched and welled in her again and her vision blurred. Gently, Charn said, 'If you cry again . . . your tears heal.'

Calliope nodded, unable to speak. She would cry, she was aware of it; not now but later, tonight, alone in her room. When she did, she would save the tears as something precious, and bring them to him when she could do so without anyone knowing. The balm, the soothing, to ease his wounds . . . it was little, but it was all she could offer him as yet.

Their hands slipped apart. Her touch had not burned him as he knew she might fear. Instead, it had nourished him. In the contact of minds there was control, but when hand touched hand, or body touched body, there was only the emphatic flow of life, without hindrance. But it would not hurt her unduly, and it would give him strength.

Calliope said, very quietly, 'I wish I could kiss you. But I fear it wouldn't be wise.'

Her words had an ambiguity which, Charn thought, perhaps she herself didn't understand. 'No,' he replied, speaking as softly as she had done. 'I fear you're right.'

Her mouth quirked, wryly and a little sadly. 'I'll speak to them,' she said. 'I won't let this happen a second time. Whatever I must do, Charn, I *won't* let it happen.'

It was what he had hoped to hear her say. Gravely, he replied, 'Thank you.' For her calm but emphatic statement had told him that, in what he meant to do, he had an ally. Unwitting; possibly even, if she had known his thoughts, unwilling. But sure. He could trust Calliope. If he was careful, subtle, artful, as he knew how to be, she would do what he wanted of her without ever realising that she had been used. Or, if realisation came, it would be too late. It was a question of loyalty, and of survival. On both those scores Charn had no scruples.

A face was gazing back at her from the meld of strange, dark reflections, and for one moment it almost stopped her pulse. But the charcoal hair and the silver eyes were her own. Not Malorn; only Selethe, an image caught and mirrored in the hall of remembrance's eternal twilight. Selethe, alone, searching, but not finding what she sought.

A child's voice was singing, prettily though a little out of tune, and the queen paused to listen to the song, which was familiar to her from her own childhood. A long-lost friend, perhaps, her memories finding a small haven in this gallery? Or perhaps not. There were so many.

But Malorn was not here, and Charn was not here. She had feared that so greatly that it had been like a hard, leaden knot under her heart. Feared seeing the glimpse of Charn's face which would tell her that the world of humans had claimed yet another victim from her own realm. Entering the hall, she had whispered his name, called to him as so often in the past she had called to Malorn. But the answer she dreaded had not come.

Yet though Charn's absence gave her hope, Selethe took little comfort from it. Not all her subjects who had lost their lives in the bright world had come back to join this quiet company; some had simply vanished and left no trace behind. Her son, possibly, was among that number, and now maybe Charn too. Ten days without word, and none of the beings who had made forays through the dark door and returned reported any sign of him. Some of her courtiers believed he must be lost to them.

One small faction even whispered that he had betrayed them, but Selethe had dealt severely with the perpetrators of that lie, well aware of their underlying motive and equally aware of the poison that spite and envy could spread if left unchecked. Yet even a few of Charn's friends were among the growing numbers who, now, tried to persuade her to seal the doorway. Not yet, they said, no, not yet; for it was still possible that Charn would come back. But time was running out for him. How long could any of their kind survive in the world of humans? Though it grieved them to distress their queen, the truth must be faced. Charn would return within a few more days, or he would never return at all. If he did not, then surely they must take no further risk?

Selethe resisted the gentle pressure, but without Charn's strength to sustain her she knew that her resistance would eventually crumble. That, intuition told her, would be the beginning of her last decline, for if Charn, too, was gone, there would be nothing left to hold her to life.

The childish singing had faded, and in the ethereal air of the gallery she seemed to hear murmuring voices, as though a great company of people were talking amiably together in a room a little way off. The echo of a wing brushed her face; then something sighed, a sound of faint annoyance as though some equation would not come right. Selethe thought: *I feel old. And in the hall they will all be waiting for me. My physician will be waiting to say his healing spells. My dancers and musicians will be waiting to entertain me. My friends – my good friends – will be waiting to speak the words they think I want to hear.* She must return to them, preside over them. It was her duty to be with them and give them the reassurance of her presence.

Music shimmered faintly in the air; two instruments blending in harmony, and a subtle hushing that might have been a skirt or cloak-hem swirling over cool marble. But Selethe's skirt and cloak and feet made no sound as she turned and left the hall.

Chapter VIII

Philome had wanted her to take a carriage; either their own if Foss wasn't planning to use it, or a hired chaise from the livery-stable at the corner of the square. But Calliope insisted that she would prefer to walk. The exercise would do her good, and climbing Charity Hill was no great hardship. She would not overtire herself.

To her relief Philome didn't argue, and she was able to leave the house without too much fuss . . . and without anyone seeing her hand. Wearing gloves at breakfast could have presented her with a problem, but one of Philome's birthday gifts to her had been a new cosmetic ointment for whitening and softening the skin, and that provided her with a ruse. She was trying it, she told her family with an ingenuous smile; and according to instruction gloves should be worn if the treatment was to have maximum effect. Philome was gratified, while Foss gave Calliope a conspiratorial wink, assuming that she was simply indulging her stepmother, and no awkward questions were asked.

The day was sunny but a brisk wind was blowing through the town, ruffling Calliope's hair and making merry with the skirt of her long coat. There was a frown on her face as she walked quickly along the street; an acquaintance hailed her from the opposite pavement but she didn't notice, for now that she was safely away from the house she was deeply preoccupied – and deeply worried.

She had, or so she fervently hoped, persuaded her father not to begin his planned interrogation of Charn until she returned, saying that she very much wished to be present to see and hear the results for herself. Foss knew nothing of her visit to the workroom the previous afternoon; though everything within Calliope had wanted to confront him with what she had seen, scream at him, berate him for what he and Nempson had done, prudence – or, more cynically, cowardice – had stilled her tongue. She tried to comfort herself with the thought that an argument would have achieved nothing of any value; with Foss, subtler measures were needed, and this time she wouldn't have been able to count on Nempson's support. Anyway, her father had agreed to leave the captive untouched for a while longer, and she believed he would keep his word.

Last night, alone in her room, she had cried again; a helpless bout of weeping as shock and unhappiness and pity had risen to the surface of her mind once more. When the rest of the house was soundly asleep, she had returned to the workroom with the tears she had collected. Charn was sleeping; he stirred but was incoherent, and Calliope dabbed the contents of her small bowl gently on his face, neck and arm before going quietly back to bed. Whether he would remember her second visit, or know what had taken place, she couldn't tell. But it eased her mind to feel that she had done what little she could for him.

Now, though, there was the other matter. She was out of the main press of the town, in the quieter streets that led towards Charity Hill, and after a brief glance about to make sure that no one was observing her she pulled off her right glove.

The hand beneath, fingertips to wrist, was grey.

The change must have taken place as she slept; when she woke this morning her arm had been resting on her pillow, only inches from her face, and the shock of what she saw as her eyes opened had gone through Calliope like an electric charge. Every trace of colour had drained from her skin, leaving her entire hand looking like that of a corpse. There was no pain, nor any loss of feeling, but when, appalled and bemused, she had cautiously reached out her unmarked left hand to touch and explore, her own flesh had felt icy, and as dry and sere and fragile as old paper.

She knew instantly what, or rather who, had caused the change. Last night she had held Charn's hand without protection. If she closed her eyes she could remember clearly how his fingers had felt as they closed around hers and gripped. So cold, yet substantial as any human touch. But it was not human, *he* was not human, and if she had begun to harbour any delusions on that score then she was a fool who was playing with fire. Perhaps literally playing with fire, for what was it that Charn had murmured to her last night when her tears soothed his injuries? *It cools. Like the flames of my own world.* Fire and water: inimical opposites. The men had burned him, and he in turn had burned her, leaving a stigma of his own on her flesh.

Had he known what the contact would do to her? Impossible to be sure; she suspected not but didn't entirely trust herself to be objective. Now though, she knew for certain what had happened to Tobery. He must have touched Charn momentarily, enough only to mark the tip of one finger. But then there had been the fever. Was that a part of the contagion? The thought was unnerving, but though Calliope had checked herself carefully for any signs of sickness there seemed to be nothing amiss. Only her hand . . .

Then, in thinking about her hand and about Tobery, her mind had strayed to something else. A memory, lodged in a forgotten niche of her mind for fifteen years but now suddenly and unexpectedly coming back to light. When the mental image became clear and unequivocal, and she was sure there was no mistake, she knew that she must go to the hospice.

Though at the time she had been plagued by guilt, she was thankful now that she had failed to make her customary visit to her mother on the last quartermoon. Charn had been newly captured then, and she was so preoccupied that she had entirely forgotten the day. This, she had told Foss and Philome, was to make up for her lapse; and no, there was no need for Celesta or Luthe to accompany her unless they wanted to; in fact she would prefer to go alone. Philome, understanding, said it was only natural that now and then she should wish to spend a little exclusive time with her poor mother, and to Calliope's relief she had diverted Celesta, who was bored and, perversely, had been half tempted to go too. So as she walked briskly up the long, steep slope of Charity Hill, where the green of the trees was already deepening as spring advanced towards summer, Calliope rehearsed in her mind what she would do, what she would say, how she would gain the information she so desperately wanted.

The morning visiting hour had already begun. The hospice gates stood open and small groups of people were about in the gardens. Calliope entered the main hall and looked about for someone who might tell her where the Hospice Master could be found. An angel approached; Calliope explained her mission and within a few minutes the Hospice Master emerged from his office to greet her with solemn courtesy.

'It's a foolish and trivial request, I know,' Calliope said when she told her story, giving him a tentative and self-deprecating smile. 'But the memory came back to me in a dream three nights ago.' White lies were becoming so easy. 'I wondered if there might be some significance in it; so I would very much like to know if what I dreamed about actually happened in the past, or if it was simply a childish misunderstanding at the time.'

The Hospice Master nodded. He was greatly interested, Calliope knew, in the nature and significance of dreams, and actively encouraged dream-divining as part of his patients' treatment. Calliope saw the approval in his eyes as he looked at her, and sighed an inward sigh of relief.

'Well, my dear, I'm only too happy to help, and as I was here at the time I do of course remember the – ah – circumstances of your poor mother's admittance. But as to that detail . . . I think we will need to consult the records to be quite certain. Perhaps you'll be so kind as to step into my office?'

Calliope did, and waited patiently while he took a sheaf of documents from a glass-fronted cabinet and sorted slowly and methodically through them. At last she had her answer.

'Yes.' The Hospice Master pushed his reading-spectacles a little further down the bridge of his nose and looked at her with quiet triumph over the tops of the lenses. 'It seems, my dear, that your dream and your memory are both perfectly accurate. I have it here; the record of our resident physician's initial examination refers to an inexplicable phenomenon. When she was admitted, your mother's hands and forearms had undergone some change. As he puts it, the skin appeared to have lost its colour and turned grey.'

Calliope's heart lurched, missed a beat, then began to pulse again, painfully quickly. 'Yes,' she said. 'That was what I remembered.' Griette, silent after the days of screaming, being carried to the litter and put inside. And, in the moment before the door closed, her hands. Moving. Fluttering. *Grey*.

'The phenomenon had apparently been visible for some time, and it was several moons before it entirely wore off and her skin returned to normal,' the Hospice Master continued. 'The malaise has never recurred, so we feel that it had no significance worth further investigation.' He smiled sympathetically. 'I understand that she was of a scientific turn of mind before the unhappy events that brought her to our care, so I would imagine that it was simply a lingering after-effect of some experiment. Perhaps if you were to ask your father, he might—'

Calliope interrupted gently. 'I don't wish to distress Father by reminding him of it, sir. That was why I came to you. It seemed more . . . tactful.'

'Ah, yes. I quite understand. Well, I do hope that I've been of service.' He paused. 'Strange that you should recall such a small detail. You must have been no more than a child at the time. But then the nature and import of dreams is a matter where I firmly believe we stand only on the threshold of understanding . . .'

Calliope steeled herself to listen politely to an explanation of the Hospice Master's theories regarding dreams and their import for some ten more minutes, until, snatching at an opportunity, she was able to excuse herself, thank him and make her way at last to her mother's room. Another angel said that Griette seemed well today and a little more aware of her surroundings than usual. She would doubtless be very glad of a visitor. Aware of the faint sting of censure in the angel's last words, Calliope looked down at the floor, murmured a faint apology, and went in.

Griette was sitting by the window, working at another sculpture. As Calliope entered she looked up and smiled; a sweet smile, but childlike and with no trace of recognition. Pushing back the sorrow that always hit her so hard at these moments Calliope kissed her brow then tried to look at the clay model, but Griette hid it quickly with her hands and Calliope withdrew a little, taking a chair a few feet away. For some minutes she made her customary small-talk, to which Griette responded with occasional nods but no other sign that the words meant any more to her than the distant background sounds of the hospice. At last Calliope allowed her conversation to die away. For some little while silence held, but for the faint, moist sound of Griette's wooden spatula on the clay, which she was crouching over now as though to protect it. Then, taking a grip on her resolve, Calliope said,

'How can fire be cold in the other world, I wonder?'

The spatula stopped. Griette sat very still.

Slowly, Calliope ran her tongue over lips that had become dry. She watched her mother. So still; as if life, or its pretence, had suddenly fled from her. Calliope drew breath.

'Our fire burns, but theirs cools. That is what he told me.'

Griette made a sound, and it shocked Calliope for it was the first sound she – possibly anyone – had heard from her since the days of screaming ended. A high, thin sound, like a small whimper, and swiftly cut off. Then, startlingly unpleasant, what might have been the beginnings of a little laugh, before Griette bent over her clay once more and the sculpting resumed.

'Mother.' Calliope rose to her feet. 'Mother, please. Look at me.' Her left hand went to her right wrist, took hold of the glove. '*Look.*'

Griette turned her head, and Calliope pulled the glove off.

'He touched me,' she said, 'and I don't know what it means. Mother, I don't know what it *means!* But you do; I know you do, because it happened to you! Please, Mother, please – for his sake and mine, I so desperately need to *understand!*'

Griette stared at her daughter's outstretched hand, at the grey skin that, beyond the wrist, mutated back to a normal, natural colour. A glassy look came into her eyes. Her mouth twitched, once, twice, the second spasm far more acute than the first. Then, so suddenly and violently that Calliope jumped back, her hand swung and smashed into the clay model, pummelling it, pulverising it.

'*Nnnh!*' The awful sound cracked from Griette's throat and seemed to fill the room. '*Nnnn – nnnh – NNNNNHHH—*'

Running feet in the corridor; the door was flung open and Calliope had a brief, irrational image of white birds of prey swooping down from a vast height as two angels ran in. There was an outcry of voices; hands took hold of her, pulling her away, and suddenly the room's dimensions seemed to spin around her as she was bodily hauled out into the passage. Image of Griette, crying out still and beating at the table and the ruined sculpture with clenched but impotent fists; then in the midst of the furore the Hospice Master was hurrying towards them, more angels at his heels, and somewhere else in the building a voice was wailing up in strange, mad excitement—

Without warning, nausea hit Calliope in a colossal wave and she reeled, clutching out for support as suddenly the floor beneath her feet bucked and distorted, hurling her off balance. Someone caught her, righted her; but then she felt the sickness coming and couldn't stop it, and she retched, violently, horribly, agonisingly, vomiting as the fever overtook her in a single, devastating rush. For one instant she saw the Hospice Master's face, a picture of agitated concern. Then a huge, engulfing darkness rushed at her out of another dimension, and she slumped unconscious into an angel's benevolent arms.

* * *

She was delirious for nearly two days; an ordeal which for her seemed like half a lifetime as she writhed in the grip of monstrously distorted dreams. Philome, after an initial bout of wild railing at her stepdaughter's foolishness and lack of care for herself which had brought her to such a terrible pass, rallied with an energy which would have surprised and touched Calliope had she been in a condition to know of it. She was almost constantly at Calliope's bedside, and the few hours which she did not spend tending her were occupied with preparing foods, drinks, potions, everything and anything which might conceivably be of help.

Foss brought all his skills to bear, but knew that the fever, if fever it was, could only be allowed to run its course for better or worse. His fears for Calliope manifested in episodes of vile and explosive temper, during which everyone in the house kept well out of his way. Celesta cried noisily and often, Luthe spent as much time away from home as he could contrive, and Tobery and Diona sulked for lack of their mother's attention.

But shortly before dawn of the second morning after the hospice chaise had brought her home, Calliope's delirium at last abated and she fell into a profound but natural sleep. Foss stayed with her for two hours until he was confident that there would be no relapse, then, with a calming word for the anxious Philome, left the room and made his way down to the ground floor.

A number of the Society members had called at the house since the incident, to convey their fervent wishes for Calliope's recovery and to check, as Foss had had no time to do, that all was well with their captive. Charn, in pain but conscious and fully mentally coherent once more, had used them to a degree he would not have dared risk before. He needed to heal, needed to regain his strength as quickly as possible; the survival instinct was driving him and in this extremity any source of energy must be taken without qualm. Ruthlessly, skilfully, he fed from his captors and visitors; listening to their conversations as he began to recover he knew that another cause had been attributed to Calliope's affliction, and he judged that when his new victims also fell ill, an infectious outbreak would be blamed and no suspicion would fall on him.

But he had reckoned without one factor.

Foss had seen Calliope's right hand as she was being carried to her bed, and it was enough for him to make the connection between this uncanny phenomenon and Tobery's equally inexplicable symptom of a few days ago. Then there was the conversation he had had with the distraught Hospice Master, which awoke a memory that took him back fifteen years.

To Foss's knowledge, Griette had never had any direct contact with a live creature from the twilight world. Throughout their explorations together he had not succeeded in capturing any specimen that survived for any time, and he had assumed that she had been no more fortunate. Now though, he was beginning to wonder if this assumption was wrong.

During the past few days he had scoured his mind to find a possible cause for Calliope's and Tobery's symptoms, but nothing, either in his experience or in any of the medical tomes in his library, answered the conundrum. This fever, or disease, or whatever it was, was a mystery. But when the records had been combed and the precedents explored, there was one factor, quite separate from all that medical science could offer, which nagged at Foss's mind. That the creature was intelligent and could understand and speak their language was now established, and under duress he had been persuaded to reveal his outlandish name. Beyond that, however, the Society knew nothing about their captive, for Calliope's illness had forced them to set their work aside until the more personal emergency was over.

But with Calliope now out of danger it was time, Foss thought, for that to change.

He opened the door of the workroom and went in. Charn seemed to be asleep, but Foss thought he detected a flicker of movement under the eyelids, suggesting that the sleep was feigned. He said nothing, only crossed to the window and with a fierce gesture opened the shutters wide. The sky was clear and the early morning sun vivid; its brilliance thrust back the shadows and Foss had the small satisfaction of seeing the captive flinch from it in shock.

'So you are awake.' He turned and walked back to the chair, stopping just out of arm's reach. 'And you don't like the light. Well, my grey friend, I'm afraid you must live with that discomfort – and a good deal more if need be – until you have answered some questions.'

Charn watched his jailer warily. He had anticipated an end to this respite, and surmised that Calliope must now be on the way to recovery. It had come earlier than he had expected. In one sense he was glad, for he wished the girl no harm; in another sense though, it alarmed him, for he knew what it must inevitably mean. Interrogation; about himself, his nature, his world. Charn had thought long and hard about how he could resist the pressure – or, to put it in blunt terms, torture – that would be applied to wring answers from him, but he was enough of a realist to know that he wouldn't withstand beyond a very finite point. Hostile silence would only serve him so far; they had broken him once and knew how to do so again.

But the approach he expected didn't come. Instead Foss stared down at him, his blue eyes hard and cold with anger. 'First my son,' he said, 'and now my daughter. I want an answer, and I assure you that you will give it. What did you do to them?'

Charn began to feel very uneasy. He had assumed that the man wouldn't have the insight to link the two incidents, but it seemed he had miscalculated. Either that, or there was something else involved here.

He had made a mask of his face, meeting the steady stare with impassive disinterest; now he turned his head away. 'I don't know what you mean.'

'I think you do,' Foss said darkly. 'I'm speaking of their afflictions. Their symptoms. Grey skin. As grey as yours. A fever that doesn't correspond to any malaise known to us.' He pivoted, paced across the floor. The heels of his shoes made an unpleasantly threatening sound. 'And something else. Something that happened years ago, but which I will never forget.' The heel-noise ceased abruptly; Foss turned again. 'I will speak a name to you, my cold friend. A human woman's name. *Griette.*'

Charn couldn't judge whether or not Foss saw the rapid tensing of his hands on the chair's arms; the reaction was reflexive and happened before he could prevent it, but he was also quick-witted enough to snatch himself under control and cancel the movement before it could be completed. He stared back, apparently impassive, and for a few moments felt a sense of stalemate between them. The man was unsure of his ground, unsure of his suspicions. *Careful*, Charn thought.

'Shall I tell you about Griette?' Foss said. 'Shall I tell you what became of her? Perhaps I shall. For if I do, then it might be—'

He broke off as a sudden and urgent knocking came at the workroom door. 'Foss!' It was Nempson's voice. 'Foss, are you there?'

Foss cursed and crossed the room in four strides, wrenching the door open. 'Nempson? What in an inferno are you doing here at this hour?' Then his expression froze as he saw Nempson's face. 'What's wrong? Is it Calliope?'

'No, no!' Nempson made a violent, negating gesture. 'She's rallying, so Philome just told me – Foss, this is something else!' He drew a hectic breath. 'The powers know I wouldn't disturb you at a time like this without good reason, but this is good reason – damn my eyes, it's *vital*!' A second gulp of air, then: 'We've got another of them.' He flicked a glance towards Charn's chair. 'Another like him!'

The two men left the house at a run five minutes later. Against the background of Philome's questions and protests Nempson had given Foss the bare bones of the tale, and they were enough to make Foss silence his wife and rush for his coat. A second creature from the twilight world had been brought to the Institute less than an hour since. By sheer good fortune Nempson had been paying an early visit, meaning to search the Institute's library for a particular tract he wanted, and had seen the furore for himself. The being, like Charn, had human form, and was a female. It had been found in the very same part of the town where their own search had borne fruit; exactly how and where Nempson wasn't sure, but those details could be verified later. What mattered was that they had another specimen. And, Nempson added delightedly, though the creature was dead when found, the body was undamaged. For the first time, the *very* first time, they had the whole and uncorrupted corpse of a twilight being to dissect and examine!

Even from the back of the house Charn heard the sounds of the two men's hurried departure, and as he listened to their diminishing footsteps he felt a dark tide move in his mind. Nempson had said enough at the workroom door for Charn to get the gist of his news, and Charn was horrified. Had Selethe sent someone to search for him? Impossible to judge which of her courtiers it might be. *Humanlike. Female.* He couldn't *think* clearly; couldn't unravel the mystery and decipher a name from the mental list of possibilities. There were so few of them, the higher orders. Surely Selethe wouldn't have risked the life of another?

He slumped back in the chair, feeling a wearying and ugly emotion wash over him. It was something new to him, alien, and made him feel as though the last vestiges of strength had been drained out of his soul. He didn't want to put a name to it; but the name was in his mind nonetheless.

Despair.

Chapter IX

Except for one brief return to reassure himself that Calliope's recovery was continuing without complications, the Agate family saw nothing of Foss the next day. But though Philome's early efforts to wring from him what he was *doing* at the Institute met with failure, it wasn't long before the news became generally known. By evening, it had reached Calliope's ears.

It was Luthe's fault, and Philome berated him for upsetting his sister to no possible purpose by tattling. But the damage was done, and though she took good care not to show it, Calliope was deeply alarmed. She tried to persuade Philome to allow her to get up, pleading that she felt well now and was tired of lying in bed, but Philome wouldn't hear of such a thing. Out of bed was one rashness that would inevitably lead to others, she said; before anyone knew what was what, Calliope would be rushing away to the Institute and making herself ill again, and Philome would *not* be responsible for a relapse. In fact she fully intended to lock her stepdaughter's bedchamber door before retiring for the night, to ensure that there would be no foolishness.

She was as good as her word, and Calliope had no choice but to stay in her room until the following morning. But though Philome might have thwarted her in other ways, she couldn't force her to sleep, and through the deep of the night Calliope lay wakeful, aching with frustration and worry. Her one small comfort was that there was little danger of her father returning for some time. If all Luthe had said was true, nothing would tear Foss from the Institute until the dissection and examination of this latest discovery was complete, and that would take a long while; possibly several days. With luck, then, there would be time for her to make investigations of her own.

She began by considering the facts of the new discovery, few though they were. Another humanlike twilight creature; female, dead. How had she died? Not at the hands of the townspeople, that was certain, for they would have burned the corpse to ashes. If the light of this world had been the cause, then surely her body would have shown the marks of it. A natural death, then? It seemed likely, but Calliope knew nothing of the natural ways in which such beings died.

Unless she had starved . . .

Under the glow of the lamp at her bedside Calliope studied her right hand. The grey was fading, giving way once more to her flesh's natural colour, but her fingernails still had an alien, silvery nacre. The theory forming in her mind was outlandish and she couldn't find any logical arguments to support it, but intuition was arguing with logic and gaining the upper hand. And it posed questions whose answers could come from only one source.

Had Charn heard about the female creature's discovery? she wondered. Was she – had she been – someone known to him? An odd feeling moved in Calliope at that thought; one which she didn't comprehend and couldn't name but which made her irrationally angry. She put it aside, vexed by it, and concentrated on the matter at hand. She needed to see Charn before the business at the Institute was completed and her father turned his attention to him again. There could be no doubt that Foss had seen what had happened to her hand and, as she had done, drawn parallels between it and Griette's eerie symptom of fifteen years ago. If he too saw a possible connection with Charn, then Charn would suffer as Foss sought to wrest answers from him. Calliope didn't want that to happen, and not only for compassionate reasons. A suspicion was taking shape in her mind, and she wanted to put it to the test before any further injury could be inflicted on their twilight captive.

It was very late and the outside world was silent and empty under the high, waning moon by the time Calliope at last finished working out the bones of her plan. She wasn't sure how she might persuade Charn to answer the questions she wanted to ask. He was too unpredictable for rules to be applied; she would have to rely on instinct and play the game moment by moment. But there was one trump card that she could produce if all else failed.

She lay in bed and reached under her pillow for the little sheaf of papers she had placed there earlier in the evening. A selection from her mother's documents; not the copies she had made, but the last few pages that Griette had written, which she had shown to no other living soul.

She thought back to her visit to the hospice and her mother's bizarre, horrifying reaction to the challenge she had issued just before collapsing with the fever. It was hard to believe that she had confronted Griette as she had; her action had been utterly out of character, as though she had been goaded beyond sense and prudence by some desperate instinct that now she couldn't begin to understand or explain even to herself. But Griette's violent response had opened a door onto new and chilling conundrums. The sound she had made . . . there had been such an awful, alien timbre to it, combining fury, repudiation and appalling psychic pain. And her hands, clenched into fists and beating, beating at the half-finished clay sculpture, as though seeking to reject what it might have become, what it might have *meant*.

The scrawled writing on the papers she held blurred suddenly before Calliope's eyes and she put a hand, splay-fingered, over her face, biting back tears. There was no *reason* to cry now. All this was fifteen years in the past; she had no more power than Griette to change it. But the words her mother had written were lodged in her memory and nothing would erase them. *The Sacrament. I do not have the courage. In failing, I will end all.*

Griette, she knew now, would give her no answers, and to try again would be to compound the cruelty that she had already, if unintentionally, inflicted. There were only two possible roads she could take. One led through the maze of her mother's papers and the cryptic equations and notations that had taken Griette beyond sanity; the other led to Charn. Calliope did not know which was the more daunting.

She slid the papers beneath her pillow again. They offered no solutions but only served to deepen uncertainty and confusion.

Nor, at present, could she face the prospect of studying the other documents and trying to unravel their secrets. Tomorrow her mind would be clearer, and the last traces of the fever should be gone. Tomorrow, she would choose her road and begin her journey.

Philome allowed Calliope to get up the next morning, but only, she said, on the clear understanding that Calliope would stay indoors for the rest of the day and not exert herself in any fashion. Calliope assured her that she had no intention of going out, and, looking pale but otherwise none the worse for her illness, joined the rest of the family for breakfast in the dining room.

Foss, to her great relief, was still at the Institute. He had sent a message shortly after dawn, saying that the work at hand was likely to keep him from home for another two or possibly even three days yet. He would take his meals in the Institute common-rooms and not neglect himself, he assured Philome, but unless some emergency should arise, such as a relapse in Calliope's condition, he would prefer not to be disturbed until his business was complete. Philome had dispatched a reply telling him that Calliope was much improved and she herself would await his return with the patience which she believed was one of her chief virtues, and did her best not to let her annoyance sour the atmosphere at table.

Luthe came to breakfast late, and excited. He had made an early foray into the town, and reported that a sizeable crowd was gathered outside the Institute, clamouring for word of the new captive. Rumour had been escalating for the past day, and fact had become increasingly confused with speculation and superstition; now, a growing faction of the populace was demanding that the creature's body should be destroyed immediately, before it could 'rise from death' and wreak havoc. The Institute had appointed one of their most respected members to publicly assure the townsfolk that such a thing could not happen and there was no possible danger; but many people, Luthe said, were far from convinced.

Philome privately wondered if their conviction might not have some foundation, but she squashed the fear down, telling herself that she was being childish, and concentrated her attention on sorting the letters which the errandman had delivered just before

107

the meal began. Luthe continued to talk, attended by a goggle-eyed Tobery and Diona, and a tolerant Calliope and Celesta.

'I don't mind telling you,' he said, 'that I was hard-pressed to hide a smile or two as I listened to all that was being muttered.' He flicked a conspiratorial glance in Calliope's direction. 'Knowing what we have under our own roof, eh, Calli? What would the townsfolk say if they were aware of *that*, I'd like to know?'

Calliope stared at him. 'Luthe, if you said a single word to anyone about—'

'About our grey friend? No, damn me, of course I didn't!'

Philome said sharply, 'Luthe! Language!' but the censure was reflexive; she was absorbed in the letter she was reading. Luthe continued.

'All the same, it seems a da— a wretched shame to have such a prize in our grasp and not be able to trumpet it, eh?' He shook out his napkin with an affected mannerism that he had recently learned from an older crony. 'That's my view. So I thought maybe I'd invite a few of the fellows round to see the thing for themselves. Sensible fellows, of course, stout friends I can depend on not to say a word in the wrong place. Tonight, maybe. Before Father comes home.' He coughed. 'Wouldn't want to get under Father's feet, after all.'

Calliope continued to stare at him, but her face was paling to an angry, ashen colour and her mouth had set into a taut line.

'Your *friends*?' she repeated.

Luthe blinked, taken aback by her tone. 'That's what I said. Why, Calli, whatever—'

She swept his unfinished question furiously aside. 'In other words, to bolster your own standing in their eyes and make them envy you!' Her teeth clenched briefly. 'How *dare* you suggest such a thing! Charn isn't a rabble-show freak to be exhibited for the sake of your vanity, and if you think for one moment that I'll allow you to use him in that way, you can think again!'

'*You* won't allow?' Luthe echoed indignantly. 'Rot it, who are you to give me orders? You don't have any right!'

'In Father's absence I have every right where Charn is concerned!' Calliope snapped back. 'If Father were to know that you were going behind his back—'

'Well he shan't know, shall he? Not unless *someone* tattles!'

'Calli! Luthe!' Philome set her letter aside and stared reprovingly at them both. 'What is this? You know I will *not* have quarrels at mealtimes.'

'But, Philome, she hasn't the right to order me!' Luthe said indignantly. 'She hasn't the *right*!'

'And Luthe hasn't the right to try to use Charn as a—'

'*Enough*.' Philome thumped the heel of her hand on the table, a rare show of anger and one that surprised them both into silence. 'I'll hear no more from either of you, *if* you please!'

Celesta, who had set down her knife and, for reasons of her own, was paying keen attention to the dispute, said pruriently, 'Calli doesn't like *anyone* to show an interest in Charn. Except for her, that is.'

Calliope shot her sister a look of pure venom, but before she could retaliate Philome gave Celesta a crushing glance and said, 'Celesta, that is not helpful. As this matter does not concern you, I will thank you kindly to get on with your breakfast.'

Celesta scowled but stared down at her plate and made a sullen show of toying with its contents. Philome turned again to Luthe and Calliope, who were now facing each other across the table and looking for all the world like two bristling cats to launch into a full-scale territorial fight.

'Children.' She used the term quite deliberately; for all that she was only a few years older than either of them it was a pointed reminder that, in Foss's absence, she was head of the household. Luthe met her gaze resentfully, Calliope uncertainly, and Philome said,

'If you wish to invite your friends to the house, Luthe, I trust you know that you are always welcome to do so.' She could have added that that would be vastly preferable to the clandestine drinking-house meetings that Luthe naively believed were a well-kept secret, but didn't wish to muddy the waters any further for the moment. 'But where the – creature is concerned,' she gave a small, involuntary shudder of distaste, 'Calliope is quite right. It is here only for the purposes of proper scientific research, and I don't believe that scrutiny by a succession of gawking young men counts as scientific research, do you?'

Luthe flushed. For all his bravado, fear of his father made him reluctant to argue with Philome, and he shrugged, trying to appear careless.

'Well, it's of no moment,' he said. 'I doubt that the other fellows would be any more interested in the thing than I am.' With a petulant gesture he pushed his plate back. 'I'll leave the table, if I may.'

'You may.' Philome watched him as he slouched out of the room, then, as he shut the door as violently as he dared behind him, she sighed.

'Luthe is becoming very difficult these days. And quite frankly, Calli, you didn't help matters at all by allowing your temper to get the better of you.'

'I'm sorry.' Calliope looked contrite.

'I'm sure you are, my dear, and I do sympathise with your view; Luthe's notion was childish and unworthy. But perhaps if you *could* try to make allowances . . .?'

Celesta made a sound that might or might not have been a hastily suppressed snigger, then set her own plate aside. 'I've eaten my fill, Philome, thank you. Might I be excused, too?'

'Yes, yes, my dear.' A little distractedly Philome emphasised the permission with a wave of one hand.

Celesta stood up. 'Shall I tell the servants to—'

'No.' Philome was looking at Calliope; an odd look. 'They may leave the clearing for a while longer. I want to have a private word with your sister.' Her fingers strayed again to the letter she had been reading.

Naked annoyance showed on Celesta's face. If anything was afoot – and clearly something was – then she wanted to be privy to it. But Philome's expression made it quite clear that private meant private, and with a sigh of frustration the younger girl left.

Silence held for a few moments after her departure. Tobery was building a tower from the remains of his fried-bread sippets, and Diona was watching his progress absorbedly. Over their bowed heads, Philome met Calliope's wary gaze.

'Calli, I have received a letter from the Hospice Master. Why he wrote to me instead of to your father I don't know; perhaps he considers that under the circumstances a woman might be better placed than a man to deal with this matter.' She paused. 'It concerns your recent visit to your mother.'

Calliope said, 'Ah . . .'

'Yes.' Philome nibbled at her lower lip, not entirely certain how best to proceed. Calliope was of age and Philome had no authority over her; in truth she hadn't the right, as Luthe might have said, to probe into this at all. But she was worried and, for the moment at least, the worry wasn't something that she wanted to bring to Foss's attention.

She said, 'The Hospice Master writes of the . . . incident that took place during your visit. Before your collapse—'

'It was the fever,' Calliope interrupted defensively.

'Yes, I know it was. But there was something else, wasn't there?' A nervous look. Philome nibbled her lip again.

'Your mother,' she said, 'has been silent for fifteen years. In fact, the Hospice Master says, it was believed that she had entirely lost the ability to make a sound. Yet when you were taken ill – when the angels were summoned to the room and found all in such disorder – your mother was . . .' She consulted the letter once more, not wanting to make any mistake, '. . . "crying out aloud, and as though in great pain".'

The faint rustle as Philome set the letter aside again seemed ominously loud in the still room. Calliope was staring at the table, not daring to look up lest her stepmother should see and interpret what was in her eyes. After a little wait Philome spoke again.

'The Hospice Master, quite understandably, is anxious to know what might have provoked your mother to break her silence after so long. So he asks if you can shed any further light on the incident.' A pause. 'Which I think perhaps you can, Calli. For the Hospice Master feels – as do I – that there is a connection between this unhappy incident and the . . . symptom about which you inquired when you spoke with him in his office. The symptom that afflicted your poor mother when she was first taken ill, and which you yourself exhibited during your fever.'

Calliope hadn't realised that the Hospice Master had related that conversation to her stepmother. It was logical, of course, that he should have done so, but nonetheless she silently cursed him.

Philome continued, gaining resolution as she steered towards the nub of her concern. 'Calli, I know that strictly speaking it's not my business to ask you about this. But I must. For Tobery's sake.'

The little boy glanced up briefly at the sound of his name, then, assured that he hadn't done anything to earn a rebuke, returned to his precarious tower.

'I saw what happened to your hand,' Philome said. 'I also remember very well what happened a few days ago when . . .' Silently her eyes indicated Tobery; she didn't want to draw his attention a second time. 'I want to know, Calli, and I really think you should tell me. Are you keeping something from me? Something that, for my own children's sake if for no other reason, I should be aware of?'

Calliope continued to stare at the table. She couldn't reveal the truth. Philome wouldn't understand; she would overreact, and her first thought would be to go to Foss and tell him everything. Calliope didn't want that. In fact the thought of it horrified her, for she knew full well what her father's response would be.

Even if he wasn't already harbouring the same suspicions himself.

Suddenly, and so unexpectedly that it caught her completely unawares, she started to cry. Tears spilled from her eyes and there was nothing whatever she could do to control them; they splashed onto the table-cloth, onto her plate, and despite the fact that it made no rational sense and she didn't even know why she was crying, she simply couldn't make them stop.

'Calli . . .' Philome got to her feet, astonished and dismayed. 'Calli, whatever's wrong? What have I said?'

Calliope covered her face with her hands. A futile gesture, she knew; it was far too late to make any attempt to hide what was happening, and she felt so *angry* with herself. Angry, bewildered, confused . . . lost. There was no *reason* for this.

But Philome was reaching across the table and taking hold of her fingers, pulling them away from her cheeks. 'Calli, Calli!' The bewildered concern in her voice nearly broke Calliope's heart, and she realised with an awful certainty that her stepmother had sensed, on some instinctive level, that there was far more to this than met the eye. 'What is it, my dear? Oh, what *is* it?'

Calliope could only shake her head. Words wouldn't come; there were no words ever invented that could express or explain.

'Tobery. Diona.' Philome looked at her two children. They had been staring in curious dismay at Calliope, but their mother's tone was such that they both focused instantly on her face. Philome smiled at them.

112

'Little ones, you may go and play now. Go into the garden. It's a fine day and I'm sure you'll think of some wonderful games.'

Diona started to open her mouth, then, as if intuitively sensing the imperative behind Philome's words, scrambled from her chair. 'Come on, Tob'ry.' She grasped her brother's hand. 'Garden. Mama says.'

The tower of sippets collapsed as Tobery allowed his sister to pull him away from the table. He gave his plate a faintly regretful glance, then focused briefly on Calliope's face.

'Calli's crying,' he said. 'Silly.'

'Come *on*.' Diona tugged again. 'Mama says.'

The two children left, and Philome moved round the table to take the chair next to Calliope's.

'Oh, my dear,' she said compassionately. 'Can't you tell me about it?'

Calliope could not. A small, sharp part of her consciousness realised, belatedly, that she had underestimated Philome's sensitivity, but that knowledge worsened the ache in her without giving her any solace.

'It's something to do with him, isn't it?' *Him*, Philome said. Not *it*; *him*. For some obscure reason it made a vast difference, and Calliope's teeth clamped savagely down on her tongue as she shook her head in mute and inexplicable anger.

'No.' The word came out with a savagely stubborn edge to it. 'No, it's nothing to do with him. Nothing. I'm . . .' she groped for the lie and was a little shocked by how easily it came. 'I think I haven't yet entirely recovered from the fever. It's no more than that.'

Philome didn't believe a word of it, but she also saw that to press Calliope further at the moment would be futile. There was a connection, she felt certain, with the incident at the hospice, and with Griette herself. A link, an association, between this and the events of the distant past that had led Calliope's mother to her unhappy fate.

For a moment she wondered if, contrary to her first intentions, she should alert Foss. But the impulse faded. She knew her husband too well to have any doubt of his response, and she had a strong intuition that, at least for the present, it would be better for all concerned to say nothing. But she believed that Griette held the answers to a great and possibly very frightening conundrum, and she wished to all the powers in this or any other world that the poor, mad woman could and would reveal them.

'Please,' she said, laying a small, soft hand over Calliope's thinner and harder one. 'Just answer me this one question. Are you, or anyone else in this house, in danger from that creature?'

Unconsciously Calliope flexed her hand as she considered. The tears were stopping, the lapse over, and though she felt foolish and a little bereft she could at least think clearly again. *In danger.* Were they? Herself; Tobery. There had been no lasting harm, only a weakness and a fever. Besides, if her theory was right then Charn had had few options.

She put a hand to her face, wanting to sniff but at the same time unwilling; it was too childish. 'No.' Her voice caught; she cleared her throat and repeated the word more clearly. 'No one's in danger, Philome. I promise you that.' And added silently: *But it's so hard to be sure.*

Philome wanted to be convinced, and fortified the desire by reminding herself that, second only to Foss, Calliope should know the truth. But knowing the truth and telling the truth were not the same thing . . . 'Well,' she said, keeping the doubt from her voice, 'if you say so, Calli, then I accept your word.' She sighed. 'Perhaps your reaction *is* just a last trace of the fever, or perhaps there's something else that you don't feel able to confide.' She met her stepdaughter's gaze and held it. 'If so, then I hope that you'll change your mind. Because if I can help in any way, you need only ask me.'

Calliope felt shamed. Wishing that she could be kinder to Philome, and not raise yet another barrier between them, she got to her feet and said awkwardly and a little distantly, 'I'll remember that, Philome. Thank you. But for now . . .'

'For now you don't want to tell me and you want to end this conversation. I quite understand, my dear. Go, then.'

Calliope ventured a faint, guilty smile. 'I'll send the servants.'

'Do that, yes.' Philome continued to watch her, but Calliope was too preoccupied to notice the slight, thoughtful change in her expression. 'Perhaps you should lie down in your room for a while. Or sit quietly in the library. I think you've overtaxed yourself a little for your first morning out of bed.'

'Yes,' Calliope said. 'Yes, perhaps I have. I'll do as you suggest.' She left the room very slowly.

Celesta was hovering in the hall, pretending to be absorbed by her own reflection in a mirror but in reality keeping a covert watch for Calliope. As soon as her sister appeared, Celesta pounced.

'Calli!' She ran up the stairs, meeting Calliope half way between hall and landing. 'What did Philome want to talk to you about? Was it something in the letter she was reading?'

Calliope looked at Celesta's face and suddenly, momentarily, hated her. She thrust the reaction away, knowing it was irrational, unjust and false, but the movement with which she shook off Celesta's clutching hand was vicious.

'It was a matter entirely between Philome and me,' she said curtly. 'Which was why she asked you to leave the room.' She brushed past her sister, jumped the last three stairs to the bottom of the flight and turned sharply in the direction of the kitchen.

Celesta leaned over the banister rail. 'Calli—'

'I'll ask the servants to clear breakfast away,' Calliope interrupted. 'Then I shall lie down. In my room. With the door locked.'

Celesta stared, nonplussed and angry, and was debating whether or not to go after her when a voice called softly to her from the floor above. Philome had emerged from the dining room; she beckoned.

'Celesta. I would like a word with you, please.'

Celesta climbed the stairs, with a backward glance or two. Philome took her arm and led her a little way along the landing. When she spoke again her voice was low-pitched and conspiratorial.

'Celesta, I want you to do a small favour for me.' A pause as she wondered whether Celesta was the ideal person for the mission she had in mind. But, ideal or not, there was no one else available; not unless she spoke to Foss himself, and she had not yet changed her mind on that score.

She continued, 'It concerns your sister . . .'

Chapter X

Philome and Luthe were out, Celesta tending Tobery and Diona, so shortly after lunchtime Calliope had the chance she had awaited. She left her room, where she had spent the morning, and made her way downstairs with the queasy edge of nervous anticipation moving in her like something alive.

The house's atmosphere was drowsy with the peaceful somnolence of a warm spring afternoon. The servants, knowing that nothing more would be wanted of them until the sun started to wester, were resting in the kitchen or sleeping in their basement rooms; quiet hung like mist in the air, and only dust-motes moving lazily in the mellow glow that suffused the hall gave any sense that time was still passing. The click of the latch as Calliope opened the understairs door was a harsh but brief intrusion on the silence; she lit the pocket-taper she was carrying, closed the door behind her and, torn ambiguously between reluctance and eagerness and striving to disown both feelings, made her way along the windowless passage that led to the workroom.

The shutters in the workroom were closed, blocking out the day, but the etherea lamp burned faintly on the table, its glow just enough to show dim contours in the gloom. Charn didn't stir as she entered, but as she moved closer Calliope saw that no further harm had been inflicted on him; he was simply sleeping. In fact the scars on his face and left shoulder and arm seemed to have faded but for a few faint striations. How could he have healed so swiftly? she wondered, and smiled humourlessly and a little grimly as she contemplated the possible answer. Yet even if she was right, she couldn't hate him for it any more than she hated herself for eating the meals that were set before her every day at the dining table. Without food, any creature would die. How could she blame Charn for responding to the most basic and natural instinct of all – the instinct to survive?

She extinguished the taper and waited for her vision to adjust to the near-dark. She could hear Charn breathing, a light, regular sound, and as her eyes acclimatised she made out the contours of his face and figure. In this dimness, which stole the subtleties of colour away, he looked as human as anyone born of this world;

in fact it was almost possible to imagine that . . .

Calliope's mind jolted and she stared harder. Almost possible to imagine a glimmer of gold in his hair; the faintest touch of pigment in his skin. But *was* it imagination?

She moved rapidly to the table, and was about to spin the wheel of the etherea lamp when Charn stirred in the chair. He murmured something; she couldn't catch what it was but to her ears it seemed to have the cadence of a name. *One of his own kind? A woman?* Calliope set aside the question and walked slowly towards him.

His eyes opened when she was four paces away. He looked at her for a few moments, steadily and thoughtfully – she found his instant transition between sleep and wakefulness disquieting – then, suddenly and sharply, a thought seemed to surge out of his subconscious mind to the surface and his eyes turned stark.

He said, 'What do you want?'

The bitter aggression in his tone took Calliope by surprise, for it was such an acute contrast to the circumstances of their last encounter that it made no sense. A raw, instinctive part of her mind thought, *What has Father done to him?* But the suspicion died as swiftly as it had risen. This had no connection with Foss.

Charn was still staring at her, and abruptly he demanded, 'What hour is it?' Then without waiting for an answer he flung a swift glance towards the shutters and tensed as he sensed what lay beyond their seal. '*Sunlight . . .*' His body twisted in the chair. 'But what day? How long since—' The question cut off and he wiped the back of one hand across his mouth. Three quick, savage breaths calmed him, then he turned rapidly to look at her again.

'Why are you here?'

Calliope's eyes narrowed. A new suspicion was forming in her mind alongside the old, and for the moment it eclipsed her original purpose. She said, 'What's wrong, Charn?'

'*Wrong?*' He echoed the word vituperatively, and it startled her. He didn't normally take such an aggressive stance with her; defence and evasion were his usual way. With the circumstances of their last encounter sharp in her memory, this change of tactic hurt more than it should have done.

She said, 'I want to talk to you.'

Something that seemed to mingle fury and terror flared in his face, then his expression closed. 'No,' he said. 'I've nothing to say, to you or to anyone. Unless—'

Silence hung briefly. 'Unless what?' Calliope asked.

Dared he? Charn wasn't sure. Yet he had to find out; had to know. And she was his only route to an answer.

He put one hand to his face, feeling the sickness of dread. 'A question,' he said, his voice calmer but still with an edge that he was finding hard to control.

She continued to stare at him. 'Ask it. I'll answer, if I can.'

She would, he knew it. She wouldn't refuse to help him. She never had.

He drew breath. 'Your people. They've found . . . another like me.' His lashes flicked and he looked at her directly. 'Your father was here when the other one – the small, thin one – came to tell him.' He paused. 'I need to know about it, Calliope. I need to *know.*'

An ugly sensation twisted under Calliope's ribs and she felt momentarily as if sand was clogging her lungs and preventing her from breathing.

'Why?' she said.

'Because . . .' Then Charn paused, realising that there was far more behind the question than was apparent on the surface, or than Calliope wanted to reveal. She thought that . . .

But what she thought, what she believed, didn't matter and couldn't be taken into account. Later, yes, he would tell her a variant of the truth to content her; but for now there was a greater imperative. She would agree to a bargain. She must.

'Please.' His tone softened suddenly, catching her unawares; he saw the immediate change in her look, the eagerness mingling with anticipation and uncertainty. Yes, he could persuade her. 'Please, Calliope. I need to know all you can tell me about what has happened. About the . . . other one of my kind.'

A fly, trapped between the shutters and the glass of the window, was buzzing monotonously. Irrationally, Calliope wanted to hurt it, smash it, *kill* it.

Aloud she said, 'If I do tell you, what then?'

'Then I'll explain my reasons for asking this of you. And I'll answer any questions you want to put to me.' Another pause. '*Please.*'

For all the confused emotions that were agitating in her she couldn't withstand the appeal and the tone in which it was delivered. He saw her turn her head aside with a painful movement, and knew that he had won.

'All right,' she said. The two words blurred, sounding as though they were choking her. 'I'll find out for you. I'll go to the Institute. See what I can discover. But . . .' She looked at him again, and her eyes had an unnaturally dark cast to them. 'You must keep your promise, too.'

Charn returned her gaze. 'I always do.'

She didn't believe that but nodded nonetheless. 'Very well, then. I'll return as quickly as I can. Before Father—' But there was no point in saying it; it would have been a piece of empty and unworthy spite.

Charn didn't speak again, only watched as she went to the shutters and released the trapped fly before she walked quickly out of the room.

Philome would be angry, but then again Philome wouldn't know until it was too late, and Calliope reminded herself forcibly that her stepmother had no real authority over her. She could make her own decisions and act on them as she felt fit. No one had the right to restrict or proscribe or persuade. No one had the *right*.

Bright, hard sunlight, a brisk wind, a freshness to the air. It reminded her uncomfortably of her visit to the hospice, but she refused to think about that as she hurried through the streets and the dome of the Institute loomed larger before her. The crowd of onlookers had thinned considerably, leaving only a few disgruntled diehards to mutter at the foot of the steps. Calliope gave her name and purpose to the attendant at the door, was admitted and started quickly towards the less public part of the great building.

She was in the long, echoing corridor that led towards the experiment-rooms when a voice hailed her, and she turned to see Nempson Trinity hurrying in her wake.

'Calliope!' Nempson raised a hand in greeting. 'My dear, whatever are you doing here? The last we heard, you were still confined to bed!' He drew level, stopped and smiled warmly at her. 'This is a rapid and felicitous recovery, and I'm heartily glad to see you about and among us again!'

Calliope returned the smile, though with reserve. 'Thank you, Nempson. The fever's quite gone now, and I was . . .

greatly curious about this latest news.'

'Ah, you've heard, have you?' Nempson's face took on an odd expression; almost sheepish, she thought. 'Well, truth to tell, the matter isn't entirely as the early evidence led us all to believe.' He cleared his throat, looking downright embarrassed now. 'It's possible – though at this stage, mind you, I only say *possible* – that we've made a wrong assumption.'

'In what way?'

Nempson coughed again. 'I've just come from the office of the City Preceptors; they received a report a few hours ago, and their inquiries have led to a possible connection with the creature that we are examining. There now seems to be some likelihood that it – she – is human.'

'*Human?*' Calliope was nonplussed. 'But I thought—'

'That she looks to all intents and purposes like one of these twilight creatures. You're quite right; she does. No colour whatever to the body, and that of course appeared to be conclusive evidence of her nature. However, an approach has been made to the Preceptors concerning the disappearance of a woman of . . . well, not to be indelicate about it, shall I say a woman of a certain disreputable ilk—'

'A prostitute?'

'Yes.' Nempson flushed, and Calliope, aware that as a childless widower he might know more about prostitutes than he cared to admit, suppressed a smile. 'The inquiry was made by the woman's procurer; a thoroughly unsavoury creature by all accounts, and only concerned with the percentage she might forfeit by the loss. But from the description given, and the fact that the missing woman lived in the same alleys where we found the body – and where, interestingly enough, the male creature was captured – it appears that she and our corpse might be one and the same.'

The same alleys . . . Calliope frowned. 'But Nempson, if she's human, then how—'

'How did she come to take on the appearance of one of the twilight beings. Quite. That, my dear Calliope, is something which we must try to establish. For at the moment I don't mind admitting that it's a mystery to me.'

But possibly not, Calliope thought in sudden alarm, to Foss. Unconsciously she flexed her right hand, and apprehension moved in her. She wanted to see the body; wanted very much to look at the dead woman's face and commit it to memory. But to do so would carry a risk, for it would mean a meeting with her father. With this news fresh in her mind that was something she greatly wanted to avoid.

Nempson's voice broke into her thoughts. 'We were alerted to something amiss when we began the dissection, for the unfortunate creature's blood was of a normal, human colour, albeit very pallid. But, knowing as little of these beings as we do, we thought it possible that in death the hue changes, or that the constitution of the males and the females differs in some way. This news, however, puts an entirely new complexion on the whole affair.' He nodded along the corridor. 'I'm on my way to the experiment-room to alert the other Society members, so you'll be able to see for yourself the—'

Calliope interrupted him. 'No, Nempson, I— won't come with you at present.' Her mind worked fast; she didn't dare see her father, for one glance at her would remind him of the circumstances surrounding her fever, and he would draw the same conclusion that she had already drawn. 'I only came to – to reassure Philome that Father isn't neglecting himself; I promised to return home without any delay.'

'Ah.' Nempson's face expressed wry sympathy. 'Of course; I suppose it's only natural that Philome should fret, and we don't want you tiring yourself unduly so soon after your recovery. Well, reassure your stepmother that Foss is perfectly fit and well and that our experiments should be concluded within another day or thereabouts.' He paused, flicked her a smile that had a modicum of shyness about it. 'I'm sorry that you're not able to join us. Perhaps tomorrow?'

'Perhaps, yes.' Calliope nodded. 'Thank you, Nempson.' She glanced back along the corridor, resisting the impulse to turn and run with all the speed she could muster, out of the Institute and away back to the house without another word spoken. 'I'll leave you to your work, and . . . and . . . yes; thank you . . .'

She was backing away as she spoke, her right hand now clenched so hard that it hurt. Nempson stared after her, looking disappointed. 'My compliments to Philome.'

'Yes. I'll tell her. Goodbye.'

Too many *people* about; they crowded the streets, impeding her.

She had to get home before Philome did, before Philome could object and argue and waste time. Another day or thereabouts, Nempson had said. But when Foss heard this latest news he might decide to return immediately and look for the truth by another route, and if he did then Calliope knew she wouldn't be capable of talking him out of it.

People stared at her as she ran towards the square but she ignored them, not caring what anyone might or might not think. Reaching the house at last she flew up the steps, raced into the hall and, without even pausing to take off her hat and coat or light a taper, was away to the workroom. The door jolted open – and Celesta jumped like a shot bird, spinning round from the table and staring at her sister with a mixture of shock and guilt on her face.

Calliope stopped dead on the threshold. 'What are you doing in here?'

Aware that she was on weak ground, Celesta took refuge in aggression of her own. 'Why shouldn't I be here? This isn't your private domain!'

The etherea lamp had been turned up, making the room far too bright for comfort, and Calliope snapped, 'While Father is away he wants Ch— the creature left in peace. You know that!'

Celesta shrugged. 'I've not disturbed it; I've done nothing more than look at it. Anyway, it's asleep.'

Calliope looked swiftly at the chair. Charn was motionless but she knew instinctively that Celesta had been fooled; he was awake, alert, and listening.

'Get out of this room.' She turned on her sister with a venom that she could not remember ever having felt in her life. '*Now*, Celesta! I won't have you meddling and interfering – and I won't tell you a second time!'

Celesta had shrunk back from the fury in Calliope's voice; she began to edge around the table, keeping a distance between them as though she feared physical assault. Five more steps took her to the door, and as she reached it, and its promise of safety, her sapped confidence returned.

'Very well. I shan't stay where I'm so obviously unwelcome.' A toss of her head, her fair hair glinting in the lamplight. 'From the way you're behaving, Calli, anyone would think that the creature was your *suitor* rather than a thing that isn't even human!' She paused, and her mouth twisted in a spiteful little smile. 'We've all noticed how possessive you've become about it lately. But then, for an old maid perhaps it's all there is left.'

Black fury surged in Calliope and for one instant she could have picked up everything on the table – even the table itself; in that single, breathtaking moment she felt the strength was in her to do it – and hurled it at her sister's head. But Celesta was gone; the door slammed shut behind her and Calliope's rage drained away as fast as it had risen, leaving only a sense of bleak misery.

Then, from behind her, Charn spoke.

'Your sister has a malignant tongue.'

Calliope turned. Charn was watching her, his expression unreadable. A muscle in Calliope's neck worked violently.

'She's young. And she knew she was in the wrong; it was only—'

'You don't need to justify yourself or defend her. I meant no slight to either of you; it was merely an observation.' His eyes focused on the etherea lamp. 'If there could be less light . . .'

Calliope moved to reduce the nutrition level of the quivering nucleus, then stayed her hand as her mind registered his appearance more thoroughly. Those earlier impressions had been right, and in this light she could see them more clearly. The subtle but unmistakable hazel-brown tint that suffused the grey of his eyes. Hints of colour in his skin and hair. The smallest shades, but they were there. He was changing. Becoming less ethereal. More like a human.

She held on to that thought, knowing it would strengthen her resolve, and said, 'Celesta's of no importance. I've found out what you wanted to know.' And a good deal more besides. All she needed now was for him to confirm it.

Charn's face tensed. Calliope walked slowly towards him.

'You made me a promise,' she said, 'and before I tell you anything, I want to be sure that you'll keep it.'

He made a sharp sound and turned his head away; a gesture with which, now, she had become familiar. 'I gave you my word. I don't see how I can prove its worth.' Then he looked at her again, and again she saw the entreaty in his eyes that could sway her so easily; *had* swayed her so easily.

'Please,' he said. 'I can only ask you as a friend.'

Calliope had been prepared to resist the appeal, but she was not prepared in any sense for such a quiet, simple statement. *As a friend.* Confusion rushed like a tide. Was that what she had become to him? Or was this some subterfuge, some trick, designed to trap her?

She put her right hand, the hand that his touch had damaged, to her face. The fingers *ached*. But despite her doubts and the cynicism that was trying to break through from an intuitive level, she couldn't dissemble any longer. Whether or not he intended to keep his promise, she must keep hers, for her conscience – or something else within her – wouldn't allow her to do otherwise. Besides, he was in danger. For that reason, if for no other, she owed him the truth.

She said, 'I've been to the Institute. There has been a development. The . . . person they found; they think now that she is human.'

Silence. Charn was suddenly very still. Then, just as she had done when Nempson told her, he said, *'Human?'*

'Yes.' Calliope's gaze didn't leave his face. 'They believe that she is a . . .' Would he understand what a prostitute was? She changed her phrasing. 'A woman who lives by . . . by pleasuring men. It's common enough in our world; it—'

'Yes,' he said. 'I know.'

Do you? she thought. *How do you know? You shouldn't.* But the thought stayed unspoken. Instead she said with deliberation, 'She was found in a district where many such women live.' A pause. 'The same district where you were captured, Charn. Does that mean anything to you?'

It did. His expression gave the truth away in a small moment before his self-control brought the mask back, and Calliope saw it.

She said, very quietly, 'Did you mean to kill her?'

Ah, yes; the arrow struck its target. 'It's how you sustain yourself, isn't it?' she continued. 'From us. From humans.' She gestured towards his face and shoulder. 'Your wounds have healed so quickly. Why didn't you kill me too, Charn? Were you afraid that to do to me what you did to her would have been too dangerous? Or did you only need a little from me because there were others here from whom you could feed, like Tobery?'

She expected him to turn his head away again, evading an answer, retreating into a shell of silence that only calculated violence had so far succeeded in breaking. This time, though, he didn't. Instead, the fringe of silver lashes (and now the silver was tinged with gold) masked his eyes momentarily, then he looked at her again with a peculiarly candid expression.

'It's the only way I *can* sustain myself in your world,' he said quietly. 'I feed, or I die.' A pause, then: 'Do you condemn me for it?'

'No.' Calliope answered before she could stop herself, and instantly felt the advantage she thought she had gained slipping away. If this was a game of wits between them, she was not going to win, and the knowledge and acceptance of that fact made her suddenly want to abandon any artifice and be open with him.

She sighed and said, 'I don't condemn you for wanting to live. How could I? If I did, I wouldn't have . . .' The words tailed off.

'You wouldn't have done what you did to help me after your father and his friends had finished their torture. I know. It's why I regret the need that drove me to feed from you. But I had no other choice.' He was silent for a few seconds, still watching her. 'The other time, the first time, it was different. I was—' He stopped abruptly as he realised that he had been on the verge of trying to justify what he had done. He hadn't known that the girl would die. If he had thought about it at all, he had assumed that she would recover in good time. Not that she might regain consciousness only to crawl from the shabby room and the shabby house and meet a sad, mindless and humiliating end in the gutter of an alley.

Yet if he had known, would it have changed anything? He had been so desperate . . .

He said: 'You say you don't condemn, but I think you do; for that at least.' His shoulders lifted in a shrug that was disturbingly human. 'How can I blame you? I could tell you, and truthfully, that I had no desire to harm her or to harm anyone. But why should you believe me? I can offer you no proof.'

Calliope didn't answer, for her own certainties were slipping. She wanted to believe what he said; oh, she *wanted* to. But Charn was highly intelligent, highly perceptive. Perhaps he had sensed her confusion, or a glimmering of it, and was playing on that and using her cold-bloodedly (the term was highly ironic, she thought) for his own purposes.

Suddenly he sighed, startling her and snapping her back to

125

earth. He had dropped his gaze and was looking at his own hands, flexing them as though testing their strength and finding it wanting in some way. Calliope had a quick, strange insight into the bitterness that his captivity goaded in him, and guilt took hold of her. But she pushed it away, telling herself that she would not be swayed.

Then he said, 'I intended only to take a little from her. Just as I took only a little from you, and from your brother.' A swift glance to confirm that he had judged her relationship to Tobery rightly. 'But when there is touch – when there is physical contact – the transfer is so much less easy to control.'

Calliope's lower lip quivered. 'Transfer . . .?'

'The drawing of energy. Of life.'

The small hairs on her arms and the nape of her neck prickled. *Draining colour from us, giving colour to you.* 'That is what you take?' she asked. 'Our life force?'

He sighed again. 'It's as good a term as any other. I and my kind can't sustain ourselves with the foods you eat in this world; they're too – substantial. Yet we must have nourishment in some form. So we find it where we can.'

Luthe's sickness. The peculiar, short-lived fever that had afflicted more than half of the family. The nameless, minor but debilitating little malaises suffered by several of the Society members. Then, far more potent, the touch. The physical contact. Her own hand, with which she had reached out to him, with which she had clasped his fingers. Tobery had doubtless done the same, too young to understand the risk he was running. And the dead woman . . .

A strange, morbid fascination crept to the surface of her mind. 'What did you do with the woman, Charn? What did you do, that was so far beyond your control that it killed her?'

Even as she asked the question she knew the answer, and wished to any and every power in the entirety of creation that she had stayed her tongue. But the words were uttered, the need to know betrayed. Charn's eyes, dark with the sting and yet the pleasure of memory, sent a burning, hopeless ache of anger and jealousy through her like the flame of the taper-torch with which her father had smashed his resistance. She had no true knowledge and certainly no personal experience of such things; of what must flare and blaze between a man and a woman when passion, whatever the energy and motivation that drove it, eclipsed reason and made all else irrelevant. Her knowledge was cold, clinical, the knowledge of a scientist. But science had no place in this. It informed, but it did not *understand*. Yet on a deep, yearning, instinctive level, Calliope understood.

Crying at the breakfast table. Making a fool of herself. At the time she had believed, or pretended, that she didn't know why. But now she did. It hurt. It *hurt*.

She turned sharply aside, unconsciously emulating his habit, and sought refuge in something more practical and immediate.

'I think my father suspects the truth,' she said. Her voice had a diamond-hard edge of self-control. 'He's not yet certain, but if it's established that the woman *is* human . . .' She looked at him helplessly. 'He's not a fool, and he isn't easily thwarted. He'll wring answers from you at any price. And I don't want—' She cut the words off, looked away again.

Charn knew what she had been about to say. She didn't want him to be tortured again, to suffer as he had suffered before. It was what he had hoped; for in that hope lay the possibility of freedom.

Calliope had regained her poise and was looking at him again. 'Why were you so anxious, Charn?' she asked. 'Did you think that someone from your own world had come searching for you?'

He saw the underlying motive in her question and it surprised him. She thought he had a lover or consort who cared enough for him to risk her own life in a bid to find him and take him home. Charn carefully masked a smile. Her assumption was wrong. There might be some who would have done such a thing, if ever he had given them the encouragement to believe that it would matter to him. But he had not, and so they would not. With one exception . . . but he was assured, now, that Selethe had not defied all duty and all reason to take that potentially lethal step.

He studied Calliope's face. For all her attempts to seem careless there was misery in her eyes, and, surprisingly, he felt a swell of affection towards her. It wasn't a feeling that would or could ever flower into anything more, but it awoke a desire in him to explain at least a part of the truth to her. He believed instinctively that he could trust Calliope, and the belief had been strengthened by her reaction to her father's brutality. If he asked her to make a promise of silence the promise would be kept, and whatever he told her now would not reach Foss's ears. That, he thought, was good enough. He owed her this.

He said, his voice low-pitched and level, 'I expected no one. But I feared that someone might come. One particular person.' His eyelashes came down briefly, and to Calliope the faint gold glint made it look as though sunlight had unexpectedly touched him. 'I haven't told you,' he added, 'about Selethe.'

Gaze fixed on his face, Calliope listened then in silent fascination as Charn told her of Selethe, of her ethereal court, and of his own place in that court's hierarchy. He said nothing of Malorn and the queen's agonised yearning to discover his fate, but he described to her the lure that the bright human world held for the denizens of his own dimension, the trouble it had brought to them, and, finally, the desperate but futile attempts that had been made to persuade humans to understand that the twilight beings were more than mindless creatures deserving only destruction. At last he stopped speaking, and for some while the only sound in the workroom was the faint hush of Calliope's breath.

At last she spoke.

'That's why you came. To try to make us understand.'

Charn nodded. It was by no means that simple, but her assumption served his purpose. 'Yes,' he replied. 'That's why I came.'

'But Father— we—' She snapped the words off with a hiss and her right hand clenched in a sharp, almost vicious movement. 'Why has no one been willing to *listen*? If I had known, I would have—' Again the abrupt breaking off, and this time she shook her head violently so that her hair flew about her shoulders. In truth she didn't know what she would have done, for whatever her own mind might dictate, she would have had Foss's will to contend with. That was hard to combat under any circumstances, and Calliope doubted if ultimately she could have summoned the courage to oppose him. Cowardice, or habit? Probably both, for all her much-vaunted independence. But now . . .

'I don't know what to do.' The words were out before she could stem them, an admission and a plea together. She looked at Charn helplessly. 'Even if Father had known what you were trying to achieve, I don't think he would have been willing to

128

change his attitude. And now that you've . . .'

'Killed someone?'

She swallowed. '*If* you have.'

'I don't think there can be much doubt of it. Do you?'

She didn't, and he saw confirmation in her face. 'Now that this has happened,' she went on, avoiding the damning words, 'he won't be content until he has all the answers he wants.'

Silence again. Charn finally broke it.

'That,' he said, 'will probably kill me.'

He heard the small, choked-off sound that Calliope made, and latched on to it, though it discomfited him. 'As I see the matter, I'll have a simple choice,' he said. 'To answer, or to die. There are some questions I can't answer, Calliope. I daren't; not even to save myself.'

'About the gateways between your world and ours?'

He had explained a little of that, of the ways in which the twilight beings moved between their dimension and this dangerous, alluring, substantial place. Not enough to imperil his world's safety; but while Calliope would not press him further, Foss was another matter.

'I won't give him that secret,' he said quietly. 'Not under any circumstances.'

But Foss would want it, Calliope thought. Would *demand* it. Her own grey hand; her mother's grey arms. It would set her father on a path from which no reason or pleading would turn him. His will against Charn's, and neither would break. But Charn would ultimately lose the battle.

She felt as though something within her had started to crumble. 'What can I do?' she said. Her voice was a whisper, anguished. 'What can I do to *stop* it?'

For several seconds the room was very quiet; only the faint susurrus of their breathing impinged on the silence, and the rhythms seemed to clash.

Then Charn said:

'There's only one thing that would save me.' His eyes, another kind of darkness blending in the bleak grey, were focused steadily on her face. 'Set me free. Let me return to my own world.'

Chapter XI

Through the night, reason and conscience and something far, far more personal were at brutal war in Calliope. Sleep was beyond the realm of possibility, but waking nightmare was not, and a parade of images stalked through her mind as she wrestled with the demons that this latest encounter with Charn had unleashed in her mind.

Set me free. He claimed it was his only hope of survival, that unless he was released from captivity then his next confrontation with Foss would be the last. Was it true? Calliope tried to tell herself that her father would not take the risk of destroying Charn, however determined he might be to have answers; but at the same time another, darker voice cast doubt. She knew how intemperate Foss could be. She had already witnessed what he was capable of doing. The risk couldn't be taken. And yet . . .

Those two words, *and yet*, were the lure and possibly also the trap. Calliope knew why she was reluctant to take the step that would ensure Charn's safety. She might argue that he was trying to use her, play on her uncertainties and her fears, convince her that his life depended on this plea and thus gain his freedom through a lie. But in her heart she knew why she so feared to let him go. For to do so would break her heart.

It was a kind of madness. It must be, *must* be: to think – to *imagine* – that she loved that cold, alien creature of the twilight world was a delusion so great that it was almost impossible to encompass. He had used her and her family, feeding from them, taking their life force to satisfy his own needs – and he had satisfied those needs in other ways. He had killed. Once? Twice? More? She didn't know, couldn't know, and crushed down a renewed pang of fury as the circle of her thoughts came full turn yet again and she imagined the woman, the prostitute, pleasuring him while he—

Calliope sat up in her bed with a wild, bitter movement; the same reflex that goaded her each time *that* phantasm rose again in her mind. It brought an ache to her, a physical pain that seemed to penetrate to the core of her body as revulsion and jealousy met in a headlong clash. She couldn't cope with such a feeling, and the floundering, bewildering sensation goaded her to an anger that made her want to hate Charn with all the power she possessed.

But that, like sleep, was impossible. As the first signs of dawn started to show, and the street-lamps were snuffed out, she acknowledged miserably that she could not bring herself to do what he had asked of her. She could not bring herself to release him and let him go back to his own world, knowing that he would never return.

Unless . . .

Suddenly a peculiar silence seemed to enclose the room. Calliope sat very still, aware of the change in the atmosphere; aware, too, that it emanated not from some outside source but from within herself, like an unexpected but powerful psychic charge. The idea had come suddenly, almost at random, but now that it was in her mind she held it fast. Would Charn agree to such a bargain, and if he did, would he keep his word? There were no guarantees; she didn't know if she could trust him. But it was a chance.

Below, somewhere in the depths of the house, busy footsteps sounded. The servants were up and about, and Calliope shivered violently, like someone waking abruptly from a frightening dream. There was light in her room; she hadn't noticed it growing but the night's shadows were sliding away and the familiar contours and furnishings were lifting into relief, gaining colour. The sun would rise soon and the day promised to be bright. There was little time to lose.

She didn't pause to change out of her nightgown, only snatched up gloves, firebox and a pocket-taper and prayed fervently that Philome wouldn't break with habit and rise early today. The stairs were empty, other bedrooms quiet, and as she moved silently towards the ground floor Calliope rehearsed what she would say, how she would put her proposition to Charn. The secret of the gateway between this world and his. That would be the price of his freedom; the secret that her mother had been searching for when tragedy – or something else, but Calliope wasn't prepared to speculate further about that yet – had struck her. Charn would have her word that she would not reveal the secret to another soul, and he knew by now that she did not give her word lightly. Foss would never find it out, nor Nempson, nor any other member of the Society. But *she* would have and hold the knowledge, and it would be a talisman which, perhaps, one day she might find the courage to use.

She reached the ground floor. There were noises from the direction of the kitchen but no one in sight, and she started across the hall towards the understairs door and the workroom.

She had taken four paces when someone rapped at the front door.

Calliope jumped and spun round. A caller at this hour? For an irrational moment she feared it was Foss, then reason took a hand and she reminded herself sharply that he would not knock for admission to his own house.

A patter of feet sounded behind her and a maid appeared. She gave Calliope a curious look but only said, 'The door, miss—'

'Thank you, Jass, I'll see for it myself.' The girl hesitated and Calliope repeated a little more curtly, 'Thank you.'

Jass retreated towards the kitchen and, taking a grip on her nerves, Calliope opened the front door.

A boy wearing the red and grey jerkin of an Institute servant was standing on the step. He stared at Calliope in her nightgown and gloves, making no attempt to disguise his baffled fascination at the sight she presented, and only when she snapped, 'Yes? What is it?' was his attention forced back to his mission.

'Message for personage by name of Calliope Agate.' He held out a small oilcloth pouch and it was all Calliope could do not to snatch it out of his hand.

'I am Calliope Agate.' She took the pouch, almost tore it in her haste to extract the paper inside. Her father's handwriting . . .

'Is there a reply?'

'What?' She was staring at what Foss had written, trying and failing to take in the entire page at once. 'Ah . . . no. No reply.' The habit of courtesy struggled to the surface from under jarring confusion and the first threat of panic. 'Thank you.'

The haste with which she slammed the door in the messenger's face confirmed his view that she was at least eccentric and probably something a good deal worse, but she neither knew nor cared. Foss's words, concise and commanding, struck dread into her.

Suddenly she moved like a cat released from a trap, back towards the stairs, running. On the first landing she collided with someone else coming down.

'Calli!' Celesta recoiled against the wall, recovered her balance and stared at her elder sister in astonishment. 'Whatever's amiss with you?'

Calliope was too agitated to ask herself what could have prompted Celesta to be up and about so early, and Celesta was thankful – as Philome would also be – that her sister wasn't aware she was being watched.

'A message for me.' Calliope pushed past, heading for the upper stairs. 'It's nothing that need concern you.'

Celesta looked annoyed. 'I'm not interested in your secrets,' she retorted, the lie coming easily. 'I only—'

'Well, don't.' Calliope had reached the stairs; briefly, angrily she looked back. 'If Philome asks, I'm going to the Institute.'

Celesta watched her departing back. The Institute . . . the message, then, was from their father. Interesting. As was the question of why Calli should have been prowling about the house in her nightgown, carrying gloves and a pocket-taper. The connection was obvious. But what had she been *doing* in the workroom? Possibly her business there was quite legitimate and had Foss's sanction. But somehow Celesta doubted it.

Calliope had disappeared. Celesta stared at the stairs for a few moments longer, then hurried away to knock stealthily, urgently at the door of Philome's bedroom.

Calliope was half way to the Institute when she suddenly realised the futility, even the foolishness, of what she was doing.

She stopped in the middle of the busy street, causing several people to veer hastily and mutter at her, and pulled Foss's crumpled message from her pocket. Though the words were firmly lodged in her memory, her eyes scanned them again to assure herself that there was no mistake. There wasn't. The identity of the dead woman had been established beyond doubt. She was human, and 'a number of factors' had convinced Foss and Nempson that she had met her death at Charn's hands. That, Calliope knew, could mean only one thing; they had made the fragile but vital connection between the dead woman's condition and the malaises which had afflicted herself and Tobery. They knew, now, how the beings of the twilight dimension sustained themselves in this world, and Foss's instructions to his daughter were succinct and clear. He wanted to confirm this suspicion beyond doubt, and the simplest and swiftest way to do that was by further interrogation. He and Nempson had a few last experiments to perform on the corpse, but they would be at the house by noon and Calliope was to ensure that all was ready. There followed a list of implements that Foss would require, and as she read it again Calliope felt something constrict to a hard knot within her. Her assistance would be required, the letter said. And Foss was certain that, in the light of this new evidence, she would agree entirely that scruples had no further place in their thinking if the future safety of all concerned was to be guaranteed.

So she was on her way to the Institute to reason with him. It was ridiculous. It was *impossible*. He wouldn't listen to reason; not he nor Nempson nor anyone else, not now. She could speak, plead, urge until the sun turned black in the sky and the world ended; it would make not one whit of difference. Anger and outrage were driving her father now, and they were powerful forces. This had become personal, and Charn couldn't hope to withstand it, for what Foss intended to do was so subtle, so slow, so cruel, that it would not kill him. Not for a very, very long time. Not until he had given them the secret of the gateway.

Calliope thrust the letter away, looked up and with a small shock saw her own reflection in the window of a confectioner's shop. Coat flung hastily over the first dress she had been able to find; hat at a rakish angle atop a tangle of uncombed hair; slippers on her feet still because in her agitation she hadn't remembered to change them for outdoor shoes. She looked like a madwoman.

Mad as my mother.

A shudder went through her. She wasn't insane. Not yet. Not *yet*. For it was not insanity, surely it was not, to stop this barbaric plan from being carried out. If reason would not stop it, she must take another way. The only other way.

She whirled, barged someone but didn't pause to apologise, only ran on down the street, retracing her route back to the house. The town clock was striking as she reached the square, and Calliope was horrified to hear the hour. So little *time* – by now Philome would be about; possibly even Luthe, too. Breakfast would soon be served, and if she tried to refuse it there would be questions and arguments, and time would march on towards noon and then it would be far, far too late.

Thoughts and terrors flurrying in her mind, but with no solutions to any of them, Calliope ran up the steps and through the front door.

'Calli!' *Oh, powers, it was the worst luck she could have had! Philome, on the stairs—*

'My dear, whatever is this great rush and mystery? Celesta said you had gone to the Institute but clearly she was mistaken! I was about to—' Then Philome stopped in mid-sentence as she saw Calliope's dishevelled state.

Calliope clenched her teeth against the furious lecture that she anticipated – what could she be thinking of to show her face in the street in such disarray; did she think nothing of her family and how making such a public spectacle of herself might shame them? But though the words were on Philome's tongue, with an effort she stilled them as she remembered Celesta's report and what she had made of it. There was more to this than seemed apparent on the surface. Until she knew more, Philome thought it best to tread with great caution.

Calliope, meanwhile, had taken advantage of Philome's hesitation to marshal her own thoughts, and desperation had come to her rescue.

'I'm so sorry, Philome!' Her voice was breathless but otherwise sounded natural enough, or so she fervidly hoped. 'A message came from Father. He is returning at noon, and we are to begin a new experiment—'

'On the . . . creature?' Philome looked uneasy.

'Yes. Yes, on Charn. There are certain materials that Father needs. He asked me to fetch them, and – and to make other preparations; and you see there is very little time, because . . .' She floundered, but only briefly. 'Because all must be ready at the meridian hour, or the experiment will fail.'

Philome didn't know whether or not Calliope was telling the truth, but her explanation seemed plausible enough. There *had* been a message from Foss; Celesta had confirmed that. And Philome knew her husband's ways, and the eccentric rules that his experiments so often demanded, all too well. She sighed.

'Well, if this is at your father's behest I suppose there is little I can say. But I do think it irresponsible of him to tax you to this degree so soon after your recovery, and when he returns home I shall assuredly tell him so!'

Calliope didn't dare to imagine the consequences if Philome should do that and thus expose her lie, but at this moment she didn't care. She had won the respite she needed; for now that was all that mattered. There was another brief tussle over the question of breakfast, but she won it by again pleading Foss's imperative, and at last was able to escape to her room.

Coat on a chair, hat flung to lie wherever it should choose to fall. Gloves, firebox, taper; they were on her bed where she had left them and she thrust them into the pocket of the apron she had put on for appearance's sake. Fingers swiftly through her hair; it would do, it was enough to dispel the image of desperate urgency. A look in her mirror, a deep breath, and she went downstairs again. Past the dining room where Luthe, yawning, was just going in and gave her a languid but uninterested 'Good morning'. Last flight of stairs, then the hall. Calliope paused again for another breath – it seemed she hadn't taken a single one since leaving her room – then lit her taper and slipped through the door to the workroom.

Charn was awake, sitting in the chair with the air of a quiet, patient sentinel. He looked at her as she entered, and knew instantly that something was amiss. Not just her appearance, though he didn't fail to notice how thin the veneer of her neatness was this morning. But something else, churning and chaotic beneath the mask, a psychic charge like fire in her.

She closed the door at her back and moved quickly across the floor. As she approached, a sudden small frisson went through him, for the shutters were fast and the etherea lamp turned very low, and in the feeble glow of the pocket-taper she seemed to be drained of colour. She had the look of an inhabitant of his own world. It unnerved him, and he pushed the reaction away with a sharp, angry mental command.

'Charn.' Calliope stopped two paces from the chair.

He looked back at her. 'You've made a decision.' It wasn't a question.

'Yes.' She must hold to it, *must* hold to it. She would try to make the bargain, but if he refused – and she believed he would – then there must be no wavering. She drew breath. 'I will let you go. But there is a condition.'

His expression remained inscrutable. 'What is it?'

'That . . .' She faltered, gathered her courage. *Be strong*, an

136

inner voice said. 'That you'll teach me the secret of the gateway.'

Silence fell. Still Charn's look didn't change. Then, as Calliope's inward tension verged on breaking point, he turned his head away and said, 'No.'

'I won't divulge it to anyone else,' Calliope pleaded. 'Not to another living soul. I give you my *word*, Charn! You know I can be trusted!'

He did; and that made the mental alarm that had already stirred in him ring harder. Why were her manner and her words so hectic? She seemed desperate, as if she were fighting some inner compulsion.

Or as if time were running out.

He continued to gaze at her, but now with far greater intentness, though he took care to conceal it. 'It's out of the question,' he said. 'You must know that, Calliope, you must understand. I made a pledge not to reveal the secret to anyone in this world. Would you ask me to do what you will not do yourself?'

A pledge. To Selethe, his queen and his liege. Calliope felt her one thin hope shattering, for he was right: how could she give her word to him with one breath and yet ask him to break his with the next?

She turned away, forcing herself not to put a fist to her mouth as a twist of emotion so painful that she could almost physically feel it rose in her. *Control*, she thought. *Control. Would you rather watch him die?*

Her shoulders, which had tightened, slumped and she made herself turn back again. 'Very well.' There was defeat in her voice now. She should have acknowledged from the beginning that this was a vain and impossible fancy and not have tried, not humiliated herself by even asking. 'Then if there can be no bargain, I must simply release you. Because, you see, I think my father is going to kill you.'

She drew Foss's letter from her apron pocket and held it out to him where the glow of the etherea lamp could illuminate the words. Charn stared at the paper, then looked up at her again.

'What is that?'

It took her a few moments to realise that the letter had no meaning to him. It was an object, a physical artefact, but no more. He didn't understand its purpose. He didn't understand the concept of writing.

'Oh, Charn . . .' Calliope's voice caught and she snatched the paper away as her vision blurred. Such a small thing, but it hurt her with shocking force for it turned him in one single moment from the powerful, alluring and dangerous half-friend and half-adversary that he had been in her eyes, to a child as young and as vulnerable as Tobery. She felt a gulf opening between them, a gulf between worlds and one for which no bridge could be built. It was a feeling akin to despair.

But the moment and the urgency must still be faced, so with a great effort Calliope composed herself and told him, in her own words, what her father intended to do. Charn listened and, though she didn't quite know why, she spared no detail. When she finished there was silence. At last Calliope breached it.

'I'm right, aren't I? He will kill you.'

'Yes.' Charn made no drama of it. He was staring at the floor.

'Then I must let you go.'

He raised his head, and their eyes met. *Now*, Calliope thought. *Now, before Father can return. Before I lose my resolve.*

'My family—' Her voice caught again; she coughed, clearing it. 'My family are at breakfast. I can get you out safely to the front door; if you wish it I'll come with you as far as . . .' She hesitated as she realised that she didn't know where he would go once he was away from the house, or how far he would allow her to accompany him. But before she could ask that, Charn shook his head.

'I can't leave in that way.' He nodded towards the shuttered window. 'The light.'

'Surely for the few minutes you'll need—'

'No, no. You don't understand.' He had to tell her this much; there was no choice. 'There must be darkness, Calliope. Utter darkness, or the gateway won't function.'

'But . . .' Then the protest tailed off as Calliope realised the dilemma. In the night, utter darkness could be found; that must be possible, or no denizen of his world would ever have broken through. But the day had only just begun; long hours must pass before night came again. Charn, grey and strange in a world of colour, could not go undetected, perhaps could not even survive under the sun, until then.

She swung round, surveying the workroom with a quick, frantic glance. 'If I shut down the lamp—'

'No.' There were cracks in the shutters, light under the door; her concept of darkness fell far short of his. 'It isn't enough.'

Where, then? Abruptly the answer came. Beneath the house, as in all houses of a similar age, was a cellar, unused for as long as Calliope could remember; and the reason why it was unused might be Charn's salvation now. Below ground level, it had no window and the door had been made to fit so well that not one single glimmer of illumination could get through. In past times, so Foss had once told her, a member of a household who had committed some misdemeanour would have been locked in such a place for a day or two; it had been believed then that wicked behaviour was invariably the work of evil spirits temporarily possessing the body, and that a sojourn in absolute darkness would drive them out as well as delivering a salutary lesson to the offender. With the dawning of a more enlightened age that piece of ignorance had been laid to rest, but the cellars proved useless for any other function. They were too small to serve as working rooms, and anything stored in them quickly mouldered and rotted in the airless damp; and so they had become redundant.

Now though, their dark, close privacy might be put to a new purpose.

She told Charn, and saw his eager reaction. 'Yes,' he said. 'Yes. I think it will work.'

Refusing to let the ache of doubt and misery take hold of her, Calliope thought rapidly and hard. The way to the cellar lay through the kitchen; impossible if the servants were about. Faint sounds were filtering down from the dining room, suggesting that breakfast was now in progress, but she couldn't judge how long it would be until the meal was over. They must wait until it was, until the dishes were cleared and washed; then there would be a respite, albeit brief, when the kitchen would be empty. She could only hope with all her soul that Foss and Nempson would not return early.

She explained her strategy to Charn. She would free him, and together they would wait in the passage from the workroom until the moment was right. Less than a minute would be needed to gain the sanctuary of the cellar. And then . . .

But Calliope didn't want to think of that, and instead turned to the table and began to search for the key that would unlock the clamp at Charn's waist. She was rummaging, making more noise than necessary, when unexpectedly he said,

'What of you, Calliope?'

Calliope stilled. As he spoke she had found the key, and she clutched it so hard that it dug into her palm, painfully. 'Me?' she replied.

'Yes. When your father finds me gone, the clamp unlocked – you'll be blamed.' A pause. 'I don't want that to happen.'

Reactions clashed in Calliope's mind. For one irrational moment she had hoped – stupidly, she now realised – that he had been about to say that he didn't want to leave her. But he had not. Nothing, doubtless, was further from his mind. Yet in another sense he *did* care what would become of her.

She said aloud, 'I'll find a way. You shouldn't be concerned.'

'But I am. I don't want any harm to come to you because of me.'

Any more harm. But she pushed that away as unworthy, and laughed a careless, brittle and contrived laugh. 'Then I shall say that you forced me to release you. I shall say I was here, and you were troublesome, so I thought it wise to replace the shackles on your arms. But as I moved to fasten them, you caught hold of me and threatened to break my neck if I didn't free you.' Oh yes, the idea was coming so quickly, so smoothly. She *hated* herself. 'The key was in my pocket, for I feared it might be lost . . . as it almost was; it was far from easy to find . . . so I had no choice.' She sniffed, wiped a hand quickly across her face. 'You fled from the house, and I don't know where you've gone.'

Silence. Then: 'Do you really think your father will believe such a facile story?'

She shrugged. 'He isn't the most complicated of men.'

Nor a fool either, Charn thought. There would be trouble in the wake of this; Calliope would suffer.

'Perhaps,' she said suddenly, trying but failing to mask another sniff, 'you should hurt me in some way.'

'Hurt you?'

'Yes. Not enough to . . . do great damage, but it would allay any suspicion Father might have that we connived.' At last she found enough courage to look at him, and even managed a faint, self-deprecating smile. 'I would have screamed, after all, and brought the household running. Unless you stopped me.' She clamped one hand briefly over her mouth, pantomiming to show him what she meant. 'I won't die of one touch. Will I?'

He understood, and knew, too, the deeper motive that was moving in her and which possibly she wasn't willing to acknowledge even to herself. He smiled back, though strangely. 'No. You won't die of one touch.'

'Then that is what you should do. If you're willing.'

'Yes,' he said. 'Of course.'

She brought the key, and unlocked the clamp. Charn did not know how many days had passed since last he had stood on his feet, and the shock of finding that his legs wouldn't obey him brought a quick stab of terror. But Calliope helped him, hating the gloves she must wear as, gradually, she coaxed his reluctant muscles back to life. He took a little of her essence, reluctant yet knowing the degree to which it would help, and at last enough strength was restored for him not to need her supporting hands as he left the chair and moved cautiously across the room.

Calliope drew back. His height disturbed her a little; she found it intimidating and yet attractive in a way she couldn't comprehend and, afraid to stand too close to him, moved to what felt like a safer distance. Charn used the minute or two needed to test his balance and strength by surveying the workroom, moving to the table, to the shelves, looking at the equipment, the bottles and jars, the papers and manuscripts. He made no comment on anything, but Calliope felt squirming discomfort as she sensed his distaste for much of what he saw.

At last he turned to her and said, 'I'm ready now.'

She nodded. 'Very well. Come with me to the understairs door, and I'll see how the land lies.'

She saw him cast one last look towards the chair as they left the room, and the feeling that emanated from him was like a slap to her mental perceptions. Trying to ignore it, Calliope led the way along the passage, apologising awkwardly for the fact that she needed the taper to see her way. A little short of the door he stopped and waited, and Calliope eased cautiously into the hall.

No sounds of clattering from upstairs; either breakfast was over and cleared or the family were taking a few minutes to sit replete and quiet before summoning the servants. Then footsteps sounded from the direction of the kitchen, and the maid Jass appeared, wearing her outdoor coat and clearly about to leave the house.

141

'Ah, Jass.' Calliope intercepted the girl. 'Is breakfast over?'

'Yes, miss, I'm sorry,' Jass said, misinterpreting the reason behind her question. 'Madam said you wouldn't be wanting breakfast today. But I could tell Cook that—'

'No, no, thank you; I haven't changed my mind. Have you cleared away?'

'Yes, miss, and there's just the dish-washing to finish before the kitchen's all to rights ready for lunch.' Jass looked uneasy. 'Cook says I can be excused early, to go to Trader Street market.'

Clearly she feared that Calliope was about to give her some new task that would put paid to her anticipated free hour, and behind the fear lay a greater terror that it had some connection with the mysterious horrors of the workroom. Calliope smiled.

'Better hurry, then, or the best bargains will be gone.'

'Yes, miss. Thank you, miss.' Jass fled before Calliope could change her mind. The front door banged, her quick footfalls diminished down the steps, and Calliope stared speculatively towards the kitchen. Five minutes or thereabouts; the clearing would be cursory, for all the servants would be as anxious as Jass to snatch as much time to themselves as they could.

She stepped back into the passage and found that Charn had withdrawn out of reach of the daylight intruding from the hall. She closed the door and said, 'We must wait just a little longer.'

He nodded, shifted slightly. Her eyes hadn't reaccustomed to the darkness yet and she could see him only as a darker shadow among many others. He was leaning against the wall, and she moved to wait beside him. She wanted to talk, to pass the time, but could think of nothing to say; all there seemed to be in her mind was the sense of his proximity and its effect on her. Her pulse was over-rapid and her hands under the gloves were perspiring; she was fighting a foolhardy yet, at moments, overwhelming urge to move closer, touch against him, make contact with the fabric of his cloak and with the solidity of his body beneath. Absurd. *Ludicrous*. She shivered, and he said,

'Are you cold?'

'No.' Strange that he should think of such a thing. Cold, to him, was like warmth to her, welcomed and sought. Yet he had thought of her comfort.

Ah, this was getting more preposterous by the moment! She was indulging in flights of fancy again, imagining significance

142

into things that had none. Wasting time, wasting *time*. Chance was that the servants were done now and gone from the kitchen. She could find no excuse to delay.

Without a word to Charn she returned to the door and looked out again. Silence reigned, and a swift foray along the hall confirmed that the kitchen was, indeed, deserted. Fiercely crushing down her mixed feelings of relief and misery, Calliope ran back to the passage and hissed through the door, '*Charn! Now!*'

He moved with a quick, lithe grace that fascinated her as she pointed the way through to the back of the house. On his heels, and glancing back fearfully, Calliope followed him into the kitchen, then slipped past him towards the back door. Light was streaming into the kitchen and sweat beaded on his face; she opened the door, then looked at him. What she saw gave her a small shock, for in the hard daylight the tinges of colour that had begun to imbue him showed far more clearly. There was a hint of flesh tones in his skin. His eyes were no longer pewter-grey but brown, almost the same shade as her own. And his hair was fair; no, *blond*, with subtle shades of hue that made her want, irrationally, to reach out and touch it.

Unease gripped her; she pushed it firmly away and said, 'We have to go outside. But only for a few moments.'

He nodded. She saw him tense as he approached the door, then they stepped into direct sunlight. Charn flinched violently, shuddering and shielding his eyes, and Calliope led him quickly to the cellar entrance a few paces away along the wall of the house.

Untouched for years, and distorted by long exposure to the weather, the door was stuck fast. Calliope wrestled with it but it refused to give an inch, and at last she turned to Charn in appeal.

'I can't free it! It isn't locked, but—'

He all but pushed her out of the way and wedged his forearm against the door. For a moment she thought even his strength wouldn't be enough, but abruptly the door gave with an extraordinary sucking and groaning sound, and jolted open. Charn was through in a moment, Calliope behind him and thrusting the door shut – though not tightly, for she must be able to open it again later – behind her. Light cut off abruptly but for the taper's faint pinpoint; she heard Charn exhale and thought that he swore under his breath.

'Are you all right?' Her voice, echoing in the stairwell, sounded hollow and unnatural. 'Did the light damage you?'

'No.' Silhouetted, he shook his head. 'It was painful, but there's no damage done.' A pause. 'Thank you.'

Calliope didn't want his thanks. She held the taper out towards the stairs, aware now of the thick, cloying and repulsive stench that filled the cellar. Stale air, undisturbed and unchanged for so long that it was barely possible to breathe it. Moisture and must and decay, like sour earth with echoes of something dead. The steps shone with an unpleasant phosphorescence, and when she experimentally slid one foot forward the stone floor felt slimy.

'The steps will be treacherous,' she warned Charn. 'Have a care.'

They started down. Twice Calliope slipped. On the first occasion Charn caught hold of her arm to save her; on the second he wasn't quick enough and she lurched against him. He said something in a strange language that sounded both soothing and amused, then, startlingly, took her gloved hand in his and held on to it. The grip steadied and reassured, and with a pounding heart Calliope continued to grope her careful way downwards.

Only twelve steps and they were at the bottom, confronted by another warped and jammed door. Charn opened it as he had opened the first, and they went into the cellar.

The smell was worse here, and Calliope held the skirt of her apron over her mouth in an effort to block it out.

'I . . . won't be able to stay long,' she said indistinctly through the apron's folds. 'The air . . .'

Charn didn't seem to be affected by the reek. He said, 'Put out the taper.'

She did, though with a nervous shudder, trying not to imagine what might be lurking in crannies and only waiting for the light to vanish before venturing forth. When the dark came it was so intense that she gave a sharp, involuntary gasp. Charn's hand squeezed hers, briefly, then he spoke again.

'Yes. Oh, yes. This is enough.'

So, Calliope thought, the moment had come. She had succeeded, and he had his freedom. She wanted to turn and run out of the cellar, blindly, out of this blackness and away to the light again.

'Go, then,' she said. 'Why wait any longer? Go, Charn. *Please.*'

His hand released hers. She flexed her fingers, which were tingling, and stepped away from him, not knowing what this would entail or what he must do, but aware that she could not be a part of it. She heard him sigh, softly, as though marshalling his thoughts or some mental power. There was a pause. Then, so unexpectedly that she jumped, his voice broke the silence.

'Light your taper again, Calliope. Just for a few moments.'

She complied, nerves jangling, fumbling clumsily with her firebox but at last getting the flame to flare into life. The light came; Charn, grey once more now, gaunt, shadowed, was looking down at her.

He laid his hands on her shoulders. No danger in it, not through her clothing, but she shivered nonetheless.

'I must leave the mark,' he said.

She had not forgotten that. 'Yes,' she said softly. 'I'm ready.'

He raised one hand towards her face and she resisted the temptation to close her eyes. She wanted to see what he did, wanted to watch his expression as he touched her. But then the hand hesitated and stilled.

'What is it?' she asked uneasily. 'What's wrong?'

Charn paused for a moment longer. Then he said, 'It will be better for you if the fever comes quickly, or your family will wonder why you didn't raise the alarm immediately after my disappearance.'

That would be safer, she knew, but she shrugged. 'It will come when it comes. We can't control that.'

'No, no.' Something odd in his voice. 'There is a way to ensure that the onset will be swift. But perhaps you won't forgive such a liberty.'

She realised abruptly what he meant, and her eyes widened, staring at him in the gloom. Perhaps Charn saw something in the look she gave him that she herself did not – or dared not – recognise; or perhaps he decided that, liberty or no, this was for the best. Or perhaps, simply, it was a whim. She would never know. But he leaned over her, bent his face towards hers. His hands cupped her jaw, flesh to flesh, then his mouth made contact with hers and he kissed her. It was a strange kiss, gentle yet with an underlying ferocity that sent a shock through Calliope. Instinctive fear tried to make her pull back, but she didn't, couldn't. She tasted something that made her think of frosty winter evenings, and coldness seemed to flow into and through her like a river. The kiss seemed to go on for such a long, long time . . .

But finally there was an end, and time slid back into motion again as Charn raised his head. His eyes were half-lidded, the colour of pewter again now behind the pale lashes. He gazed at her, a thoughtful look, assessing, unfathomable.

'Goodbye, Calliope,' he said. 'I owe you a great debt. I hope you believe that if I could repay it, I would.'

'Yes,' Calliope's whisper was barely audible. 'I believe that.'

She snuffed out the taper and stood motionless, listening to the small sounds as he moved across the cellar floor. There was another faint sigh, but this time she did not think it came from him. A breath of cold air flittered across the room, raising gooseflesh on her arms, and she hugged herself. Then . . .

A scent. Not the stink of the cellar but something quite lovely, if a little dangerous. Heavy, sweet, like an opiate. Like a night flower.

White flowers . . .

Calliope stared into the dark but saw nothing. Not the gateway opening, not Charn's tall figure as he moved silently into its portal. She wasn't aware that he looked back, and that his last sight of her was one which he committed carefully to memory. She only knew that there was suddenly an emptiness in the cellar where moments before there had been a living presence, and that he was gone.

She lit the taper. Climbing the stairs was less hazardous than descending, and the door to the garden opened easily. No one in the kitchen; only the fire in the black cooking-range crackling and murmuring to itself. A smell of soap.

Through then to the hall. Upstairs, Tobery and Diona were playing a game with Philome, and their laughter brightened the house. Calliope paused to listen for a few seconds, then went on to the workroom. It all looked so *tidy*; nothing disturbed, even the chair still perfectly aligned, though empty now of course. This wouldn't do, for it wouldn't convince.

She threw papers, upset a few implements, and dragged the chair out of position, though it was too heavy for her to risk trying to tip it onto its side. Better. The mess could easily be taken for the signs of a struggle, and all she needed to do now was prepare herself for Foss's return.

Tentatively she touched one hand to her lips, remembering as she did so how Charn's lips had felt. No difference, except that her skin seemed cold. Or perhaps that was just anticipation.

Then without any warning the room seemed to swim, and suddenly Calliope found herself leaning heavily against the table without any knowledge of how she came to be there. Had she blacked out? In her mind, she seemed to hear Charn's voice: *A way to ensure that the onset will be swift.* Gripping the table edge to steady herself, Calliope smiled. Oh, yes. Oh, *yes.* The device was working with a vengeance; everything in the workroom looked alien to her and she was beginning to feel *distinctly* strange, as if a dream were rushing up over her and eclipsing reality. Which perhaps it was. Which perhaps it had. Perhaps it had all been a dream. Charn, and the chair, and the torture, and her tears, and the cellar. All a dream. Like an opium.

White flowers . . .

She was unconscious when Foss came home and found her. She lay at the foot of the chair, one hand still clasping a spent pocket-taper while the other arm, by some extraordinary means, had become entangled with one of the shackles. Her face was grey. And from her expression it looked as though, at the moment of collapse, she had been trying to stop herself from laughing.

Chapter XII

More than a moon since Charn had gone. Calliope had suffered five days of fever which, now, seemed like nothing more substantial than a momentary bad dream. Then had followed a seemingly endless procession of physicians and alchemists and members of their own and other Societies, as Foss set sternly about the task of finding out exactly what had happened, and what depth of harm the creature of the twilight world had inflicted on his daughter in the minutes before his escape.

For an entire quarter-moon Calliope suffered the questions

and the examinations with meek resignation. Her story was accepted, not doubted for one moment, and although Foss and Nempson both lectured her – Foss sternly, Nempson worriedly – on her foolhardiness in attempting to subdue the captive without help, they also clearly admired her courage in the face of his 'violent assault', and assured her that she could in no way be held to blame for the loss of their prize.

Outwardly Calliope thanked them for their exoneration; inwardly, she felt as if something at the core of her had rotted. Guilt, shame and relief fought constant battles, together with a powerful feeling that she wanted to be rid of anything and everything to do with this. She didn't want to hear Charn's name spoken. She didn't want to think about him. She didn't want to acknowledge the fact that he even existed. But that, of course, was impossible.

A search was mounted, but no one had any serious hope of finding Charn again, and after two days the efforts were abandoned. Clearly he had escaped to his own world, and it was generally agreed among the Society members that he was extremely unlikely ever to return. Most were content to turn their attention to plans for finding and capturing another such prize, so that the experiments could continue. Foss, however, was not so sanguine, for to his mind the attack on Calliope had given the entire affair of the twilight creatures a new and very specific dimension. Charn had committed an outrage against a member of his own family – and that was an affront which Foss would not tolerate under any circumstances. No matter how much time and effort it might take, he wanted revenge.

Calliope realised the depth of her father's fury and determination one day when, shortly after she had been allowed out of bed for the first time, he summoned her to the library, saying that he wished to speak with her on a serious matter. When he told her of his intentions, she was horrified. From now on, Foss said, his alchemical work would have one purpose and one alone: to break the secret of the gateway between this world and that of the twilight beings. Let it take a year, or ten, or twenty, he would do it. And when he had succeeded, he would enter that world and take reprisal for the offence that had been committed against Calliope and thus against himself.

Calliope didn't argue with him. She didn't dare; in this mood his temper was on a dangerously short fuse, and besides if she made any plea, however small, on Charn's behalf, it would instantly arouse his suspicions. She said yes when he asked if she was ready to help him in the work, and she agreed when he told her that he believed her mother's notes would prove invaluable, knowing with a sure sense of dread that he was right. When he had gone, leaving her alone in the library, she stared out of the window at the bright day and felt as if the world had turned black.

She had no doubt that her mother's notes did contain the key, for she was certain now that Griette had unravelled the secret, and had used it. A heady, opiate scent. The scent of white flowers, white as the moon's face, blooming in a hot summer night. For as long as she lived, Calliope thought, she would never forget that perfume and the way in which, briefly, it had eclipsed the reek of the cellar in the moments before Charn stepped through the portal. Foss might never make that connection, for he had not witnessed what she had witnessed. But if one road led to the answer there would surely be other roads, and in time, enough time, he would find one.

Unless she could find it first. Unless she could warn Charn.

So, with a moon past and life at least in theory returned to normal, Calliope was walking a delicate and perilously narrow path between outward compliance and the inner demands of her own resolve. Foss was surprised by the energy and dedication with which she threw herself into her work so soon after her recovery, but only assumed that she shared his desire to strike back in vengeance. He knew nothing of what Calliope did, what she studied, how thoroughly and carefully and meticulously she thought, during the time that she spent alone in her room, or in the library when he was away visiting his patients.

Philome, though, was another matter, for Philome saw the strange, frenetic light that burned behind Calliope's eyes in unguarded moments. With an unformed yet acute intuition she sensed that all was very far from well with her stepdaughter, and that the cause of it was not what Foss so gullibly believed. She counted the hours Calliope spent alone, and the tally was high. She watched, covertly, Calliope's mood and manner, and realised how remote and private she had become. She knew how often Calliope went to the workroom when her father was out. And, like a small but hungry maggot at the core of her mind, she had the knowledge of what Celesta had seen – or thought she had seen – on the day of the twilight creature's escape.

Celesta had proved to be an excellent foil. She loved nothing better than an intrigue, and the added spice of sisterly rivalry had given her efforts on Philome's behalf an extra edge. In a perverse way Celesta had been jealous of the rapport which Calliope seemed to have struck with Charn; though she professed to find the creature alien and repulsive, she had obviously been fascinated by him, and Philome had no doubt of the motive behind her frequent malicious remarks about Calliope's possessiveness – or worse – where he was concerned. So Celesta had watched and Celesta had followed, and, as Philome suspected, Calliope had been too distracted to be any the wiser.

Then the captive had escaped. Or perhaps *disappeared* was more accurate. For Celesta, making her way quietly along the first floor landing shortly after breakfast, had heard a murmur of voices in the hall. One she recognised immediately as Calliope's but the other was not familiar. A male voice, Celesta reported later to Philome. She had moved as quickly as she could to the banister rail and leaned over, but whoever was there had gone before she could catch a glimpse of him. Then minutes later Calliope returned from the direction of the kitchen, alone but clearly distraught – and, in Celesta's opinion, looking very furtive. She disappeared through the understairs door, and after a brief wait Celesta took a taper and followed her. She didn't enter the workroom, but she stood outside the door and listened, and what she heard baffled her. It sounded as though Calliope were moving things, throwing them about. Then came the sound of something very heavy being dragged across the floor, and after that, silence.

The rest of the story, of course, was known, for not long afterwards Foss had returned and Calliope had been found unconscious in the workroom. Attacked by the twilight creature, and forced to free him in order to preserve her own life. It was very plausible. But Philome felt certain that it was not the truth.

She knew she should have told Foss of her suspicions now; matters had surely gone too far for him to be left in ignorance. Yet still, for reasons she couldn't quite pin down, Philome was reluctant. Possibly it was guilt, for she felt that Calliope had a right to privacy and her surveillance was already intrusion enough.

Or possibly it was a conviction that with the twilight being gone (and well rid of in her opinion) he was no longer a threat to anyone. In that sense, if Calliope had released him she had done no harm, least of all to herself. All things considered, Philome decided that discretion was still the better course, and she continued to wait. But she also continued to watch.

Then, during the sixth quarter-moon after the furore, Foss cast a new and unexpected card into the game.

It had not been a good day. Tobery had had bad dreams and kept Philome awake half the night, and in addition she had a sore tooth to contend with which did not put her in the best of moods. A new spat with Luthe on the subject of the company he was keeping had ended in sour stalemate – and then there had been the quarrel with Calliope.

It was over nothing more serious than the untidiness of Calliope's hair, but it had flared suddenly and vitriolically into a stormy confrontation in which a great many unpleasant things were said. Philome was honest enough to acknowledge that she had a temper, but she was in no doubt that for once she had had no part whatever in triggering the argument. It had been entirely Calliope's doing, and even when the storm was over and they both calmed down and apologised for their hard words, Philome had the distinct impression that Calliope's remorse was a sham. As happened on occasion, she had a sharp and piercing insight into what that actually meant. It wasn't just that Calliope did not feel sorry for what she had said. It was that she felt nothing at all. No interest; as if the entire incident had been none of her concern. She said the right words, she made the proper amends, but neither the quarrel nor its aftermath had touched her. She was remote, distant, as cold as a midwinter icicle, and Philome knew that nothing she might say or do could break through to her.

Afterwards, Calliope retreated to her room, to do whatever it was she did during the long hours she spent there these days. Reading, she said. Studying. Philome could neither confirm nor refute it. But she would have staked a heavy wager that the subject of Calliope's studies – or at least, the motivation behind them – was not what Foss fondly believed.

Foss himself came home late in the afternoon. He had spent most of the day visiting some of his wealthier patients, presenting this moon's account while he was at it, then had paid a brief call at the Institute where, Philome gathered, some new contraption or other had just been installed and was causing great interest. He came in, kissed his wife perfunctorily and sat down in his favourite chair before inquiring after Calliope's whereabouts.

'Calliope is in her room,' Philome said. 'And in truth, husband, I think it's high time something was *done*.'

Foss looked at her. 'Done?'

'Yes.' She wouldn't tell him all of it, Philome thought, but in the wake of today's argument there had to be some ground for intervention. 'The fact is, Foss, I suspect that she simply isn't rallying from this illness as she should. I don't mind admitting that I'm worried.'

Foss grunted. 'Physically, she's well enough. The fever has long gone, her colouring is normal again and she's regained her strength.'

'Yes, I know. But however healthy her body might be, there is still something *wrong* with her. We had an argument today—'

'Ah—' Foss began.

'I know what you're thinking, and you've said it so often that it's tiresome. Women squabble. Well, perhaps we do. But you have to admit that it is not like Calliope to be quarrelsome.'

'That's true.' Foss frowned. 'However, if there's a malaise still infecting her, I'm damned – pardon me, my dear – if I know what it is. I've conducted all manner of tests on her, with no material result. To all intents and purposes she's as well as you or I.'

Philome was of the opinion that tests were no substitute for instinct, but she didn't say so, only approached the point more obliquely. 'It has occurred to me,' she said carefully, 'that what afflicts Calli might be a form of shock. I profess no knowledge of such things, of course, but speaking as a woman, and thus knowing women's weaknesses, it seems a possibility.'

'Shock? In the wake of the creature's assault, d'you mean?' Foss stared at her.

'That's precisely what I mean. Calli has become waspish, snappish and withdrawn, and that, I understand, is often a symptom among women. I remember my own mother, when my father lost the last of their money in that ill-fated—'

'Yes, yes.' Foss also remembered Philome's mother, and had no wish to be reminded of her. Calliope was made of sterner stuff, far too stern for such nonsense, and he felt his patience beginning to ebb.

'Philome, speaking both as Calliope's sire and as a physician, I think I'm in a better position than you to interpret her symptoms; as you said yourself, you have no knowledge of such things. I assure you, if these strange moods of hers have any cause at all, shock is not at the root of it. However,' holding up both hands pacifyingly as Philome made to protest, 'if matters are as you say, then I agree that something should be done to rectify them. I'll speak to her. If there's anything amiss, any private trouble or grievance she's nursing, she'll tell me.'

If he believed that, Philome told herself, then he didn't know Calliope half as well as he thought he did. But she kept the observation, and the speculations that accompanied it, to herself.

'Well, of course, you know best,' she said with a sigh. 'But until things do improve I shall continue to worry.' She paused, then, 'Truly, Foss, in this past moon she's become like a stranger. I feel I can't reach her any more.'

Foss grunted again, but this time it had an edge of wry amusement. 'If she were Celesta – which thank the powers she's not – I'd think she were lovesick.'

Philome gave him a very peculiar look which, perhaps fortunately, he didn't notice. 'Lovesick?'

'Yes. If the symptoms are as you describe them, then you'll find the answer clear as day in any medical textbook ever written. Withdrawn and inattentive, yet also combative and temperamental. We see the signs in her sister every day; all romance and foolishness, swinging between one extreme and the other and no sense to any of it.'

'Well,' Philome said carefully and slowly, 'I suppose that is a possibility . . .'

'Calli? Living spirits, Philome, you know as well as I do that that's nonsense! She's far too level-headed.' Foss paused. 'Mind you, I'm not saying that marriage wouldn't be good for her.'

That did take Philome aback, and she stared at him in astonishment. 'Foss! You've never encouraged Calliope to take suitors; in fact quite the opposite! Time and again you've told me that she's better off unwed, because marriage would interfere with her work!'

'Rot me, my dear, I've never said anything of the sort!' And as Philome tried to recover from this barefaced untruth, Foss went on, 'I have simply said that a *wife's duties* would interfere. However,

153

in the right circumstances the two need not be incompatible. For example, if Calliope were to find a husband who shared her enthusiasm for science . . .'

The coin dropped. Philome's eyes narrowed. 'Foss. What's in the wind? What haven't you told me?'

He looked back at her, and instantly she recognised the significance of the faint, sly smile on his face. There *was* something. Foss had been making plans; and he was very pleased with the result.

Her earlier preoccupations flew out of the window as her mind latched on to this new and utterly unanticipated development. 'I think,' she said, 'that you had better tell me *exactly* what is going on!'

'Very well.' Foss's smile broadened. 'Someone – someone we both know – has intimated to me that he wishes to ask for Calliope's hand. He doesn't need my permission to ask her, of course; she's of age and may choose for herself. But he is a little shy, and he also wishes to go about the matter with my full knowledge and approval.'

'Well, that's reassuring at least.' Philome was beginning to look very interested. 'Who is he? A gentleman?'

'Oh, most certainly. A professional man like myself. Older than Calliope, but, as we both know, that is no bar to happiness. A widower, but with no children to turn him grey before his time.' He raised one eyebrow, an amused comment on his own situation, and Philome smiled. 'He is well-off, with a great deal to offer. And, like Calli, a dedicated seeker after knowledge.'

'Who *is* he?' But Philome thought she already knew. Foss beamed.

'Nempson Trinity.'

'Well, well,' she said. 'Well, *well*. Nempson. I can scarcely credit it.' Yet, thinking back, she recalled the way Nempson often looked at Calliope. A little like a hapless dog hoping for an encouraging word. Was that too unkind? Perhaps, but no matter. Nempson. A good man. Educated, intelligent, wealthy enough to provide his wife with a very fine home. In fact, Philome thought, he had everything that Calliope could wish for; even the age difference was no real obstacle, as Foss had pointed out. Besides, he looked younger than his years. In a way, he was quite handsome – and he and Calliope shared so much common ground. Nempson

Trinity was, in fact, eminently suitable.

But for one thing.

Realisation struck Philome like a chilly shock, and she started as the truth of it came home to her. What had Foss said . . . withdrawn and inattentive, yet combative and temperamental. He described Calliope's oscillating moods to perfection. The symptoms of a very particular ailment, he said. She could see it now. Oh, she could *see* it. Calliope was, indeed, lovesick. But the object of her love was not Nempson, nor any other man in this town . . . or in this world.

Celesta's spiteful aspersions had struck their target far more accurately than she knew. Calliope had pledged her heart to Charn, and the knowledge of it struck dread like a knife-blade into Philome's soul.

Oblivious to his wife's disquiet, Foss said, 'I'll go up to her room now. As I said, if anything's amiss with her she'll talk to me about it; and at the same time I'll sound her out a little on the matter of Nempson's suit.' He grinned at Philome. 'A fine thing, don't you think? Nempson and Calli. It will be an excellent match for them both.'

Philome noticed that he said 'will', not 'would', and thought fleetingly what a blind fool he was. However, her expression remained composed and she only replied, 'Yes, Foss. I entirely agree. *If* Calliope is willing.'

'Well, naturally I wouldn't dream of coercing her in any way. But there's time enough, and once she's accustomed to the idea I think she'll see how well it suits her. Calli's no fool, my dear. She'll make the right decision.' He heaved himself out of the chair, then consulted the elaborate timepiece that stood on the mantel above the fireplace, squinting a little and making a calculation. 'We'll dine in an hour. Will that be convenient?'

'Yes, Foss,' Philome replied. 'Whatever you say.'

At dinner, Calliope was silent. Foss was untroubled by it, but Philome watched her stepdaughter uneasily, wondering what was going on in the mind behind the mask of her face. Later, of course, Foss would tell her all that had transpired during their talk, but Philome doubted if she would learn anything of real value. Whatever Calliope might have said to her father, it would be far less than the whole story.

Celesta, with an animal-like instinct, knew that something was in the wind, but didn't have the temerity to ask questions in Foss's presence. Luthe, as always, was preoccupied with his own concerns, and Tobery and Diona were too intent on their food to be interested in anything else. As for Calliope . . .

She had listened to what Foss had to say to her. Part of it had been no less than she expected; she had had no doubt that Philome would report their quarrel to him and that he would not be pleased to hear of it. But the other, prime reason for his approach had shocked her to the core.

Under no circumstances, in no conceivable future whatever, could she ever have the least desire to marry Nempson Trinity. She had not even been aware of his interest; naive of her, perhaps, but then she wouldn't deny for one moment – especially in the light of recent events – that she *was* naive. Of course, of course there would be no pressure. None at all. But though he didn't realise it, Foss's obvious approval of the idea was pressure in itself; subtle but telling.

What had she said? She couldn't remember clearly now. Something about how surprised she was, and flattered, naturally, to think that Nempson was fond of her in that way. Beyond that, careful evasion. It had been enough to content Foss, for she certainly hadn't given the impression that she rejected the idea out of hand. Inwardly, though. *Inwardly* . . .

The plate of food, which she didn't want but was forcing herself to eat for Philome's sake, blurred suddenly before her gaze and she realised that she was in danger of crying. With a sharp effort she held the tears back, blinked several times and felt the perilous moment pass and fade. Nempson. Sheer impossibility. Sheer *insanity*. Or, perhaps more accurately, a kind of sanity which she did not want.

Ah, yes. There was the nub of it, the worm in the bud, the *truth*. Slowly, gradually, Calliope's mood began to change as she realised that Foss had done her a great service by saying what he had said this evening, for unwittingly he had mapped out, in clear and unequivocal terms, the choices that lay before her and which until now she had been unable to resolve. The attraction of the known factor: her home, her family, her work; all the rules and suppositions of the world to which she had been born and bred. In this world, Nempson's hopeful suit was a pinnacle.

Everything that, being the person she was, she could ask of life.

Then her mind turned the coin over and she saw the other side. Darkness. The unknown. An alien place, an alien way. Danger; *abominable* danger. No security, no warmth, no comforting human harmony; no promise and little hope of any future at all. In the midst of that cold, colourless maelstrom, haunting her dreams and her daydreams in equal measure, grey and strange and distant and yet in another way so close, so *close*, stood Charn.

In her mind she saw his eyes, saw his face with that edge of anger that never entirely left him. Memory conjured the grip of his hand and the touch of his mouth, both of which had brought the fever and done her such harm. Her imagination conjured his voice, though he didn't seem to be speaking to her; seemed, already, to have forgotten her. But that made no difference. Foss's words had brought home the truth. There was no choice to be made.

'Calli?' Philome's voice intruded suddenly, and Calliope snapped from the vortex of her thoughts with a start.

'I – I'm sorry, Philome. I didn't hear.'

Philome smiled. So sweetly, so fondly. 'I simply said, my dear, that if you've eaten your fill of the pie there's a lemon syllabub to follow. Would you like some?'

Warm reality and friendship and congruity. When she was little, she would have committed any crime for a taste of lemon syllabub, and that recollection made Calliope return Philome's smile with an affinity that surprised them both.

'Yes,' she said. 'I think I would. Thank you, Philome.'

The house was dark, the streets outside silent and still, and as she made her way like a ghost down the stairs Calliope knew that what she was about to do was an act of madness. But the compulsion and the desire were driving her, and she also knew that to resist would be a far greater folly. Better to go mad, to be mad, than to fail or, worse, fear even to try. *I do not have the courage.* Her mother's words, desperate, broken: Calliope understood the depth of them now. She would not follow where Griette had led. She would not take that road. Not while there was life and hope and possibility.

Through the kitchen, to the garden. The night outside was

warm, a little stifling now that summer had really come and the weather was holding fair. No taper this time; instead Calliope carried an old-fashioned lantern which would be far safer on the slippery cellar stairs. When its light went out it would be harder than a taper to rekindle, but no matter. It was a pledge of her good faith. She would not *need* to rekindle it. Pray she would not.

This time, the cellar door opened without difficulty. The foul smell assailed her again but she did her best to ignore it and felt her way slowly, carefully, down the twelve steps to the room below. Absurd, the images that came to her as she entered the cellar. Charn's hand gripping hers to steady her; the touch of his cloak's fabric against her forearm where the glove didn't cover it. She wore no gloves tonight; wouldn't need them, because he was not here.

She thought of her family sleeping. Foss snored, and sometimes the sound reverberated through the entire house. Luthe had probably had too much wine again and would wake in the morning with hammers in his head. She hoped Tobery would have no more nightmares. And Celesta would dream of lovers. Calliope almost, but not quite, laughed; though if she had given rein to it the laughter would have had a fond dimension.

The door closed behind her and she felt the cellar's atmosphere close in like the claustrophobic sense before the breaking of a thunderstorm. Tonight there would be another kind of storm, or there would not. In a strange, fatalistic way she felt that it was out of her hands now. She had read, she had studied, she had prepared. From here she could do no more, for what she had learned from her mother's notes was that there must be an extra dimension to this that no reason or science could embrace. The dimension of human will and human emotions, infusing the secret notes, the ones she had never shown to Foss or Nempson or anyone else, like the perfume of white flowers.

She held the lantern before her and slowly, slowly, turned down the wick. The light sank; shadows drew in closer, so close that she fancied she could reach out and touch them. She watched the little flame until it died, its after-image dancing before her vision for a few moments before the utter dark descended. Then for several seconds she listened to her own breathing, counting the beats of her heart until it steadied and settled to a calmer rhythm. There was nothing to fear. Darkness was not her enemy, it was her friend. It was the gate.

She set the lantern down, irrationally annoyed by the metallic sound it made, for that disturbed her concentration. Never mind, never mind; it didn't matter. Thick blackness, like a cloak, heavy and suffocating. But in another way the dark was empty, and thus alive with possibility. *Any* possibility.

The sound's echoes faded and silence reclaimed her. *Her*. Calliope Agate. Not the wife of Nempson Trinity but the daughter of Griette. Griette, who had sought the way, who had yearned so powerfully to find it. White flowers. A scent of opium . . .

It came, like mist, touching her face and then filling her nostrils with its strange, fragile perfume. Memory surged back to the night of Charn's going, and in her mind Calliope saw him again, saw his face in the moment before she had extinguished the taper for the second time and the gateway had opened to admit him and carry him away. *Silver*. There was a glint of silver, out of a dimension that shocked and momentarily terrified her with its alienness. So far away . . . *ah no*, she thought, *don't close your eyes; resist that temptation*. She must look; she must see.

She didn't know how it happened; what strange and fathomless magic was snared by the currents of her mind in that moment. It could never be replicated; perhaps, indeed, it could never be repeated for as long as she might live. But in one single, perfect instant the fragrance of white, moon-drenched flowers swirled around her and her consciousness drowned in it, gave way to it, yielded will and awareness and the entirety of self to its call. True dark, utter dark, opened before her like a soft, gentle mouth. The gateway engulfed her, welcomed her, and Calliope was gone from the only world she had ever known.

Chapter XIII

Cold enveloped her. Bitter, bitter cold, that struck through clothes and skin to her bones. Calliope gasped, and the sound cut the silence thinly, like the breath of a weak child. No one and nothing answered her.

She could see her own hands, pale and vague as ghosts, pressed to the paving on which she knelt. She must have fallen, for there was the echo of a jarring sensation in her hips and shoulders, though she had no memory of losing her balance at any point during the transfer. All else in her field of vision was darkness, but the stone slabs beneath her struck an unexpected and discordant resonance in her mind. A street . . . she was in a street. Surely, that wasn't right?

She raised her head and stared through dishevelled strands of hair at her surroundings.

The darkness was not complete, for there was a source of light ahead. She couldn't judge its distance; perspective was distorted and it might have been a handspan or a hundred paces away, but from here, although no pole was visible, it looked perplexingly like a perfectly ordinary street lamp; one of the new kind that worked on a similar principle to the etherea lamps and burned without colour. Its illumination was poor (the innovation had not yet been perfected), but it was sufficient to show her that she was in a narrow lane, almost an alley, lined with unremarkable houses. Slowly Calliope scanned the scene around her, and the tumultuous anticipation that had filled her in the cellar began to turn to something bleak and sick. This wasn't what she had expected; wasn't what she had looked for. It was too familiar – in fact if memory would only trigger she was sure she could name this street. Something had gone *wrong*.

She started to stand upright – and gasped again as her legs felt suddenly as if their veins were filled with lead instead of blood. For a moment she thought that her feet would refuse utterly to obey her; but then they moved, with a dragging reluctance that sent cramp stabbing through her. Swaying, desperate for a point of reference, Calliope latched her gaze onto the light that hung dim and disembodied down what now seemed a narrowing vortex. Twenty paces, maybe thirty, but no more, no more than that. She could reach it, if she tried. She could make herself move. *What was the matter with her?*

A scuttering, slithering of leather on stone cracked the quiet as she put too much strength into the effort to move and almost lost her balance again. She was so *cold*: it was numbing her, body and mind together. But this was summer; even at night the town streets should be warm.

160

It was then that revelation struggled up through bemusement and told her the truth that she should have grasped from the beginning. Cold. *Cold*. Of *course*. That lamp, drifting as incorporeally as a dream before her; it wasn't one of the imperfect new devices. Its lack of colour had another cause.

Her pulse moved thickly, sluggishly, as she stared around again. No lights showed in the windows of any of the houses. There was no noise of footsteps, voices, carriages; none of the mundane and customary sounds of an active town. Even at dead of night there was always something to keep absolute silence at bay. But not here. Her first conclusion had been wrong. She had not failed. This image of her own world was no more than that; it was a parallel, an imitation.

She had succeeded. She had found the doorway, and had broken through.

Shock hit her then, so powerfully that she sagged to her knees again. This was Charn's world, and he was here somewhere in the cold, grainy, monochrome maze that so closely mimicked the streets of her home town. Calliope's mind spun hazily – was this similarity design or chance; was the one dimension a mirror image of the other, or did someone know of her coming and was it all a trick contrived to confuse and disorientate her? But the questions were sluggish and tangled and she couldn't think clearly. *So* cold. She must move, and keep moving, or the lead-and-ice sensation within her would crush her to the ground again, and next time she would be unable to rise.

Shivering violently, she started to make her way towards the light. Progress was unsteady and erratic; she must look like a drunkard, like Luthe when he came home from a riotous evening with his friends. Thought of her brother slammed home the realisation that he and all her family were beyond reach, separated by far, far more than physical distance, and Calliope came close to panic as a sense of terrible isolation swept over her.

But this is what you wanted, an inner voice said. *To escape from them, and from their plans and expectations. To break free. To pursue your own dream, even if it is a form of madness.* Easy at this moment, in darkness and loneliness and without any clue to what the next minutes or hours or days might hold, to believe that she *was* mad. What would her father have said? Or Philome? Or Nempson Trinity, in whose misguided imagination she was the ideal of a sober, companionable and tractable future wife?

Laughter rose in her then, and once it had begun she could not stem it. It was soft laughter, not unpleasant, but it was also a clear sign that she was losing her grip on self-control. Calliope put a hand to her own throat, wanting to physically stifle the sounds she was making. To her surprise the contact hurt, and suddenly the slight pressure made it seem as if there was no air to be had anywhere. She stopped, trying to regain breath—

There was quick flurry of movement under the halo of the lamp ahead, and something pale and ghostlike darted into the deeper gloom to her left. Calliope jumped, recoiling; then another insubstantial shape – much larger; and it had wings – flitted to her right. Fear surged; she floundered, not knowing which way to look, which side to try to defend; then as she wavered there was a hiss of displaced air and what looked like a vast, flying cobweb rushed at her out of the darkness. She glimpsed a strange, sweet, childlike face, its eyes wide and avid with curiosity; as she stumbled backwards it hovered over her and a thin, bell-like cry rang on the air; a cry that sounded absurdly like a word: '*Who? Who?*'

Trembling, Calliope stared back at the creature. She was confused, confounded and wanted to laugh, scream and cringe away all at once. The thin air sawed in her throat; over the noise of her efforts to breathe, the being uttered another eerie call and started to drop downwards.

Fear ignited into panic, and Calliope ran. For the first vital seconds terror gave her strength; though her body felt like solid stone she somehow made her limbs move, and as the cobweb-thing recoiled in surprise she flung herself towards the refuge of the houses, seeking cover, seeking an escape and not caring what might lie before her. A gap seemed to open up in her path; she plunged into darkness that was near absolute – and then the tearing agony hit her, shooting through her legs and torso as though her blood had caught fire. With a cry she collapsed to her knees, vision blurring as the shock of the pain slammed into every nerve. Her own weight was a crushing, overwhelming force; she couldn't bear it, had to be rid of it; and somewhere behind her was the cobweb-creature and its cohorts, and she had to get away—

Half-crazed with pain and fear Calliope dragged herself

forward, on into the sanctuary of darkness. On her feet, on hands and knees; it didn't matter just as long as she kept moving, for if they caught up with her they would – they would – she didn't know what they would do, but she was remembering the creature in the Public Garden, and what the mob had done to it merely because it was alien and *different*. Onward, fighting the agony, *fighting* it . . . but something was wrong, because where moments ago there had been blackness and close, confining walls to shield her, suddenly the walls were melting, and a pale, unearthly sphere was swimming across her vision as the lamp floated into view again. A gossamer shape sailed on the air above the lamp, and a distant call – '*Who? Who?*' – drifted down like something out of nightmare.

This was insane, impossible! Calliope scrabbled to turn her leaden body around and writhe away, back into dark, back into hiding. Before her, a solid wall loomed; then as she struggled towards it, it twisted in on itself and blew away like smoke, and the pale sphere, with the cobweb creature undulating in its glow, came gliding out of nowhere towards her.

'Ah, no—' She choked the words out uncontrollably through clenched teeth, and from the air around her came a shimmering chorus of echoes. '*Ah, no – ah, no.*' The sound was mindless, meaningless, pantomiming her speech but without any understanding; and now she could see the uncanny choir, tiny, darting things no bigger than fireflies, dancing above her head. Calliope's mind teetered on the brink of hysteria; she tried to cry out a denial, a protest, but there was no breath in her lungs and no rationality in her head, and the fireflies were swooping closer and she didn't have the strength left to flee from them . . .

From behind, something touched her.

It was like a feathered cloak stroking the length of her back, and the cold that emanated from it was so huge, so stunning, that it went beyond pain. Every nerve of Calliope's body locked, paralysing her with her mouth open in a shocked rictus. She did not feel her legs giving way; she *could* not feel them, for all sensation was gone. She only saw black solidity rotating towards her, coming to meet her as she keeled to the ground. And, like a storm of grey and silver snow, the denizens of the otherworld, Charn's world, closing in to shroud and enfold her in their consuming embrace.

* * *

She could not tell how long the journey lasted. Time had lost cohesion; they might have travelled for days or hours or merely minutes, and distance had no meaning either, for the greater part of her senses had shut down and all that registered was the cold and the colourless darkness and the endless, lurching sense of motion.

They had wrapped her in a billowing shroud of some strange, soft substance that felt like moist silk and clung like fine down. At first, when the paralysis began to abate, she had tried to fight them off; but then shrieking cramp assailed her legs and arms, and the twilight creatures closed quietly, resolutely in to subdue her. Immobilised by pain, Calliope could only stare blankly as with meticulous care they manoeuvred her body into the shroud, all the while calling to each other and perhaps even to her in their sweet, thin voices. Then, still careful, they had gathered the folds like a sling and lifted her into the air. A brief spinning, a sense of disorientation, and Calliope, enveloped and helpless, was borne away on a small tide of wings.

She lay now in her clinging prison, too stupefied and exhausted to be anything but passive. The part of her mind that still functioned told her that there were some ten or twelve of the twilight-dwellers attending her, from the cobweb being with its child's face to three flittering creatures like ghostly birds. The cradle of fabric in which she lay was translucent, giving her glimpses of a vague, shifting world beyond its confines, and above her, where her captors flew with a slow and steady pulse of wings, was a narrow oval of emptiness; a starless, moonless sky. They passed beneath the disembodied lamp and she could not judge whether it truly was a lamp or something far stranger, for she only saw its glow surround her briefly, and felt a sensation like ice-cold sleet raining down on her skin. Then the light was behind her, and darkness was a little warmer, and she was carried towards an unknown destination with the bewildering feeling that she was lost in a dream and had forgotten how to wake.

On and on. The creatures were still calling, their voices sounding like the chimes of the town clock mingling with the twitter of birdsong. For a while one of them did sing, and Calliope almost, though not quite, identified words of her own language in the song, though they made no coherent sense. She listened, fascinated in a peculiarly detached way by the sounds. Questions

164

she might and should have asked herself, such as where they were going and why and what would happen when – if – they reached their destination, did not occur to her. She wasn't even afraid any more. Only cold, and languid, and weary to the bone. Perhaps she even slept as her captors flew on, for at last she slipped into a dreaming limbo in which the borders between reality and fantasy had no true distinction.

At last there came change. A gentle sensation of dropping, falling, and with it a slowing in the momentum of their flight. Calliope stirred from her torpor as the sling began to shake and sway, and on a subliminal, almost primal level sensed an intensifying in the darkness around her, a new feeling of density and enclosure. The twilight beings' voices began to echo as though from the walls of some huge, strange cavern, and now there were lights, chilly and colourless, that danced and streamed above her like a rush of bright water. Beyond the lights, shapes undulated; contours of walls, dark ceilings, shimmering, flowing draperies shot through with silver . . . vaguely, dreamily, Calliope realised that they had left the night outside behind; then she felt herself start to drop again, skimming lower and lower, a sharp glide downwards—

The lights coalesced, flared, and her captors let her fall. The distance was no more than an armslength, but as she hit solid ground pain exploded through her and she screamed, rolling, flailing at the folds of the shroud as it billowed down on top of her. The scream died away; she lay motionless, unable to move or breathe for the throbbing agony. Then, as it began to recede, she became aware that everything around her was acutely still. The twilight creatures had fallen silent; there was no sense of their presence and for a moment she believed that they had gone, dissolved away as though they had never existed. Had they existed? Had they ever been there at all? She couldn't think; couldn't rationalise this.

Something moved; she felt it brush lightly against her through the fabric. Then more movement, and more. Dimly discernible through the clinging shrouds, shapes were gathering, drawing nearer, closing in. She heard soft breathing, gasps, whispers, and faintly, bizarrely, strains of phantasmic and melancholy music drifting on the air. Confused and apprehensive and unable to make sense of anything, Calliope lay mute, capable only of waiting for whatever fate would befall her.

The shroud around her rustled and moved. Something was leaning over her and lifting the folds away; she felt a surge of bitter cold and suddenly a clamour of bell-like voices began to flute and twitter and exclaim. The shroud fell aside. Eyes looked in at her, a host of them, alien and incredible, and beyond the eyes were towering black walls and an arched ceiling decorated in silver, and thin, grey fog that moved and flowed with a life of its own.

Shock tumbled in on Calliope, and a cry that sounded harsh and guttural amid the twilight creatures' sweeter tones broke from her throat. In panic she sat up, flailing at the forms surrounding her, trying to push them away, drive them back, break out of the circle they made, the horrifying, ice-cold circle that threatened to crush her. The creatures fell back in consternation, and a small crescendo of sound erupted from them. Then a new voice called out, and as the circle broke and scattered Calliope had one stunned glimpse of the black dais at the hall's centre, and of the shockingly humanlike figure enthroned there against the backdrop of a silver-grey gossamer cascade. The queen was rising, gesturing urgently – and as her gaze and Calliope's met and clashed, an icy breeze sprang up from nowhere, and with it a heady, inundating perfume. *White flowers – the sweet fragrance of the gateway between worlds.* Overwhelmed, Calliope swayed violently, felt her legs start to give way—

Behind the throne a shadow moved among shadows, and a dark shape broke from the throng. Through blurring senses Calliope saw the fluctuating light streak silver into grey hair, heard a voice snap out an order in a strange tongue, felt the creatures around her draw back further. On her knees, she doubled over as the newcomer reached her. Then a voice that struck through her with the power of a sword-thrust said incredulously,

'*Calliope!*'

Slowly, a part of her mind still refusing to believe that this was real, Calliope raised her head.

She hardly recognised him. Oh, the figure was the same, and the face, and the pewter eyes behind their fringe of pale lashes. But the nuances that in her own world had made him seem so human were gone. In the ethereal clothes of the twilight court he

166

was outlandish, alien; a creature from some strange, dark vision. His hair – all grey now; that first burgeoning of colour had vanished without trace – was swept back and tied in a severe knot at the nape of his neck. And his eyes burned with an arctic light, as cold as the eyes of a corpse.

She whispered, all but choking on the words because there was no air and she could barely breathe, '*Charn . . . oh, Charn, help me . . .*'

He cut through her plea with a caustic force that bordered on savagery. 'Damn your stupidity, what have you *done*?'

A black chasm opened between Calliope and her wild hopes and dreams. Terror collapsed, swept aside by the anguish of disillusionment, and she could only stare dumbly at him, searching desperately for some sign of feeling, of compassion, but finding nothing. For a moment Charn gazed back. Then with a violent movement he pulled the cloak he wore from his shoulders and flung it around her. She tried to protest, arms stretching towards him, but he stepped out of reach and spoke rapidly and sharply to the hovering creatures at her back. Three of them hastened to take hold of her through the cloak's folds; Calliope tried to resist but her limbs were leaden weights; wrapped in the cloak she was as helpless as an infant. Another command and the beings lifted her between them and bore her away from Charn, away from the black throne and the agitated queen, towards a towering door that wavered like a mirage in the shifting gloom.

In that moment the last of Calliope's defences collapsed, and with it the last of her strength and will. Numb with cold, with the monstrous burden of her own body in this world and with the misery of Charn's hostile rejection, her overstrained mind gave way. Darkness and silence closed in on her, and she knew nothing more as she was carried from the hall of the twilight court.

Philome heard Foss's heavy step in the street, then the slam of the front door as he entered the house. The ferocity of the sound told her all she needed to know. As she had feared, as she had dreaded, he had not found Calliope.

She looked at her own reflection in the bedchamber mirror. What she saw made her squirm inwardly, for though her demeanour was as calm as usual, her eyes gave the truth away. They *burned* with guilt, or so it seemed to Philome; guilt and shame and the deep, ugly fear that she had made a terrible mistake for which no amends were possible. If her suspicions were right, Calliope was by now so far beyond reach that no human resource would be enough to find her, and it was probable – indeed, almost certain – that her family would never see her again.

From the hall below came the rumble of Foss's voice. Philome licked her lips nervously. She didn't want to face him; but her cowardice, as she now saw it, had already brought one disaster and to procrastinate would only compound the folly. It must be done, and the sooner the storm broke, the sooner it would be over.

Philome smoothed the skirt of her morning gown, quelled an impulse to change it for something more attractive (that was, after all, only an excuse to delay the inevitable), then walked out of the room and towards the stairs.

Foss's voice came into focus as she reached the first floor landing.

'. . . to think once again, and think *carefully*! If Miss Calliope said any word to you that might have—'

Philome leaned over the banisters, and interrupted quietly, 'Husband.'

Stopped in mid-flow, Foss looked up belligerently. 'Philome, can you not see that I'm—'

'Foss, *please*. I must speak to you. Now.'

The two maids whom Foss had been quizzing looked uneasily from their master to their mistress. For a moment they and Philome all thought that Foss's temper would erupt, but perhaps, with more perception than usual, he saw something in Philome's face that gave him pause. He hesitated, then made an impatient gesture in the maids' direction. 'Go back to your work. I'll send for you later.'

They curtsied and fled, and Foss placed fists on hips and stared at his wife. 'Well?'

With a cautious delicacy that suggested she was mentally and physically walking on glass, Philome started to move down the stairs. 'Foss . . . about Calliope . . .'

His eyes lit instantly. 'Have you heard something?'

'No, I— I've not. But—'

He swept through her halting efforts. 'Damn it, I've tried everywhere I can think of! The Institute, the homes of all her

168

friends; even the Hospice in case she'd taken it into her head to visit Griette.' He swung round, staring about him as though suspecting that Calliope might be hiding behind a piece of furniture. 'I've told Nempson. Had to; he was at the Institute when I arrived there. He's greatly concerned, of course; in fact he'll be here at any moment and then we'll discuss what steps to take next.'

Philome gave silent and heartfelt thanks for the prospective buffer of Nempson's presence when she told Foss what she knew. Gaining a little in confidence, she began again, 'Foss . . .'

Foss, though, was still intent on his grievance. 'Simply to disappear, without a word to anyone – I don't mind admitting it, Philome, I am *angry* with her!'

'And worried,' Philome ventured, her tone hovering uneasily between statement and question.

He stared at her. 'Rot me, of course worried, what d'you take me for? But that's only a natural reaction, and it isn't logical; if anything ill had befallen her, you can be sure we'd know of it by now. No, Philome, Calliope's disappearance is quite deliberate, I'm sure of it. She's taken some notion into her head, though the powers alone know what, and has gone off pursuing it.' An exasperated grunt. 'It's inconsiderate of her – and damned discourteous, when we're in the midst of such vital work! When she comes back, as I don't doubt she will as soon as she's satisfied whatever foolishness has overtaken her, I shall have some *very* firm words to say to her about reliability and integrity!'

Now or never, Philome thought. 'Foss,' she said quietly, 'I don't think she will come back.'

Foss stopped still. 'What?'

'I don't think she will come back,' Philome repeated. She didn't dare meet his gaze. 'You see . . . there is something I haven't told you.'

The house was suddenly very, very quiet but for the sound of Foss's breathing. 'What,' he said with icy control, 'do you mean?'

Bleakly then Philome confessed it all: her early suspicions as to what lay behind Calliope's aberrant behaviour, the recruiting of Celesta and the information that had yielded, and, hardest and worst of all, the reasons for her decision to say nothing to Foss but instead to wait and see how matters progressed. When she finished, her face was scarlet and her hands, gripped tightly

169

together, white. Her last words fell away, and she whispered, 'I'm sorry, Foss . . .'

Acute silence reigned for several seconds. Then Foss said, 'You are sorry.' Momentarily, his tone was calm, normal. Then the storm began to grow on the horizon. 'You are *sorry*. You come before me as bold as daylight with this outrageous confession of deceit and betrayal, and you have the effrontery, the audacity, the sheer, unabashed *gall*, simply to say that you are SORRY?'

'Oh, Foss!' Philome wailed.

'Don't whimper and lament at me like a half-witted sheep!' Foss roared. 'Damn you, woman, damn you and the past five generations of your ancestors, don't you possess a single grain of loyalty, or even *sense*?' He could have struck her. He could have taken his belt to her, knocked her down the rest of the stairs and kicked her as she sprawled on the floor. '*I am Calliope's father! Her blood kin, her sire – what right do you have to conspire with her against me?*'

Before Philome could protest the injustice of that, a loud knock came at the front door. Purple in the face, but just managing to drag his temper back under control, Foss stamped to answer it and Nempson came in.

'Philome.' He bowed to her but his expression was wary; clearly he had heard something of the altercation, and Philome wished that she could melt into the wall and vanish. 'Has there been some . . . development?'

Foss said, 'Ha!' and with a great effort Philome tried to rescue a shred of her pride. 'Yes, Nempson, in – in a sense there has. Foss, I think, is better able to explain than I am . . . so if you will both excuse me . . .'

She would have turned and retreated upstairs, but Foss said in a voice like controlled thunder, 'You will kindly *remain*, Philome, and confess to Nempson what you have already confessed to me.' He hunched his shoulders ominously. 'The library, I think. Tell Jass to bring tea.'

'Yes, Foss,' Philome said in a small, chastened voice. She watched as the two men headed away into the depths of the house, and only when she heard the library door close behind them did she wipe her face, smooth her skirt and walk with what dignity she could muster towards the kitchen.

170

Chapter XIV

'How did she *come* here?' Selethe stared across the hall, her hands clenching and unclenching as her gaze focused restively on the spot where Calliope had been laid down by her winged escort. The tension she radiated charged the air around her, and eddies of light and shadow stirred agitatedly. 'No one from the human world has ever found and used the gateway before now! How has this girl, this Calliope, succeeded where the rest failed?'

'I don't know, madam.' Charn's face, lit starkly by the lights' flickering, was grim. 'But I'll find out; be assured of it!'

He was unpleasantly aware that every face in the huge, dim expanse of the hall was watching the dais intently, and though the spectators kept their distance their scrutiny put him on edge. In the first chaotic minutes after Calliope had been carried from the hall, the entire court had been in turmoil, for there was hardly a soul present who did not realise the significance of the human stranger's arrival. An agitated throng had besieged the throne, and amid the hubbub of noise Selethe, who was as shocked as any of them, felt suddenly as if her self-control was about to give way. She called for silence. Silence fell, and she had called Charn to the dais, with a clear implication that she wished to speak with him uninterrupted. He knew then that she was aware of the interloper's identity, and cursed the lapse of restraint that had made him utter Calliope's name aloud. The queen would have had to know the truth before long, but Charn wished fervently that he could have had time to recover from his own shock before this interview took place.

'She must have discovered how to open the gateway by chance,' he said. 'Though how she achieved it—'

'Is hardly relevant.' Selethe was calmer now. 'The fact is that, whatever means she used to reach us, she is here in our domain. And where she has led, it is possible that others might follow.' She looked directly at him. 'Do you think she has betrayed the gateway's secret to her people?'

Charn hesitated for a few moments before replying. 'I can't say with any certainty. I think it unlikely that she would have done so deliberately . . . but I can give no guarantees. She is, after all, her father's daughter, and he has no scruples – as I discovered to my cost.'

Selethe frowned. 'But father and daughter are not necessarily of the same mettle.'

'They are both human.'

'Yes . . . and that, perhaps, is at the nub of this question.' Selethe's gaze strayed across the hall again, thoughtfully. 'I've heard so much about her world's strangeness; but to *see* it, embodied in a living creature . . . Her eyes, her hair, her skin – I didn't think such things were *possible*. She is more alien than I imagined, Charn, and that has given me some insight into the reasons why her kind react to us as they do. To them, we must seem as bizarre as they are to us. People fear that which they do not know, and when fear and ignorance combine, it can sometimes give rise to unintentional destructiveness. That makes me wonder . . .'

Her voice tailed off. Charn looked her obliquely, queryingly, and said, 'Madam?' but abruptly she shook her head, dismissing her speculations and making a negating gesture.

'No: this isn't the right moment to pursue such a train of thought. We must consider the implications of what this girl has done, and whether her presence is a hazard to us.' She met his gaze, and suddenly her eyes were decisive. 'I am inclined to believe that she can be trusted.'

Charn's mouth hardened. 'I'm sorry, my lady, but I can't agree with you!'

She raised her dark eyebrows. 'You say that with great vehemence; yet Calliope befriended you, and but for her kindness and courage you would not have returned safely to us. From what you've told me, it seems that she helped you at considerable risk to herself. Don't you think that is proof of her integrity?'

'No, I do not.' His eyes narrowed. 'It isn't enough.'

'Oh, but I think it *is* enough – at least, where you are concerned.'

Charn's face muscles tautened as he realised what she was implying, what she had seen and interpreted in the few brief moments when he had faced Calliope in the hall. They looked at each other, her eyes searching, his suddenly acutely wary. Then Selethe smiled a small, bitter smile. 'Charn, I saw her face and I heard her voice when she tried to speak to you. I saw and heard an artless child who had neither the guile nor the experience to

172

disguise the emotion she was feeling and her anguish when you turned away from her. I don't know how she came here – but I do know why, and so do you.'

The chagrin that Charn couldn't mask in time confirmed her suspicions. He was well aware of Calliope's feelings; indeed, he had probably used and manipulated them to gain his freedom and escape from the human world. Something inside the queen seemed to clench and tighten as she remembered another time, another human woman, but with a skill long practised she thrust her pang away. There was a further question she wanted to ask of Charn, but even as it formed she thought better of it. If forced into answering at this moment, Charn would have lied, to himself as much as to her. Let it bide, she thought. It would keep for a while.

Charn said suddenly, harshly, 'Whatever Calliope may feel for me, or have deluded herself into believing that she feels, it can have no bearing on this situation. Trustworthy or not, she threatens our security by her mere presence here.' He turned fully to face her, a sharp, quick movement, and his voice became urgent. 'If she revealed her intentions to any of her fellow humans, then doubtless she also revealed the means by which she intended to reach our world. I need say no more about the consequences of *that*. Even if she told no one of her plan but simply disappeared, her father and his friends won't sit and wait passively for her to return of her own accord. They'll search for her. They'll stint nothing in the search. However careful Calliope might think she has been, there's every likelihood that she unwittingly left traces of her going which could all too easily be followed.'

Selethe considered. She knew his assessment was right; though his apparent cynicism about the integrity of one who loved him so patently and painfully saddened her. But perhaps there were other factors involved in that . . .

'She can't be permitted to stay,' Charn insisted. 'It's too dangerous. She must be sent back to her own world.'

Selethe continued to reflect for a few more moments. Then, quietly but decisively, she said, 'I think not.'

'*Madam*—'

'No, Charn. Or at least, not yet.' There was an odd gleam in her eyes; something that Charn couldn't interpret but which made him feel suddenly ill at ease. 'My reasons are twofold,' the queen continued. 'Firstly, if you are right in fearing the consequences of her coming – and I'm only too afraid that you are – then to simply return her to her own people would not negate the danger to us. What she has done once, she might well do again. I think instead we must take time to make her understand our predicament. She is obviously honourable and has strong sensibilities; I believe that when she knows the truth she will sympathise, and be willing to give her solemn promise that she will never attempt to return to our world and never divulge her knowledge of the gateway to another living soul. Then, and only then, will we send her back to her people.'

Charn stared at her for a few moments, his face unreadable. Then, heavily, he sighed. 'My lady, I understand what you're trying to achieve – but it isn't *feasible*. Oh, she may promise; she may promise anything in *words*. But in deeds? We have no guarantees at all!'

'You're saying, again, that we can't trust her?'

'Yes.'

Selethe nodded. 'Then I see only two other options. The first is that we send her back and then seal the gateway between our worlds, finally and forever.'

He looked aghast. 'But, my lady—'

'There's no need to remind me, Charn. You have argued vehemently against that course from the start, and you know that I won't do it; not while the old question, the old enigma, remains unresolved.' Her face clouded briefly; with an effort she forced the look to clear.

Charn said, 'And the second option?'

She smiled, thinly and without humour. 'To kill her.'

'*What?*' Shock flared in his eyes. 'Lady, no! I won't—'

'Hush, my dear, hush,' Selethe interrupted him, then her smile faded and her expression became deadly serious. 'I wouldn't countenance any such thing. I said it simply to shock you, to make you realise that my plan is the only reasonable choice open to us. You say we can have no guarantee that Calliope will keep any promise she makes to us. That's true. But can you suggest a better alternative, Charn? *Can* you?'

She saw the answer in his eyes. He could offer nothing less drastic than the alternatives she had already suggested, and though he hated to admit defeat, he was cornered.

'Calliope trusted you not to harm her when she set you free,' she added more gently. 'In a sense, we will be repaying that compliment in kind.'

Something dark flickered in Charn's eyes. Selethe waited but he made no comment, and she continued, 'It will take a little time – time to build up Calliope's confidence and trust in us. But I think it's the best hope we have.'

There was another pause, then at last, reluctantly, Charn nodded. 'You're right, my lady. There is no other way.'

'Then go to her, Charn. Talk to her.'

'I . . .?' He looked horrified.

'You would rather not?'

'In the circumstances, I . . . I would find it hard, madam. In fact I – would prefer not to see her at all.' His gaze met hers with a mute plea. 'It would be kinder.'

To whom? Selethe asked herself. Aloud, she said, 'I'm sorry, my dear, but I must command you. No one else in our world knows Calliope as you do – and her feelings for you will give you an advantage that no others could have. That's hard-hearted of me, I know, but I must use any and every means possible to persuade her. You understand, don't you?'

'Yes, my lady,' Charn replied pallidly. 'I understand.'

'Then go. Do what you can for our cause.' She paused, seeming briefly to see far deeper into his thoughts than she felt she had any right to do. 'I will meet her and talk to her myself, in time. Tell her that; and tell her that she has no need to be afraid.'

Charn left the hall a few minutes later. As the doors closed behind him a cool, green scent wafted on the shifting air; it had a strange edge of melancholy and, caught off guard, he felt his chest constrict with an unlooked-for emotion. He stopped, pressing fingertips to his brow and shutting his eyes momentarily; when he opened them again the lapse was under control and he felt only anger with himself. An instant's aberration . . . and even if it were more than that, there was nothing he could or wished to do about it. He had no choice but to obey Selethe and face Calliope. Beyond that, though, his obligation would end.

Composure restored, he walked on.

Calliope regained consciousness to find herself lying on a wide couch in a grimly imposing room. Ornate black panelling clad the walls, overlaid with diaphanous draperies of silver and grey through which chill, colourless lights glowed feebly from their sconces. In a strange, circular hearth at the room's centre a fire was burning, but its flames were silver and it radiated not heat but a pitiless cold that drove into her bones like knives. Stunned and numb and still not fully conscious, Calliope tried instinctively to shrink away from the flames, but found to her shock that she could barely move. Her body was a terrible weight dragging at her, pinning her down; she was gasping for breath but the air was so thin and tenuous that she couldn't inhale enough of it into her lungs. Panic and confusion flooded through her; she gave a choking, mewing cry – and instantly, shapes moved from the shadows to surround her. She had a blurred impression of strange faces, alien eyes staring hugely down at her; and through the slow, thick throbbing of her own pulse in her head she heard an incoherent buzz of voices, chirping and purring and thrumming in an eager chorus that made no sense to her. Then something that was and yet was not like a thin, grey hand reached out to touch her face. The icy shock was so enormous that Calliope cried out again, and the creature that had touched her gave a shrill shriek of pain and fluttered backwards. They all backed away then, milling agitatedly; briefly their voices rose to a hubbub – then suddenly they flowed from the room and were gone.

Calliope lay motionless, dazed, her mind and body gripped by a haze of pain and cold. Somewhere deep inside her a thread of reason was struggling to make some sense of this, but shock had driven it so deep that she could not grasp and hold on to it. No warmth, no air, nothing but aching agony; and there was no one to whom she could communicate her distress, for the twilight creatures had fled and Charn had turned his back on her, and they didn't understand, they didn't *understand* that *she* was the one who was so very afraid . . .

She had begun to shudder as though with a racking fever, and that was how Charn found her when he came from the court hall in obedience to his queen's command. Her eyes under half-closed lids were glazed and barely able to focus, and at first sight of her Charn uttered a searing oath and turned on the lesser beings who had been hovering in confusion outside but now, heartened by his arrival, had slipped back into the room at his heels. He snapped out a furious order and four of the creatures hastened to douse the silver fire; then at another harsh word three more darted out on some frantic errand. Curiosity overcoming their fear, the rest began slowly and cautiously to close in on Calliope, murmuring in their sweet, bell-like tones; Charn's arm jerked, once, in a savage gesture, and they too were gone, leaving him and Calliope alone.

Calliope stared up at him. She had recognised his voice but she was beyond the reach of any outward reaction, and as he walked slowly towards the couch she made no attempt to move or speak. In the gloom he looked stark and threatening and she could not see the expression on his face. But when he spoke to her, his tone, though reserved, was gentle.

'They don't realise that you are different.' He indicated the hearth, dark now, the fire put out. 'They meant you no harm; they were simply misguided.'

Words were tumbling through Calliope's mind; a cataclysm of questions, accusations, entreaties; but though she fought to articulate them she could only stutter through clenched and chattering teeth, 'C . . . c . . . cold.'

'I know.' Charn made as though to reach towards her but thought better of it and withdrew his hands. *Yet he was wearing gloves. He could have touched her; surely he could have touched her?* 'I've ordered clothes and coverings to be brought to you. Our fabrics don't harm you, it seems, so at least we can make you warmer.'

We. So impersonal. Huddled in his cloak Calliope strove to control the shuddering and so preserve some tiny shred of her dignity. 'Ch-Charn . . . I . . .'

'Don't try to speak. The queen's own physician has been sent for; he'll do all he can to help you.'

She didn't *want* a physician, royal or otherwise; she wanted only to talk to Charn, to reach out to him, to make him *unbend*. But her mind wouldn't work and her tongue wouldn't obey her. Feebly, hardly aware of what she was doing, she pushed one hand to the edge of the couch, thinking to stretch it towards him and try to convey with a gesture what she could not convey in speech. The effort was so great that she gasped, and a thin, rattling sound came from her throat as the small exertion cost her lungs the little air they had. A quick frown came to Charn's face and he demanded, 'What is it? Are you in pain?'

'Nnh.' She tried to nod. 'Feel like . . . stone . . . like lead . . .'

She didn't know whether or not he had understood, for the pain and the cold were combining and crushing in on her again, and her senses swam giddily with the renewed onslaught. Memory of his own experiences in her world sprang into sharp focus in Charn's mind. The weakening, the fading strength – there had been only one way to alleviate it and survive, and it had had dire consequences for his human victims. This, though, was an inversion; and intuition told him that what had done harm in Calliope's world might have a very different effect here. A part of him didn't want to do it, for it would re-forge a link that was better broken. But another and more powerful part overrode the reluctance and thrust it aside.

Calliope was in a stunned daze now, but when he knelt down beside her and touched gloved fingers to her eyes, enough of her consciousness remained for the lids to flicker and open in startled confusion. Their gazes met, locked. Charn exerted his will . . .

She was asleep when Thimue, the queen's physician, arrived. Thimue was among the higher beings of the twilight world; a rotund little figure, indisputably human in appearance, though no more than half Charn's height. He was wearing his customary garb of a long, black robe with a decorated silver collar and sash, and his face was that of an old man, yet the skin of his cheeks and hairless pate looked incongruously unlined and youthful.

'Charn.' Thimue inclined his head courteously, then turned to look at the couch. His black eyes widened. 'Is *that* the . . .?'

'The human girl.'

'Ah.' He started forward, seeming to glide rather than walk, as though he weighed no more than a feather.

'Don't touch her without gloves,' Charn said.

'No. No, indeed. Even her aura burns, does it not? I can feel it from here. Is she sleeping?'

'After a fashion. Awake, she is in constant pain, so it seemed kinder to give her relief.'

'You induced the sleep yourself? I see, yes . . . that was probably wise. What a very strange creature she is. Does she have a name?'

Thimue did not join overmuch in the life of the court hall, preferring his solitary studies and contemplations, and so had not heard the details of Charn's sojourn in the human world. 'She does,' Charn said. 'It's Calliope.'

178

'Calliope . . .' The physician tested the unfamiliar syllables on his tongue. 'Stranger still . . . well, Charn, you had best tell me all you can about her. Then we must see what we can do to ease her affliction.' He paused, glancing shrewdly up at Charn's face. 'You look none to the good yourself, my friend. More rest would be of benefit to you. Rest for the burdens of the body, and perhaps a little music now and then, to ease the burdens of the mind?'

'My mind is well enough,' Charn replied tersely. 'I need no cures, thank you, Thimue. Now; I have demands on my time, so if we can proceed with this as quickly as possible . . .?'

The twilight-dwellers had thought only to do their best for Calliope, and it was no fault of theirs that their first attempts to minister to her had misfired. It was fortunate, as Thimue later concluded, that Charn had intervened when he had, and, armed with the knowledge he had gleaned, he set about undoing the damage that had unwittingly been done.

The first and most urgent priority was to ease the cold that had lodged deep in her marrow and which, in Thimue's view, was the greatest threat to her. The clothes and blankets ordered by Charn were put on and around her, and though the materials were as fine as gossamer their layers warmed her as efficiently as any wool or linen. Calliope lay throughout in a blank, unnatural lethargy. She was awake now, but her mind seemed to be trapped in the uneasy no-man's-land between waking and sleeping. Sometimes she asked for Charn; Thimue would tell her gently that he had gone, had not had time to stay, and she would nod as though understanding, only to ask for him again minutes later. Her state of mind worried the old physician. She seemed dazed, almost witless, and he couldn't help but wonder if the transfer through the gateway had harmed her reason in some way; or, alternatively, if she was simply a dullard. Charn had told him no personal details about her, and Thimue could only hope that eventually her wits would rally enough for him to communicate with her and make his own judgement.

But for her occasional pleas, Calliope bore Thimue's ministrations with passive docility. Much of the activity around her barely registered; her senses had collapsed under the onslaught of pain and cold, and even when she was given the blessed relief of warmth, the weight of her body in this world of thin, colourless

179

fragility was a leaden burden that she could hardly bear. Her only comfort, had she been capable of appreciating it, was that she was no longer afraid of the twilight beings. In her erratic and unpredictable lucid moments she realised intuitively that the inhabitants of this shadowed world did not wish to do her any harm. Thimue was in almost constant attendance, a quiet but substantial presence, and many others came, drawn by the lure of the unfamiliar and eager to see the new wonder for themselves. Her strangeness fascinated them, and her mind was filled with vague images of faces, poignantly innocent, and alien eyes, wide with curiosity, that gazed on her from a cautious distance. Frail forms, grey and silver countenances, soft, murmuring voices speaking a tongue that she would never understand . . . to Calliope their presence was like a haunting dream from which she could not summon the strength to wake.

At last, though, came a change. Under Thimue's care the paralysing cold in her turned slowly to warmth, at least of a kind, and the pain that racked her began to abate. With its hold loosened her mind grew clearer, and at last she struggled up from the realm of nightmare into rationality. Thimue, greatly relieved by her recovery and also by the realisation that she was not a half-wit as he had feared, set out at once to win both her trust and her friendship. Calliope took an immediate and instinctive liking to him; he spoke her language well, and as soon as she was able to comprehend, he explained the nature of her affliction. She felt pain – constant pain, as though she were carrying some intolerable weight? Yes; from what he had learned he judged that this was natural and, unhappily, inevitable, for it seemed that the twilight and human worlds were inimical and it was impossible for the natives of one to thrive in the other. But if there were no cures for that problem, he told her, he could at least help her to gain a measure of relief.

The anomalies between the twilight and human worlds fascinated Thimue. As he explained, it seemed that the bodies, and possibly also the life essences, of the human race were in some complex way more tangible than those of his own people. In this dimension Calliope was too heavy, too solid, almost too *real*; just as Charn had found her world's substance too strong for him, so for her this world was too tenuous. Their light was, to her, an ominous, perpetual half darkness, while their eyes were seared by the sun and even the moon of her dimension. Their silver fire, whose coolness they welcomed and enjoyed, drove cold unbearably into her bones; yet to them she seemed to burn with heat, projecting an aura that radiated palpably from her and which they could not tolerate, except at a distance, for long. If they touched her without the protection of gloves their skin was scorched, just as direct contact with Charn in the human world had turned her hand chill and grey. Their natures were in conflict, and the gulf could not be bridged.

There were exceptions to the rule, however. The fabrics were a case in point, and once Calliope was a little better Thimue was eager to discover whether she could take the food and drink of the twilight world. He was disappointed. One experiment with wine brought her retching and choking to her knees; at first this alarmed Thimue, but after some thought he came to the conclusion that even if anything ingestible could be found for her it might do more harm than good. If life in this world was to be tolerable for Calliope, her constitution needed to be weakened rather than fortified; for the present, at least, she would do better to fast.

Queen Selethe had been kept closely informed of Calliope's condition, and when Thimue reported that his charge was probably now as fit as circumstances would allow, she reminded Charn of his obligation. Uneasy in mind, and not looking forward to the encounter, Charn went unannounced to Calliope's room.

Calliope was alone and had until a few minutes earlier been sleeping. She had dreamed an anguished and disturbing dream about Charn, and now was lying on the couch and trying to unravel a confusion of emotions, chief of which was an aching sense of grief that he had not been near her, or to her knowledge even inquired after her, since her recovery began. Each time she asked for him Thimue had soothed and distracted her with gentle evasions, and finally she had given up her efforts and retreated into private and miserable recrimination at her own foolishness. After all, she told herself, what claim had she on Charn? She had trespassed uninvited into his realm and had no right to expect anything of him. Yet in her own world, in the cellar beneath the house moments before his final departure, he had said to her: *I owe you a great debt, and if I could repay it, I would*. She, gullible simpleton that she was, had believed him; but when they met again his only response to her was one of contemptuous anger, as to a troublesome and unwelcome nuisance. No, she had no claim whatever. But she felt betrayed, and shamed, and bitterly, bitterly unhappy.

So when she heard her door opening, and looked up to see him on the threshold, she could only stare at him with confounded astonishment.

He closed the door behind him and stood returning her gaze reservedly. 'Calliope.' His tone was courteous but distant. 'How are you?'

Calliope sat up, wishing to all the powers that she too could manifest the inhuman skill with which he controlled his reactions. His expression matched his voice, impassive, undecipherable, and with a small flare of anger she sought for words that would smash down the barrier he had raised between them. But the right words were not there, and all she said was, 'I'm well enough, thank you. Thimue has been very kind.'

'Thimue is dedicated and meticulous.' The way he said it made it impossible to judge whether he was paying the physician a compliment or an insult. He looked around, indicated a low chair. 'May I?'

'Of course.' She ferociously quashed irrational disappointment at the fact that he did not choose to sit on the couch beside her, and watched as he seated himself. Looking physically and mentally uncomfortable, he asked,

'Are your needs being cared for? Do you have everything you want?'

The irony was doubtless unintentional and Calliope ignored it. 'Everything that I can use, yes,' she replied. 'It seems that my difficulties in your world are much the same as your difficulties in mine. I can't eat or drink; the light seems like half-darkness to me and I am never truly warm.'

For the first time Charn unbent a fraction, and the ghost of a smile caught at the corners of his mouth. 'I sympathise,' he said with some feeling. Then the smile was gone.

Trying to keep the spark of conversation alight Calliope added, 'If nothing else I've gained an insight into what you must have suffered in my father's house.'

Charn doubted it. 'Possibly,' he said non-committally. 'And, speaking of that . . .'

'My father's house? What of it?' Calliope looked wary, and in that moment Charn's careful sanguinity began to crack. He had resolved to approach her coolly, detachedly, gaining the answers to his questions by calm reasoning; now though, a kind of helpless anger was rising in him and he couldn't control it. The emotion welled, surged – and suddenly broke out as he demanded furiously,

'Why did you follow me here, Calliope? What did you think you could possibly *achieve* by breaking through the gateway?' With a violent movement he was on his feet again, pacing across the room, his tension a palpable aura. 'I didn't ask you to come; I didn't ask you to pry into my world's secrets! Why couldn't you have left well alone?'

The outburst took Calliope by surprise. She stared at his back, dismayed – then abruptly the dismay was swept away by a flood of anger that matched his own.

'*Why?*' she echoed, her voice rising harshly. 'Great powers, do you think I'm going to humiliate myself further before you by answering *that*?' For he shouldn't have to ask, she thought bitterly; he shouldn't, he *shouldn't*. 'You ought to be answering *my* questions, Charn! Why did you pretend friendship, only to turn on me when I was brought here? Why didn't you come near this room in all the time that Thimue was tending to me?' Her lungs constricted as the anger swelled. '*Look at me, damn you!*'

That surprised him, and before he could stop himself his head turned and their eyes met. What he saw made him hesitate, and for one instant Calliope glimpsed a hint of something else beneath the blaze of anger. Charn was frightened.

The new outburst that she had been about to hurl at him shrivelled on her tongue. 'All right,' she said, ferociously willing her voice not to shake. 'All *right*. I know you didn't want me to follow you. You refused to teach me how to use the gateway, and when—'

He interrupted her, fiercely and combatively. 'Then why did you ignore what I said? I'd told you about my world. You knew it was no place for your kind, just as your world is no place for mine!'

'*Yes*, I knew that.' Calliope's fists clenched involuntarily. 'I didn't even think I could *do* it, Charn! But when Father told me that Nempson wanted—' She stopped abruptly, realising that

Nempson's plans could be of no possible interest to him; if she tried to explain, it would sound only like a pitiful and unconvincing excuse. Which, in truth, it was.

However, she had said enough to alert Charn, and his eyes glinted edgily. 'Nempson – that little satellite of your father's? What has he to do with this?'

'It's not important,' she said miserably. 'A family matter; it has no connection.'

'If you've told them about the gateway—'

'I *haven't!* They know *nothing* about it – do you think I'd break the promise I made?'

For all that he had said to Selethe, in truth Charn didn't think it, and he made an impatient, dismissive gesture. 'All right; I accept that. But you haven't answered my question.'

'You haven't answered mine.'

They regarded each other like two cats on a disputed territory border, and for some time it seemed that the stalemate couldn't and wouldn't be broken. Finally, surprisingly, Charn was the first to speak.

'Very well. You ask why I'm hostile and angry; I'll tell you bluntly. By coming here, by breaking and blundering through what should have been an impregnable gateway, you have put the future stability, security and possibly very existence of this world at risk.' His full mouth hardened. 'Is that answer enough for you?'

'How can I have done? No one else knows that I'm here! I left no word, no trail that could be pursued, no clue at all!'

'So you think. But can you guarantee it?'

Dismay filled Calliope's eyes, giving him his answer. Charn continue to stare at her for a few seconds, then said, 'How did you break through, Calliope? How did you discover the secret?'

If Calliope had been less distracted at that moment, she might have been alerted by the change in his voice; the sudden edge of something akin to suspicion and the shard of keen vigilance that accompanied it. But it eluded her, and she only shook her head.

'I didn't discover the secret, Charn. I told you; I didn't even believe that I could do it, and I don't know how I succeeded. I simply . . . *willed* it to happen, and somehow it did.' She put her hands to her face, pressing fingers hard against her brow. 'I can't even remember any more how I came through. There was a perfume, and—'

'A perfume?' Charn took a step towards her, then thought better of it and drew back. 'What perfume? What do you mean?'

'A scent of flowers,' Calliope said very slowly. 'Heady, and sweet . . . I don't know what kind of flowers they were . . .' *Though they were white, white as the moon* . . . She blinked, as though emerging dazedly from a dream. 'I only imagined them. But for a moment they seemed real, and that was the moment when the gateway opened.'

Charn said tautly, 'That was all?'

'Yes, that was all. I don't possess the secret of your gateway. I succeeded by pure chance, nothing more.' Her hands dropped to her sides again and she turned her head away from him. 'And I wish now that I'd failed!'

There was a long silence. Finally, Charn spoke.

'You must go back. You know that, don't you?'

Calliope nodded mutely, still not facing him.

'Before you do, though . . .'

Now she did turn, and he saw the flicker of hope in her eyes. Refusing to respond to it in any way, he went on, 'Queen Selethe wants to meet you . . . and to ask a favour of you.'

She had not expected that and was confounded. 'Of *me*?'

'Yes.' He smiled thinly and, perhaps, a little sadly. 'It's no great matter. But it is important to the queen.'

'And to you?' Calliope queried softly. 'Is it important to *you*, Charn?'

A pause. Then: 'Yes. It is.'

She dropped her gaze, focusing on the dark floor and hoping, desperately hoping, that she would not cry. 'Very well,' she said, her voice low-pitched and husky. 'Ask. If I can do what you and Queen Selethe want of me, I will.'

Chapter XV

When Charn left, Calliope finally allowed herself to cry. The tears came quickly, steadily, falling on her hands and on to the fabric of his cloak, which she still wore wrapped about her like a keepsake. Now though, the keepsake had a bitter significance, for it was all she had of him and soon, when she was gone, it would be all there would ever be.

She had given the promise he wanted. It made no difference to the inevitable course that events must take, so what point would there have been in withholding? An empty act of spite; or petty revenge for the ruin of her dreams? She wanted neither, for her dreams had been impossible from the start and it was not Charn's fault that they had turned to ashes. She would keep her promise. She would return home, and the knowledge of what she had done and where she had been would never, ever be divulged to another human soul.

And for as long as she lived, she would never see Charn again.

The tears stopped at last, and a strange, chill calm came over Calliope. She believed she understood Charn a little better now, for as he had told her, explained to her, about the queen's fears and the dangers that humankind could ultimately pose to the twilight world, the mask of indifference had slipped and she had seen the undercurrent of emotion that lay beneath. For a brief span there had been echoes of the small but potent empathy that had formed between them in her father's house when he was at his lowest ebb, and because of it she knew, now, the reason for his more customary cold reserve. He did not hate or despise her. He had simply accepted, as must she, that their worlds and their natures were too alien for the gulf between them ever to be breached. He was not capable of loving her. He was out of her reach; always had been, always would be. Better that she should go, quickly and without turmoil, and try to forget him.

Though that was something Calliope knew she would never do.

She was motionless in the gloom, hunched taut and preoccupied on the bed and staring at the floor, when Thimue softly opened the door and looked in. Seeing that she was unaware of him the physician made to greet her; then hesitated as another form of sight stirred in him and a sixth sense awoke. Clothed in the familiar fashion of his world, yet with hair and skin so ingrained with alien colour, she had a look of some outlandish hybrid, at home neither in one realm nor in the other . . . and the metaphor went deeper than mere physical appearance. Thimue felt a sudden, acute sense of premonition, and though he couldn't

186

define its nature it filled him with foreboding. For a moment more he continued to watch her. Then he drew back, closed the door again, noiselessly and without disturbing her, and glided away.

Selethe said: 'Please forgive me, Calliope, if I seem disconcerted. It's simply that your appearance is a little . . . astonishing to me.' She smiled a benign but faintly uneasy smile, her eyes flicking their focus constantly from Calliope's hair to her skin to her fingernails, back to her hair again. 'I hope you don't think me too discourteous.'

Calliope tried to return the smile, but it was a pallid effort. She had not wanted this, not wanted to come before Selethe and accept her personal thanks for the decision she had made; to her it was a charade and its kindly intentions were misplaced. Yet Selethe *was* trying to be kind; and despite the feeling of listless depression that hung over her, Calliope had taken an immediate and instinctive liking to the queen that was growing by the moment.

They were in a small, private anteroom abutting the court hall. Selethe felt that a private meeting would be less daunting for Calliope, so Charn had escorted her here by a little-used route, where she would not be the object of too much curiosity. He sat now on a chair at some distance from the couch where Selethe and Calliope were seated, and since making the formal introduction had not spoken a word. Now and then Calliope glanced uneasily at him, but he seemed preoccupied with his own thoughts and didn't so much as glance at her.

'I understand from Thimue,' Selethe continued, her tone sympathetic, 'that you are not finding it easy to adjust to our world.'

Calliope gained her voice at last. 'I – I have adjusted a little, madam. It's just that I feel so . . . *heavy*. Everything is a great effort for me.'

'You can't take any of our sustenance, I believe?' Selethe leaned forward, still gazing in a fascinated, almost mesmerised way that Calliope found unnerving. She tried to rationalise her disquiet, reminding herself that the queen had never in her life before seen anything that was not monochrome, and managed, 'That's so, madam.'

'And our fire chills you beyond bearing?'

A nod.

'Yet even from here I feel an aura of heat from you, as if you were burning with fever . . . this, of course, is hard for me to comprehend.' Selethe's eyes glinted wryly. 'It rather brings home to me how narrow my experience has been – and the depth of my ignorance as a result.' She started to reach towards Calliope, then, remembering, quickly drew back her hand. 'Tell me, my dear, are you suffering from being unable to eat?'

Calliope shook her head. 'Thank you, madam, but I'm well enough,' she replied. 'I don't seem to feel hunger, and Thimue believes that fasting is better for me. It reduces my vitality, he says, and that is all to the good.'

Selethe touched her lower lip with the tip of her tongue. 'I see . . . yes; it is, then, like a mirror of my own people's experience, isn't it? In the world of mankind we lose strength rapidly, but a human in our world is *too* strong, and must be weakened.' She was staring at Calliope's hair again; abruptly she blinked, broke the thrall with an effort and sat back on the couch. 'Yet the weakening surely has its limits? No one can live indefinitely without nourishment. If it is allowed to go too far, what then?'

Charn spoke up for the first time. 'She will die,' he said.

Calliope and the queen both looked at him, and Selethe said with a touch of reproof, 'You are very blunt, Charn.'

'I am also honest, my lady, for I see no point in equivocating. For all Thimue's undoubted wisdom, we don't know how long Calliope can continue to survive here.' Now Charn did meet Calliope's gaze, with a strange, hard stare. 'As you have just said, no one can live indefinitely without nourishment, and we have no way of judging where, for Calliope, the borderline between life and death lies, or how quickly and unexpectedly it might be crossed. That is why, madam, I've been urging you to allow her to return to her own world without any further delay.'

There was a faintly combative note in his voice, and Calliope felt curiosity stir. Had there been some dissension between Charn and his queen? she wondered. Charn looked uneasy, almost worried, and Calliope was puzzled. She had given Selethe the promise she wanted, and now that it was done Selethe must surely be as anxious as Charn to see her go. Yet Charn implied that the queen had been procrastinating.

Curiosity began to turn to disquiet, but before she could formulate a careful question, Selethe spoke again.

'Of course, Charn, I understand and share your concern,' she said. 'I wouldn't dream of endangering Calliope in any way, and I have no intention of delaying what must be done. But it has occurred to me that we might be able to achieve something more through Calliope's kindness.' She paused, and her gaze, cautious now, slid to Charn again. 'Something that is of very great importance to us.'

Charn tensed. 'Madam . . .?'

'I am speaking, Charn, of Malorn, and the key.'

For a moment it was as though Charn had not taken in her words. He stared at her blankly, uncomprehendingly – then the blankness was replaced by a look of horrified disbelief.

'Madam—' His voice caught. 'You can't mean this as a serious proposition!'

'Can I not?' Selethe spoke mildly but there was a steely edge underlying her tone. 'Why?'

'Because— because it—' He had been about to say *it is insane* but checked himself in time, belatedly and horribly aware that he should have seen this coming. Selethe's sudden keen interest in Calliope had coincided with an equally sudden reluctance to send her back through the gateway. The queen had been preoccupied, with an air of suppressed excitement – the warning signs had been there, Charn thought; and he had failed to recognise them.

Forcing his voice under better control, he tried desperately to make her see reason. 'My lady, it can't be contemplated! To even think of it – the risk is *monstrous*!'

'No, Charn.' Selethe spoke quietly, but with such absolute authority that Calliope looked at her in surprise. Her tone stopped Charn in his tracks and she continued, 'I've thought long and hard about this, and now that I've met Calliope for myself I am resolved. She gave you her trust. We will repay that compliment in kind.'

'Madam, *please*—'

'I said, *no*. You won't sway me, not this time.' She smiled at him, leavening the rebuke, then before he could collect himself enough to even try to argue again she turned to face Calliope.

'My dear, I won't dissemble with you any longer. I want your

189

help, and if you are willing to give it I shall owe you a debt of gratitude so great that it can never be repaid. You see . . . many years ago, my son went to your world, and vanished there.' From the corner of her eye she saw Charn put a hand to his face, covering his eyes. She ignored him. 'We have striven to discover what became of him, but all our efforts have been in vain. I ache to know the truth. I *must* know the truth!' Suddenly, forgetting or not caring for the risk to herself, she reached out and grasped Calliope's hands. Her own hands were gloved; even so, Calliope felt cold striking through her fingers and numbing them.

'Help me, Calliope,' Selethe pleaded. 'You can succeed where we have only failed. Please – help me to find Malorn!'

The queen told the story of her lost son with a painful, almost childlike candour that wrenched Calliope's heart. Listening in the quiet room, with Charn a silent, motionless spectre behind her, she heard of how Malorn had first gone to the human world to discover why so many of their kind had never returned; how, once there, he had met a woman of the human race and had come to love her, and how finally he had gained his mother's reluctant permission to give his love the key that would enable her to cross the threshold between dimensions.

'He hoped to bring her back,' Selethe said in a small, broken voice. 'Malorn hoped that she might survive here as he could not do in her world.' Her great silver eyes lifted to Calliope's face with a look of such grief that Calliope could not hold her gaze. 'We know now that his hope was unfounded, for we have seen the truth in you. But at the time we did not realise it. *He* did not realise it. So he went to her, to give her his gift, and he did not return.'

She told Calliope then of the distraught and increasingly futile efforts that had been made to solve the mystery of Malorn's disappearance; of the emissaries who had gone to search for him and vanished in their turn, and of how, finally, she had given in to Charn's urging and allowed him to risk his own life in the world of humankind. Four times Charn had gone through the gateway, she said. He had learned, or surmised, the fate of those who had preceded him, but he had found no trace of Malorn. Then on the fifth occasion he himself had been captured; and the rest of his tale they all knew only too well.

Now though, Selethe said, her tone changing and a note of eagerness creeping into her voice, Calliope had given them a chance that they had never had before. She could move in the human world as none of the twilight-dwellers might ever do. She had knowledge they could not match, and she could use that knowledge. She could search. She could solve the mystery that had haunted Selethe for fifteen years.

'I used to tell myself that my son might still be alive,' Selethe said quietly. 'Now, though . . . I believe he must be dead, for he could not have survived in your world for this long a time. Not unless . . .' But then she shook her head, pushing away whatever wistful thought had come to her, and looked steadily at Calliope. 'So I am not asking you to work a miracle for me by finding him and bringing him home. I want only to know what happened.' She shivered. 'However ugly the truth, I want to *know*, for even the worst truth is kinder than the torment of uncertainty.'

There was silence. Then, still watching Calliope's face, the queen said, 'Will you help me, Calliope?'

Calliope looked at Charn. He had risen from the chair and stood at the far side of the room, his back to them both. For a few moments he remained motionless, but then as if aware of her scrutiny he turned his head and their eyes met.

She said, 'Charn, I . . .'

'The decision is not mine to make.' Charn's voice was tightly controlled.

Calliope hesitated. There was one question she wanted, needed to ask, but to voice it in Selethe's presence might not be wise. Yet what choice did she have? If she was to decide, if she was even to make any sense of this, she had to know the answer.

She said: 'The decision may not be yours, Charn. But you don't want me to accept, do you?'

He turned sharply, quickly to face her. 'No, I don't.' His gaze flicked from her to Selethe and an edge came into his voice. 'The queen knows why.'

Selethe remained calm. 'Charn does not trust your people, Calliope,' she said. 'He doesn't even trust you.'

Calliope was still watching Charn but he refused, now, to return her gaze. 'I see,' she said. Her level tone was almost but not quite betrayed by a slight unsteadiness.

Suddenly, angrily, Charn spoke. 'It's not a question of trust,' he said sharply. 'I don't believe that Calliope will break the promise she has already given. But I do believe that to ask more of her – to ask *this* – is foolhardy.'

'Why?' Selethe queried gently.

'Because it demands too much of us all!' Now Charn did force himself to look Calliope in the eye, though it was clearly at a cost. 'From Calliope, who owes us nothing, it demands a loyalty which she has no reason to feel, and a search for which she has no clues and can receive no help; while from us it demands the revealing of a secret which in human hands could bring ruin on our world and everything in it!'

'Not in her hands,' Selethe countered. 'We already have her promise.'

'What if she doesn't keep her promise? What if she *can't* keep it?'

Calliope spoke up. 'I don't make promises lightly – you of all people know that.'

'Yes,' he said. 'I do. But if your father were to learn anything of this matter, your promise would be worth nothing – he'd see to it, whatever the cost to you!'

Incensed, Calliope flared back at him. 'That is a *despicable* thing to say! Whatever he might have done to you, Charn, he's not a monster!'

Charn said, 'As to that—' but Selethe interrupted.

'Charn. Calliope.' Her tone brought them both to heel and they turned, chagrined, to look at her. Calliope's cheeks were flushed, Charn's face as hard as marble. The queen glanced from one to the other and continued, 'This quarrelling achieves nothing. In one sense Charn is right, Calliope, for I am asking a great deal of you, and without justification. As he says, you owe us nothing; in fact the onus of debt is entirely upon us.'

'I don't look at it like that, madam,' Calliope said, then frowned. 'Besides, you've already revealed to me the secret Charn spoke of. And if . . . forgive me, but if your son . . . no longer lives, then how can my father and his Society pose any threat to him or to you?'

Selethe and Charn exchanged a look. Charn's eyes were apprehensive, for he knew what was in her mind, and he projected a silent, urgent warning to her not to voice her thoughts. But the appeal was fruitless. Selethe was resolved and, as she had said, would not be swayed.

The queen turned to Calliope again. 'My dear,' she said, 'I'm afraid that he could. You see, even if Malorn is beyond the reach of harm, the key is not.'

'The key?' Calliope didn't understand.

'The key that can unlock the gateway between dimensions without need for the skill to open it by other means. It was to be Malorn's gift, as I told you, to the woman he loved, but now it, too, is lost in your world. If, as Charn says, the human scientists and seekers should ever come to know of its existence . . .' Her voice trailed off, and from the shadows Charn said grimly,

'They would spare nothing and no one in the search for it. That was what I meant, Calliope, when I said that any promise you might make to the queen would be worth nothing.' He moved a little nearer to her, and the drifting, pallid light momentarily etched his face with silver. 'Consider the power such a key would give to the men of your father's Society, and how they would use it. Consider how deadly a weapon it would be in their hands!'

'A *weapon*?' Calliope's eyes were stark. 'Is that how you see them, Charn; as mindless destroyers?'

'What reason did they ever give me to think otherwise?'

She couldn't deny that, but it made her ache inwardly; ache for Foss's prejudice, for his intractability, for the tragic mistake he had made in refusing to *understand*.

Voice cracking, she said, 'They are not evil.'

'Perhaps not. But they chose of their own will to be blind and deaf to reason. To them I was nothing more than a thing without sentience, to be mangled and tormented and experimented upon for no better reason than to satisfy their curiosity. Even when they discovered that I had intelligence, their attitude didn't change one whit. They only intensified their efforts to force information from me by any and every means they could devise.'

Calliope's anger was wavering, but a spark still burned in her, kept alive by the bond she shared with her father and the loyalty she felt to him. To be judged so harshly when he could not answer for himself was unjust; she was his only ally against Charn's bitter indictment, and suddenly, fiercely, she wanted to defend him. Not to make excuses, not to plead; simply to explain.

'You gave them little option, Charn,' she said. 'From the

beginning you were hostile, unyielding, as violent in your way as they were. The fault wasn't all on their side.' Suddenly she turned to Selethe. 'Madam, my father is not an evil man! I know he did Charn a great wrong, but – but if only he had understood, if *I* had understood and had told him, shown him—' The flow of words stopped as suddenly she heard the tinge of hysteria in her own voice and realised that she was in danger of betraying her cause with the vehemence of her protest. She swallowed, and the thin air had a taste of metal in her throat. 'Forgive me.'

Selethe's silver eyes gazed calmly back at her. 'You're very loyal to your father,' she said.

Calliope's gaze dropped. 'Yes.'

'You and he have a deep affection for each other, I think.'

A pause, then Calliope nodded. 'We've always been close. Especially so since my mother – my real mother – was . . .' she hesitated, and Selethe's look intensified.

'You have lost your mother?' she asked gently.

It was as near to the truth as made little difference, Calliope thought. 'Yes,' she said.

'So since that sad time, you have taken your mother's place as your father's helpmeet.'

Calliope was close to tears, though she couldn't begin to fathom why. Foolish of her; there was no *reason* and it was just weakness . . . She bit at the insides of her cheeks to control the reaction and said, 'Yes, madam. At least, I have tried to.'

'Of course you have; and no doubt succeeded. I think I'm beginning to understand you a little better, my dear; and to understand your anxiety that your father should not be unfairly judged.' She flicked a glance in Charn's direction. 'I don't condemn him, Calliope. Charn, I know, has good reason to be hostile; but Charn cannot claim to know your father as you do. So I will ask you one thing, and trust that you will answer me honestly.'

Calliope raised her head. 'I will, madam.'

'Then tell me: whatever his faults or failings might be, is your father an honourable man?'

Calliope thought of Foss; of his dedication to his work and his family. She thought of his unstinting generosity to her mother in her desperate affliction; generosity that he was not obliged to give but which he saw as far more than a duty. She thought of his largesse. And she recalled her own birthday, when he had placed her mother's legacy, sealed and untouched, in her hands. He had sworn to keep faith with her last request to him, and he had kept that oath for fifteen years . . .

She looked without flinching into Selethe's eyes and said, 'Yes, madam. He is.'

For a moment or two more Selethe sat unmoving; then, slowly, she rose to her feet.

'I have the assurance I hoped for,' she said, 'and it is enough. Charn – I believe that in your anger you have wrongfully exaggerated the case against Calliope's father.' She smiled at him, kindly and a little sadly. 'You were overwrought; indeed, we all were. But now my doubts are at rest. If Calliope is willing to help us in our search, then I believe we have nothing to fear from her, or from her people.'

Charn made no attempt to argue, though Calliope knew from the look in his eyes that he was far from happy. A worm of disquiet moved suddenly in her own mind as she recalled the intensity with which he had denounced Foss and Nempson and the others of the Society. Though his words had had the venom of prejudice, his conviction was deep and genuine, and for a moment Calliope's confidence wavered. Then reason and the old affection for Foss reasserted themselves. She pushed the doubt away and felt it crumble to nothing.

Charn was watching her face, and possibly he had seen or sensed something of her momentary turmoil, for he said, 'But is she willing, my lady? We don't yet know.'

Selethe turned her great eyes to Calliope, searching her face. 'My dear, I won't press you for a decision now. That would not be fair. But . . .' She left the word hanging in mid-air, almost but not quite a question, and suddenly Calliope felt a desperate need to dissemble.

'Madam,' she answered haltingly, 'I . . . still don't know what you would expect of me; what this – this search would entail.' She glanced uneasily at Charn, saw that he wasn't about to help her and floundered on as best she could. 'If your son is – is dead; and the key lost – where could I begin?'

'I will give you what help I can,' Selethe told her. 'It's little enough, but it might have some value.'

'The woman,' Calliope ventured. 'The human woman . . . if she could be found, might she . . .?'

Selethe sighed. 'We've searched for her, but have never discovered any trace of her.' She made an odd, bitter little sound. 'If I had only been less stubborn, and helped my son instead of hating his human love and opposing him at every turn . . . She is probably dead, Calliope. Dead, or she has forgotten Malorn.' Another sigh. 'Even if she lives, and remembers, it's of little use. I would not listen when Malorn tried to tell me of her, you see; I did not want to hear of her beauty, or her gentleness, or the way she lived her life in her bright, alien world. So there is nothing of her in my mind. Nothing at all.'

'Not even her name?' Calliope asked.

'Oh, there was a name. But only one. Your people, your kind, have two, do they not? A name for their family, by which they can be recognised, and another, lesser name whose only significance is personal. I don't know her family name, you see. If I had *listened* . . .' She made a quick, angry gesture. 'Ah, I repeat myself to no purpose; and I despise self-pity . . . But no. I know only her other name, her lesser name, as I know yours.' She smiled without humour. 'If someone wanted to seek for you, how many other Calliopes might lead them on a fruitless road before they found the right one?'

Calliope returned the smile. 'Not all names are widely used, madam. Mine is quite rare.'

'Is it?' Selethe shrugged. She looked dejected, discouraged. 'Ah, well then; I suppose there is nothing to be lost by telling you. Though what purpose it will serve . . .' She pulled at one of her gloves. 'Long ago, I used to say the name aloud to myself over and over again, hating it, *loathing* it. But I haven't uttered it for many years now. My anger faded with time, and I felt only a lingering distaste.' She drew a quick breath, as though steeling herself to break the taboo she had created. Then she said, quite calmly,

'Her name was Griette.'

Chapter XVI

'This is intolerable!' Foss lurched angrily up from the stool, and with a convulsive swat of one hand sent half the papers on the workroom table scattering chaotically to the floor. 'We are getting *nowhere*, Nempson! Six days, six *days* since Calli went missing, and we've found not the slightest trace of where or how she went!' He swung round and glared savagely at the chair from the Institute, seething at its useless emptiness, hating Charn for escaping and, perhaps above all, furious with Calliope for all that she had failed to do.

Nempson bent down, carefully picked up some of the fallen documents and returned them to the table. 'You're overtired, Foss,' he said. 'We both are; we've barely slept beyond the odd snatched hour or two since her disappearance, and no brain can hope to be at its clearest when the body is exhausted from lack of rest.'

Foss transferred his glare from the chair to the other man. 'Thank you, Nempson, but as a physician I'm perfectly capable of judging that for myself!'

Nempson eyed him. 'And your temper's on a short fuse; that's a sure sign that you're taxing yourself too far. We're both in need of a respite, my friend. One of Philome's excellent dinners, a bottle of wine and a sound night's sleep, and we'll stand a far better chance of solving this conundrum.'

For a moment it seemed that Foss would round on him again, but abruptly he saw the sense of the advice. His big shoulders sagged, he shook his head and uttered a gusty sigh that dissipated the rush of his anger.

'I suppose you're right ... though blast it all, it galls me to have to admit it.' He scrubbed at his face, as if trying to erase his weariness and confusion. 'I don't know what Philome has planned for dinner. Didn't ask her. But there'll be something . . . and wine would be welcome. More than a mere bottle, too. Very well, Nempson. Let's leave this damned room and its contents to rot until morning – and if we both end up in our cups, you're welcome to sleep in one of the unused bedrooms.'

'Thank you. I might take advantage of that.' Nempson smiled pallidly. 'As matters stand, it's a preferable prospect to my own empty house.'

Foss spun the wheel of the etherea lamp, and as the glow began to fade the two men left the room, locking the door carefully behind them.

Philome was in the kitchen, where to the discomfort of the servants she had been hovering distractedly for the past two hours as she waited for some word of when her husband might require food. The last six days had taken their toll on her; though her 'transgression' in failing to tell Foss of her suspicions about Calliope had been forgiven, it was most certainly not forgotten, and Philome now fluctuated between guilty penitence and half-mutinous and half-defensive reproachfulness. She worried constantly and acutely about Calliope and, though she would not have dared to voice it under any circumstances, she couldn't banish the feeling that, with the possible exception of Nempson, she was the only one who had any true concern for Calliope's health and wellbeing. Tobery and Diona, of course, were too young to understand; but Celesta seemed indifferent, Luthe treated the whole thing as a novelty with a fast-diminishing amusement value, and Foss was now so angry at the failure of his efforts to locate his daughter that he seemed to have no room for any other consideration.

When the men appeared in search of their meal, Philome complained fretfully but briefly about the late hour and spoiled meat and further burdens on her nerves, then subsided and ordered the long-delayed dinner to be served. They sat down in the dining room in strained silence. The younger children had been fed and put to bed long ago and Luthe, as usual, was out with his friends, so only Celesta joined them at table. The saddle of mutton was crisped at the edges and the vegetables had suffered from the cook's efforts to keep them hot; Celesta began to wrinkle her nose at the fare, but Foss gave her such an ominous look that she thought better of saying anything and picked at her plateful with fastidious resignation.

Philome did not ask how the men's explorations had gone, for their faces told her the answer she would have received. Foss was drinking a lot of wine and Nempson, normally moderate, was almost matching him. Philome sipped uneasily from her own glass, keeping a wary watch on her husband for any early sign of temper or other trouble and wishing she could think of some innocuous small talk to ease the atmosphere.

Outside, the burgeoning summer was having one of its fits of petulance, and when something flurried against the window Philome uttered silent thanks for a conversational opening and said, 'I do believe it's raining.'

Celesta groaned. 'Oh, it *can't*! I'm supposed to be going on a picnic tomorrow, and now the weather will spoil it.' She hunched her shoulders sulkily. 'It's *unfair*.'

'Unfair?' Foss looked bellicose. 'What strikes me as unfair, miss, is your preoccupation with frivolity while your sister is still missing! You have a selfish and shameless disregard for the sensibilities of others, and I'm damned if I know where you get the trait, for it certainly isn't from me!'

Celesta opened her mouth to retort, but Philome pedalled on her foot under the table and said, 'Your father's quite right, Celesta. How you can even *think* of picnics at a time like this is beyond my comprehension!'

Foss grunted and muttered something about lack of discipline, giving his wife a resentful glower as he said it. There was another buffeting at the window, and Nempson, who was carefully attending to his food and trying not to show the embarrassment he felt, said tentatively, 'There is a new device at the Institute, Philome, which predicts the weather for some days ahead. The early trials have been most encouraging, and—'

He got no further. As he started to speak there had been a new sound, like a rising of the wind – and suddenly, with a shattering crash, the window pane was smashed in from outside.

'*What by all the*—' Foss leaped to his feet, his voice rising in a roar and eclipsing Philome's shriek of terror as the curtains billowed and shards of glass scattered across the floor.

'Oh! Oh!' Philome wailed. 'What is it, what's happening? Is there a riot?— Celesta, quickly, summon the servants!'

'Stop babbling, woman!' Foss had already pushed the table aside and was striding towards the window. Philome cried, '*Foss, be careful!*' but he ignored her and hacked the curtain back, staring out into the night.

It wasn't raining. The street below was quiet. But . . .

'Living spirits, there's something flying—' The words cut off and Foss stumbled back with an imprecation as the vague, pale shape beyond the broken window suddenly launched itself towards him. There was a commotion, Foss flailing, Nempson on his feet, Philome screaming again and covering her eyes – then with a turmoil of beating wings and shrill, piercing cries, a winged creature as long as Foss's arms burst into the dining room. Foss made a wild grab for it, but it eluded him and flew up to the ceiling, where it hovered, flapping and shrilling in agitation as the room's bright light assailed its huge, colourless eyes.

Nempson said, '*Great powers!*' and Philome, who had shrunk back on her chair and was now clutching at her hair in fear that the intruder would dive at her, cried tremulously, 'What *is* it?'

'It's one of those creatures!' Nempson's eyes were wide with incredulity. 'Foss, quickly – have you a snare or net or—'

'Wait!' Foss said as Nempson seemed about to climb on the table after the frantic intruder. 'Look – it's holding something.'

The being, they all saw now, had hands of a kind, and clutched in one of them was what looked like a tightly-rolled scroll. As if it understood Foss's words, it shrilled anew, then manoeuvred itself until it was directly above the table's centre and let its burden drop. The scroll fell into the dish of mutton; Foss snatched it up before the half-congealed meat juices could stain it, and started feverishly to unroll it.

'Don't tear it!' Nempson's attention was split between the messenger and its message, and suddenly the being moved again. It swooped down; Philome yelped, Nempson tried convulsively to snatch at it, and his hands closed on air as it darted to the window, through the shattered pane and away into the night.

Red-faced, hair awry, Nempson stared at the window with a mixture of disbelief and frustration. Philome was gasping, Celesta seemed frozen on her chair, her mouth open in shock, and Foss stood motionless, staring at the now opened scroll in his hand.

It wasn't made of paper or anything resembling it, but had a texture like stiff, fine fabric. Nor was the writing upon it in ink; in fact even the most knowledgeable minds at the Institute would have been unable to identify the substance. But it was addressed to himself. And the hand was one he recognised instantly.

He raised his head and looked at his companions. One by one they realised that something momentous was afoot, and three pairs of eyes stared back at him. Nempson said uneasily, 'Foss?' and Philome ventured, 'What is it, my dear?'

The pulse in Foss's temple was throbbing visibly. 'It's a letter,' he said in a peculiar, strangled tone. 'From Calliope.'

When Philome had been brought round from her faint by means of a burnt feather held under her nose, the three of them read the letter together. Tobery and Diona, woken by the commotion, had come to investigate, and Celesta, to her fury, was ordered to shepherd them back to bed, leaving the three adults alone.

There could be no possible doubt that the writing on the strange material was Calliope's; but for that, Foss would have been hard pressed to believe that the letter was not a hoax. It ran:

'Dearest Father,

I know that you and Philome must have been greatly worried for me these past days, so before I say more, I assure you that I am Safe and Well and among Kind Friends. I am sorry to have caused you Trouble and Anxiety. But I dare to believe that you will understand and forgive my Offence when I am able to tell you all upon my Return.

Though it is hard to give Credence to such a statement, I am not at present in our World. I have travelled to the habitation of those beings we call the Twilight Creatures, and here I have discovered something of great Moment. I cannot Explain fully as yet, for the nature of my adventure is greatly Complicated. But I can and must tell you now that it has a connection with my own Mother and with the sad Mystery of the legacy that she left behind her. I dearly hope, dear Father and dear Philome, that it does not grieve you to read of this, for I do not wish to bring you Unhappiness by referring to the past. I am impatient to return home to you, so that the whole Story may be told. But before I can do so, I must beg of you, Father, a promise. It is no Burdensome thing, I believe, but the giving of it will be a great Boon to me in the matter of my Departure from this place.

I have for my own part Pledged to the creatures of twilight that upon my return to you I shall carry out a certain mission that is of great import to them and to their world. It is something that I alone can do, and until it is Completed I may not tell my story. My vow is a solemn one, given of my own free Will, and I Cannot and Must not Break it. Therefore I entreat you, as my Father and as one deserving of the sincerest Love and deepest Respect which my heart can offer, to grant me your own promise in this same regard; that you will allow me the Freedom to accomplish what I must without hindrance or questioning, and manifest that Patience which I know is one of your many merits until the task is done and I may tell you Everything. I ask nothing

else of you, but only that Word which I know is your unfailing
bond. I in my turn Pledge to you that no harm but only good
shall come of what I do.

The messenger to which this letter is Entrusted will return to
you before the next Sunrise, and will carry your reply to me. I
have assured the creature of safe Passage in its errand, and I will
wait in the earnest Hope of your Goodwill, which if granted will
see me very soon among my cherished Family once more.

From your loving and devoted daughter,
Calliope.'

Philome said, in a very small voice, 'Oh, dear spirits . . . dear
spirits . . .' She sank into the nearest chair, dabbed at her eyes
then looked up at Foss in distraught appeal. 'What are we to *do*?'

Slowly, Foss lowered the letter. He was staring towards the
broken window, but his gaze was focused on something else
entirely; something visible only to his mind's eye.

Nempson, who stood at his elbow, said softly, 'Is it *possible*? Or
is this some . . . some . . .' Options failed him then and he shook
his head.

'It's no fraud.' Foss squeezed the letter convulsively, unaware
that he did so. 'This is Calliope's writing; no doubt of it. And the
creature that broke into this room was real enough.' He glanced
briefly at his wife. 'For the sake of all the powers, Philome, stop
whimpering! At least we know now that Calli's alive and well!'

'But *is* she?' Philome countered melodramatically. 'Alone,
among those – those *things* – oh, Foss, when I think what might
be happening to her at this very moment—'

'Damn it all, nothing's happening to her; doesn't she say so
herself in this letter? Pull yourself together!' He glanced at
Nempson. 'We have some thinking and planning to do, and little
time in which to do it.'

'You're going to reply?' Nempson asked.

'Indeed I am. When that winged monstrosity comes back for
its answer, it shall have one.'

Nempson began, 'If we could capture it—' but Foss shook his
head emphatically.

'There's no point. From what I saw of it I doubt that it can
even speak, let alone understand our tongue, so it's of little use to
us. It goes against the grain, I know, but we shall give it safe

passage, as Calli asks.' His face creased into a frown in which speculation, curiosity and a good degree of rancour combined. 'I won't be satisfied until I've got to the root of this, Nempson.'

'You mean . . .' Nempson shifted his eyes briefly but meaningfully in Philome's direction, then mouthed in a near-whisper, 'Griette?'

'Yes.' Then with a calculated shrug Foss shook off his darker thoughts, and his expression became more pleasant as he turned again to Philome, who had been following their talk with agitated if bemused attention. 'My dear, Nempson and I will decide what to do for the best, and how to bring Calli home by the safest means. When the messenger returns it will doubtless come to this room again, so we shall discuss our strategy while we await it. Go down and tell the servants that they are not to come up here until they have my leave. Then fetch us a bottle of brandy from the library, and leave us alone.'

Confused and frightened, Philome clutched at the straw of domestic triviality in an effort to anchor herself. 'But the meal, Foss, the clearing—'

'Can *wait*. Do as I ask, Philome, and stop making difficulties.' He forced a smile, though his teeth were clenching. 'If I were you I should go to bed, for we'll need nothing more tonight.'

'To *bed*?' she echoed incredulously. 'Foss, do you think I could sleep for one *instant*? And what about Celesta? She will want to know what has happened, and—'

'Then tell her! Or read, or comb your hair, or anything else that pleases you; but kindly leave us to *confer*! That is, if you want Calliope back safe and sound?'

Philome bridled. 'Of course I want her back! To say such a thing – truly, Foss, you are very unfeeling at times!' Summoning her dignity she rose to her feet and with a flounce of skirt walked towards the door. Opening it, she paused and looked back, reproach in her eyes. 'I'll fetch your brandy. And when you have made your decisions, I will be gratified if you have the kindness not to keep me in an agony of suspense for a *moment* longer than necessary!'

The door slammed behind her. Foss said something under his breath, then waved impatiently towards the table.

'Sit down, Nempson, do! Push that mess aside; the servants can see for it later.' Despite his irritation, the time spent in pacifying Philome had had the effect of allowing his own mind to settle and clear after the first shock, and the bones of a strategy were already taking form. He waited until Nempson had seated himself, then plumped into an adjacent chair and said briskly, 'Very well: let us sum up what we know.' He splayed one hand, began to count off finger by finger. 'One: that Calliope has somehow reached the place where these twilight creatures have their lair. How the deuce she accomplished it we don't know, and for all our experiments and searching among her mother's papers we can't find out.' He grunted. 'Though I'd take any odds that that devious creature Charn had a hand in it somewhere.'

Nempson's mouth pursed into a tight line and he thought, as he had done many times over the past few days, of Charn and Calliope together. 'I would give a great deal to have him in captivity again.'

'So would I, my friend, but that's neither here nor there for the moment. Where was I? Ah, yes. Two: Calli has formed some kind of liaison – she claims even friendship – with these entities. Three: from them, or through them, she has "something of great moment" that is connected with Griette and all that happened in the past. Lastly, four: she cannot, or will not, reveal what it is until she has carried out some secret assignment for these new-found allies of hers. A matter on which she asks – *demands*, damn it – my solemn word to ask no questions!'

'She claims that no harm can possibly come of it,' Nempson said. 'In other words, she expects us to trust in the integrity of these creatures and be utterly compliant to their wants!'

'Quite. Calliope seems to have run away with the notion that they are the equals of humans and have the right to be treated as such . . . and that, Nempson, is what raises my suspicions.'

Nempson leaned forward, his eyes keen. 'You think she might have been coerced in some way? Threatened, or even brainwashed?'

'I don't merely think it, I'm certain of it. Blast my eyes, I'm Calli's *father* – if anyone thinks they know her better than I do, I'd like to see them dare say it to my face!' Foss shoved his chair back, stood up and stamped towards the window, bull-like in his aggression. 'They've gained control over her,' he continued balefully. 'Whether she's been intimidated or whether it's some subtler form of indoctrination, I don't know. But her mind has

204

been warped, Nempson.' Suddenly he swung round and made a violent gesture towards the letter lying on the table. 'Read that again if you doubt me! Promises, pledges, words of honour – to creatures like *those*? It's madness! But Calliope is not mad! She is *not* like her mother!'

If Nempson perceived the note of desperation in Foss's anger, the note that betrayed a rising dread, he was very careful not to show it. Voice and face calm, he said,

'I agree entirely. So we must do something about it.'

'Indeed. Oh indeed, we must.' Foss glared at the window again. 'And will.'

'You have a plan in mind?'

It was crystallising, becoming clear. Foss had no qualms about it, for to him this was a form of war, and wars were not won by playing to the rules. 'Yes,' he said. 'I'll send a letter back to Calliope – or to whatever evil entity is manipulating her. I will do what she asks, and pledge my word of honour, couched in such terms that no one can be in doubt of its sincerity.'

Nempson understood, and began to nod slowly. 'Of course. But once Calliope is safely home, matters will be a little . . . different.'

Foss flicked him a conspiratorial glance. 'Two gloves on the one hand, Nempson. Or perhaps even three.' He smiled a hard smile, recalling their use of the same metaphor during their discussion on the night before Calliope's coming of age, and reflecting on the momentous changes that had taken place since then. 'We shall have Calli back. We shall discover the nature of this "mission" and the mystery behind it; and we shall turn the tables on these twilight creatures, in ways that ensure they never *dare* to tamper with humankind again!' He drew a deep breath, shoulders hunching with the grim pleasure of anticipation. 'As you say, my good friend, matters will be different then. They will be very different indeed!'

Awaiting the messenger's return was becoming all but unbearable for Calliope. With no distinction between day and night, the court's dreamlike atmosphere made her feel that she was trapped in a mesmeric, languorous no-man's-land which negated any sense of urgency. Hours might pass in the twilight dimension just as in her own, but to her it seemed that time had slowed down and finally crawled to a halt, leaving her suspended in limbo.

Selethe had tried her best to be kind, encouraging Calliope to find distractions that would make the waiting easier. She had been invited to the great hall where the black throne stood, and encouraged to join the queen's courtiers in one of their strange and solemn revels. But though she had stayed for a short while and even danced a little, the diversion could not hold her. If Charn had been there it might have been different. But Charn, again, had withdrawn from her. When the story was told he had asked Selethe in a tight, remote voice if he might be excused from her presence, and when she consented he had gone without a further word, not even glancing in Calliope's direction as he went. It was as if in the light of what he had heard he could not bear the taint of being near her. Calliope had not seen him since, and when her irrational hope that she might find him in the court hall was dashed, the storm-clouds closed in on her mind again. Knowing she could not banish them, she had pleaded to be released from the revel, and now she sat alone in her room, staring into the empty hearth at its centre, and brooding.

The shock she had felt at Selethe's final, unwitting revelation now seemed as if it had happened to someone else. In truth it had not *been* so great a shock. Somewhere deep in her subconscious mind a faint chord of premonition had been sounding since the moment Selethe began to tell her son's story; and in a chillingly logical way this turn of events had surely been inevitable.

The image of her mother's face had risen like a ghost before her inner vision as, in a shaking voice, she told Selethe everything. Her mother's experiments. Her sudden withdrawal into strange and secretive moods that grew more frequent and more prolonged as time went by. Then the final shattering of her sanity and, when the screaming finally ceased, her removal, serene but mindless, to the care of the Hospice and a future without hope.

And, lastly, the legacy she had left behind.

Malorn was dead. For all the queen's brave words Calliope knew that she had still clung to a frail thread of hope, but Griette's last writings laid that hope to rest. Selethe had asked point-blank if Calliope had certain knowledge of his fate, and Calliope could not bring herself to lie. She told Selethe of the papers that she had shown to no other living soul, and of what they had contained.

The words were fixed in her memory; as she recounted the references to 'utter darkness' and 'the elusive border between dream and reality', Selethe had turned to gaze at Charn, a strange, helpless gaze, and said softly, 'She tried, Charn . . . she tried to find the gateway.' Charn nodded once, tautly, and looked away; and Selethe had pleaded then with Calliope to tell her all, *all* she knew.

Sombrely, and with an ache in her that she felt nothing would ever banish, Calliope obeyed. *White flowers. I cannot do this . . . the risk is too great . . . I must fail this last test, and in failing I will end all . . . the Sacrament . . .* At this Calliope glanced uneasily towards Selethe, wondering if her expression might give away a clue to the meaning of that cryptic allusion, which she did not understand. But the queen's face was as empty as the face of a statue. So, dropping her gaze again, Calliope had spoken of the last page, and the one word written so carefully and precisely in its centre. *DEATH*. It was final confirmation of the thing that Selethe had dreaded to know.

And it was then that Calliope had made her decision.

Tears started to spill onto her hands. She blinked them away but more came, and they cast her thoughts unwantedly back to the workroom in her father's house, Charn injured and semi-conscious in the chair, and her crying which had soothed and healed his hurts. Hating the memory, she uttered a thin sound of protest and put a clenched fist to her mouth, biting the knuckles until pain distracted her and made the tears stop. *Weak fool.* She had no *choice*, for anything else was impossible, as her mother, finally, had learned. Did she want to follow the path Griette had taken to the living hell of insanity? Of course not, of *course* not; so all she could do was to find the key that Malorn had given to Griette, and let it be returned to its rightful place. Close the gate. Close it for ever.

So, the letter. The twilight-dwellers had no concept of writing (that, too, sent memories stabbing through her) but with Thimue's help she had contrived substitutes for pen and ink and paper that served well enough. Selethe had watched, fascinated, as she wrote, then had stared at the finished message in great wonder, touching it here and there as though it were some strange and powerful talisman. She did not ask Calliope to read it to her, for which Calliope was thankful. She had only taken the rolled scroll, stroked it one last time, lightly and thoughtfully, then given it into the care of her messenger. As the winged creature departed with a soft sound, Calliope had felt as if a part of her soul were departing with it.

It had been, she knew, the hardest letter she had ever written or would ever write in her life. If Foss agreed to do what she asked of him – and Calliope believed he would – then she must say her final farewell to Charn and go back to her home and her old life, where she would remain for always. She could never return here; and nor would he ever set foot in her world again. As Griette had lost Malorn, so she would lose her love. But Charn, at least, would live. She, unlike her mother, had that comfort, and if she was wise then it would be the saving of her.

If she was wise . . . Calliope raised her head suddenly, pushing her hair from her eyes, and a small, poignant and very private smile caught at the edges of her mouth. Time, perhaps to practise what she was preaching to herself, and translate a little of that supposed wisdom into deeds. She didn't know the hour, but it could not be long before Selethe's messenger returned with her father's answer.

Provided that no harm had befallen it . . .

Ah, no. She would not consider that possibility, for to do so would be to deny the integrity that she knew was Foss's watchword. Whatever Charn might think or say, she trusted him and was certain that he would not fail her. So she in her turn must not shirk her part of the bargain. However much she might wish it otherwise, there could be no more procrastinating. She must prepare herself, and be ready.

She rose and crossed the room to where a part of the wall shimmered faintly in the eldritch glow of the ever-burning lights. This was a looking-glass of sorts, though of a substance and effect never dreamed of in the human world, and she placed herself before it, facing her own reflection.

Even if fate had taken a different twist, she knew as she gazed at herself that her stay here would soon have come to an end. The mirror told the inescapable truth – for the figure that looked back at her from within its depths was losing its colour and turning grey.

She had known for some while that she was beginning to weaken. It had brought her relief, as Thimue had predicted; the excruciating sense of grossness had all but gone, and with it the pain and effort of movement. She no longer suffered from the cold, and even her vision was adjusting by slow degrees to the tenebrous and unchanging dusk of the twilight world. But for all the respite, she was still human. The hiatus could not last indefinitely, and before long there would be a new affliction; the creeping malaise of debility and enfeeblement as her body, starved of nourishment, began to fail. Slowly but surely her strength would fade, until the fatal borderline was crossed and she was beyond the point of no return.

Greying eyes, greying hair, greying skin. She could pass now for a denizen of this world, and the knowledge brought the old yearning back. But it must not be. It could not be. She must *live*.

A sound made her turn then, and when she looked towards the door she saw that it was swinging noiselessly open. A name started to form on Calliope's lips – then the door opened fully and she saw Thimue on the threshold.

The old physician gazed at her compassionately and said, 'My dear . . . the messenger has returned.'

Calliope tensed. 'Is there a reply?'

'Yes. It was given to the queen. She is waiting for you, in the room behind the court hall.'

She nodded, swallowing back something that tried to rise in her throat and suffocate her. 'Very well. I – I'll go to her.' Her heart was pounding. It *hurt*.

Thimue held out a gloved hand to her as she moved towards him. She hesitated; then on an impulse laid her own hand on his arm. Strange, so strange, that this was possible now. Her touch no longer seared him; his no longer struck cold to the core of her being. But it was not, and could never be, enough.

The door swung softly to behind her as she let him lead her towards the room where Selethe waited.

Chapter XVII

The meeting between Selethe and Calliope lasted only a few

minutes. When it was over, and Calliope had walked slowly from the room to where Thimue waited solicitously to escort her back to her own chamber, the queen sat for some time alone among the shadows. Her bearing was serene but her eyes told another story, and her mind was steeped in thoughts not only of the past but of the future.

At length she summoned a servant to her, and when the ethereal being appeared she commanded that a fire should be lit in the room, and that word was to be sent to Charn that she wished to see him.

Charn duly came. When she saw his face Selethe made no reference to what she read there but only said quietly, 'Sit down, my dear. I don't doubt you know why I have sent for you.'

'Madam.' Charn inclined his head but did not answer the question. He took a chair far enough from the fire to be out of reach of its silver light, and Selethe continued, 'Calliope's father has given his word. She has returned to her room and is preparing to go home.'

He nodded, said nothing. One hand began to toy with the filmy black cuff of his sleeve.

'Before she leaves us,' the queen said, 'I think that you should talk to her.'

He looked up. 'I have nothing more to say to her, my lady.'

You poor, sad, stubborn fool, Selethe thought with an inward sigh. She had not wanted to do this brutally, but Charn's recalcitrance was robbing her of options. She would risk a great deal; above all she would risk losing his friendship and trust, which meant more to her now even than they had done before her last hope for Malorn had died. But it must be done. She would not, *could* not, allow the tragic mistakes of the past to happen once again.

She said, 'I think you have a great deal to say to her, Charn. But you're afraid to say it, for you are afraid to admit the truth even to yourself.'

'Madam,' Charn replied in a tone that verged on bitter anger, 'I believe that you would do better to leave well alone. In a very short time Calliope will be gone. She will fulfil the promise she has made – and no, I don't doubt her integrity; I believe she will do it – and when the task is completed we shall not see or even hear of her again. Knowing that, what can I have to say to her

210

that will serve any purpose at all? She'll never return. That is a fact.' His eyes narrowed, as though with pain. 'It can't be changed.'

'Though you,' said Selethe, very gently now, 'wish that it could.'

Charn's fingers clenched and the cuff tore suddenly. Selethe saw him bite back an imprecation, and he crushed the scrap of fabric into a tight ball, wishing he could do the same with his own rising emotions.

'Oh, my dear,' she said with a wealth of sorrow in her voice, 'you love her, don't you? Charn, Charn, don't look away like that. Don't pretend; not to me.' She rose to her feet and crossed the room to where he sat. As her hand came to rest on his shoulder Charn covered his face, fingertips pressing mercilessly on flesh and bone as if he were trying to drive out thoughts and feelings that beset him.

'My lady, please . . .' he said indistinctly.

But Selethe had trespassed too far to turn back now. 'I've known since your last return from the human world that something was amiss,' she told him gently. 'How could you hide it from me? I've seen it before, in other eyes and in another time – how could I fail to recognise the same sadness in you?' She shook her head slowly, knowing no other way to convey her distress. 'Oh, my dear, I am so sorry for you both!'

'For us *both*?' The words came out harshly before Charn could check himself.

'Yes.' She forced a small, sad smile. 'I realise that you're remembering my anger, the hatred I felt for the human woman who took Malorn's heart; you know that though I never saw her face, I did hate her for a long, long time. But you also know that my view has mellowed in the years since Malorn was lost. Now, the realisation that his love was – is – Calliope's own mother, and that she lives on in such straits . . . ah, Charn, it changes everything. Now, you see, I ask myself: if all those years ago I had tried to help instead of to hinder, what happy outcome might there have been?' She swallowed convulsively. 'Not just for my son and Griette, but also for you and Calliope.'

'My lady,' Charn said tightly, 'there could have been no happy outcome. It wasn't possible then, and it isn't possible now!' He made a husky, choking sound, like a bitter laugh quickly and rigorously stifled. 'You've heard the ending of Malorn's story from Calliope's own lips, and you *must* know in your heart that our own could be no different. Malorn and Griette were inimical, and so are Calliope and I. I can't even touch her without inflicting harm on her; and if either of us stays for more than a short time in the other's world, we will *die*.' He met her gaze with a savage challenge. 'Knowing Malorn's fate, as we now do, neither of us can delude ourselves that there could be any other future for me and Calliope. So whatever I might feel, whatever I might want, I will send her back to the home where she belongs and forget that this – this *aberration* ever happened. That's the only solution. For all our sakes.'

There was a long pause. Then Selethe said:

'It's not the only solution, Charn.'

His head came up sharply and he stared at her. She smiled, and the smile was suddenly hesitant.

'There could be a way for you. The way that it seems Malorn intended to take.'

Charn's pewter-coloured eyes narrowed. 'No, lady – oh, *no*. Not *that*.'

'Listen to me!' Selethe snatched hold of his left hand before the denial could become more vehement; he tried to pull away but she clung on, squeezing with all her strength. 'Charn, I beg you, *listen* before you reject what I'm saying out of hand! The words are in Griette's own writings. *The Sacrament*. Malorn must have meant to try, Charn! He planned to take the Sacrament of Night – and if he had succeeded—'

'But he did *not* succeed!' Wrenching his hand free at last Charn jackknifed to his feet and swung away from her. 'Malorn failed, my lady, and he *died*!'

'He failed because, at the last, Griette did not have the courage to take that irrevocable step!' Selethe retaliated. 'You heard her words, Charn, you *heard* them! But Calliope is different!' She sucked in breath and her voice modulated. 'If she were given the choice, I believe she would be willing – and I believe she is strong enough to give what the Sacrament demands.'

She was standing behind Charn now, fists clenched, willing him with all her power to pay heed to her. For several seconds Charn stayed motionless, then, slowly, he turned to face her. His shoulders were sagging with weariness or defeat or both, and his face looked haggard.

'Madam,' he said, 'I understand what you're trying to do . . .

but I must ask you, *please* not to cling to this vain hope.' He closed his eyes and pinched the bridge of his nose, trying to banish the pain of the throbbing pulse in his head. 'Even if Malorn's woman had not lost her courage, what chance is there that the bid would have succeeded? Oh, we know what the Sacrament is said to do, and we know how it must be performed. But beyond that . . .' His hand fell to his side and he looked at Selethe again. 'We understand nothing of its true purpose or nature. Where and how it originated is a closed mystery to us, and though we *believe* that it can work, we cannot be *sure*, for no one in living memory has ever put it to the test.'

'There are stories,' Selethe said gently. 'In the past . . .'

'There are stories, yes. But they may be nothing more than legend – or wishful thinking.' His mouth contorted for a moment before he wrenched himself back under control. 'No, my lady, no; I will *not* consider it. Not under any circumstances. It's a mirage, a treacherous lure and an illusory hope. I won't expose Calliope to such a deadly risk!'

'Shouldn't Calliope be allowed to choose for herself?' Selethe asked quietly.

He shook his head forcefully. 'No, madam, she should not! How could she choose wisely, when she knows nothing of what the Sacrament entails? How could either of us choose, when no one in our world or hers can say with any certainty what it might lead to and what we might become?'

'Malorn was willing,' said Selethe.

'I am not Malorn. Perhaps I don't love Calliope as he loved Griette.' Charn shrugged. 'So be it.'

His tone, his manner, everything about him, told Selethe that the careless words were a sham; but she also knew that to argue any further would be hopeless. Maybe she was deluding herself. Maybe in truth she had no more faith in the Sacrament than he did, but was unconsciously using him in a pitiful, selfish effort to revive the snuffed spark of her own hopes and dreams. If that was so, it was an evil thing to do, and with a sudden sense of shame she drew back from him, turning away so that her face could not betray her thoughts.

'I'm sorry,' she said in a low voice. 'This was wrong of me; I should not have tried to . . . to meddle.' She clasped her hands, crushing her knuckles together. 'Please, forgive me.'

213

'There's nothing to forgive.'

But there was, Selethe thought. And yet . . .

'It will be for the best, I think, if Calliope leaves as soon as possible.' She made herself say the words before temptation could overcome her again. 'There's no reason, is there, to delay?'

'None.' Charn's voice was level.

'Then if you can bring yourself . . . oh, Charn, at least say goodbye to her! At least do that, for me if not for yourself!'

Her back was still towards him but she could imagine his expression and she shut her eyes against the image. There was a pause, then at last he said, 'Very well, my lady. For you.'

And for her, Selethe thought unhappily. *Poor child . . . poor child.*

'I will send her through the gateway myself,' she said. 'It seems right, somehow.' With an effort she straightened her shoulders. 'Go to her now. Make your farewells, and when she is ready let her come to me here.'

Charn did not answer, but she sensed him moving toward her and then a hand came to rest lightly on her shoulder. He kissed the crown of her head, once and gently, as a son might salute a mother, then she heard him go out of the room.

Selethe moved to the couch, sat down and stared into the fire's silver flames. She had done all she could; though perhaps for all her good intentions she had only brought unnecessary pain. But she had had to try, for to let Calliope go without some kindness, some word of comfort and understanding from Charn, would have been crueller still. She had made that bitter mistake once, and it was possible that Malorn had died because of it. He had never told her of his resolution to take the Sacrament of Night. Through her stubbornness she had lost his trust, and he had not dared to confide in her. If he had, and if she had been willing to understand and to help him, then that terrible, irrevocable step into the unknown might – just might – have been the saving of him and of Griette.

But what was done was done. Facts, as Charn said, could not he changed by wishing. Malorn's life was ended, and Griette's life was broken, and Charn and Calliope must go their separate ways and try, in time, to forget. Shrouded in her thoughts, Selethe continued to gaze into the fire and wondered what it was like to be able to cry.

Calliope said, 'Your cloak. No doubt you'll have need of it.'

Charn shook his head. 'No. Keep it, if you wish to.'

She hesitated with her hand at her throat, then quickly, as though fearing she might change her mind, loosened the fastening and slipped the cloak from her shoulders. 'I think it will be better if I take nothing back with me.' The expression in her eyes was masked by half-lowered lashes; she held the garment out, watched him take it and tried not to speculate on the reason for his reluctance. She was dressed now only in her own clothes, and the room felt wintrily cold.

'Did the queen persuade you to come?' she asked him. The question discomfited Charn; he didn't answer immediately, and suddenly Calliope's lashes flicked open and she gave him a startlingly candid look. 'There's no need to pretend that you're here of your own will, Charn; not unless it's true. I'd rather you didn't demean me by pretending.'

She wanted the truth; very well, Charn thought savagely, she should have it. 'Queen Selethe does want me to say goodbye, yes,' he replied. 'But I wanted to see you, Calliope. So the choice was mine.'

She nodded quickly, nervously. 'I suppose I should be comforted by that, shouldn't I?'

He made an odd, almost disparaging sound. 'I see little comfort in it for either of us. It seems . . . pointless. A formality.'

'Yes. Well, then . . . perhaps we should seal it formally.' She smiled brittly, unconvincingly. 'In my world, when people make their farewells they shake hands, or – or kiss. But that wouldn't be appropriate for us, would it? We must think of something . . .' Her voice started to quaver. 'Something else, and . . . and . . .' Then suddenly the words cracked and collapsed, and Calliope put a clenched fist against her mouth, shutting her eyes as the emotion she had been trying to repress came shattering through her defences. '*Oh, Charn, Charn, I don't want to go!*'

It was the reaction Charn had dreaded above all else, and he swung away from her as he felt the ramparts he had built against his own feelings starting to crumble. Unbidden, unlooked-for, a fierce imprecation broke from his lips; the anger was directed at himself, but Calliope, her passions overstrung almost to breaking point, misinterpreted.

'I'm *sorry*!' She choked the words out bitterly. 'But I don't care any more; I don't *care* if it discomforts you to hear the truth!' For the first and only time, she told herself with the miserable defiance of desperation, she would not be cowed by his disdain! This was the last chance she would ever have to tell him what she wanted to say and bring it into the open – if she let the moment slip away from her she would condemn herself to a lifetime's regret. She didn't want that. She would be unable to *bear* it.

'I know you care nothing for me,' she went on, her voice low but painfully intense. 'Not in any way that matters. But for me it's different, and I'm not going to hide it any longer!'

'Calliope—' Charn started to turn towards her but she interrupted him.

'*No*. I *will* speak. I know I must go. I know that I couldn't stay here and survive. But leaving you is going to break my heart, Charn!' She hugged herself, gripping her own upper arms as though she wanted to bruise them to the bone. 'Why should I spare you by saying nothing, or pretending that I don't feel what I do? I didn't want this to happen – it was the *last* thing I wanted; because it's crazed and futile and it *hurts*! But it's happened, and there's nothing I can do to change it.' Her head turned quickly and she stared, almost glared, at him through the strands of her hair. 'For what small satisfaction it might give you, you've gained a hold over me that no one has ever done before – or will ever do again!'

Tight-lipped, chest constricting, Charn said, 'It gives me no satisfaction whatever, Calliope. Why do you think it should?'

'Oh yes; why do I.' She laughed, and the laughter had a grotesque edge. 'How could I possibly imagine that it has the slightest effect on you for good or ill? What a *very* foolish mistake. I must be more naive even than—'

'Calliope!' Charn said ferociously. 'In the name of all that's cherished, *stop* this!'

He cut through her flow of words and momentarily silenced her. But before he could say any more – and his own defences were caving in, self-control teetering – she flared at him again. 'Why should I stop it, Charn? Why *should* I?'

Her challenge smashed Charn's last bastions, and he fired back, 'Because I too have feelings, and they're no different from yours!'

216

Calliope froze. For several seconds she stood absolutely motionless, and then, as her mind finally took in what he had said, a blend of devastating emotions – shock, anguish, disbelief – brimmed in her eyes.

'Don't play games with me,' she whispered. '*Don't.*'

'This is no game!' Charn's heart was pounding under his ribs as his raw emotions coalesced into a kind of helpless fury. 'Don't you understand what I'm trying to tell you, trying to *show* you? You say you didn't want this to happen. Well, neither did I – but it seems we've both been too witless or too weak to prevent ourselves from falling prey to it!' He looked at her stark expression, aware that she must be seeing its match in his own face. 'I can't control what I feel any better than you can, Calliope. I'm just more skilled at hiding it.'

She said falteringly, 'That's why you were so cold towards me.'

'If that's how you interpret my behaviour, yes. Although I have a different term for it, and that term is self-defence. But whatever fine words we choose, the purpose behind it was straightforward enough.' Charn's hands flexed; there was an ache in him, burning in him, and he wanted to give rein to it. But that was impossible. 'Do you want to know why I behaved as I did?' he demanded. 'Shall I tell you? Look!' He held his hands angrily towards her, the palms upturned. 'If I were to touch you, ungloved, I would injure you! Even now, at our last meeting, we can't have so much as *that* small token by which to remember each other! So answer me, tell me if you can, what would have been the *point* of showing what I feel?'

'Charn—' Calliope started forward, reaching out to him, but before their fingers could connect he pulled quickly back.

'Don't, Calli!' For the very first time he used the diminutive of her name; it touched and yet hurt her and she flinched, seeming to shrink in on herself. More gently, Charn continued, 'It would only harm both of us to no purpose. We can't hope for anything; you must know that, even if you don't want to accept it. There's no future for us and we have to go our separate ways. The alternative . . .' He paused, then forced himself to say it. 'The alternative is to have no future at all. Like Malorn and your mother.'

Even though her time in this world had stolen so much of the colour from her, he still detected the flush that came to her cheeks in response. Ignoring it (for he had to, and it was a skill he had learned well over the years) he hardened his resolve.

'I'm sorry. Those were harsh words and I didn't say them to hurt you. But it's the truth.' Another pause, longer this time. 'If we tried to stay together, as they did, one or both of us would die. What would that achieve? It's better that we part, and try to forget—'

'I won't forget!'

He sighed. 'All right. In truth neither will I.' A pause. 'I suppose that frightens me.'

She nodded, calmer after the momentary outburst, and in a tangled way grateful that he was honest enough to admit his weakness. 'It frightens me too, Charn,' she said. 'But yes; you're right and I can't deny it. So . . .' A sniff; she wiped the back of one hand across her eyes with a quick, undisciplined movement, then appeared to collect herself. 'We can at least pretend, can't we? Pretend that we'll forget. Who knows; it might work.' *Don't say that time heals, Charn. Don't say it, don't, don't . . .*

Charn didn't, nor thought it. He only continued to gaze at her, until, fearing that something inside her would implode if she didn't break the silence, she flicked her hair back and said in a good approximation of her normal voice, 'We ought to be formal and civilised. That would be for the best, wouldn't it?'

'Perhaps, yes. For the safest, anyway.' Then, seeing something in her eyes that he felt he had no right to intrude on, he looked down at the floor. 'I should leave you now. Drawing this out; it's . . .'

'Pointless. Like all the rest.' Her face contorted with a brief, humourless mockery of a smile. *Say it,* she told herself savagely. *Say the word. Let him go, once and for all.*

'Good . . .' The word stuck in her throat half uttered, and it took all her strength of will to force the obstruction of it down. At last, though: 'Goodbye, Charn. I . . .' *love you.* But that wouldn't come. No matter. He knew it, and to speak it aloud would only hurt them both. *Pointless.*

It would have been safe enough, Charn knew, to hug her, just briefly and taking care that their faces or hands did not touch. But he made no move, and neither did she. He said quietly, 'Good luck.'

'And to you.' *Inane response.* 'That is . . .'

'Yes. I know.'

She pressed her hands together and touched them to her mouth, letting out breath slowly through latticed fingers. 'Please go now. *Please*.'

He hesitated, then nodded. He felt as if something inside him had shut down and would never be reawoken. 'Goodbye, Calli.'

Though his feet and the door made no sound, and her eyes were closed, she knew when he was no longer in the room.

One look at Calliope's face told Selethe the story that no words would ever reveal. Dark shadows, sunken cheeks, her eyes scarlet-rimmed . . . she was making a brave effort to appear composed, but to the queen's acute senses her inner turmoil was a storm on the verge of breaking. Selethe's conscience was rebelling. She had sworn to Charn that she would keep the secret, not let slip even the smallest clue that might give Calliope false hope; but to see her like this, bereft, almost bereaved, tore at Selethe's heart.

No, she told herself, *no*. Charn was right: to tell Calliope of the Sacrament would be a cruel injustice. The hazards were too great for the risk to be taken. She would be playing with Calliope's life, and that she had no right to do. Let it rest, she thought. Let it be put aside and forgotten.

Calliope was waiting. All that needed to be said had been said, and tomorrow, when the sun rose in her world (Selethe had tried so hard to imagine what daylight must be like, but the enormity of it defeated her and she wished, only *wished*, that she could see it for herself) her search for the long-lost key would begin. Calliope knew, now, the nature of what she sought. So small, so apparently insignificant . . . and, she believed, still vouchsafed in Griette's keeping. The finding and the taking of it would not be easy, but Selethe had faith that it would, with time and care, be done. She trusted Calliope – and wished with all her heart that she could have given her more than mere thanks and gratitude in return.

So, then: the fond farewell was made and this was the moment of parting. In the tiny chamber she had chosen Selethe spoke softly to the air, and the light, already sombre, began to dim. She saw Calliope stir restlessly, a silhouette among shadows, and said, 'Don't fear the dark.'

'I'm not afraid, madam. Only . . .' But that was something private and she did not finish. Knowing what had been left unsaid

Selethe thought recklessly, *Tell her!* but, again, quashed the impulse.

The last faint gleam faded and died, and darkness was complete. Selethe had opened the gateway for others on so many occasions, but suddenly, for the first time, she felt a flicker of yearning. Just to *glimpse* that bright world; just to peep in and *see* . . .

She tried to crush the impulse in her. Calliope would enter her world from the point whence she had left it; in the blackness of the cellar beneath her home. It sounded to Selethe like a dismal and dreary choice, but Charn had said it was by far the safest. It was harder to visualise a particular location and create the gateway there than it was to simply allow the portal to open at random, as most who made the journey did; but Charn had forged the link with the cellar once, and had schooled the queen carefully until the picture in her mind's eye was clear. Safest. Dreary, but safest. There was nothing there for her, Selethe told herself, and hardened her resolve.

'Good fortune go with you, my dear, dear child.' In the blackness she opened her mind, opened the path, felt the shift and the mutation as the currents of dimensions subtly altered their flow. There was a scent, heady, sweet; the scent of flowers; and with one hand Selethe made a gentle gesture. 'Turn,' she said, her voice as soft as a breath.

Calliope turned. Without drama or tumult she was gone, leaving only the scent and a still, profound silence. Selethe raised her hand again to make the sign that would close the portal.

And paused as bitter regret rose like a surge-tide in her mind. No right, she had told herself. No *right* to tell Calliope the truth, for she could not choose wisely. But those were Charn's words, not her own, and suddenly Selethe could no longer believe them. Calliope's choices were not Charn's to make, and her future was not his to ordain. The right of it was hers and hers alone, just as it had been Malorn's so long ago.

She saw Calliope's face again in her inner vision. Such grief . . . It was an emotion Selethe understood only too well, and she knew that it would never truly be assuaged unless the spark of hope could be kept alive. She herself had nurtured that spark all through the years of Malorn's absence, and it had sustained her when all else had lost its meaning. Now though, the spark had finally been extinguished, and with it had gone the last remnant of purpose in her life. She was an empty shell. For her it did not matter, for she was old now and her life was moving quietly towards its natural end. But Calliope's life lay before her. Or should.

The war in her suddenly came to a climax. Charn's words; her own arguments. She had *promised* him. But. *But.* Then, in her mind, she saw another face, and the question formed: what would Malorn have said? What would Malorn have done?

Selethe knew the answer, and it crystallised everything. She breathed in. The perfume was still strong, and she could feel the faint vibration of the way between worlds, still open, still waiting. How long might it take? Minutes only; that was all she would need, and Calliope's spark of hope could be rekindled. Charn would not know; indeed, no one would know, for she had given instructions that she was to be left undisturbed until she should send word. Minutes. For the sake of a life.

Selethe glanced over her shoulder, guiltily, as though expecting to find that she was observed. How foolish of her: in utter darkness how could there be a watcher? She smiled to herself, and a small, piquant shiver went through her at the incidental thought that she would see the bright world for herself, just once, just once.

She closed her eyes, savouring her excitement.

Then stepped into the gateway.

Chapter XVIII

It had not been an agreeable time for anyone in the Agate household. The messenger from the twilight world had returned as promised to collect Foss's reply, and after its departure Foss and Nempson had sat discussing their strategy over the brandy bottle until they were interrupted by a distraught Philome, who berated them both for their selfishness in failing to bring her news. Foss and Philome had quarrelled tempestuously enough to bring Celesta hurrying to the commotion, then as Nempson made to retreat tactfully from the scene of battle Luthe came home and, bolstered by drink, made a sardonic comment that turned the full might of Foss's wrath on him. The rumpus abated eventually and they had all retired; but no one slept well, if at all, and the atmosphere the following morning was highly uncomfortable.

Tension, of course, was at the root of it, amplified by a sense of helplessness that put Foss in particular on a knife edge. Never patient at the best of times, he was now like a simmering volcano only awaiting the smallest excuse to erupt. Celesta and Luthe took good care to go unseen and unheard about the house, and even Tobery and Diona seemed anxious to avoid him. Philome spent most of the day in bed with a diplomatic headache, so it was left to Nempson to make the best he could of the situation. By lunchtime Foss's precarious temper had improved a little, but the respite was not destined to last, and as the late dusk closed in there was more trouble. This time the arena was the kitchen. The family had sat down to dinner and Foss decided to use, almost for the first time, the innovative but unreliable bell-rope to announce that they were ready to be served. No answer came, and after ringing three times Foss stormed downstairs with Philome and a reluctant but obligated Nempson at his heels. Without giving the servants a chance to explain that the bell had not sounded in the kitchen, he berated them for their lazy incompetence in such terms that within minutes they were threatening to leave their posts on the spot. Philome, struggling to make herself heard, was just pleading, 'Can we not discuss this *reasonably*?' when from outside came an extraordinary sound that cut through the altercation as she had been unable to do. Voices tailed off, and everyone looked towards the window.

'What by all the stars . . .' Foss began.

Philome licked her lips nervously. 'It sounded like . . .' But then she realised that she did not know what it had sounded like. A door slamming, perhaps. But no door in the world could shut so loudly.

Nempson, thinking of some of the experiments that he and Foss had recently carried out, said uneasily, 'Foss, the workroom . . . Do you think we should—'

He didn't finish the question, for Foss silenced him with a sharp wave of one hand. Then he beckoned. 'There's something moving outside,' he said in a low, hoarse voice. 'By the door of the old cellar.'

Philome gave a muffled little squeal, but Nempson had stepped to Foss's side and was peering through the window glass. 'I see it,' he hissed after a moment.

Foss's mind was running riot with thoughts of the twilight messenger. There were no holds barred now that his letter had been delivered; if the creature or another of its kind had been foolish enough to return, he would not let it elude him this time. He signalled with his eyes towards the door, and Nempson, whose thoughts matched his, nodded. They moved across the floor, ignoring the wide-eyed stares of the now silent servants; Philome put her fingers in her mouth and bit them as she saw Nempson pick up a heavy poker from beside the range. The latch lifted; the door opened – and from outside in the darkness a voice said indistinctly, 'Father . . . ?'

Philome screamed '*Calli!*' and rushed for the door, pushing Foss and Nempson aside in her haste. Calliope stood midway between the house and the cellar entrance. She was unsteady on her feet, and as light from the kitchen spilled over her Philome gave a second cry, this time filled with horror.

'Foss, look at her! She's grey! Oh, Calli—'

Foss said, 'Living spirits!' and ran forward as Calliope swayed suddenly and seemed about to fall. He caught her under the arms, then swore with shock. 'Damn my eyes, the girl's half rigid with cold! Help me, Nempson, quickly!'

Calliope, though, was rallying. The worst of her disorientation was momentary, caused only by the sudden and, to her altered vision, intolerably violent explosion of light as the kitchen door opened. Now that there were hands on her, steadying her (though they were so hot!), she felt at last as if she was coming back to earth.

The transfer through the gate had been swifter and far simpler than she had anticipated, and within moments she had found herself in the dank, foul-smelling cellar, from which she had entered the twilight world. Feeling a wash of nausea as the cellar's stench eclipsed the perfume of white flowers, she had not lingered to find her abandoned lantern but fumbled her way to the inner door and away up the slippery steps to push the outer door open and stumble out into the night before bile could

223

rise in her throat and choke her.

It was then, as she reached the outside world, that the dizziness hit her. She seemed to have no weight, no stability, no *substance* – she was like a sapling in the wind, staggering and tottering and feeling, horribly, as if her body were made of feathers. She clutched for support at the wall of the house, but there was nothing there to grasp; only flat, rough stone that scraped her palms and gave her no purchase. She veered away, her steps carrying her impotently into the middle of the yard; and then the kitchen door opened, and Foss's face looked out, and she had called his name and—

'Calliope!' He was trying to shake her and hug her and look at her all at once, and Philome was there, clasping her arm and sobbing, and in the background was Nempson Trinity and a gaggle of servants— Impressions swarmed in on Calliope and swamped her; she didn't know whether to laugh with relief or cry with misery or scream with confusion or—

Behind her, from the direction of the cellar, came a noise.

It didn't register on her mind at first; or, if it did, it was as nothing; only the door she had left open swinging back on its hinges. But suddenly Foss's hands on her arms convulsed as though with shock. His stare focused beyond her; at his side Philome took a stunned pace backwards.

Calliope turned her head. She took one look at what the others had already seen, and her eyes widened incredulously.

'Madam—'

Selethe, a phantom of black and grey and silver, had emerged from the cellar behind her and stood, stricken, in the yard. Her eyes were vast with bewildered awe; then she saw Calliope and called out to her.

'Calliope . . .' Her voice rang in the air like a thin, fragile bell. 'Oh, Calliope, please help me . . . I did not imagine *this* . . .'

Philome made a dreadful, inarticulate sound, and Foss's eyes bulged. 'By the powers, it's another of those creatures!' His voice rose to a bawl. 'Nempson, catch it! Catch it and bind it, before it can elude us!'

Horror hit Calliope. 'Father, no!' she cried. 'Nempson – don't don't touch her, let her be!' She twisted in Foss's grip, fighting to free her arms. '*Nempson!*'

But Nempson had shouldered past her where she battled

against Foss's hold. He was reaching out, eager, acquisitive—

'*Selethe, go!*' Calliope shrieked. '*Go back, get away from them!*'

'Quiet, girl, quiet!' Foss flung one arm about her and suddenly she was pinned in a wrestler's hug, crushed against him. She heard Selethe's scream of fear and pain and she howled a protest, but Foss was dragging her back towards the house, and though she flailed and kicked and struggled she was no match for his strength, and all the while he was gasping, almost shouting, in her ear: 'Calli, Calli, daughter, it's all right now, it's over, you're safe, you're home, and I'm going to heal you, I'm going to break the spell these demons have put on you and make you well again!'

One frantic effort; just one; she had no strength for more. '*NO,* Father! You don't *understand*—'

Foss hit her. He had never before done such a thing, beyond the occasional slap when she was too young to respond to any other form of discipline. To him, though, an extreme situation called for an extreme remedy, and the blow to the back of her skull was calculated with a physician's knowledge and precision, not to harm but simply to incapacitate her. Calliope felt the strike, felt the rush of blackness coming at her out of nowhere – in a last instant of consciousness she tried to protest, but it was far too late. The blackness engulfed her, the world was blotted out, and she sagged like a sack of flour in Foss's arms.

For a short while there was pandemonium in the house. The servants were alarmed, Philome nearly hysterical, and the commotion, with the terrified Selethe at the heart of it, spilled from the kitchen through to the entrance hall, where the rest of the family arrived to add to the confusion. Foss, his attention torn between Selethe and Calliope, was trying and failing to command both emergencies at once; but as Nempson and the hastily-conscripted Luthe bore the new captive away through the understairs door to the workroom, some order at last began to struggle through the chaos. With only the briefest of distracted glances after Nempson, Foss carried Calliope to her bedroom, while Philome, Celesta and the younger children hurried like a noisy comet-tail behind him. She was stirring when he laid her on the bed; Tobery and Diona were sternly shut out of the room and Celesta was sent running for Foss's medical pack. As her footsteps diminished, Calliope groaned, mumbled something and started to open her eyes.

'Calli!' Philome swooped compassionately and tried to gather Calliope into her arms. 'Oh, my dear – are you all right, are you injured? What did those creatures *do* to you?'

'Leave her, Philome!' Foss said sharply. He was pulling the sashes from two of Calliope's dressing-robes, and as he came back with them to the bedside he caught Philome's arm and drew her away. 'Don't touch her!'

He bent over the bed. Calliope murmured groggily, 'Father . . .?' and Philome's face registered shock as she saw what her husband was doing. 'Foss! Dear spirits, you're surely not going to *tie* her?'

'Father?' Philome's words had registered and Calliope's voice was suddenly stronger. 'Father, what are you doing . . .?'

'It's for your own good, Calli.' Foss had tied the sashes around her wrists and was now lashing them firmly to the bed frame. 'Don't question me – you're in no fit state, and nor will you be until I've cured you of the evil influence that's infected you!'

'*What?*' Convulsively Calliope tried to sit up and found she could not. Her eyes, their dazed look rapidly clearing, focused wildly on Foss's face. 'Father, what are you talking about? I'm not under any influence! Stop this; untie me – *Father!*'

Foss ignored her. 'Where's that wretched girl with my pack?' he demanded through clenched teeth, then raised his head and shouted towards the door, 'Celesta!'

'Foss,' Philome pleaded, 'this surely isn't necessary! Calli's ill, and—'

'Which is precisely why she must be restrained!' Foss interrupted. He was breathless. 'It's not just a malaise of the body, Philome; her mind has been warped by these creatures, and for her own safety she must be protected! Help me now; fetch another cord and we shall bind her ankles so she can't struggle and injure herself.'

Calliope cried, 'Father, *no!* Please, listen to me, you have to listen!'

'Now, daughter, be calm,' Foss told her sternly. 'I know what's for the best, and you must trust me.'

'But you promised – in your letter, you gave your word not to interfere!' She pulled again, ineffectually, at the cords, then suddenly a mixture of panic and real fury flowered in her face. 'Father, untie me!' Her voice rose wildly and she started to writhe on the bed. 'Untie me, now, *now! You can't imprison me like this; I won't allow it! FATHER!!*'

Celesta heard the screaming from the landing, and burst into the room to find Foss and Philome wrestling with a shrieking, threshing Calliope. Foss shouted, 'Insensator pad – in the lacquered box – hurry, girl, *hurry!*' Celesta fumbled in the pack, thrust the box into his hand and he snatched the pad from it. An acrid smell sharpened the air, and Philome jerked back, turning her head aside to avoid the fumes as Foss pressed the pad over Calliope's mouth. Her cries were muffled; belatedly she realised what he was doing and tried to resist. But the anaesthetic worked fast; already her eyes were watering, and the smell in her nostrils was impossible to escape. There was vagueness, dizziness, a fog spreading through her mind . . .

Her body went limp and she sagged among the pillows as though gently and naturally falling asleep. Philome, pink-faced and dishevelled, let out breath in a gasp of relief and Foss put the pad away.

'Open the window,' he told Celesta, and coughed, waving away the lingering stink. Celesta obeyed, then they all stood looking down at Calliope.

'What is it, Father?' Celesta whispered. 'What's wrong with her?'

A full explanation would take time, Foss thought, and he had other priorities. 'She has been harmed by these twilight creatures,' he said. 'She can be cured, but we must all take the greatest care. Which means,' he turned a severe gaze on her, 'that no one must come near her, at any time, without my express permission. No matter what happens, no matter what the circumstances, you are to stay *out* of this room until and unless I tell you otherwise. Do you understand, Celesta?'

Celesta's rebellious instincts had vanished in the wake of this, and she nodded soberly. 'Yes, Father.'

'The same rule will apply to Luthe, to the little ones and to the servants. I shall rely on you to help me enforce it.'

Celesta's gaze flicked to Calliope again. 'Yes, Father.'

'Very well. Go downstairs now, and convey my instructions to the rest of the household. Then see that Tobery and Diona have some supper, and put them to bed.'

She didn't argue, only gave her sister a last, frightened glance and left the room.

Foss put his medical pack on Calliope's table and began to search in it. Philome sat down on the bed and took one of Calliope's hands, anxiously stroking her fingers; seeing it, he said, 'We must bind her more securely. And I shall prepare a draught to ensure that she remains quiet at least until morning. That will give me time to examine her more thoroughly and decide how best to begin her cure.'

Philome nodded. She had as yet only the barest grasp of all that had happened but was only too glad to put her trust in her husband's wisdom, for it was the one rock of sanity in a world gone suddenly mad.

'*Can* you cure her, Foss?' she asked. 'She looks so *dreadfully* thin and frail; I can hardly dare believe that she'll ever recover.'

Foss privately reflected that there had been nothing frail about Calliope's struggles of a few minutes ago. That, though, was doubtless part of the evil inflicted on her; and something to bear in mind when he began his treatment. Aloud, he said, 'Oh, she'll recover, my dear. Rest assured. She just needs a little time, that's all.'

'What of that . . . that thing; the female that came after her . . .' Philome shivered.

'Don't worry about it. Nempson knows what to do; by now it will be safely confined in my workroom and no danger to anyone.'

'Yes. Yes, of course.' She tried to feel reassured. 'But why did it come, Foss? Why did it follow Calli?'

'It's my suspicion,' Foss said, 'that it intended to spy on her, or perhaps even to continue exerting control over her. I also think that it did not mean to reveal its presence. That was a grave mistake on its part – and a piece of good fortune for us.'

'It called Calli by name,' Philome remembered. 'And she called it "madam". As if it was *human*.'

'So I heard.' That could be a very valuable clue, Foss thought. His fingers twitched and he flexed them, feeling the stirrings of impatience and excitement. Nempson would do nothing without him, of course, but this new prize had much to yield.

'Foss,' Philome said, 'if what you say is true – if the creature does have some control over Calli – then to have it in the house is surely dangerous? What if it can . . .' she waved her hands indecisively, searching for the right word but unable to find it '. . . if it can *do* things to her, at a distance?'

'We'll take all precautions to see that it can't,' Foss told her reassuringly. 'Now, Philome, stop fretting. I shall mix a draught for Calli, then you may help me settle her and we'll leave her to sleep while Nempson and I begin our work.'

'Your work?'

'On the twilight creature. I doubt I'll see my bed tonight, but you mustn't mind that.'

From sheer habit Philome's mind filled with small caveats about lateness, tiredness, the uneaten dinner; but she pushed them resolutely away. This was *important*.

'I'll sit with Calli,' she said in a small voice. 'At least I can do that.'

'As you please, my dear; although she won't wake again tonight. Now: fetch me a glass, if you will, and some water, and we'll see about making her more comfortable and more secure.'

'Please . . .' Selethe twisted in the chair, her head turning from side to side as she strove to escape the agony of the restraints. 'Please . . . I do not understand . . .' Sweat streaked her face, mingling with the tears of pain and fear that ran in rivulets down her cheeks. 'I am not your enemy . . . Oh please, where is Calliope, let me talk to Calliope . . .'

Foss, his face lit harshly by the etherea lamp which had been turned to full strength, watched her impotent and increasingly feeble exertions with concentrated interest. Behind him at the workroom table, Nempson was preparing a piece of apparatus; the rectangular brass frame was in place now, together with the cylinder of glass prisms, and Nempson was carefully slotting into place two perforated discs, one of zinc and the other of silver. As yet neither man had addressed a word to the captive; for the moment they were content merely to listen and to monitor. Most of her utterances so far had been no more than confused and incoherent protests interspersed with pleas to see Calliope, but among the ramblings she had revealed her name and the fact that she held a high position in whatever peculiar and alien hierarchy pervaded the twilight world, though her exact status was unclear. That excited Foss, for it suggested that she had been one of the prime movers behind Calliope's corruption. He looked forward to the moment when she would be fit for a proper interrogation to begin – and when it did, he had some new methods in mind to ensure that she co-operated more readily than Charn had ever done.

Their observations so far had confirmed a few small but useful facts. Like Charn, the new captive could not bear bright light, and contact with many everyday substances, including metal, seared her skin. Further experiments would be made as a matter of routine, but it seemed likely that the two creatures were similar enough in essence for the men to make some basic assumptions about Selethe and proceed accordingly. There were, however, precautions to be taken that Foss considered vital, and he looked over his shoulder to where Nempson was now completing the apparatus. In the glow from the etherea lamp the twin discs had a dull and faintly ominous patina, and a reflection from their surfaces was mirrored in Nempson's eyes as he glanced up.

'It's ready,' he said.

'Good.' Foss looked at Selethe again. She had fallen silent; her eyes were closed, her head lolled and she seemed to have slipped into semi-consciousness. That was to their advantage; while he had reasonable faith in the device they were about to use, its efficacy could not be absolutely guaranteed, and where Calliope's safety was concerned he intended to take no chances.

He checked that Nempson had aligned the device accurately, then between them they manoeuvred the etherea lamp until it stood directly behind the machine, where its light shone through the slots in the discs. Two handles protruded from the device's base; at a nod Nempson turned one, while Foss grasped and spun the other. The discs and the glass prisms began to revolve, slowly at first but rapidly gathering momentum, until the patterns of lamplight blurred together into a bizarre, flickering glimmer that danced across Selethe's form slumped in the chair. Selethe stirred as though in the throes of a nightmare and uttered a thin, piteous whimper. But she did not wake.

'I think we can safely leave the creature unattended for a few hours,' Foss said. 'The metaphysical inhibitor will block any influence its mind might still be trying to exert over Calliope, and should help to weaken its resistance into the bargain.'

The apparatus was humming faintly as the discs and prisms

continued to spin. Once wound up to its full speed the momentum would keep it operating for five or six hours. Gently, Nempson released his hold on the handle, then, careful to avoid crossing and breaking the light beam, he moved round the table and the two men left the room.

'I told Philome to set us a cold supper in the library,' Foss said as the door closed behind them.

'That will be welcome.' Nempson flexed his shoulders to ease weary stiffness. 'Philome's abed, I expect?'

'No, she's sitting up with Calli tonight. Nothing she can do, of course, but it makes her more contented in mind.'

They emerged into the hall, where a lamp had been left burning, and as Foss extinguished his pocket-taper Nempson said, 'Touching on Calliope . . .' He still felt it would be a liberty for him to use the diminutive of her name. 'Do you think you *can* undo the damage these creatures have wrought on her mind?'

'I'm as certain as it's possible to be.' Then Foss frowned. 'Providing, of course, that it hasn't gone too far. The human brain is a very singular mechanism, Nempson, and I'll confess freely to you that even as a physician I don't claim to understand all of its workings. I could cite cases . . . but that's by the by. In this instance, however, I'm confident that the disorder can be repaired. Calli is at least lucid, if not rational; that's an excellent sign. And she's a strong, sensible girl. I believe that once I can get through to her and make her comprehend the fact that she *has* been put under a compulsion, her own willpower will rally in her favour. She'll *want* to be cured; and that, as with any disease, is half the battle.'

They walked on towards the library. Above them, the stairs rose away into gloom and then darkness; Nempson looked up and thought of Calliope confined in her bed with Philome watching over her. The feelings of anger and outrage that had been simmering in him since Calliope's disappearance rekindled, and with them came a desire for vengeance. Not so much on Selethe, though if she had been instrumental in this then she too deserved fitting punishment, but on the other being, the one whose face was etched indelibly in his memory and for whom grim, smouldering hatred burned in him like a slow fire. Foss, he knew, shared that hatred. But Foss was Calliope's father, and however deep his feelings ran they did not, could not, encompass the furious ache of jealousy. This was *different*.

'Nempson?' Foss had opened the library door and was waiting for him. Nempson blinked as his thoughts spiralled back to earth.

'Your pardon – I was distracted for a moment.' Another glance towards the stairs. 'In the morning, perhaps you'll permit me to see Calliope? There might be something I can do to assist . . .'

'Of course.' Foss gave him a look that mixed sympathy, approval and reassurance. 'I'll appreciate your help, my friend. And so will she when she recovers her proper senses. Depend on it; so will she.'

Chapter XIX

With the impromptu supper finished, Nempson dozed off in one of the library's more comfortable chairs. Foss, though, had no thought of sleep, and after checking that the captive was still insensible and the metaphysical inhibitor still operating, he went to Calliope's room, gently roused Philome who had dozed off at the bedside, and told her that he would relieve her until dawn. Gratitude overcame Philome's guilt and she retired sleepily to her own bed, leaving the way clear for Foss to do what must be done without question or objection from any observer.

Calliope was still oblivious to the world. Knowing the nature of the narcotic that he and Philome had earlier eased down her throat, Foss doubted if she was capable even of dreaming. She looked very peaceful, but the greyness of her skin and hair gave the lie to any impression of normality. It was grotesque, Foss thought. And – though he had not been so tactless as to say anything to Nempson on the subject – he had a very unpleasant suspicion as to the cause of it.

That fear, at least, proved groundless, for an intimate examination of Calliope showed that she was still a virgin. Foss's relief was profound: aside of the implications for her proposed marriage, any congress with a twilight creature (and he had no need to speculate on which one) could have had far more obvious and alarming consequences. On a detached level it occurred to him that the possibilities of interbreeding between alien races might be a subject for valuable experiment in the future, but for now he felt only gratitude that he would not be forced to deal with the reality of it under his own roof.

He then turned his attention to the question of the cure. Though Calliope was physically safe from outside interference or attack, her mind was quite another matter. Until the thrall on her could be broken she was a danger to herself, and must be treated accordingly. Foss replaced the makeshift dressing-robe bonds with rope restraints, tying Calliope by her wrists and ankles to the four corners of the bed frame. She would be able to change her position as comfort demanded, but any further movement was impossible. Then from his medical pack he took a bundle of fine copper wires, knotted together into a filigree net, and placed it carefully over Calliope's skull, looping her hair up beneath it. Copper was the finest known conductor of the brain's effervescences and helped to expel harmful influences in the psyche; this treatment, combined with controlled and administered doses of certain drugs, would speed the elimination of Calliope's sickness and, he judged, return her to her normal self within a few days. Calliope would of course resist the treatment at first, and it was possible that in the early stages before recovery began her protests would become violent. Hence the need for restraint; unfortunate, but the misfortune would be greater if she should break free and possibly do mischief to herself or someone else before her reasoning powers were restored.

Calliope began to wake from her stupor as Foss completed his preparations. She stirred in the bed, mumbled an inarticulate query, then started to struggle feebly as her mind and body reacted with vague but instinctive fear to the presence of the ropes and the copper net. Foss made soothing noises, at the same time turning to his pack and fetching out two phials and an oilskin pouch. He mixed the draught he wanted into a beaker of water, and as he took it back to the bed Calliope's eyelids fluttered open.

'Father . . . ?' She couldn't yet focus on anything in the room. 'Wh . . . what time is it . . . ?'

'It wants two hours to dawn,' Foss told her.

'To dawn . . .' She frowned. Her mind wasn't yet functioning and memory was elusive. She knew that she was at home, in her

233

own bed, and that was normal, reassuring. But there was a feeling in her, a conviction, that an interval of time had become misaligned or even mislaid.

'Where did I . . .' she began; but couldn't find the words to finish her question.

Foss patted her hand, forcing himself not to recoil at the coldness of her flesh. 'You've been ill, Calli,' he said pacifyingly. 'But you are beginning to recover, now that you're back safe with us.'

Back? Then there *had* been a hiatus. Minutes? Hours? Days? She couldn't *remember*.

'I can't think . . . can't clear my mind . . .' She tried suddenly to rub at her eyes as confusion and frustration combined. Her hands jerked against the ropes that bound them; for a moment she froze, staring at Foss in bemusement. Then: 'Father, what have you done to me? I can't move. *I can't move!*'

'Hush, daughter, be calm! There's nothing to be afraid of; it's simply a precaution and will do you no harm. Here, now; I've prepared something for you to drink, and you must take it to please me.' He held a beaker to her lips and was gratified to see her obey him without question. Half the nostrum went down, then she said, 'My throat . . . so *dry* . . .'

'This will ease it. More, now. Drink it all, like a good child.'

Good child . . . she had always been a good child. Until . . .

Then memory came back. Calliope's eyes opened wide, and her face contorted into a look of appalled horror. 'Oh no, you can't, it isn't – *Father, what have you done?*' She fought with all her strength against the bonds, and her voice rose to a shrill scream of panic. '*Where is she, what have you done with her? Father, untie me! UNTIE ME!*'

The bout of screaming, spitting, pleading hysteria that consumed Calliope during the ensuing minutes was deeply painful to witness. The insensator pad could not be used in combination with the new drugs Foss had given her, and he was forced to muffle her shrieks as best he could, lest she should wake the entire household. Eventually though the dosage took effect, and Foss, unkempt and sweating, stepped back from the bed as Calliope at last sank into complete and helpless unconsciousness. His face was grim, for although this reaction was only to be expected at such an early stage, it had nonetheless been more

234

extreme than he had hoped. Clearly it could not be allowed to recur, or her recuperation would suffer a serious setback. Time was the key, he thought. Time for the copper net to do its work of dissipation; time for the malignancy to be eclipsed by the cool, clear balm of Calliope's natural reasoning powers. Until they could come into play she must be kept senseless. It was frustrating, but it was the only safe and sensible course.

He sighed a sigh in which concern and irritation vied for precedence, then looked towards the window. The first watery signs of dawn were showing – he and Nempson must have spent longer in the library than he had realised – and footsteps and a distant sound of hooves outside suggested that the world was waking up. The servants would be about soon. If he woke Nempson and ordered an early breakfast for them both, no precious time need be wasted. He had done all he could for Calliope, and until this first and drastic stage of her recovery was over they would elicit nothing of any use from her. Downstairs, though, was another potential source of information. They had not planned to begin the interrogation until the captive had had a little longer to resign herself to her new situation and become tractable, but that, perhaps, was taking unnecessary pains. Foss suspected that Selethe could be coerced to talk without too much difficulty. And if verbal coercion failed, there were other methods in plenty.

He paused for a final, professional scrutiny of Calliope's inert form in the bed. Best not to allow anyone else to see her today. Celesta would ask too many foolish questions, and Philome would be distressed by the precautions he had taken and doubtless argue about them. He would tend her himself, and order that a proper quarantine was to be observed until he gave further word. This evening, when she woke from the narcotic, he would see how the land lay.

Satisfied, Foss left the room, locked the door behind him and pocketed the key before making his way downstairs to wake Nempson.

No one had seen Charn, or dared disturb him, since Calliope's departure. For many at the twilight court his absence was not unwelcome. But Thimue, who had a deeper understanding of and sympathy for Charn than most, decided at last that the taboo should be broken, and took it on himself to make the first move.

He found Charn alone and uncommunicative, both of which he had expected. No light and no fire burned in his quarters; he was simply sitting in the cheerless dark, and acknowledged the old physician with a glacial politeness that made it clear the intrusion was unwelcome. The tactic did not work with Thimue, who had never been daunted by Charn's manner. He sat down, uninvited, and after a few moments' stiff silence said,

'It won't do, Charn. You achieve nothing by withdrawing from the court and your duties in it; and with the queen still closeted away—'

Charn looked up sharply. 'Closeted away?'

'Yes. Like you, she wishes to have time alone for solitary contemplation; she has retired from the hall and sent word that she doesn't wish to be disturbed. However, in her absence someone must of course stand proxy for her, and that obligation, as I recall, falls to you.'

Charn hesitated for a moment, then shrugged as though he neither knew nor cared whether that were true. 'The court won't disintegrate for want of a focus,' he said. 'It can look to itself until the queen comes out of seclusion.'

'Unfortunately, it cannot,' Thimue countered. 'Affairs which were left in abeyance during Calliope's sojourn here' – he noted the way Charn's face tightened as he spoke the name – 'now need to be attended to.'

'Then let someone else attend to them.'

Thimue spread his hands. 'As you wish.' He paused. 'I'm sure her majesty's other senior advisors will be happy to offer their services.'

Though Charn affected indifference, Thimue knew that his point had gone home. Charn was at loggerheads with his fellow councillors often enough for them to enjoy this opportunity to the full, and the reminder of it might be the one thing that could shake Charn out of his melancholy. Thimue had sown the seed; it only remained to give it a little time to germinate.

He rose to his feet again and said aloud, 'Well, the choice is yours of course, my friend. I simply felt that you should be aware of the situation.'

Charn gave him an unfathomable look. 'I appreciate your concern.' Then, as Thimue wondered whether or not the thanks were weighted with sarcasm, he frowned. 'Where is the queen, precisely?'

'In the anteroom where she said her farewells to Calliope.'

A strange choice, Charn thought. But though a faint note of alarm sounded somewhere on an intuitive level, in his present mood he felt too disheartened to pay it any attention.

Thimue said softly, 'I'll leave you to your contemplations.' He glided to the entrance, then looked back. 'My door is always open, Charn. For anyone, and for any reason.'

Charn did not answer, and Thimue went out.

The interrogation of Selethe began an hour after dawn.

She was conscious when Foss and Nempson arrived in the workroom, but her huge silver eyes were filled with pain, and as soon as the men appeared she began to plead with them to release her. Ignoring the entreaties, Foss crossed to the table and touched the handles of the metaphysical inhibitor. Its momentum was broken; the rotating discs began to slow down, and the oscillating light-beam lost cohesion and finally faded. Foss rubbed the bone behind his right ear as the abrasive hum died away. Then he looked speculatively at Selethe.

She fell silent under his gaze. What she was thinking he couldn't begin to guess; she looked bewildered and agonised, but Foss had no intention of trusting any expression on that grey, alien face. He said, speaking slowly and clearly, 'Do you know who I am?'

Selethe's mouth trembled. 'You are . . . Calliope's sire . . .'

'Calli told you that, did she? Well, well. I wonder what else you wrung from her.' He hunched his shoulders and thrust out his jaw menacingly. 'Perhaps you would care to tell me?'

She whispered, 'I don't understand . . . I came only to – to see . . . Calliope said . . . she promised . . . ohh, please, I cannot bear this!'

'Promised?' Foss echoed. 'What did she promise?' He took a step towards the chair. 'What?'

'I c-c . . . she said . . . you would honour . . . oh, *please* . . .'

'It appears to be in pain,' Nempson observed, with a hint of vindictive satisfaction in his voice.

'Indeed it does. Perhaps it's not as resilient as our first guest was, eh? Which is all to the good, for it makes our task easier.'

237

Foss spoke with deliberate savour; psychological intimidation, especially when the victim was already showing signs of fear, was a valuable tool. Then he made a show of relenting and waved a hand towards the table. 'Dim the etherea lamp a little, Nempson. The light seems to hurt it; let it have a few moments' respite.' Another pace towards Selethe; he loomed over her now, staring down at her as a bird of prey might stare at a mouse pinned under its talon. 'Then we shall increase the level again. Unless, of course, it proves willing to co-operate with our wishes in the meantime.'

His words reached Selethe through a haze of agony. Nothing Charn had said about his own ordeal at human hands could have prepared her for the sheer, torturing horror of the reality. She felt as though her body were on fire – not the kindly fire of her own world but a ravening, consuming blaze of furnace-hot pain that seared her to the core. The skin of her wrists and ankles was blistering where the shackles held her, the ferocious light stabbed like swords into her eyes. Calliope had not come to help her, and these men, these *monsters*, they would not listen but had only hatred and cruelty in their minds. They were going to torture her as they had tortured Charn, and she could not withstand it. She could not do what he had done and resist the torments they would inflict on her, for she hadn't Charn's strength and she hadn't Charn's will. A wild and incoherent perception spun in Selethe's mind: *betrayal – not Calliope, no, not Calliope; but she herself – she would have no choice but to give these men what they wanted; she would betray her world, betray all her people, because she was weak and terrified and in such pain that there could be no other way for her* . . .

Foss said with a gentleness that even in her extremity did not deceive her, 'Well, creature? *Will* you co-operate with us? I think you have intelligence enough to know what a refusal must mean for you.'

They had dulled the light, and even that small relief was a spar to which Selethe clung desperately in the vast sea of her anguish. She could not resist. She *could* not.

'Ask . . .' The word cracked from her throat. 'Nnn . . . anything you will of me . . . anything . . . I will answer . . . help me, oh help me, I will answer!'

* * *

'Unless she has destroyed them, those papers must be somewhere in the house.' Foss stared out of the library window, turning the brandy-glass he held slowly, methodically in his hands. Dusk was falling, darkening the view of yards and gardens and giving them a faintly sinister look; though the setting sun wasn't visible from here, there was a smear of its reflection in the sky above the rooftops. The afterglow looked angry, and it reflected Foss's mood.

'She deceived me, Nempson.' He moved at last, returning to the table and the papers strewn across it. 'Her own father. She *deceived* me! Calli, of all my children . . .'

Nempson was examining the box, Griette's box from which the papers had come, probing at it with a small brass tool. He was thankful now that they had resisted their colleagues' pressure to house the legacy at the Institute, whence it would have been difficult to retrieve it without questions being asked. This development, at least for the present, was better kept private.

'It's possible, of course,' he said, 'that the creature is lying.'

Foss shook his head. 'What motive could it have? Besides, the story makes sense. Griette was already becoming deranged when her later notes were written; we know that from the last papers we have. So it seems logical that there might well be more, and that their content is much as the creature described.' He paused. 'Rot it, man, what are you *doing* with that box? Your scritch-scratching is getting on my nerves!'

'It occurred to me that there might be some hidden inner compartment,' Nempson said.

'There isn't. I've looked. So kindly put that damned instrument down and concentrate.' Foss tilted the brandy-glass to his mouth and drank half its contents in one draught. His anger with Calliope was sawing at his mind and he felt considerably out of sorts. 'As I said, unless Calliope destroyed those other documents – which is highly unlikely, as the creature knows of them – they must be somewhere in this house. I'll take any wager that she's hidden them in her room.'

'We can hardly search among her personal possessions, Foss. We've no right.'

Foss snorted. 'Haven't we, damn it? If it's rights we're debating, what right did Calli think she had to hide them from us in the first place?'

Nempson could have pointed out that it was only through

Calliope's good graces that they had been able to see the box's contents at all. But with Foss in his present frame of mind he restrained himself – besides, whatever the principle of it, he too would give a great deal for a sight of the missing papers.

Trying to justify that thought, he said, 'We may be misjudging Calliope. Perhaps she felt those papers would stir the fires of unhappy memories, and that's why she concealed them.' He saw Foss's expression and added coaxingly, 'Don't you think we should at least give her the benefit of the doubt?'

'That's as may be,' Foss said sourly, 'but whatever her reasons, it doesn't change the fact that she *cheated* me.' As Griette had cheated him. Griette, who had turned her back on husband and family and all she should have held dear, to run like a lovesick adolescent after a fantasy, a moonbeam, a will-o'-the-wisp . . . Well, he thought with bitter fury, there was rough justice in it. Will-o'-the-wisps had a partiality for luring travellers to disaster, and Griette's had proved no exception. She had made her choice of her own free will. If she preferred the mire of madness to the ties of fidelity and obligation, so be it: let her rot there, and let Calliope rot with her if that was the course she was set on. The sands of his compassion had run out.

'Foss?' Nempson said. 'Are you unwell?'

Foss realised that he had put one hand, splay-fingered, over his face and that the glass in the other was shaking violently. Snatching back self-control he put the glass down, a little too hard, and let out breath in a grunt. 'No.' The tone vetoed any contradiction. 'I'm perfectly all right. Perfectly.' Griette should have died with her unnatural lover; with the son of that filthy entity now strapped shaking and whimpering to the chair in the workroom . . . His hands balled unconsciously into hard fists. He was glad they had hurt her in the getting of information. He wished they had killed her. He wanted to return to her now, return and take vengeance on her mind and body, make her the scapegoat for the true transgressors, the ones he could not punish.

'Foss?' Nempson said again, uneasily.

'What?' He snapped back to earth. 'I— ah— your pardon, Nempson; I was thinking of— hiding places, yes . . .' His face had broken out in a sweat. 'Blast it, this room's hot.' Striding to the window he jerked it open, letting in cool evening air. Foolish lapse; and quite illogical. The creature was of more use alive than dead, and until and unless that changed, thoughts of retribution were not constructive.

If it *did* change, however . . .

His skin prickled and he mopped at his forehead. *Away with that.* 'I'll search Calli's room,' he said aloud, decisively. 'It's time I looked in on her anyway; Philome keeps badgering me not to leave her alone for too long. If those papers are there, I'll find them.'

Nempson nodded. He had some inkling of what had been going on in his friend's mind and was not surprised by it. 'Will you tell Philome about this?' he asked.

'No.' Foss's back was to him, so Nempson couldn't see his expression. 'Philome is an excellent wife. An *excellent* wife—'

'Indeed.'

'But she is not . . . a complex person. You take my meaning?'

'I believe so. It's no slight to her.'

'Quite the reverse.' Choking anger was in Foss suddenly and it took a great effort to force it back down into darkness. 'This tale of the key and the doorway and what Griette tried to do . . . it would upset Philome to no purpose to hear of it. She wouldn't *understand*, Nempson.'

'She would sympathise,' Nempson suggested tentatively.

'Oh, yes. Yes, she would sympathise. But sympathy without understanding strikes me as having very little point to it. So it will be a greater kindness to her to say nothing, and I trust I can rely on you to keep a still tongue.'

'I trust you know me well enough for an answer to be unnecessary,' Nempson replied stiffly.

'Hm? Oh, damn it; I didn't mean to put it that way. I spoke clumsily. No offence intended.'

Nempson inclined his head. 'None taken.'

'Good. Then make yourself comfortable, and have another look at those papers. Brandy's on the mantel. I'll go and see Calli, and see what I can unearth.'

Foss found the missing documents where Calliope had hidden them among her shawls. His twinges of conscience at rummaging among private belongings while their owner lay insensible not two paces away vanished when the papers were revealed, and for some time he stood staring at them in the lamplight while a

241

confusion of emotions tumbled through him. *White flowers. The Sacrament. DEATH.* It was all as Selethe had told them during her interrogation; frantic, garbled messages from a mind rapidly losing its grip on the last vestiges of sanity. But Selethe had also told them that before her final collapse into madness Griette had hidden away one artefact more precious than all her writings. The key to the door between worlds. To Foss, that was a prize beyond price.

Selethe had sworn that neither she nor Calliope knew the key's whereabouts. Foss hadn't believed her at first and had tried to force the knowledge from her, but when she held to her story even under the touch of a lit torch, he had accepted that she was telling the truth. The secret, it seemed, was Griette's alone. And Calliope had been charged to unravel it.

He raised his head and looked at his daughter, who had not stirred throughout his noisy search of the room. He doubted that she would wake until morning, for the last narcotic dose had been very strong; probably he hadn't been concentrating fully and measured too much. A pity, but Foss quelled the temptation to administer an antidote and wake her from her stupor, reminding himself that too much interference with the brain's natural processes was not advisable. He must contain his impatience and wait until she woke of her own accord. If his judgement proved correct – and he was confident that it would – then much of the corruption inflicted on her by the twilight-dwellers would have been purged by his treatment and by the severing of whatever psychic link the creature downstairs had forged with her. She would be, if not entirely in her right mind, at least rational enough not to rant and shriek as she had done before. He would be able to reason with her. He would be able to question her. And in the light of this, he would *insist* on some answers.

'I would not normally dream to do such a thing,' Thimue said, 'but I can't shake off the uneasy feeling within me, Charn. My bones tell me that something is wrong, and in all my long life I've learned to listen to such warnings.' He paused, looking up into Charn's pensive face. 'I believe we should go to the queen and make sure that all is well. Will you sanction it?'

They stood together near the great doors of the hall. Music imbued the air; figures drifted amid the gently shifting framework of light and shadow, and a few were even dancing desultorily, but without the familiar focus of Selethe's presence the court had a sluggish, directionless air. At the hall's centre the cobweb-curtains stirred around the empty throne, and an ominous sensation stirred in the pit of Charn's mind.

He said, 'Yes. I will sanction it. In fact I'm beginning to have similar feelings to your own.' He paused, scanning the hall speculatively. Was he simply catching Thimue's disquiet? It was possible, and he wanted to believe there was no more to it than that. But a deep-rooted intuition told him otherwise, and abruptly the bud of it flowered into something ugly.

'I'll go to her myself,' he said. 'Now, before others start to sense something in the wind. Say nothing to anyone, Thimue; I hope I'll not be long.'

'I'd like to come with you,' Thimue said. 'With your leave?'

On the verge of a refusal, Charn suddenly changed his mind. If there was anything at all in their shared suspicion, he would prefer not to face it alone. Besides, Thimue's skills might be needed.

'Yes. I'd be glad of it.'

They left the hall without drawing attention to themselves, and made their way by a lesser route to the anteroom. At the door an ethereal servant hovered as it had done since Selethe's withdrawal; Charn dismissed it with a quiet word and gesture, then he and Thimue stood listening. There was no sound from within the room, and at last Thimue said uneasily, 'Perhaps if we knock?'

Charn rapped sharply, twice. 'My lady? It's Charn, madam.'

Silence. They waited, then Charn called softly, 'Madam, I must speak with you. It's a matter of urgency.'

No response came, and Thimue said unhappily, 'If something has befallen her . . . I think we should abandon the proprieties, Charn. I think the queen needs help.'

This, Charn thought desolately, was something for which he had tried over the years to prepare himself, but now that he was actually facing the stark possibility he realised that no amount of preparation could ever be enough. Selethe had often made references to her own death; sometimes lightheartedly and sometimes in seriousness. She was old, she had lived her rightful span and it was known that her tenure could not last much longer.

The end, when it came, was likely to be peaceful; simply a quiet slipping away into oblivion. But if that moment had arrived its timing, with Calliope's mission unfulfilled, seemed a tragic irony. Charn suddenly did not want to be the first to bear witness to it.

His hand had stopped inches from the door. Thimue, gleaning something of his thoughts, said compassionately, 'Shall I?'

'No.' It took a good deal of resolution but Charn shook his head, then tempered the sternness of his reply with a bleak smile. He pushed at the door. It swung silently open, and with a sensation that his pulse was about to suffocate him he went in.

The room was empty. Confounded, Charn stared around for several seconds, then called sharply, 'Thimue!'

The physician hurried after him and his eyes widened. 'What? But this isn't possible!' He started to cast about as though expecting Selethe to materialise from the air. 'She can't have emerged, Charn – the servant would have known and would have sent word!'

Charn was searching the room, but even as he did so he knew that the search was pointless. Selethe was not here.

'I'll call the servant back—' Thimue began.

'Don't bother. All her servants are too reliable for there to have been any mistake.'

'But where *is* she?'

It was crazed, unthinkable; surely it was *unthinkable* . . . but a terrible foreboding was beginning to form in Charn's mind. He struggled to tell himself that Selethe would never countenance such a thing; but the reassurance didn't ring true. He believed he knew where she had gone.

'Thimue.' He spoke so sharply that the physician looked at him in surprise. 'The queen herself sent Calliope back through the gateway to her own world. Where did she say her farewells?'

'In this very room. She thought that a private place would be kinder and . . .' Thimue's voice tailed off as he realised what Charn was implying. 'You don't think that she . . .'

Charn didn't think it, not now. He knew. There was no other possibility. Selethe had gone with Calliope to the human world, and had walked unsuspecting into the hands of Foss Agate and his friends.

He looked at Thimue, and the expression on his face made an answer unnecessary. 'Go back to the court hall,' he said. 'Set the servant on watch again, and give instructions that *no one* is to open this door until I return.'

'You're going after her?'

'Yes.'

'Then you think she is in danger.'

'I'm certain of it.'

They continued to stare at each other for a few seconds longer. Then Thimue said, very quietly. 'Fortune go with you, Charn.' He shuddered, feeling that a vast, dark hand had suddenly cast its shadow over them both. 'And may it preserve our queen!'

Chapter XX

To Philome's relief, Foss and Nempson heeded her pleas to take a night's respite from their work. In fact they did not take a lot of persuading; with Selethe too weak for further interrogation and Calliope unlikely to wake until morning, there was in any case little more they could do, and Foss reasoned that a good meal and a night's uninterrupted sleep would benefit them both and restore their depleted energies. Nempson stayed for dinner then went home, and Foss and Philome retired at what Philome considered a gratifyingly civilised hour.

By the time the clocktower in the market square chimed the first hour past middle-night, the entire Agate household was sound asleep. In the workroom Selethe had slipped into pain-racked delirium, while in her attic bed Calliope muttered in drug-induced nightmares, her body twisting feebly and without co-ordination against the restraints that held her.

And in the yard behind the kitchen, Charn cautiously opened the door from the cellar and stared with a hard, angry gaze at the bulk of the house rising before him.

There was no moon tonight. Glancing up, he could see the shapes of clouds scudding across the sky, blotting even the stars from view. Well and good; the lack of light would make departure easier when the time came. He moved forward, forcefully quelling the sick, almost feverish agitation inside him and telling himself that it was only one of the unpleasant effects of this world. However great and however deep his fury, he *must* maintain absolute self-control now.

The kitchen door was bolted on the inside, but a catch on the window was loose and yielded to Charn's probing and twisting. The casement swung open; rubbing at his hand – even through gloves the metal of the catch had stung him – he climbed lithely on to the sill and, eyes unhindered by the darkness, jumped down to the kitchen floor. No signs of life; no sounds of movement. Family and servants alike were oblivious to the world.

He stalked across the floor and out into the passage that led to the entrance hall. The route brought back a sharp stab of memory, and the feeling intensified when he reached the hall and saw the understairs door. Beyond it lay the workroom, and his goal.

He knew in his heart that there was no justifiable logic behind the impulse that had brought him here. He had no evidence that Foss Agate had broken the promise given in his letter to Calliope. But against logic and evidence Charn believed he had done just that, for he remembered Foss all too well, and despite Calliope's heartfelt assurances he trusted the man no further than he could have bodily hurled him. Calliope swore he was wrong and that her father was a man of honour, and Charn didn't doubt that her faith in him was genuine. But – to invert something that Selethe had said – daughter and father were not necessarily of the same mettle, and by now Calliope might have discovered just how naive her judgement had been.

He paused and looked towards the stairs, wondering where Calliope was and how she fared. She had told him once that she slept in a room on the house's topmost floor, and suddenly Charn was pulled by a strong desire to climb the stairs and go in search of her. He crushed the thought; though there was no point in pretending that she had no part in the impulse that had goaded him here, his priority – and imperative – was to find Selethe.

A board creaked under his foot as he headed towards the understairs door. Charn froze, listening, half expecting the sound to trigger a response. But there were no raised voices, no noise of footsteps, and after a few seconds he allowed himself to relax. He had overreacted; it was easy to forget that human senses were far less acute than his own and that it would take a good deal more than a mere creak to disturb the house's sleeping occupants.

On then, through the door and into the narrow passage beyond. As he moved noiselessly towards the workroom it suddenly and unpleasantly occurred to him that he might have made a dangerous assumption in presuming the entire household was asleep. Foss could be in the workroom at this moment, alone or with colleagues . . . Charn slowed his steps as the door came in sight, scanning, listening. There was a glimmer of light under the door; the greenish glow of the etherea lamp. But no sound impinged; no voices or shuffling or clink of equipment, not even the telltale hush of breathing.

Or was there something?

He leaned towards the door, holding his own breath. There it was again, faint and thin but unmistakable nonetheless. A quavering exhalation . . . and mingled with it, a woman's soft moan of pain.

Black fury erupted through Charn like an explosion. He didn't hesitate, didn't consider, didn't *think*; his arm came up violently and he burst the door open and shouldered through it into the workroom.

'*My lady!*' His voice rose in outraged horror as he saw Selethe. She was pinioned in the chair – that monstrous chair with its shackles and its copper hood – and her face was a raddled mask of torment, eyes tight-shut, mouth distorted and drooling, skin nacrous and leprous with the searing effects of light. Her hair had collapsed from its coils and was draped in sweat-soaked black strands over her shoulders and breasts; her gown, too, was wet, and torn in places, exposing her arms and one thigh. Blood crusted her fingers, and the skin of her hands and wrists was blistered as though she had been burned.

'*Madam!*' Charn's second cry was a choking, near-inchoate sound, and he crossed the room in three strides to drop to his knees at her feet. Ripping the gloves from his hands he took her face between his palms, and words spilled desperately from him, beseeching, comforting, exhorting; anything that might give her strength and help. The queen uttered a small, piteous sound; then her eyes half-opened – the whites were streaked black – and through a daze of affliction she recognised him.

'*Charn . . . ?*' Her tongue was swollen; she could barely form words. '*Oh, Charn . . . you should not . . . you must not . . . ohh, Charn, they have hurt me so . . . the light burns, it burns . . .*'

247

Charn's rage rose like a tidal wave; jackknifing to his feet he swung round to the table, where the green glass sphere of the etherea lamp glowed. It was turned low; to his eyes, as to hers, it seemed to glare like the midday sun, and his forearm smashed into it with a force that sent the entire lamp hurtling from the table. The sphere hit the floor and shattered with an explosion of noise and flying shards. The gas inside vaporised; an eldritch whine shrilled in Charn's ears momentarily as the tiny nucleus ricocheted away, then the room plunged into darkness.

For the space of a heartbeat Charn stood motionless, his eyes focused with a blank, blind stare on the place where the lamp had stood. The surge of uncontrolled fury had gone, and its vanishing had left a void in him. Then with a jolt sense returned, and he spun back to Selethe.

'Lady!' He was at her side again. 'What did they *do* to you?'

With the dousing of the light Selethe's will had rallied; she drew in a ragged breath and said, 'They wanted . . . answers. To questions that I . . .' She coughed; spittle flecked her lips and chin and Charn wiped it gently away with his sleeve. 'I told them, Charn. I c-could not withstand, and I . . . *told* them.' Her eyes met his with a mute, desperate plea. '*Forgive me* . . .'

Charn uttered an oath that could not even begin to express his disgust and loathing for Foss and all he represented. 'There's nothing to forgive, my lady!'

'But there is; there is . . . I was reckless. I wanted . . . wanted only to . . .'

'Hush.' He touched a finger to her mouth. 'Say nothing; you have no need to explain.' Explanations, if there were to be any, would come later; for now all that mattered was to free her and get her away. Pulling on his gloves again he started to examine the shackles, and Selethe whispered,

'I believed in him, Charn. The human man; Calliope's father . . . I *trusted*.'

'And were betrayed.' *As I tried to warn you.* That was an unworthy thought; he thrust it away but on its heels came another, and one he couldn't ignore. Abruptly his hands stopped moving and he looked into her face once more.

'Did Calliope have a hand in this?' His mouth tensed and he couldn't breathe properly. 'Did *she* betray you?'

Selethe's eyes widened. 'Calliope . . . oh no, no! Charn, you

248

mustn't think – she tried to stop them, she *tried*, but they would not listen! He – the man – she was screaming, and he struck her, I saw him strike her down, and they carried her away – I pleaded, I begged, but they won't let me see her . . .'

Charn's pulse pounded like hammers through his body. 'Madam, where is she? Do you know?'

'Th-they said . . . they th-think we— I— cast some compulsion on her; that we have infected her mind . . . I heard them say she is ill and— and must be cured . . .'

The topmost floor. Calliope's room . . . Charn's mind roiled and he attacked the shackles with renewed energy, careless of the burning pain that assailed his hands. *Only get Selethe to safety and he could return—*

'Even if you open them, you can't free me.' The queen spoke again, suddenly and with a calm that startled him. Again he looked up, and she smiled a wan smile. 'The band at my waist. It is locked.'

He had forgotten. The chair's wrist and ankle shackles were merely clamps and could be unfastened if he could just find the knack of them. But the waist restraint had a lock, and the solidity of the iron would resist any effort he could make to break it.

'The key—' He started to his feet, looked wildly around. So many shelves and boxes and hiding places—

'He took it,' Selethe said. 'I saw. He took it away.'

'Then I'll take it back!' He would tear Foss limb from limb if he had to, and take joy in it—

'No, Charn!' Selethe's protest stopped him even as he turned impulsively for the door. 'No,' she repeated more quietly. 'You must not even try, for you wouldn't succeed. You must leave—'

'I will not!'

'*Hear me.*' She swallowed, struggling to gain proper control over her tongue. 'You must leave me here, as I am, and look for another way to set me free. Find Calliope. She is the only one who can give us hope. If you try alone, if you challenge them without her help, they will kill you. Charn, *please* . . .'

'I won't abandon you to their mercies!' Charn said ferociously.

'You must.' Selethe drew herself upright with a tremendous effort. 'Whatever my straits, I am— am still your queen. I *command* you to obey me.'

He looked at her, at the feeble, pitiful wreck that Foss and

249

Nempson had made of her, and felt a helpless sense of reverence for her dignity and courage. She *was* his queen, and submission to her will was inborn in him. He could not gainsay her.

'I think,' Selethe continued, 'that my life is not in immediate peril. I think that I am . . . of some better use to them alive than dead.' Exhaustion washed over her suddenly and her head sank back against the chair, her eyes closing. 'I can survive this for some while yet. Give me hope, Charn. Find Calliope. *Find* her!'

Charn knew he had no choice. He knelt before Selethe, took her hands in his. 'My lady, I'll come back!'

She nodded. 'I know you will. Don't make farewells to me, Charn. Just go – for both our sakes.'

At the door he looked back. But she had turned her head away, and he was powerless to offer her anything. He left, went like a shadow through the passage and emerged into the hall with the sound of his own breath sawing in his throat. Hatred filled him – but it was impotent. She was right; he could not challenge the likes of Foss and his friends and hope to prevail. *Think clearly*, he told himself. His breathing slowed, and with it the shivering that had started to overcome him lessened. Calliope was upstairs. Ill, they had said. She had tried to help Selethe, but her father had refused to listen and had struck her down. His own daughter . . .

Charn moved like a predator to the foot of the stairs and began to climb.

Calliope knew instinctively that she was awake, but still she couldn't shake off a sense of bizarre and dreamlike unreality. Her head itched as though spiders were spinning webs across her skull, and her body seemed either unwilling or unable to respond to the commands her mind tried to give. Even her arms would not move. She could feel them spread out to either side of her, but when she attempted to draw them in, something held them back.

Perhaps she had a fever. A little while ago she had tried opening her eyes, to find that the world beyond her eyelids was almost as dark as the world within. Only a faint rectangle relieved the gloom; the outline, she soon realised, of her bedroom window. Which meant that it must be night. Fevers were always worse at night, and if she was ill, she reasoned, it could well explain her apparent inability to move.

She wondered how long she must wait for morning. The house and the square outside were silent, suggesting that it was well past midnight. Dawn soon, then, so if she could not get back to sleep the waiting would not be too arduous. *If* she was ill, her father would be here early to see her, and then he would no doubt explain.

She yawned. Her mind was very hazy and the idea of attempting to clear it seemed too great an effort to trouble with. Maybe her father had given her a nostrum to dull her senses. Maybe she *would* sleep for a while longer. Maybe—

The thought broke down as she heard a scraping sound from the far side of the room. Then, very softly, a voice whispered her name.

Calliope frowned. The movement provoked the itching in her skull again, but she could not raise her hand to scratch. Someone or something was outside the door, calling to her. The voice had seemed familiar and she thought to reply, but when she tried, her mouth and tongue were so dry that she couldn't make a sound. Water – was there some water by the bed? She usually left a jug there.

'*Calliope!*' The voice came again, urgently. '*Calliope, can you hear me?*'

Yes, yes; she wanted to say; I can hear you. It wasn't her father, or Luthe. Someone she knew, though. Was it worth the effort of looking for the water and taking a drink and . . .?

The door rattled sharply and the handle turned, but it did not open. She couldn't remember locking it; she rarely did lock it, for what was the point in her own home? Maybe it was Tobery, who could lift latches but not, yet, twist handles. But no; Tobery had a child's voice to match his child's stature. This was an adult. A man. Someone she *knew* . . .

Outside on the landing Charn stared at the door in mounting frustration. This was the right room; he knew it with a sure and unerring instinct. But if Calliope was there, she either did not hear him or for some reason could not answer. A riot of possibilities went through his mind: she was gagged, she was drugged, she was unconscious, she was dead – and the frustration began to turn into an anger that carried a measure of panic. With no means

251

of judging time he feared that its sands could be about to run out; at the first sign of dawn he must abandon the house, or the servants would be stirring and the danger both from them and from the growing light would be too great.

Keys – always there were keys to thwart him! He grasped the doorhandle again and wrenched at it. In the room beyond, Calliope's eyes widened in alarm at the renewed noise. Who was outside? Anyone who knew her would surely not attack the door as though it were an enemy. The thought occurred to her that she *should* call out, not to the unknown, unseen intruder (her mind latched suddenly and fearfully onto that word, *intruder*) but a warning to the household, a cry for help.

'*Calli!*' Forgetting caution in a reckless moment, Charn all but shouted her name suddenly. Calliope felt a stifling surge of terror – and on the floor below Foss started out of his sleep.

There was only one thing Charn could do. Bracing himself, he rammed his shoulder against the door with all the strength he could summon. A heavy thud echoed through the house; the lock and hinges strained, but held. There was a scuffling noise on the next floor, voices rising in alarm, then another door banged loudly and Foss bawled, 'Who is it? What's going on up there?'

Charn swung round, and was in time to see light flare in the stairwell below him. Footsteps thumped – then Foss, a robe thrown hastily over his nightshirt, appeared at the foot of the stairs.

'*What?*' It began as a shout, then became a roar of incredulous fury as he recognised Charn. Behind him Philome was calling, 'Foss, what is it, what *is* it?' but her husband ignored her as he and Charn both stood immobile, staring at each other. Then Charn's paralysis snapped, and Foss's shock gave him the only chance he would have. He launched himself at the stairs, plunging down them so fast that Foss was taken completely by surprise. Clasping his fists together Charn swung them at Foss's breastbone; they connected, Foss gave a bellow of pain and fell backwards, and Charn was past him and running for the next flight of stairs. A woman's petrified face skimmed at the edge of his vision; he heard her terrified shriek but ignored it, raced on. A child wailed somewhere; another door opened and a fair-haired girl – Calliope's sister – appeared, her stunned expression a burlesque that was almost comical. He thrust her from his path, and then they were all shouting, yelling for the servants to wake, to come, quickly, *quickly!*

Charn reached the top of the stairs and took the flight three or four at a time, trusting to luck and innate agility to get him to the hall with his balance still intact. He reached the bottom, turned instinctively towards the front door – but no, not that way; there were bolts and they took time, and outside was the square and the street lamps and no chance of finding absolute darkness—

He skidded round and darted towards the kitchen. Footfalls thundered on the landing above him, but Foss was no athlete and Charn had a good start. The kitchen door was ahead of him, he could be through it and gone before anyone else reached the hall.

Then, as it seemed he must get safely away, a side door was flung open and new light glared out into the hall. Shocked, Charn recoiled, and as he lost momentum two figures, one carrying a hand-lantern, rushed at him.

The servants had been roused from their beds below stairs by the commotion and Foss's shouting, and while the women huddled in the basement two men had come pounding up to the hall in answer to the alarm. Charn kicked out, sending one of them staggering back; the other grabbed hold of his arm but he wrenched himself free, feeling the sleeve of his shirt rip from shoulder to elbow. He cannoned into the kitchen door and was through it before they could come at him again; as he spun to smash the door shut in their faces a burly body rammed into it and the impact jarred through him. Charn lost balance, stumbled, collided with a table and sent it juddering several feet across the floor. Dishes and utensils set ready for the morning's breakfast preparations slid from the table with a resounding clatter, then over the racket of their falling came Foss's stentorian voice.

'*Stop him! Stop that creature!*'

Foss and Luthe piled into the room on the heels of the two servants, and Charn realised instantly that odds of four against one were too great. The door to the yard was bolted and would take time to open, and in desperation he snatched a stone mortar and heavy wooden pestle from where they stood on a shelf beside the sink. The mortar he flung at the head of the nearer servant. The man ducked and the hurtling bowl struck Luthe as he threw up his arms to ward it off; recovering quickly the servant made a

253

lunge, and Charn's attempt to hit him with the pestle went wide. The pestle was grabbed by the other servant; for a moment they wrestled in a violent tug-o'-war, then Charn let go and, evading a wild swing from Foss, who had armed himself with a long-handled copper pan, drove one hand, fingers rigidly extended, at the throat of his first assailant. The man made an awful sound and ploughed backwards into Foss and Luthe, and Charn seized a handful of spice pots from the shelf and threw them in his wake. Pepper erupted in a choking cloud, and it choked Charn too, searing his throat and nostrils like fire. He saw Foss swing the pan a second time, tried to swerve, and his chest and one arm met the full force of a blow from the pestle in the hands of the second servant. Pain exploded through him and for an instant every sense blanked out – then skill and discipline broke down in a single, ruthless surge of his survival instinct. His other hand closed on something – it was solid iron and it burned into his flesh, but he was far beyond knowing, let alone caring – and he heard the sound as it cleaved the air with all the strength he could summon behind it. It struck flesh and the bone beneath with a lethal impact. There was a sickening crunch, someone's horrified yell, and Charn spun on his heel and threw himself to where, half blinded as he was, he thought the window must be. Fate was with him; he felt the sill and, with a savage will that overcame the pain blazing through him, launched himself upwards and forwards. There was a shatter and crack as both the glass and the wooden frame gave way, and Charn plunged outside into the yard, sprawling on hands and knees on to solid ground. Ribs feeling as though they were on fire, he scrabbled to his feet and stumbled towards the cellar. The skin of his face was blistering from the pepper; everything was a blur before him, and when he burst through the cellar door he almost went headlong down the slimy steps to the bottom. The agony redoubled, pulsing through his torso; but he forced himself on, expecting at any moment to hear the trample of feet and the shouting of voices and knowing only that he must get away, open the gateway between worlds and go through it to sanctuary. *Darkness, the key in his mind, the narcotic perfume* – his mind latched on to the art of it, the art he knew so well, and he felt the shift, the change—

He was gone. For a few seconds the scent of the white flowers hovered in the air. Then it blended, briefly and horribly, with the stench of the cellar, before fading to nothing.

And no one had followed him.

In the house, Luthe met Philome as she approached the kitchen door, and barred her way.

'Father says not to go in, Philome.' Luthe's face had lost all its colour and he looked as if he might be sick at any moment. 'Will you please prepare a room, quickly, for someone injured.'

Philome was appalled. 'Who is it? Not Foss—'

'No, no; Father's unharmed. One of the servants. He was hit with the iron raker from the cooking-range; it broke his skull and worse, and Father says he has to repair him in minutes. There's a lot of blood, you see, and . . .' He swallowed then as reaction started to catch up with him, and put a hand to his mouth. 'Excuse me . . . I think I—' He ran past her and away towards the front door and the outside air. For a moment Philome hovered helplessly, torn between hurrying after him, braving the horrors of the kitchen or obeying Foss's order. Then abruptly the urgency of the situation sparked her common sense. Care for the wounded – there must be blankets, a fire, Foss's medical pack, cloths for mopping—

'Celesta!' she called shrilly as she turned for the stairs again. 'Celesta, come quickly! Come and help me!'

Chapter XXI

The injured servant would live, but, as Foss said later to Philome, his survival was a miracle of providence and his life henceforth was unlikely to have great value to him. Damage to the material of the brain: he would never be fit to work again. Foss arranged that the man should go to an institution where he could stay until the worst of his injuries were healed, and then he would be dispatched for good to his family home in the country. By way of compensation he would receive three years' wages; Foss could well afford it, and it was a more than generous settlement.

Further injuries were minor. The other man had suffered a

badly bruised larynx, and Luthe's arm was swollen and stiff where the flying mortar had struck it, but beyond that everyone was unscathed. The servants assumed that the intruder had broken into the house intending to rob it. Foss didn't disabuse them, knowing that the ensuing inquiries would be simpler if the whole affair was treated as a straightforward crime. The authorities would never catch the felon, of course. But that was something Foss intended to deal with in quite another way.

In the turmoil of calming the household, tending injuries and putting the kitchen to rights, it was past dawn before anyone thought of Calliope. The lamps in the square were being extinguished, and a closed litter from the institution had just arrived to carry away the wounded servant, when Philome realised that no one had so much as looked into the attic bedroom. Foss was supervising the litter-bearers and she didn't like to interrupt him, so she took Calliope's key from the library where he had left it and hurried upstairs. Outside the dining room she was waylaid by Celesta, who had been detailed to distract Tobery and Diona from events downstairs but was finding them impossible to control. Tobery wanted to see 'all the blood' and Diona was egging him on; they simply wouldn't *obey* her, Celesta said, and *please* wouldn't Philome deal with it? Philome hesitated, remembering Foss's injunctions about Calliope, but a sudden childish yell from the dining room, followed by a thump and then an indignant howl from Tobery, settled the matter.

'I'll see for them,' she told Celesta soothingly. 'Here, my dear, you can look at Calli for me; here's the key to her room. If she's conscious, you'd best let your father know as soon as the litter has gone.'

With a sigh of relief Celesta hastened up the stairs to her sister's bedchamber. As she turned the key in the lock she heard a stirring on the far side, then Calliope's voice called weakly,

'Who's there?'

'Calli?' Celesta opened the door and looked in. 'Oh, you're awake!' She started forward, then stopped as she saw the restraints and the copper net over Calliope's hair. 'Whatever has Father *done*?'

Calliope, lying flat in the bed, ran her tongue over her lips. Her vision was still hazy – but, for the first time since her return from the twilight world, her mind was not. 'I can't sit up,' she said. 'I woke a few minutes ago, and I can't move. Could you untie me, Celesta?'

Celesta tiptoed towards the bed, her eyes wary. 'I'd better not, Calli. Father says you've been very ill, and this must be part of his treatment. He'll be angry if I do anything without asking him first.' Little wonder that he had barred everyone from the room, she thought, awed; this was clearly serious. 'It's not catching, is it?' she added uneasily.

Calliope's slender hope had been dashed by Celesta's refusal, but she took care not to show it and only shook her head as best she could. 'No; it's all right, you can come near me. In fact I wish you'd stay and talk. It's so dull just lying here with nothing to do.'

Celesta came closer. 'How are you feeling now?' she asked.

'Oh, much better.' Calliope paused. 'How long have I been like this?'

'Two nights and a day.'

Calliope was horrified: her father, she realised, must deliberately have kept her unconscious through all that time. Now, though, the drugs' effects had finally worn off – and in the minutes since she woke from her sleep, she had remembered everything. Her return through the gateway, then Selethe's appearance and her father's reaction . . . she had tried to protest; there had been a fracas and he had hit her before pressing an insensator pad to her face, and later he had tricked her into taking a stronger narcotic that had rendered her completely senseless until this morning.

Or almost completely. For unless she had been dreaming – and she was certain she had not – someone had come to her door in the dead of night. She believed she knew who that someone had been.

Charn must have come looking for Selethe. What had happened to them both? Was Selethe alive, had Charn found her, had they escaped, or were they both now captive or, worse still, dead? Feeling sick, Calliope slid her gaze sidelong to her sister, who was looking at the ropes and the net with dismayed fascination. She had to find out as much as she could before she faced Foss again, and, seeking an opening, she said.

'My mouth's so dry . . . is there any water on the table?'

'There's a jug here,' Celesta told her, then frowned. 'But I

257

don't know if I'm allowed to give you any. Maybe I should call Father—'

'No!' Alarm filled Calliope; then with an effort she forced her voice to be calmer. 'Water can't hurt me, Celesta, and I'm so thirsty. Please . . .?'

She was surely right, Celesta thought; a drink could do no harm. Anyway, their father was busy at the moment and wouldn't take kindly to being interrupted.

She poured water into a beaker and held it to her sister's lips. It wasn't easy, as Calliope could not sit up to drink, but a little went down, then a little more. After the third sip Calliope said, 'I wish I knew what's been happening. No one's told me anything at all since I was put to bed.'

Celesta stared at her in consternation. 'You mean you don't know? Father hasn't – oh, of course, how could he have done when you've been ill?' She set the beaker aside and added melodramatically, 'Oh, Calli, what you've *missed*!'

There was so much Calliope desperately needed to know – and Celesta, who could never hold her tongue for long, was the ideal source of information. 'Tell me!' she urged.

'*Well*.' Celesta plumped down on the bed, her eyes shining. 'The *real* excitement happened last night. How you slept through it all I can't begin to imagine; but then I expect Father gave you something . . . Anyway, he – Father, that is – and Nempson Trinity had been occupied all day with that new creature in the workroom, and they were very tired, so Nempson went home and *we* all went to bed early . . .'

'. . . So he got away, and Father says there's no hope of catching him. And poor Bannor; he'll never properly recover and may not even be able to walk again. And the most awful thing is, Calli, he – the creature, that is – was outside *your* room when Father heard him!' Celesta leaned forward avidly. 'I think he meant to abduct you, and carry you away back to his world!'

Nothing, Calliope thought, could have been further from the truth; but if Celesta and others in the household thought it, it might be to her advantage. As her sister recounted the story of the night's events, she had had a chance to think, and to plan. Celesta, being Celesta, had eagerly tattled every detail she knew, and Calliope realised now that Foss genuinely believed she had been brainwashed in some way by the twilight-dwellers. It explained his outright refusal to listen to her frantic pleas and protests, and it also explained this 'cure' to which he had subjected her. She had been utterly hysterical, Celesta said. Calliope recalled that all too well, and for once Celesta wasn't exaggerating. Little wonder that Foss reacted as he had.

But then, she had had good reason. Her father had broken his word. He had betrayed his solemn promise. For that, she could not and would not forgive him.

Selethe, at least, was still alive; though in what condition Celesta didn't know. Only Foss could tell her. But would he? He would come to see her soon, and when he did Calliope knew that she must tread with the very greatest care. A strategy was formulating in her mind, and she would need to act her part skilfully if it was to succeed. She must convince Foss that his treatment had worked and the twilight-dwellers' 'influence' had been eradicated. He would be sceptical and would no doubt test her thoroughly; she must pass the tests, and pretend to a sense of outrage that matched his own. He wanted retribution; she needed to make him believe that she shared his desire and would work unstintingly to achieve it. It was the only way to win his trust and his confidence again – and the only hope she had of helping Selethe.

Celesta was expanding keenly on her theory of Charn's malevolent intent, but paused as she saw that Calliope wasn't listening.

'Calli?' she said. 'Are you all right?'

'What? Oh— oh, yes; I'm sorry. I *did* hear you, and I wouldn't be at all surprised if what you suspect is true. But Celesta, I— I really do want to get up. Couldn't you loose these ropes? Please?'

'Calli, I daren't. If Father knew . . .'

'I'm sure he'd understand. You see – it's a little indelicate of me to say so, but I need to relieve myself.' This with a sheepish smile, and Celesta looked embarrassed.

'Oh! Oh, well, that's different . . .' She glanced over her shoulder at the door. 'Perhaps I should call Philome. If she says it's all right—'

'Then Father can be angry with her instead of with you?' Calliope grinned conspiratorially, gratified by the ease with which her sister had accepted the explanation, and accepted, too, her apparent return to her usual self. She had a potential if unwitting ally in Celesta, she thought. It only remained to be seen whether Foss would prove as easy to beguile.

Philome came hurrying at Celesta's call, abandoning a game of bricks with Tobery and Diona. She was torn between delight and anxiety to see her stepdaughter awake and aware, and Calliope bore her kindly if smothering ministrations as she was untied and shepherded like a small child to the close-stool on the floor below. Philome hovered outside until she emerged, then started to lead her back towards her room. They were half way along the landing when Foss came up the stairs. He saw Calliope and his jaw dropped.

'Damn my eyes, wife, what d'you think you're doing? I gave strict instructions – *strict*, mark you! – that no one was to disturb Calli without my permission!' He hastened towards them. 'Get her back to her bed at once, do you hear me?'

'That is precisely what I *am* doing, Foss, if you would only contain your temper long enough to see the facts for yourself!' Philome said with surprising spirit; then added primly, 'We have merely been along the landing. There are certain necessary functions which cannot be set aside indefinitely.'

'Ah.' Foss frowned. 'Ah, I see. In that case . . .' He stopped, looking harder at Calliope as he realised suddenly that she seemed calm. 'Daughter? Can you speak? Do you know me?'

'Of course she knows you, Foss; what nonsense!' Philome retorted before Calliope could answer for herself. 'In fact she is feeling greatly recovered, aren't you, my dear?'

'Yes.' Calliope looked into her father's eyes and made herself smile at him. 'I think I *am* recovered, Father. Completely.'

Foss caught the significance in her words, the implied message that Philome would not comprehend, and his expression, though still wary, began to change. 'Do you remember what happened to you, Calli?'

She touched her tongue to her lips as though considering carefully. 'I remember a little, Father, but not clearly. I'd greatly like to talk to you, if you judge me fit enough . . . and I think I have a great deal to thank you for.'

Foss continued to gaze at her, and she covertly watched the play of reactions in his eyes. Caution, speculation, but also a measure of encouragement.

'Do you think,' he said, 'that you could eat a little broth?'

Despite the fact that she had had nothing since her return, food was the last thing Calliope wanted, especially from his hand. 'Yes, Father,' she said. 'I would like that.' A smile. 'I feel that I've not eaten in days.'

'Possibly you've not, though I suspect you're unlikely to recall.' Foss glanced at his wife. 'I'll take Calli back to her room myself, Philome. Perhaps you'll be so good as to bring her a bowl of something nourishing?'

'Of course, Foss.' Then Philome's face clouded. 'But you're not going to tell her about all the . . .?' She signalled the rest with her eyes, not wanting to utter it aloud in Calliope's presence. 'She's not strong enough, not yet!'

'Let me be the judge of that, my dear, hmm?' Foss's look implied strongly that he would prefer not to have any argument on the subject. 'Some food. That is what she needs, and I'll be obliged if you'll see for it.'

Philome sighed. 'Very well. You know best, I suppose.' She retreated, and Foss turned to his daughter.

'Well, Calli. I find you in very different spirit to your earlier condition – and I don't mind telling you that the change is for the better!'

Calliope affected puzzlement. 'I'm sorry, Father, I don't understand.'

'No. No, I see you don't.' Suddenly he reached out and put an arm fondly, proprietorially, about her shoulders. 'Come along. We'll return to your room – there'll be no more need of the restraints, but we must have no over-exertion to begin with. Besides,' he looked back to the stairs to assure himself that Philome had disappeared, 'we can be assured of privacy there. I think, daughter, that we have a great deal to discuss.'

The backlash of tension as Charn stormed out of the court hall made the shadows dance and leap momentarily before the atmosphere calmed to something approaching normality. Silence fell; and by the empty throne the members of Selethe's council exchanged uneasy looks. Nothing was said, for no one knew where best to begin. Then Thimue moved quietly from his place among the group and glided towards the black doors in Charn's wake.

Hampered by the injury he had suffered, Charn could not walk at his customary pace, and Thimue caught up with him in a narrow corridor where coruscating patterns of light moved ceaselessly across walls and ceiling.

'Charn.' The physician's voice was troubled. 'This achieves nothing – and you'll not alter the others' minds by a show of temper.'

Charn stopped walking and pressed the hand that wasn't bound against his torso to his face. 'Spare me your good advice, Thimue. I'm not in any mood to listen.'

'Then you should remedy that, my friend, for it is good advice. You can't gainsay the will of the entire council—'

'Thank you; I've discovered that for myself!'

'The *entire* council,' Thimue persisted, 'and their will is unanimous. We must *not* act precipitately, Charn. Your bid to rescue the queen, though courageous and noble, almost ended in disaster, and we cannot risk a second attempt in the same vein. We need time to think, time to plan—'

'Time wasted, while the queen remains in peril of her life!'

'She believes she is not in danger.'

Charn turned combatively to face him full on. 'And if she's wrong, Thimue? What then?'

'We must trust that she is not wrong. We've no *choice*, Charn! Think reasonably, my friend – what can we actually *do*? We can't overwhelm these humans by physical force, and nor would we wish to' – Charn snorted at that but Thimue ignored the interjection – 'and until your injuries have healed, you are restricted and so cannot return more covertly.'

'It's bruising, nothing more,' Charn said.

'Maybe so, but it hampers you nonetheless. You were nearly captured on your first foray. Are you so reckless that you'd try a second time, with the odds against you worsened? I ask: how would that serve our queen?'

There was a tense pause; then Charn sighed heavily. 'Very well, Thimue. You're right, and I have to acknowledge it.' He made a helpless, frustrated gesture back in the direction of the hall. 'But if the council fondly believe that they serve her any better by their timid procrastination . . . they seem to think that if they simply sit by and take no action, the dilemma will miraculously solve itself! I despair of them, Thimue. I *despair*.'

'That,' said Thimue gently and sadly, 'is something you must *not* do.'

Charn laughed bitterly. 'How not? Our queen is captive and we are powerless to help her. If you had seen her with your own eyes; seen what they have done—' Unthinkingly he tried to clench the fist of his injured arm, and winced as the hand refused to close.

'Charn.' The old physician laid a hand on his opposite forearm and patted it. 'Your own injuries are healing. As you say, it's bruising, albeit severe; and it won't be long – a few days, no more – before you are fully recovered. When you are . . . well, the council has no jurisdiction over your personal actions, has it?'

Charn looked at him sharply, shrewdly. 'Are you suggesting—'

'I'm suggesting nothing, for I've no intention of compromising myself,' Thimue said with a note of censure. Then he focused his gaze away from Charn and into the middle distance. 'In fact, this conversation is not taking place.'

Charn understood. He was in no mood to smile, but the look in his eyes altered.

'Very well,' he replied. 'A few days, you think?'

'Provided you don't do anything foolish in the meantime.'

Silence held between them for several seconds. Then Charn said, 'Thank you, Thimue. I shall ponder your advice very carefully.'

'I offer it merely as a physician, of course. And as the queen's friend.'

'Yes. I see that you do.'

With mind and heart calmer than they had been at any time since his return, Charn walked away.

It took two nerve-racking days for Calliope finally to convince Foss that her 'recovery' was complete and that there would be no relapse. The fact that Foss wanted to be persuaded helped her cause greatly, and so did Nempson, who perhaps for personal reasons seemed the most ready of anyone to believe in her return to her old self. There were tests to be undergone, of course: as both physician and scientist Foss insisted that his faith in his daughter's deliverance must be backed by rational and demonstrable proof. But with Calliope's meek compliance the tests were passed and his doubts allayed, and in a small but almost absurdly formal interview in the library, she was welcomed back into their Society's fold – and, more importantly, into its confidence.

Foss's view of recent events was that Calliope's sortie to the twilight world had been a rash and impulsive mistake which, but for his own intervention, could have ended in disaster. He believed Charn had lured her into following him, warping her mind while he was still a captive; and that once beguiled she had been an easy target for Selethe's predations. The twilight-dwellers' motives, to Foss and Nempson, were clear; they had intended to use Calliope as an unwitting agent for their own activities in the human world, and those activities boded ill. Calliope pretended ignorance – it had been easy to convince her father that she could remember very little of her experience – but agreed with their judgement, soberly expressing her relief at the narrow escape she had had.

However, the fact that his daughter had been saved from the twilight-dwellers' evil machinations was not enough to content Foss. The creatures had made a similar attempt fifteen years ago, he reminded Calliope and Nempson, and the tragic result of that first campaign now languished in hopeless, broken misery at the hospice. Calliope had been their second quarry, and although their scheme had failed again, he was in no doubt that the matter would not end here unless stringent measures were taken. They could, of course, kill Selethe, but whatever her rank she was only one of many and, as Foss put it, an ants' nest was not eradicated by the removal of its queen. The taint must be properly cleansed – and Foss believed that the means to achieve it lay in the form of the lost key to the doorway between dimensions; the key that had been entrusted to Griette all those years ago. With that in his possession, he could turn the tables on the beings he now thought of as his sworn enemies. He could punish them. He could take revenge for the affronts, the *crimes* they had committed against his family. He could, and would, wreak havoc on them and on their grim, colourless and unnatural world.

He questioned Calliope closely about the key, half convinced at first that for all her denials she must know more than she had thus far told him. For once, Calliope did not need to lie to him. There were no more notes from her mother, no more secrets that she had left behind. Griette, and Griette alone, knew what had become of the key, and she had never divulged the knowledge to a living soul. At last, satisfied if not contented, Foss said, very well, then they must contrive a new strategy. Griette was unlikely in the extreme to be of any help – although by all the powers, he'd at least try – and so they had only their own wits and resources to rely on. They must dedicate all those resources to solving the conundrum. The mystery could be unravelled, he was certain of it, and until it was, he and Nempson would stint nothing in the search. Could they count on Calliope to do the same?

Calliope's pulse was racing as her father asked the question. His hostility towards the twilight-dwellers was becoming more and more malevolent and obsessive, and she knew that he would trample any and every principle into the dust to gain the vengeance he believed was his rightful due. The prospects of the lost key falling into his hands didn't bear contemplation – and if she complied, or appeared to, then any discovery she made might be impossible to conceal from him. Yet if she refused, the ground she had gained would be lost; his suspicions would be aroused and her freedom curtailed. Without freedom, she could achieve nothing.

It was a gamble, and the stakes were dangerously high. Calliope thought of Selethe, of Charn. What choice would they have made? Even Griette: if she could understand, what would she have wanted her daughter to do?

Doubt fled. Whatever the risk, Calliope knew there was only one decision she could take, and her eyes lit with an angry zeal whose true significance she hoped with all her strength that Foss would never know.

'Yes,' she said. 'Oh yes, Father. When I think of what they tried to do to me; what they so nearly achieved . . . You can count on my help in every way. Be *assured* of it!'

Foss and Nempson were assured, and work began immediately. Philome raised objections to Calliope's involvement, insisting that she was still convalescing, but Foss swept them aside. Had much of Calliope's strength not returned? Was she not eating heartily? Even the alarming greyness of her skin and hair was rapidly vanishing and being replaced by her normal colour. Work would do her good, he said firmly; and if Philome doubted the verity of that she might do well to look at Luthe as an example of the effects of bone idleness on the human constitution. With a touch more sensitivity for Philome's feelings, Nempson took her aside and promised to personally see that Calliope did not overtax herself, and Philome, ruffled but partly mollified, gave way, to Calliope's great relief.

That afternoon Foss paid a visit to the hospice. He was gone for three hours, and when he returned was not in the best of tempers. Oh, he had seen Griette, and had tried gently and patiently to talk to her and make her understand what he wanted. But Griette had ignored him. She simply sat at her table, Foss told Nempson and Calliope, working on yet another of those futile clay sculptures that seemed to be her only interest and which she never even took the trouble to finish. When the visiting bell tolled and the angels benignly but firmly steered Foss out, she was still working, scrape, scrape, scrape, as though he had never so much as set foot in the room.

Nempson, who had held out little hope that the visit would be of any use, expressed his sympathy and suggested that if Griette was unable to help them, their next line of approach should be to question Selethe again. Hiding her alarm, Calliope ventured cautiously that they should perhaps be gentle; the creature (she had been about to say 'the queen' but corrected herself before the slip could be noticed) was not robust and, as Foss himself had said, she had more value to them alive than dead. Foss concurred, though with some reluctance, and it was agreed that he and Nempson would visit their captive that evening after dinner. He would prefer it, he added, if Calliope was not present.

'It isn't that I don't trust you, my dear; quite the reverse. But we haven't yet discovered the full extent of these creatures' powers, and it could be that you're still vulnerable to some etheric influence that they exert. For safety's sake I think you should stay away from the workroom for a day or two yet.'

Calliope nodded. In fact she did not want to come face to face with Selethe in her father's presence, for she feared that the queen's reaction might inadvertently betray her. She needed to see Selethe; but she must see her alone.

'Yes, Father, I quite understand,' she said, and feigned a shudder. 'To tell the truth, I'd prefer not to have any more contact with the creature than I must.'

'That's only natural.' Foss smiled at her with fond confidence. 'Very well, then. After dinner, Nempson, we'll begin. Meanwhile, Calli, you might take some more time to study your mother's last equations, and see if you can find anything we've overlooked.'

So the pattern went for two more days. Calliope worked long and diligent hours with her father and Nempson, and in her few private moments tried not to give way to the fear and dread that lurked in her like a maggot at the core of an apple. The men had learned nothing of any further use from Selethe, and for all their determination to keep her alive, her vitality was beginning to fail. Hearing their reports, Calliope was deeply disturbed. She believed them when they said that they had done no more to injure the queen; that in fact they had made conditions as comfortable for her as they could. But they had no means of nourishing her, and without sustenance she was declining quickly.

Calliope knew that there was one recourse open to Selethe. She could have fed, carefully and subtly, from her captors' own life-essences; but for some reason it seemed she was refusing to do so. Whether it was through fear or for some darker reason, Calliope couldn't guess. But it made the need for a secret meeting all the more imperative.

Her chance came on the evening of the third day, when Foss unexpectedly announced his intention to visit the Institute. He had been making his own further study of Griette's cryptic equations, and had latched on to a theory that they might be a map of some kind, couched in a mathematical guise which, if unravelled, could provide an important clue. The Institute had a correlation machine for members' use, and by spending an hour or two among its wheels and dials he could check all the possible correspondences far more quickly and efficiently than he could do with ink and paper. Nempson had a mathematical bent and Foss would be obliged to him for his help, and Calliope could accompany them if she wished.

It was the opportunity Calliope had been waiting for, and she pleaded tiredness, championed by Philome who said that an early night, just for once, would do the poor child a power of good. Foss was too engrossed by his theory to say anything more than 'Yes, yes, very well, as you please,' and he and Nempson left the house a short while later. When they had gone, Calliope agreed for appearances' sake to play cards with Philome and Celesta for a while. She waited, curbing her impatience, until Celesta was winning and would thus be determined to carry on, then excused herself. Philome, she knew, would indulge Celesta in a few more games, and with Luthe out as usual and the younger

267

children in bed, there would be no one to witness her foray to the workroom.

Entering the passage beyond the understairs door, Calliope felt a sharp frisson like cold claws in her spine as memories and associations crowded in on her. She pushed them away, trying to quell the thumping of her heart, as she made her way towards the inner sanctum.

Foss had not yet replaced the smashed etherea lamp, and the workroom was unlit, the shutters closed against the moon's intrusive glow. By the feeble light of her pocket-taper Calliope saw that Selethe was asleep. She moved quietly across the floor, dropped to a crouch before the chair, and said softly, 'Madam . . .'

The figure in the chair stirred. Her eyes opened – Calliope saw the taper's reflected glimmer in their silver depths – and she whispered, a soft sound hardly more than a breath, '*Calliope? Oh, Calliope, have they captured you, too . . .?*'

Her look was vague, and Calliope realised that her grip on reality was fading as her strength faded. 'No, madam,' she whispered. 'I'm not a prisoner. But you . . .' She choked back something that tried to block her throat. 'I'm sorry. I'm so *sorry* . . .'

She was trying to convey everything in the word; pity, grief, remorse, anger, and it seemed that Selethe understood on some instinctive level, for her eyes cleared a little and filled with compassion. 'You mustn't blame yourself, dear child. You did not know. None of us knew. Except Charn, perhaps. Yes; Charn . . .' Then suddenly she blinked. 'Oh, but he was here! He came back— I saw him; he . . .' A frown, as though she were struggling to remember. 'But I sent him away. He tried to release me; he could not, and I told him . . .' She drew a breath, with difficulty. 'I told him to find you, and— and to—' She swallowed. 'Did he escape? *Did* he?'

'Yes, he escaped.' Unthinkingly Calliope reached out towards Selethe, then realised that in her haste she had forgotten to bring gloves. Withdrawing her hands, clenching them, she recounted all that had happened, warning Selethe of Foss's intentions and striving to make her understand the danger. 'Madam, he *must* not find the key!' she finished. 'If he does, it will spell disaster for your world!'

Selethe did not seem to comprehend. Her gaze was straying hazily across the room and her mind had drifted into reverie. 'It was so long ago,' she said reflectively. 'I didn't listen, you see. I was unkind . . . my own son . . . but you have promised to find the key, and I know you won't betray me. You have never betrayed me, Calliope. Nor has Charn. You and Charn. Malorn and Griette. It is all so sad, so sad . . .'

Calliope's heart twisted in her; she forced the pain of it away, forced herself to hold to her purpose. 'Madam, try to understand what I'm saying! I don't *know* how to find the key, and I'm so afraid that my father will succeed before I can! Please, *please*, is there anything more you can tell me that might help?'

'Anything more . . .' A frown of concentration creased the queen's brow, then she shook her head slowly. 'No. There is nothing else; nothing at all. It is all told; all gone.' She paused. 'Only Charn . . . if . . .'

'If?' Calliope prompted urgently.

'Charn and Griette.' Selethe swallowed again. 'Yes; Charn and Griette. Charn is so like Malorn. If Griette still remembers . . .'

If she remembered Malorn. If she should come face to face with another like him . . . Chill sweat broke out on Calliope's skin, and suddenly she was queasy and terrified, and hurting on a deep, deep level that she couldn't even begin to comprehend.

'Madam, I must find Charn! I must reach him!' If only she could release Selethe, get her away, get her back to her own world – but her father had the key to the waist clamp, and even if she could have retrieved it, Selethe's mind and body were too insecure. She would be unable to use the gateway, or even understand what was needed. And if by a miracle she did succeed, what would happen when Foss found her gone? He would know she had not escaped without help, and that only one person could have aided her. All the ground that Calliope had gained would be undone in a moment, and she could not afford that, whatever the cost.

Tears of miserable frustration stung Calliope's eyes. Charn would surely come back; he had failed once to rescue Selethe, and she was certain he would not let matters rest there. But time was against her; with Selethe's life declining and each hour that passed increasing the danger of her father breaking the code of

Griette's legacy she could not afford to sit by and wait for his return. Once, yes, she had opened the gateway for herself, but she knew in her marrow that she would not succeed a second time. The power that had touched her then, whatever it was, could not be called to life again now.

She concentrated on Selethe once more. The queen's eyes had closed and she seemed to be slipping into an uneasy doze. There was nothing Calliope could do to help her, and she could not afford to stay with her much longer. But before she left, she must try just once more to make her understand.

'Madam!' Again she started to reach out; again remembered in time and drew back. 'Madam, can you hear me?'

Selethe's eyelids fluttered and opened, though her eyes did not focus clearly. 'You are Calliope . . .?'

'Yes, yes, I am Calliope . . . oh, please, *try* to hear me and understand! If Charn returns, if he should find his way here and come to you, you *must* tell him—' She stopped suddenly as she realised that Selethe was paying no heed but instead was gazing towards the shuttered window. There was a faraway look on the queen's face, and she said,

'Charn will return. But he cannot stay, and Griette cannot go with him. They must part. Unless they dare to take the Sacrament . . .'

Her mind was straying towards the borders of delirium as times and identities became confused in her thoughts. But her last words sent a shiver through Calliope that raised gooseflesh on her arms.

'The Sacrament?' she echoed, very softly.

Selethe nodded. 'Oh, yes. Oh, yes. She would not try, you see. She did not have the courage.' Her head turned and she gave Calliope a steady and shockingly lucid look. 'But you are different. You and Charn. You can be together, stay together, if you are willing to take the step that they could not take.'

There was a roaring pulse in Calliope's ears, the sound of her own blood suddenly racing in her veins, and a constricting, suffocating sensation swelled in her lungs and throat. She could barely speak, but she forced the words out.

'*What do you mean?*'

Selethe's silver eyes closed and her head sagged back against the chair. 'That is why I came,' she whispered. 'To tell you. Charn said I must not, for the dangers of temptation are too great. But Charn is wrong. There is hope. In the Sacrament . . .'

Her consciousness was fading, slipping away, and in panic Calliope finally forgot all the strictures between them and took hold of her arms, almost shaking her. 'Queen Selethe – Queen Selethe, wake up!' she cried, anguished. 'I don't understand – in pity's name, *tell me what the Sacrament is!*'

Selethe sighed, and the sigh became a moan; not of pain but of something else; something far older and deeper than any mere physical affliction. 'How can I tell what I do not know?' Now her voice had a strange, sing-song quality, as though she were reciting some arcane litany. 'We do not know, and we have never known its meaning. But it is there. It is a part of our world and our history and our being . . . perhaps a part of our souls, though who can ever tell the secrets of the soul . . .?' She sighed again. 'So ancient. So very ancient. Yet it is a perilous road . . . Charn understands. He knows it is why Malorn died, and so he will not let you make the choice . . .'

Unsteadily, Calliope released her arms and drew back. The first shock was receding; but in its place was the sickness of excitement, and of a hope that she dared not let herself recognise.

'But you,' she whispered, 'do not agree with him?'

Selethe uttered a peculiar, mewing sound. 'I do not know. I cannot say. How greatly can two souls love one another? For Malorn it is not enough, you see, and so the Sacrament will fail and I believe he will die of it.' A frown flickered. 'Has died. *Has* died. I grieve so for him . . . but you must not grieve with me. Unless you, too, should fail . . .' Suddenly then her eyes opened once more, and this time their gaze seemed to penetrate to the core of all Calliope was, or could ever become. 'Charn must tell you. You must *make* him tell you, for it is the one hope and the one chance you and he will ever have. Make him tell you about the Sacrament of Night – and you and he must choose.'

Silence clamped down on the room as though a vast, invisible hand had closed around it. For several seconds Calliope could not speak, could not even breathe. Selethe's eyes were shut again, her body motionless, and at last Calliope broke her own paralysis.

'Madam . . .'

No reply.

'Madam . . . Queen Selethe . . .' She touched Selethe's arm

271

again. There was no response, not even a quiver of movement. The queen still breathed, though shallowly. But she was unconscious.

Slowly, so very slowly, Calliope backed away from the chair. On the table her pocket-taper still glowed, and she fumbled blindly for it, held it up so that its small light illuminated the queen's face. Perspiration gleamed on Selethe's brow but still she did not stir. Calliope sensed that nothing she might do would wake her, and it seemed a vain cruelty even to try.

Moving like a sleepwalker, and feeling suddenly old and burdened far, far beyond her years, she left the workroom, closing the door softly behind her.

Chapter XXII

By the time the public conveyance drew to a halt at the top of Charity Hill, Calliope was unsure that her resolve would be enough to carry her through what lay ahead. She felt sick, she was perspiring, and her legs were so numb and unsteady that they seemed barely able to support her. Alighting, she paused for a moment, breathing fresh air in an effort to rally herself, then started like a frightened animal as one of the conveyance horses snorted unexpectedly. Heart pounding, she stared after the vehicle as it lumbered into motion and on along the road, and thought: *Great powers, what sort of spiritless weakling am I?* Calm; she must be calm. Organise herself. She had Philome's and Celesta's presents, and one of her own; her alibi for making this visit without arousing suspicions. She had rehearsed (and rehearsed and rehearsed, late into the night until exhaustion overcame her) what she would do and say. All was prepared. She had only to keep her nerve.

The visiting bell was sounding as she walked through the hospice gates and up the gravelled drive. Ahead of her were several other people who had travelled on the same conveyance, and Calliope pushed away an irrational fear that they might recognise her. What matter if they did? Her presence here was legitimate, and her secret did *not* blaze out around her like an aura for the world to see. Look at things; distract herself. The fountain was playing, its jets catching the sunlight in glittering cascades. The grass of the lawns had been newly cut. The willow trees beyond the lawns were in full leaf now, and their leaves rippled as though imitating the fountain and trying to surpass it.

The entrance door lay ahead and in the hall beyond angels were waiting to escort the visitors. Calliope glimpsed the Hospice Master in the background but turned her head aside, not wanting him to see her. Then along the blue-walled corridors, an elderly angel sailing like a plump, white bird before her, and into the small, familiar room.

Griette was not working at her sculptures. Instead she was sitting on a chair by the window, gazing out at the sunlit garden. She did not look round when Calliope entered, and Calliope saw that an uncompleted clay model stood on the table, with the wooden tools ranged neatly beside it. She ventured a closer look, but the model was formless as yet and it was impossible to judge what it might become. Doubtless it would never be finished.

'Mother?' She spoke softly, and to her surprise Griette turned round. Her eyes met her daughter's and she frowned as though some tiny spark had flickered in her memory. Then it vanished, and the frown was replaced by a pleasant but empty smile.

'Dear Mother, I have so much to tell you.' That was a harmless beginning, Calliope had decided, and she moved closer to the chair, displaying her parcels as she did so. 'But first, I've brought you presents from Celesta and from me and – and from Philome.' Even after so long a time she still felt uncomfortable whenever she spoke her stepmother's name in Griette's presence. Griette, though, was as unmoved by it as by anything else, and as Calliope set the gifts down on the window ledge she looked at them detachedly.

'Shall I unwrap them for you?' Calliope's fingers were clumsy with nervousness, and she tore the paper. Her gift was a block of fine clay, Philome's a lace mat for Griette's table. Celesta, however, had departed from her usual choices and sent a box of coloured oil-crayons, reasoning with a flash of inspiration that if her mother liked to sculpt, she might also like to draw. Griette stared at the crayons with dawning interest, then reached out and picked one of them from the box. Its colour was dark blue, almost grey, and she began to draw long, sweeping but careful strokes with it on the white-painted sill.

Calliope sat down, her hands twisting nervously together. Now that she was ready to begin, her courage was wavering again. In a surge of optimism – or perhaps of desperation – she had convinced herself that she would find a way to reach her mother's mind; but now that she was faced with the prospect of putting intent into practice the task seemed impossibly daunting. She had resolved to approach Griette obliquely, with gentleness and caution, so that the terrible mistake she had made once before wouldn't be repeated. Yet what chance was there that gentleness and caution would make any impression on Griette's shuttered mind? *Look at her now*, Calliope thought. *Engrossed in her small diversions, uninterested in anything around her. She doesn't even know who I am.*

She forced the thought away, knowing that it could all too easily discourage her to the point where she would give up without even trying, and started to talk to her mother. The one-sided conversation was innocuous to begin with; then carefully and by degrees Calliope began to turn it towards the subject she wanted to raise. Griette ignored her and worked on absorbedly. The crayon lines were growing and merging; they looked like tresses of blue-grey hair now, and covered a quarter of the sill.

At last Calliope paused to rest and re-think. She was dejected and discouraged; this was achieving nothing, and she felt that she could talk on inconsequentially all day without any effect whatever. Yet somewhere in her mother's memory was the knowledge she so desperately needed. There *must* be a way to reach her.

Then, abruptly, the crayon paused. It was worn down to half its original size, and Griette's fingers were stained blue; for a moment Calliope thought that she was about to begin work on a new pattern, but instead she set the crayon aside and stared at what she had drawn as though something about it puzzled her. Then, quickly, she cocked her head towards the window, her expression alert. Calliope listened but could hear nothing out of the ordinary – yet Griette's attentiveness was increasing, and underlying it was a growing air of excitement.

Suddenly, Griette smiled. Calliope had never seen such a smile before; it was a wide, manic grin, almost akin to a snarl, and

Griette's eyes had lit with hectic energy. She looked directly at Calliope, and a strange, brilliant awareness flooded into her look. Then she said, with absolute and unambiguous clarity:

'*Dead.*'

As Calliope's own eyes widened in shock, Griette picked up the crayon, snapped it in half and threw the pieces down with such force that they rebounded across the room. Then she started to laugh. The laughter rose hysterically, louder and wilder, and there was screaming in it, and crying, and Griette's fingernails were digging savagely into her own upper arms as she rocked back and forth on the chair, her body jolting and jerking as though a fit had seized her.

The angel alerted by the commotion found Griette struggling like a wildcat against Calliope's frantic efforts to calm and control her. The woman shouted urgently for assistance, and in a frenzy of screaming and kicking Griette was carried away to the infirmary. Calliope, dishevelled and breathless and distressed, hastened out of the room after the party, but as she emerged the Hospice Master stepped into her path.

'Calliope.' He held up a hand, barring her way. 'A word, if you please.'

Other doors had opened along the corridor, and inmates and visitors alike were peering out, concerned and curious. Calliope felt her cheeks flaming, told herself that it was only the heat of exertion and shrank back into the room, away from the spectators. The Hospice Master and the angel who had first come to the rescue followed, and the Hospice Master closed the door.

'I think,' he said, not unpleasantly but with a firmness that brooked no argument, 'that an explanation is in order. Hmm?' He looked from Calliope to the angel and back again, and haltingly Calliope told him what had happened. He questioned her closely, wanting to know every detail of what she had said and done since her arrival, then questioned the angel, and at last seemed satisfied that, whatever the cause of Griette's fit, it was not Calliope's doing.

'I have to observe, however,' he said, and there was a coldness to his tone now, 'that this is, shall we say, a rather unpleasant repetition of the episode that occurred on one of your previous visits.'

Calliope flushed again. 'I've visited my mother since then, sir, and nothing untoward happened.'

'I appreciate that. Nonetheless, it's not a coincidence that I like, and it most *certainly* is not helpful to your mother's condition.'

She nodded miserably. 'Yes, sir, I realise that. But truly, I said and did *nothing* that could have brought it on!' *Only intended to . . . but surely I'm not to blame, when the words were never spoken?*

The Hospice Master relented. 'I believe what you say, Calliope,' he told her more kindly. 'But it does seem, does it not, that something about your presence upsets your mother on occasion. We can't tell what it is, and there's little point in attempting to analyse it . . . but I'm afraid I must draw the conclusion that it might be better for her wellbeing if you were not to visit her again for a while.'

There was a tightness in Calliope's lungs, and she was horribly afraid that she might make an utter fool of herself by bursting into tears. 'I understand,' she said unhappily.

The Hospice Master nodded. 'Then the best thing all round would be to let the matter rest and say no more.' He indicated the door with a courteous gesture. 'I'm sure you'll wish to stay until the physician can tell us that all is well. But after that . . .'

He did not need to say the rest; it was a dismissal, and a tacit admonishment. Calliope said, 'Thank you, sir,' in a small voice and, unable to meet his gaze, walked slowly out of the room.

She waited in the hall until the physician emerged from the infirmary. The fit, he reported, had passed; in fact it had vanished as suddenly as it had begun. Griette was calm, had been given something to ensure the calm was maintained, and was now peaceably asleep. No lasting harm had been done, and in his opinion it had been simply an unfortunate and isolated lapse.

Calliope knew that the Hospice Master was watching from his office window as she walked slowly away down the drive. She had tried to ask him, obliquely, not to tell her father of this, but had no way of knowing whether or not he would do so. If he did . . . she refused to let herself dwell on it; it was a problem she would face if and when it arose. For the moment she was too disheartened to care.

She had a return ticket for the public conveyance, but could not face the thought of sitting among strangers who might stare at her and draw conclusions from her unhappy face and dejected manner. She walked down Charity Hill and into the busier streets of the town, trying to give her attention to the pleasant day and blocking out all other thoughts. She felt weary to the bone; she needed sleep and wanted to lie down in her room for an hour or two before even considering anything else. Not that there was much to consider, for this abortive plan of trying to coax information from Griette had been the only idea she had that was of any use. She had been filled with such pent-up excitement this morning; the tumult of hope, the sense of being on the brink of a wonderful discovery. Now, the feeling was gone. There was nothing.

She reached the square where her home stood, crossed it and climbed the steps into the house. In the hall she met Philome.

'Calli, my dear.' Philome smiled compassionately at her. 'How is your poor mother today?'

With an effort Calliope dredged up a pretence of normality. 'She's much the same,' she replied, then as a tactful afterthought added, 'I think she liked all the presents.'

She started to take off her hat, and Philome said, 'Your hair looks very untidy. I hope you didn't go out with it like that?'

'What?' *Fighting with Griette; wrestling with her* . . . 'Oh, no . . . no, I didn't. The wind disordered it, that's all.'

'I wouldn't have thought there *was* any wind today.' Philome craned to see through the small window beside the front door, but her interest was momentary and she turned to another subject. 'Oh, Calli – if you intend to see your father now, I'd best warn you that he is not in a good mood.'

'Isn't he?' Half way to the stairs Calliope paused. 'Why? What's happened?'

Philome pulled a discomforted face. 'That creature in the workroom died a little while ago, and your father is highly displeased about it.'

She spoke so unceremoniously that for a moment Calliope did not fully take in what she had said. Then it hit her, and she felt as if someone had punched her in the stomach.

'*What?*' She couldn't believe it. She didn't believe it, and her mind floundered, reaching desperately for a denial. 'Philome— Philome, did you say that—'

'Quite why Foss is so annoyed is beyond me, I must say,' Philome continued. 'After all, he knew it might happen; he was saying so to Nempson only yesterday. Personally . . . well, I know

277

I should feel a little sorry for it, and I suppose I do, but I honestly admit that I'm relieved, after what the creature tried to inflict on you. Foss might claim to have rendered it harmless, but while it was under our roof I simply didn't have a single easy moment.' She stopped suddenly. 'Are you all right, Calli? You look very pale.'

'Yes.' Calliope heard her own voice. It seemed to come from a long, long way off. 'I'm all right, thank you, Philome.' She was going to cry. She knew she was. 'What has Father done with the . . . the . . .'

'The remains? I really don't know, and confess I don't want to. I should imagine that the safest thing is to burn it; though Foss and Nempson will probably want to take it to the Institute for more of their horrid experiments.' Philome shuddered squeamishly. 'How they can *enjoy* such things . . .'

Queen Selethe. A corpse on a marble slab; an object for cold-blooded dissection and examination . . . The threat of tears had vanished. Instead, Calliope thought she was about to be sick.

Some reserve of strength inside her came to her rescue and again she heard herself speak as though another agency were controlling her. 'I think in that case I won't disturb Father until he's in a better frame of mind,' she said. She was smiling at Philome. How could she have found the resources to do that? 'I'll go upstairs and rest for a while.'

'Do,' Philome agreed approvingly. 'I'll call you when lunch is served, and then this afternoon perhaps you'd like to go shopping?'

Calliope didn't answer. She was climbing the stairs, glad on a numb and prosaic level that the house was as familiar to her as the contours of her own hand. For she was feeling her way by memory, nothing more. She could see nothing, she was blinded by a hot, scarlet fog of grief and rage and anguish – and by the knowledge of what her mother had meant when she uttered that one, unequivocal word before the fit took hold of her. Selethe must have died at that very moment, and Griette had known. Somehow, she had *known*.

Calliope levered herself up the next stair, and the next, and the next. She felt like a doll, an automaton, all feelings and emotions blotted out and only an appalling void remaining.

Except that in her mind, silently and incessantly, she was screaming Charn's name.

He would have no ceremony. It had been his first edict, and every courtier, from highest to lowest, felt sympathy with the decision. So the rites that by tradition should have welcomed a new ruler were set aside, and Charn had taken his place on the black throne in an atmosphere of grim and bitter sorrow.

He would never forget the sensation that had hit him at the moment of Selethe's death. They had all known; by some means long accepted but not understood, the queen and her predecessors had had an arcane psychic link with the people they ruled, and her passing sent a massive shock-wave through the entire realm. For Charn, who perhaps was closer to her than any other living soul, the effect was like a tornado ripping through his mind; a screaming tumult first of pain and then of fury as he fought violently against acknowledging what he knew in his marrow to be the truth. Later, when the worst of the storm was over, Thimue told him that for a while he had been demented and the court had feared not only for his life but for the lives of anyone who came within his reach. The madness had struck others, too; but Charn's affliction was the worst . . . and his burden, now, the greatest.

So he sat, as he must, among the dim lights and soft shadows of the great hall, while the observances of the court, though subdued, went on around him. He felt like an alien and a usurper. No matter that Selethe had named him as her heir, and bequeathed him her trust and her confidence. He did not *want* this; he never had. He only wanted to turn back time and see his queen, the rightful queen, restored to her place. Or, when harsh reality dragged him from the refuge of that dream, to be avenged on those who had brought about her death.

No one in the twilight world knew how Selethe had died; the psychic link, though potent, was not great enough for that. But in their minds they were certain of one fact – directly or indirectly, deliberately or otherwise, humans had murdered her. For a short time there was brave talk of a mass assault on the bright world to claim reprisal; Charn crushed it relentlessly, knowing better than anyone what the result would inevitably be. But in his heart he yearned for it as fiercely as anyone. Justice – for their queen, and for themselves; a salve for the wound that had been inflicted on them.

The rage that infected the court, though, soon began to fade. The grief and the aching sense of loss had not diminished, but the twilight-dwellers had no truly warlike instincts, and before long their hatred inevitably gave way to quiet, bleak inertia. Charn's rulership was accepted, listlessly but unquestioningly; Selethe was mourned, but in time the sadness would pass. Life continued.

Even Charn himself might have fallen prey to the attitude that was overtaking the realm as the early shock of their loss wore off. Certainly his mood invited it; he was withdrawn, reserved, uninterested in anything beyond the bounds of necessity, and spent much time lost in his thoughts, which he shared with no one. Many of those thoughts were of Calliope. Like Selethe he believed that she had not betrayed her promise, and the belief was his one shred of comfort. But as to how she fared now . . . he had no way of knowing. And he wanted to know, for without that knowledge he could have no peace of mind. There was no possible future and thus no possible point in his feelings for Calliope; but love allowed for no contingencies, and could not be set aside simply because it could never be fulfilled. By a grotesque irony, he was snared by the same trap that had held Selethe for so many years: the trap of uncertainty and fear and the need to discover the truth. It undermined everything; it gnawed at him, ate at him, corroded every waking hour. Yet he could not and dared not follow where impulse wanted to lead. He had new responsibilities which could not be ignored; his place was here, as Selethe's had been, and duty must come first.

But then the deputation came to him. Charn had not expected this, at least not so soon, and what the councillors had to say took him by surprise. They spoke to him, discreetly but emphatically, of the gateway, and their view was unequivocal. The door between this world and the human dimension must at last be sealed. While Selethe lived and Malorn's fate was unknown there had been a reason, albeit disputed in some quarters, not to take that step. Now though, Selethe and Malorn were both gone and the reason had died with them. For the sake of his people, they said, Charn *must* act.

Charn heard the petition in pensive silence. Only a short time ago he would have argued ferociously against what the advisers were urging him to do, but now he knew they were right. There could be no justification for delaying any longer. Perhaps partly from habit he reminded them that to seal the way was no sure safeguard; the key Malorn had taken was still missing, and if it should fall into human hands the gate could be unlocked again. Even as he spoke, however, he knew what the response would be. There could indeed be no certainties, but as matters stood there was an ever-present danger that, by chance or design, humans would find the way into the twilight world as Calliope had done, and there would be no barrier to stop them. If the gateway was sealed, only a key could break it; without that, humans would be powerless and their world was safe. The hazard would still exist, but the risk would be greatly reduced.

On an oddly detached level Charn was almost amused by the councillors' surprise at his response to their plea. They had expected opposition and were prepared for it with arguments and speeches; instead, they found him willing to listen and to give their advice serious consideration. They wondered at the reason for his apparent change of heart – but they could not see beyond the outward mask, to where an inner fiend was driving Charn and setting light to the fire of a reckless idea.

It had come to him on the first night after his formal accession, as he sat in the otherwise deserted hall with the closed curtains of the throne shifting like ghosts around him and only silence for a companion. At first he had dismissed it, aware that he was in a dangerous state of mind and not fit to make rational decisions. But as his mind calmed, the concept had persisted, growing and evolving until it had too strong a grip on him to be ignored. Nonetheless he had continued to fight it – but when the councillors came with their appeal, suddenly everything fitted into place. Charn knew that as ruler of the twilight world he had, potentially, a long life ahead of him; as long as Selethe's had been. But the prospect of spending it as she had spent her last fifteen years filled him with a feeling of dread that stabbed so deep that he believed he would not endure it and stay sane. Unwittingly, the councillors had shown him an alternative; and he intended to take it.

For the sake of form he pretended to deliberate a while on the petition, then called his advisers to him again. He would grant their request, he told them. The gate would be sealed, and he would carry out the deed himself, as his last tribute to Queen Selethe.

Their gratitude set a worm of discomfort twisting in him when he thought of the trick he was about to play on them and on all his new subjects. In truth this was no tribute to Selethe but a personal mutiny against everything she had stood for. Duty, responsibility, loyalty: he was abandoning them all. Except, possibly, loyalty . . . but the loyalty Charn had in mind took another form. Selethe would have been grieved by his decision. But he wanted to believe that she would also have understood.

Charn fully intended to close the way between worlds; that much, at least, was not a deception. But when he performed the ritual, he would perform it from the other side. He would enter the human world one last time – and only then would he seal the gate that had allowed his people to move freely between the two dimensions.

He had thought long and deeply about what such a step would truly mean. Perhaps it was his way of evading the other and more selfish consideration; but if it was, he did not allow himself to acknowledge it. He was about to nullify something that had existed for more centuries than anyone knew; a quirk, a phenomenon, which since its discovery had been a source of danger and fascination in equal measure. It should have been done long ago, Charn thought. The course was simple enough; a charge of psychic force that would send a cross-current through the gateway and turn its own energies back on themselves. Those energies would cease to flow, and no inhabitant of the twilight world – not even its ruler – would be able to open the way between dimensions by will alone. Only a key could grant the power to awaken it again. A key such as Malorn had made, capturing a spark of the gate's own essence and enshrining it in corporeal form, as a gift of hope to his love.

And now Malorn's key would also become the sole symbol of hope for Charn. If it could be found, it would grant him the power to return to his own realm. If it were not, then when time ran out for him he would die in the bright world, and a new successor would take the black throne. In either case, whichever way fate moved and however brief a span he might have, he would be with Calliope again. It was a choice that sprang from madness. But better madness, Charn told himself, than a life of irresolvable regret. Malorn had made that same choice, and now he understood why. He would follow where his old, dear friend had led . . . for Malorn, it seemed, had been his mentor in more ways than either of them could ever have foretold.

He made no arrangements and gave no clue of his intentions to any soul. He might have named a successor, but could entrust the knowledge to no one: even Thimue could not be taken into his confidence this time, for he knew that the physician would be forced to put duty before all else and give warning to the court. His people would have to choose for themselves, and he was confident that their choice would be sound. The sealing of the gateway, he said, would be done in the hall, from the throne, and he commanded courtiers and servants alike to leave. Watching them go, he felt a pang of doubt to which fear added spice; fear of an unknown future, fear that he would bitterly regret what he had done. Above all, the rational fear of death. Almost gently, he pushed it away. The die was cast. He would not and could not turn back now.

The great hall was empty, silent, still. Charn looked at his own hands where they lay on the arms of the throne. This was not his natural place. It felt wrong. It *was* wrong.

With a smooth, calm gesture he bade the shifting play of light to be gone. It faded; shadows swept in on him, darker, darker, until there was only darkness, complete and perfect.

Charn closed his eyes, and the scent of white flowers swelled on the motionless air.

Chapter XXIII

In the past few days Calliope had called on reserves of strength that she did not know she possessed. To keep up a pretence of normality was imperative; more than ever now she had to hold on to the ground she had won with her father and Nempson; and if inwardly she was being torn apart by grief and fear she dared not show the smallest sign of it. She must continue to work. She must continue to pretend allegiance to their cause. Above all she must continue to hunt in secret for a clue, any clue, to the fate of the lost key.

All this she had resolved on the night after Selethe's death, alone in her room with sleep as far from her reach as it was possible to be. She had cried uncontrollably for two hours, and when the outpouring was over she went to sit at the window, gazing out on to the square as calm returned. The sky had been clear and the moon strong; though she couldn't quite see its orb from her vantage point, its glow bleached the sky from charcoal to a flat pewter, blotting out the stars. The light seemed to mirror her own frame of mind; like the sky, her thoughts now were stark, cold, empty of everything but a strange, colourless clarity that put aside emotion and replaced it with something far more impersonal. She had told herself then that there was no point in grieving for Selethe. The queen was dead, nothing would bring her back – and Calliope had a promise to keep. *That* should be her tribute; not tears and lamentations but the fulfilment of the pledge she had made.

So she had rallied herself. She felt like a player in a pageant-show, looking and speaking and acting from behind the disguise of a painted mask; indeed, it was easier to think of her behaviour as a role to be performed to the best of her ability, and the ploy worked. Even Philome was taken in, while Foss, self-assured as ever, did not consider for a single moment that things might not be entirely as they seemed.

Foss had eventually reconciled himself to the loss of the captive. Most of his anger had been triggered by the fact that Selethe had cheated him of his personal vengeance, and he declared more than once that he thought it likely she had deliberately willed herself to die. He found some consolation in the fact that they at least had undamaged remains to dissect and examine, and had Selethe's body removed to the Institute, where the full resources of science could be brought to bear on their research. He was toying with the possibility that the carcass might yield some clue to the nature of the key they were seeking; it was unlikely in the extreme, as he said to Calliope, but in the absence of any other trails to follow it was at least worth trying. Calliope nodded, voiced agreement, and politely declined when he asked her if she would like to join in the experiments. There was bile in her throat and nausea in her stomach at the thought of the butchery about to be perpetrated on Selethe. But it would keep Foss occupied at the Institute for a while, and for that she could only be thankful, for it granted her just a little more time to pray that Charn would return. That, now, was the only hope she had left.

She had not attempted to visit her mother again. The Hospice Master's veiled warning had gone home; he had not reported the incident to Foss on this occasion, but Calliope dared not put his forbearance to the test a second time. Foss himself had seen Griette again, but his attempts to coax anything from her had fared no better. There had been no fits or frenzies, it seemed, but neither had there been anything else; in fact, Foss said testily, she seemed to have developed an obsession with the crayons Celesta had sent her. Not that she did anything worthwhile with them; just filled in shapeless blocks of colour and went over them time and again until the paper the angels had given her – to save the room's paintwork – was worn through. Celesta, in his opinion, should have foreseen the consequences of her action, and he trusted she would consider future gifts carefully and not make any more foolish choices.

So the search continued fruitlessly, with Calliope torn between relief at the lack of progress and intensifying frustration at her own impotence. In the sanctuary of her room she had tried to send a telepathic message to Charn, begging for his help, but even as she willed herself to concentrate she knew that her efforts were futile. No one had ever proved satisfactorily that mind-communication was even possible; and even if it was, the idea of transmitting her thoughts between *worlds* was madness. Charn could not hear her. She could only wait for him to act of his own volition.

Late on the evening of the fourth day after Selethe's death, Foss, Calliope and Nempson gathered in the library. Everyone else was abed, the servants included, but Foss had insisted that he did not want to wait until morning. This afternoon he had lit upon a new theory, or the skeleton of one, and he wished to discuss it without any delay.

Calliope was not looking forward to the encounter, for she knew what the main topic of conversation would be. Both men had spent long hours at the Institute, engrossed in their examination of Selethe's corpse. The dissection had gone well enough, if inconclusively, to begin with; but then certain anomalies had emerged which, if Foss's notions were right, might be of some use to them. Wishing that she had avoided even the small amount she had eaten at dinner, Calliope steeled herself to listen to what her father had to say. The creature's remains, he told her, appeared in essence to be very little different from a human body. It had a heart, lungs, stomach and other mess of vital organs, and all were located in the proper places. They had removed the brain to examine it (Calliope gripped her glass of brandy and strove to maintain a dispassionate expression), and even this was much the same as a human's, barring some differences in its outer contours and folds. He himself had cut it open, and—

'Excuse me, Father.' Calliope got hastily to her feet. 'It's a little . . . airless in here. Would you object if I opened the window?'

'Do, my dear.' Foss smiled indulgently, and Nempson said,

'I suspect Calliope finds the subject a little repellent, Foss. She isn't yet experienced in these matters; perhaps we shouldn't dwell too much on the fine details?'

Foss looked at Calliope's back where she stood by the window. 'Nonsense,' he replied equably. 'Calliope's made of sterner stuff, aren't you, Calli?'

She said, 'Yes,' hoping that her voice sounded normal. The fresh air was helping, and there was a faint scent of honeysuckle drifting in from the garden. Away to her right she could just make out the dark bulk of the extended kitchen and the outhouse beyond. The outhouse above the cellar, where she had found the gateway. *Could* she open it again? Every instinct denied it; but in her desperation had she anything to lose by trying . . .?

Foss said, 'Calli?' and she started, turned round and saw him frowning at her.

'I don't believe you heard a word of what I just said, daughter.'

She hadn't, that was the truth of it, and she felt her face reddening. 'I'm sorry, Father. I was diverted for a moment.'

'Well, kindly pay attention from now on. I'm sure there's nothing visible in the garden, let alone diverting, and it's a plaguey nuisance to have to keep repeating myself. I was *saying* that there appear to be some very notable differences in the corrugations of the brain. The network of nerve-matter follows a quite unfamiliar pattern, and . . .'

Somewhere nearby Calliope thought she glimpsed a peculiar

flicker of light. It lasted only a moment, but it snagged her attention. Too faint for lightning, unless the storm was a very long way off . . . she listened abstractedly for a distant growl of thunder, unconsciously thankful for anything to distract her from what her father was saying, but no thunder came. Foss continued with his discourse; then, suddenly and belatedly realising that she was still not listening, broke off in mid-sentence and said reprovingly, 'Calli! Living spirits, girl, wake up and concentrate!'

The light flickered again. It was much brighter this time, and Calliope blinked, stepping quickly back from the window as an after-image danced before her eyes. Foss paused on the brink of a sharp reprimand and instead demanded, 'What's amiss? Is it an insect, have you been stung?'

Nempson, though, had glimpsed the light for himself. 'There's something outside—' He started to get to his feet; Foss said, 'What?' and heaved himself out of his chair, striding after him to the window. They peered out, but the light had vanished again and there was nothing to be seen.

Nempson leaned over the sill, peering to left and right. 'Whatever it was, I can see no obvious cause.' He ducked his head in again. 'What did you make of it, Calliope? I thought for a moment it was lightning, but there's no feeling of any storm in the air.'

Calliope returned to the window. She was uneasy and couldn't fathom why. It was like a sense of premonition.

She said: 'I don't think—'

Then the explosion came.

It happened in absolute silence, but was no less spectacular for that. Light seemed to erupt from the ground in a single, huge detonation, and though Calliope knew it was incredible and impossible, the light was black. It seared their eyes, it blinded them – but it was *black*.

Nempson, who took the full brunt of it, reeled back with a cry of shock, clapping both hands over his face in a frantic attempt to block the shattering brilliance out. For an instant the entire library lit up in stark monochrome, like an artist's etching – then the light was gone.

Outside in the silence that followed came the sharp, unmistakable sound of a door shutting.

'Calli! Nempson!' Foss's hands found them as they lurched

helplessly. By sheer luck he had turned his head away at the crucial moment, and in a rapid, unthinking reflex had protected his face with an upflung arm. His vision was unimpaired, and he jostled them aside to reach the window, his voice rising in a furious challenge.

'*Who's out there? Show yourself!*'

Calliope tried to look, to see what he had seen, but starbursts were pulsing in front of her. She heard her father shout for the pressure-lamp, then swear when no one brought it to him; he barrelled back across the room to fetch it himself, and held it out of the window at arm's length, peering into the dark.

There was a flick of movement by the outhouse wall, and something darted into the deeper shadows. Foss roundly cursed the lamp's inadequacy and groped in a coat pocket for his firebox. 'Nempson! Great powers, man, you can surely see well enough now – there's a torch on the mantel; hand it to me, quickly!'

The after-effects of the blast were wearing off, and Nempson hurried to comply. Foss lit the torch, and as it hissed into life he headed across the room to the door. There was a side passage to the garden, used mostly by the children; shouting for the others to follow, Foss ran along it. Bolts grated – Calliope, last of the trio, was just beginning to focus her eyes again – and they all hastened outside.

'Over there, in the corner!' Foss pointed and started towards the spot where a lilac bush had encroached over the high wall that separated the kitchen yard from the garden beyond. 'That's where it went, whatever it is!' He turned up the torch and as the flame leaped its sulphurous stink tarnished the freshness of the night air – but not before Calliope's senses had caught a hint of something else.

White flowers . . .

'*Ah, no . . .*' The words were out before she could stop herself, and though her voice was no more than a whisper, Foss heard. He pivoted on his heel. 'What's that? What do you mean?'

She gazed helplessly back at him, realisation dawning and with it horror. She knew where the blast of light had come from, and she knew what, or rather who, had caused it. *Show yourself*, Foss had challenged. He would not. But he was here, only a mere few paces from them, hidden in the deep shadows – and cornered.

288

'Father . . .' But there was nothing she could say. Quickly she glanced towards the wall. Charn didn't know the garden and would not realise that he could escape that way. He might try, in desperation. But if he did not, there would be no escape. And if Foss shouted for the servants—

Her body seemed to be one vast, beating pulse as she watched her father walk slowly, cautiously towards the lilac. He was perhaps five paces from it when there was a sudden, violent flurry in the bush and a figure erupted from it. The torch illuminated pale hair, a wild-eyed face – then with a bellow born of fury and triumph together Foss launched himself across the running shape's path. They collided, staggered, cannoned against the wall; then Nempson was rushing to Foss's aid and the two of them grappled with Charn. He fought back like a savage animal, but to him the light and heat of the torch were deadly weapons, and he was forced to use half his skill and energy in a ducking, weaving effort to avoid it.

'Pin it, Nempson!' Foss roared. 'Pin its arms – hold it back so I can strike for its skull!'

He was swinging the torch like a sword, the flame carving through the air with a baleful whining sound. A window banged open on an upper floor and Philome's agitated voice called out, but no one heeded her, nor heeded the lamps that were coming on in adjoining houses as neighbours were woken by the commotion. Calliope had stood paralysed, unable to grasp that this was real, that it was happening – then with a jolt that shook her to the core everything snapped into focus and she heard her own voice going up the scale in a hysterical shriek of fury.

'*No! NO! LET HIM ALONE!*'

She hurled her body like a stone from a catapult across the space between herself and Foss. Her nails clawed for his face, for his hair; then as he turned in astonished outrage she snatched the torch from his hands and flung it away with all her strength. It flew from her in a spinning, slicing arc, and she screamed out again: '*Charn, run! Over the wall; it's the only way out! Go – if you love me, GO!*'

With a ferocious reflex Charn broke Nempson's hold on him and sent him staggering back. In the moonlight and confusion Calliope glimpsed his face just for a single second, and the look he flung to her sparked joy and agony together. Then, before

Nempson could recover, he turned, sprang like a cat – she saw him catch a lilac branch, swing himself up, then the bush agitated wildly and he was gone.

Foss bellowed, '*Get after him!*' and Nempson ran for the iron gate let into the wall. He grasped it, rattled it – 'Foss, it's locked! Where's the key—?'

'Damn the key!' Foss knew that by the time it was fetched Charn would be far too long away for them to have any hope of finding him. Above, Philome cried, 'Foss, Foss, what is *happening*?' and a neighbour called another anxious inquiry. Foss ignored them both. Breath rasping from exertion he turned, very slowly, and stared to where Calliope crouched on the ground like an animal in a trap.

'You heard her, Nempson. You heard what she said.' He took a step towards Calliope. '"If you love me". She, and that creature— they are— they are—' The words broke down incoherently and Calliope knew that his rage was building, towering, almost suffocating him. She felt herself starting to shake – it was reaction, nothing more; she wasn't afraid of him, she wasn't— and her mouth widened in a trembling, defiant grimace.

'D-don't say it, Father. I don't want to hear you. I d-don't want to know.'

'You treacherous little liar . . .' Still Foss's voice did not rise. That would come soon, and when it did it would be devastating, but as yet the calmness of incredulity still gripped him. He could not believe that Calliope had done this. He could not believe it was possible. 'You *cheated* me! Cheated and deceived and betrayed—'

Calliope laughed, a shrill, unnatural sound. A part of her mind, working feverishly and independently of all other considerations, registered the fact that Philome had gone from the upstairs window. She would be plucking up the courage to come downstairs. She would wake the servants. Calliope didn't care.

'*I* betrayed *you*?' She knew that she sounded demented, and reason told her there was no time for this. Yet at this moment her fury was so all-consuming that reason had no say. She had to break the dam that had built up inside her. She had to release the poisoned river it contained. 'How dare you?' she hissed. 'How *dare* you? *You* are the betrayer and the cheat! And you are a hypocrite! And you care nothing for anyone or anything that does not suit your own convenience! I . . . I despise you and I *hate* you!' She hurled a look of sheer loathing at Nempson. 'I hate you *both*!'

Foss's face twisted. 'Oh, you show your true colours at last!' He took another step towards her. 'You are your mother's daughter!'

'Yes!' Calliope fired back savagely. 'I am! And like her I tried to love you and be loyal to you; and like her, I finally found the task too great!'

'*Love?*' Foss snarled. 'What do you know of love, you wretched child? You're a thankless pair alike, you and Griette – powers help me, I should have *known* what you were from the start! You always had the look of her, the aura – and now the birds have finally come home to roost.' He advanced another pace. 'You are mad. You are as insane as she is, and you belong with her, and with all the other abject and contemptible cripples who cannot face up to responsibility!' As he spoke he flicked a quick, evaluating glance in Nempson's direction; Calliope saw it, guessed the reason for it, and rationality slammed back. She saw what he intended, and her muscles tensed . . .

'You have disillusioned me, Calliope.' Now Foss's eyes gave Nempson a clear signal; appearing casual, Nempson sidled a little to his left. 'You have destroyed my faith and my belief in you, and you have proved yourself – *Nempson!*'

The command came a split second too late, for as he shouted Nempson's name Calliope leaped to her feet, spun round and ran for the door. Into the passage; she could hear Foss shouting, hear them both pounding after her, but she had a start on them and desperation gave her speed. Into the hall – a light was wavering at the foot of the stairs and as she threw herself towards the front door Philome's voice rose in an agitated wail.

'Calli! Calli, what has happened? Oh, please—'

She bore no grudge against Philome – far from it – but Foss's voice was bawling in the passage and there was nothing she could say, no chance, no *time*. With a sudden rough impulse Calliope grabbed Philome's arms, and her mouth bruised her stepmother's cheek in a desperate kiss.

'Forgive me!' she pleaded, hoarse with the tears that were suddenly and violently welling. Then as Philome cried her name again she slammed back the bolts of the door, wrenched it open and was away, down the steps, onto the pavement, and across the square into the night.

From the shelter of a deserted shop doorway Calliope stared up at the sky and tried to will the dawn not to break. But the wish had no more power than little Tobery's efforts to banish the monsters that he sometimes believed lurked under his bed, for the moon had set, the last stars were fading, and away to the east there was a smudge of pale green-gold above the rooftops. Day was coming, she could not prevent it. And she had found no trace of Charn.

When she fled from the house she had run blindly, not caring where she went but knowing only that she must run until she was far enough away for her father not to find her. Instinct had steered her clear of all the places where he might search; above all she had avoided the area where the Institute stood, though in her overwrought imagination the great dome of the building had seemed to loom over every twist and turn she took, watching her like a huge, omnipotent and unhuman spy.

She had stopped at last, drained of the strength to run any more, and for the first time took stock of her surroundings. She was close to the edge of the town, in a district of tall, crowding buildings; houses and shops all mingled and jumbled together without any particular semblance of order. The Institute dome was no longer visible; too far away, and the buildings between too high. Good; that was good. Foss would never think to search for her here.

If he was searching at all . . .

Calliope dismissed the thought instantly. Her father would search, she had no doubt of it. If for no other reason than his own injured pride, he would scour the town for her and would not rest until he had tracked her down. A grim sense of satisfaction flared at the thought of his frustration, but it was short-lived. She had not meant to say what she had said to Foss. Or, if a part of her had meant the essence of it, she had not truly wanted to hurl it in his face so cruelly. She didn't hate him. How could she? He was her father, and they had always been so close. But if she had shown her true colours, as he accused, then so had he. He had shown them on the night she returned from the twilight world, and because of it, Queen Selethe had died.

Calliope cried then, crouching down at the entrance to an empty alley and burying her face in her arms while the tension and bewilderment of her flight flooded from her in a wave of sheer, miserable relief. It passed after a while, and when she felt better she wiped her wet face, blew her nose on a kerchief that by lucky chance she had in her pocket, and tried to think.

She had to find Charn. He might still be in the town; or he might already have fled beyond its boundaries to take refuge in the surrounding countryside. Or – and her stomach turned over at the thought – he might have returned to his own world, through the door of darkness to sanctuary. But somehow she did not believe that, for she did not believe Charn would leave with his purpose unfulfilled. He must have come back for one of two reasons; either to rescue Selethe, if he did not yet know that she was dead, or to see Calliope herself. He had achieved neither end. He was still in this world; she was certain of it.

So, then: how to find him? Like her, he would avoid the areas where he might risk discovery; that ruled out the heart of the town, the district of the Institute, the market, the elegant residential squares. He would look for dark places, where he could move freely and be anonymous. If he needed to feed, he must find sustenance where it would go unnoticed. As he had done once before . . .

A shudder went through her at that memory, and with it a peculiar pang that blended anger, pity and a sharp note of jealousy. Refusing to let herself dwell on it, she faced the conundrum again. The poor quarters were Charn's obvious refuge; places where questions were rarely asked and anonymity could be guaranteed. Places that the town's more well-to-do inhabitants preferred to ignore unless circumstance or convenience decreed otherwise. Calliope knew such places by location and reputation, if not by experience, and so she chose one at random – or almost, for she remembered where Charn had first been captured, and suspected that he would avoid going there again – and made her way in that direction.

She didn't know what hour it was when she reached her destination, for she was unused to judging by moon and stars, and the wind, though light, was blowing in the wrong direction to carry the chimes of the market-square clock. This neighbourhood, which consisted largely of lodging-houses, taverns and eccentric shops selling little of value or quality, had grown up around a playhouse that once had been popular but was now run down and reduced to giving dumb-shows and burlesques. The last performance had just ended, and the motley audience was spilling out into the night, many of them the worse for drink. A tall, elegant man of Foss's age passed Calliope on the pavement and made a foully obscene remark; his companion, shorter and stouter and with red face and beaming smile, shook a purse and asked what her fee might be. She turned her head away, cheeks flaming, and the men shrugged and walked on towards a carriage that waited for them at a discreet distance.

After that encounter, she took care not to be seen by anyone. Not that there were many people about once the last playhouse stragglers had gone; a few female shadows hovering ghostlike and despondent in the glow of inadequate street lamps, occasional young men too tired or too drunk to find their way home, a solitary older woman with noisy, wooden-soled shoes, hurrying on some private errand. Somewhere a baby was grizzling ceaselessly, but no one troubled to soothe it. Calliope could feel the pavement through the soles of her own shoes. Every stone seemed to bite into her, and a dank sensation was numbing her feet as the damp of the small hours condensed on the cobbles and seeped into her flesh. Her ankles ached with it, and with the hours – it must be hours now – of fruitless walking.

And, still, no trace of Charn.

As the first touch of the sun brought the facades of the buildings opposite into relief, she finally stopped wishing for the night to continue and compelled her weary mind to face the reality of her plight. She had fled from her home without any plan or preparation, and had nothing to sustain her but the clothes she stood up in. A flimsy asset they were, too; the dress she had worn at dinner, summer undergarments, silk slippers with kidskin soles. When she looked at the slippers (filthy now) she saw that they were already worn through in places, and her ivory silk stockings beneath were in holes. She didn't even have a shawl, for the weather was warm and the house cosy and she had had no need, no *thought* for such things. Nor did she have any money – did she? Calliope felt in the pocket of her dress, and to her surprise brought out a few coins. For a moment she couldn't recall what they were doing there, but then she remembered. Celesta had asked her to give a letter to the post-messenger when he came to the house this morning. There had been great drama over it; the missal was to some new gallant of whom Celesta feared Foss and Philome might disapprove, and she had sworn Calliope to secrecy, pressing the payment on her and extracting in return a promise that she would walk through fire sooner than give her away. Calliope had been too preoccupied to argue, but the post-messenger had not called and she had forgotten to return Celesta's money. The coins added up to little enough, but they would buy her a loaf of bread. Enough to sustain her for a few days at least.

But after that, an inner voice said. *What then, Calliope? What then, if you fail to find Charn?*

The question frightened her, for she had no answer to it. Certainly she could not go home – she could never go home now, unless she was prepared for the consequences that Foss would force on her. His trust and respect were gone forever; he might even have her declared insane and committed to the Hospice, which in his position – and with her mother's history – he could easily arrange. Fleetingly, Calliope thought of Nempson. If she threw herself on his mercy . . . but that was out of the question, for Nempson had already chosen to take her father's part in this; she had seen clear evidence of it during the confrontation last night. Even if he had been willing to champion her, the price for his help would be one she would never agree to pay. Besides, she reflected with a flash of cynical amusement, it would never do for him to have a wife with a streak of madness in her.

Without Charn, then, she was alone, with only her own wits and resources to rely on. For a moment the prospect seemed almost exciting, but then sobriety eclipsed the excitement. This was no game. She was alone, and unfitted for it, for she had no experience in the necessities of survival. She *had* to find Charn. If she did not, her future would be very bleak indeed.

For two days and nights Calliope searched. The fact that it was summer was both curse and blessing: Charn would not dare to be abroad in daylight, and her only real hope of finding him was during the short hours of darkness; yet the fact that the nights were short, and the weather warm, made her own subsistence easier.

The curious looks she received during the first morning of her quest made her realise that she must be less conspicuous. Her slippers were in tatters now and she threw them away; bare feet were more vulnerable but less noticeable. Then in a back street she came across a small, shabby emporium that sold discarded clothing. She had never seen such a place before, and in her present straits it was an answer to her prayers. Celesta's few coins, however, were not enough to buy her what she wanted; for a while she was stymied, but then she found an ornament in her hair, overlooked until now. She had worn it at dinner; it had been a present from Philome and was made of gold with a pattern of garnets set into it. A jeweller bought it from her; not at anything approaching its true value, but Calliope was too grateful to care. The jeweller was clearly intrigued by his unlikely-looking customer and might have asked awkward questions, but Calliope's well-bred speech and manner convinced him that she was the ornament's rightful owner and not a thief. With the money in her pocket Calliope returned to the shabby emporium and bought a worn but still serviceable coat and a pair of shoes that almost fitted her. As an afterthought she also purchased a comb from among a tray of trinkets. Some of the teeth were missing, but it would do. She could pass as respectable, and she still had enough coins left for a little food.

Her sense of achievement, though, did not last long. By the end of the first day she was giddy with tiredness and every muscle in her legs ached from walking. Still avoiding the areas where she might meet someone she knew, she had roamed through streets and alleys and squares and market-places, watching for any sign, listening for any snatch of conversation that might lead her to Charn, and she had found nothing. As the sun westered she found herself a secluded cranny behind the bulk of a tavern building and, meaning only to rest for a few minutes, fell soundly asleep. When she woke it was past middle-night; the tavern had closed and the streets were all but deserted. Cursing herself for wasting the critical hours of darkness, Calliope resumed her search, but without success.

The second day was worse still. Her money ran out; it had bought less food than she had expected, for she was a novice at shopping frugally and had made the mistake of going to the more expensive vendors. Stiff, weary and growing ever hungrier, she traipsed on, still watching, still listening, still achieving nothing. During the afternoon she fell asleep again, this time on a bench in a Public Garden, from which she was shaken roughly awake by a lamplighter who called her a vagrant and something worse before driving her ignominiously away. Night came again; she fared no better, and by the third morning she was close to despair. Images of her family haunted her: she missed them and longed for the comfort of their company, or even, simply, for the chance to explain to them why she had done what she had. Yet for all the ache of reminiscence, and the loneliness and fear that were building up inside her, one thought kept her to her resolve. Charn. Beside him, nothing mattered. *Hold to that*, Calliope told herself. *Hold to it, and be strong.*

On the third day, she stole food. It wasn't much; just a small, round seed-cake placed carelessly at the very edge of a market stall; but afterwards she was plagued by agonies of conscience so great that she almost threw her prize away. Common sense prevailed – she could hardly return the cake, and what was the point in waste? – and she ate it, but she tasted shame in every mouthful.

It was late afternoon when the idea came to her, and when it did she was both appalled and astounded that she had not considered the possibility before. By chance she had overheard two women talking, and one of them mentioned Charity Hill. Reflexively, Calliope thought of the Hospice . . . and her eyes widened. Charn knew about Griette. He knew where she was. Might he, *could* he, have gone there?

She tried to tell herself that there was no logic to her suspicion, but logic was crumbling under a sudden onslaught of hope. If nothing more it was a chance, and it gave her search a focus where before there had been none. It was a long walk to the Hospice, and Charity Hill was a steep and wearying climb. But she could do it. If it took the last of her strength, she could do it.

The walk almost did take the last of her strength, and by the time she finally reached the top of the hill and saw the Hospice gates rising before her, she was close to exhaustion. Sunset had become dusk as she climbed; the road with its lines of trees was empty, drained of colour, and beyond the gates the windows of the Hospice's imposing facade shone with yellow light, like cats' eyes in the gloom. Two great etherea lamps burned on the gateposts; staring past them Calliope felt momentary panic as she pictured her father appearing suddenly on the gravelled drive, heading homeward from a visit to Griette. But the visiting hour was long past. No outsiders would be in the grounds now . . . except, perhaps, for one.

The gates of the Hospice were always locked at sunset, but the bars with their decorative finials were set far enough apart for a slender body to squeeze between them. Throwing her coat ahead of her, Calliope wriggled through the gap. Her shoes crunched on the gravel; for a moment she froze, but then laughed at herself as she realised that the sound was too small to disturb a mouse, let alone the angels far away at the end of the drive. Relaxing, she gazed around her. The formal gardens looked strange in the dusk; the eye played tricks, and familiar shapes took on new and sometimes disturbing aspects. The fountain was a deformed human figure with horns growing from its brow, the box hedges a long, giant snake, dormant but only waiting for full darkness to come before it writhed into life. Disturbed by her own imagination Calliope started across the lawn, heading away from the building and towards the garden's far and more neglected side, where dense bushes and small, crowding trees formed a natural boundary. Their cover would provide a perfect hiding place for someone anxious not to be discovered.

The willows in the wild garden, which Griette could see from her window, were rustling, whispering in a strange, thin chorus. The sound they made was melancholy, almost human, and Calliope shivered as she paused to look at their tall silhouettes against the darkening sky. On an impulse which she did not try to interpret, she sent a silent invocation towards the willows: *help me now. Let Charn be here, and let me find him.* Then she smiled ironically at her own foolishness. Perhaps she belonged here after all . . .

She walked on. It was hard to see anything now; true night was falling and until the moon rose the dark would make searching near-impossible. She had reached the bushes; better to stay here a while, find a secluded vantage point and wait for the new light to come. Long grass rustled and twigs snapped dryly under her feet; last autumn's debris, left to lie uncleared. She took another step – and heard an answering rustle to her right.

Calliope stopped still, listening. She told herself that the sound meant nothing; it was just an animal or a ground-nesting bird, disturbed by her presence.

Why, then, was her heart pounding as if it was about to break through her ribs?

She would never know why she did it; intuition, perhaps, or merely an unfounded hope. But, softly and hesitantly, she spoke Charn's name.

And from the denser darkness between two crowding quickbeam trees, the voice that she had prayed to hear whispered, '*Calli* . . .'

Chapter XXIV

He was so weak that Calliope knew at once he was close to death. Falling to her knees beside him where he lay under the trees' shelter she could feel the shuddering ague in his body beneath the heavy cloak he wore, and when she clasped one of his gauntleted hands in both of hers he barely had the strength to respond with a clenching of his fingers. But he knew her, and from the little he was able to say she pieced together his story. As she sought him, so he had been seeking her – but since his escape from her father's house he had not dared to venture close enough to any human to feed. Without sustenance his own strength had rapidly declined; to avoid the sun's deadly touch he had hidden by day and only ventured out at night, but even the moon's light had been enough to exhaust him and deplete what resources he had. Now, cramped with pain and fever, he could not even recall what had prompted him to find his way here; all he remembered was an impulse that linked the hospice to Calliope, and the increasingly desperate need to find her.

Kneeling beside him in the darkness, Calliope felt the slow and precariously faltering beat of the pulse in his wrist, and knew that if she did not find for him what he needed now, he would soon be beyond the power of any help. She was crying again, but that was of no use; tears might soothe but they could not strengthen. He needed more.

Her own pulse had begun to race violently as she realised there was only one thing she could give him. The thought of it kindled a blend of excitement and dread; for it was what she wanted, and had wanted for so long, and yet the fear of what it might mean and do, the *terror* of that . . .

'Charn . . . Charn, can you hear me?' Her voice was husky and her fingers tightened on his. For a dreadful moment he did not respond, and she thought that he had slipped away beyond her reach. But then he stirred, and she thought – though in the dark it was impossible to be sure – that she saw the glimmer of his eyes opening to look at her. A huge, suffocating emotion constricted her heart and her throat, and suddenly all fear and doubt were eclipsed by a desire, a yearning, that blotted out all else. She leaned over him, laid her hands on his cloak (the material felt so soft and fine, and he was shivering, *shivering* beneath it) and pressed her body close against him as her mouth sought his in an ardent, artless kiss. She sensed his lips, felt the shock of cold that they conveyed, and against his cheek whispered fiercely, 'Take what you need, Charn! Take *all* you need from me!'

'Calli . . .' He tried to twist free, shoulders hunching and head turning aside as he realised what she meant. 'Calli, no—'

'*Yes!*' Her hands tightened on him, nails pressing, digging, urging him not to flinch but to accept her gift of life. Every nerve in her felt as if it were on fire. She had never been so close to him, perhaps would never be so close again, and she was half crazed with the joy and the terror of it. 'Listen to me, oh, my love, *listen* – you *must* take, it's the only hope you have!' She was straddling his supine body now, and suddenly, wildly, she cupped his face between her hands, feeling his skin so cold, so cold, as the desperate, fervent protest broke from her: '*Charn, I won't let you die!*'

She felt it then; the tiny shift, the change, that transcended all rational senses and sent a tremor through her psyche. Charn had tried to fight her, tried to resist his blazing need, but he could not deny his own nature, or the craving of that nature to survive. Calliope bowed her head to his chest and he held her, gripped her, welcoming the incredible heat of her against him, for the pain of it would pass and there would be relief and release and strength. He fed with a hunger he had never known in even his worst extremity as Foss's prisoner, and the feeding was like a

300

compelling tide flowing through him. He could hear and feel Calliope sobbing, but knew it was passion and not fear that drove her. And at last, at last it was over, and it was enough. As the grip of his arms relaxed he raised his head to look at her and saw, with his unhuman sight, the raw emotion with which her eyes sought his face in the darkness.

She said, barely audibly, 'Ch . . . Charn . . .'

'Hush.' Charn touched her hair. She grasped for his hand, and she was shaking now, uncontrollably. Then, not thinking or not caring for the consequences, she kissed him again; not as she had kissed him before but slowly, gently and with an implicit passion. Charn knew the fervour that was alight in her, and felt himself responding with a desire that matched hers. He started to pull her towards him again . . . and froze as he realised where his mind and body were inexorably leading him. He wanted her – and unless he held back, *now*, the longing would go too far and pitch them both over a precipice to disaster.

'Calliope!' His grip on her changed and became rough suddenly. Calliope's body arched; she uttered a sound midway between a sigh and a moan, and in alarm Charn shook her. '*Calliope!* Look at me!'

She did, though he thought she could not see him in the gloom. Her hands, moving fitfully over his shoulders and arms, were grey.

'Calli, move back.' His own hands clamped on her wrists and he pulled her fingers away from him. 'Don't touch me. *Don't.*'

She swung her head from side to side like a drunkard. 'No— no, Charn, don't push me away—'

'I *must*! Don't you understand?' Had he miscalculated, taken too much from her? The fever would come, he knew, but he had not thought it would happen yet. In dismay Charn scanned her face for the signs, and to his inexpressible relief saw that his judgement had been sound. This was not a fever of the feeding but of her own emotions. 'Calli, we must stop this!' he went on urgently. 'We can't touch each other; not now, not *ever.*'

'No—'

'*Listen* to me! You saved my life by allowing me to take a part of yours. But it can't go any further; and if we give way to what we're feeling, it *will* go further, because I won't be able to control it! You'll die, Calli, as I nearly did! Is that what you want?'

301

His words were harsh but deliberate, and they broke through the intoxicated turmoil in Calliope's mind. Cold reason came back, and with it a prickling sweat of shock that shattered the dream and hurled her back to earth.

She whispered, 'Oh, Charn . . . oh, by the powers . . .' A racking shudder went through her and she clutched herself, shaking her head violently, trying to deny the misery of frustration surging in her mind and body. 'I didn't mean— I only wanted—'

'I know.' Charn's voice grew gentle, and she perceived that he, too, was in torment. Sombrely, wordlessly, they both drew back until there was no contact between them. Calliope wanted to cry again but fought it. She was *always* crying, she *loathed* herself for it, she wasn't a child any more but a woman, an *adult* . . .

Charn said: 'I must see Griette.'

Self-reproach collapsed and Calliope felt breath catch in her throat. She had forgotten, forgotten the mission and the purpose that had brought Charn into her life at the very beginning. Forgotten, too, the promise she herself had made to Selethe.

'Can you help me, Calli?' Charn asked softly. '*Will* you? You see . . . I sealed the gateway. Without the key, I can never return to my own world.'

For a deranged instant Calliope felt a flare of elation. *If he could not return, then he must stay*— But then she remembered what that would mean. Unless . . . Selethe had talked to her of the Sacrament of Night; that same Sacrament that might have saved her mother and Malorn. *But you are different, you and Charn,* she had said. *You can be together, stay together, if you are willing to take the step that they could not take.*

Could they? Excitement swelled agonisingly in Calliope – then died stillborn. A terrible, covetous impulse had moved in her momentarily; the impulse to deny Charn what Griette might give him, and so force him to stay and face the choice between the Sacrament and death. She must not listen to that deadly temptation. Forget the Sacrament, whatever it was, whatever its power might be. She must not even ask him; she must *forget* it. Selethe had been ill, deranged; there was nothing in this, no precious and blessed prize to be won. Even if there was, she had no right to force the choice on Charn. If she did, then her love would be a contemptible thing and not worth the having.

Crushing down the grief that welled in her, she turned her

302

thoughts to the hospice. There were angels on duty at night, of course. But they could be avoided, for doors were not the only means of entry. The night was warm; windows would be open, and Griette's window had no bars, for in all her years as an inmate she had never tried to escape. Calliope put her hands to her face; a gesture to calm herself. Her fingers felt *cold*.

'I can show you,' she said. 'I can take you to where my mother's room is.' A last pang assailed her; she pushed it away. 'We'll find a way to reach her.'

They waited until all the lights in the hospice windows had been extinguished. It was a strange, quiet interlude after the turmoil that had gone before; they sat, not touching, hardly talking, for there was nothing to say that either of them could bring themselves to voice. After a while the moon rose, and Charn drew back deeper into the shadows of the trees. Calliope wanted to stay and watch the moon's bland, remote face as it slowly climbed into the sky, but instead she too moved into the darkness, to be close to Charn.

There was a little talk then, for he asked her about Selethe and how she had died. She told him everything, sparing no detail; for all the bitterness of the story she sensed, rightly, that he needed to know all there was to be gleaned. He made no comment when she had finished, only sat for a few minutes with his head bowed and hands steepled before his face. She thought he was making some private invocation, his last respects to the queen. Still she did not mention the Sacrament of Night. It would have been possible, for her account of her last meeting with Selethe gave her the chance to speak of it; but at the last her courage faltered and she stilled her tongue.

Finally, the last distant lamp went out, and the hospice building was no more than a black, inert silhouette against the moonlit sky. Charn stood up, his movement shaking the leaf-canopy around and above him, and said, 'They'll all be sleeping by the time we reach the house.' He looked down at her. 'Shall we go?'

With an odd, sad lassitude Calliope rose to her feet. At this moment she should have been filled with hope and eagerness, but they were absent; all she felt was a sense of cheerless detachment. They stepped from the trees' cover on to open ground, and she saw Charn shudder as the moonlight touched him. It wasn't quite at the full, but in tonight's clear atmosphere its luminescence had the power to hurt, and she reached out to touch his arm tentatively and say, 'Was it enough, Charn?'

He knew what she meant, and nodded. 'Enough, love. I couldn't have taken more without endangering you.' He glanced at her. 'And you . . . do you feel any ill effects?'

She shook her head. Strange that as yet there was no sign of fever; she had expected it to happen quickly, as it had done on the night when she freed him from her father's house, but instead she felt only an extraordinary sense of calm.

'It will come,' Charn said sombrely.

'I know.'

'When it does . . . when it begins. Tell me.'

They exchanged another glance; one that conveyed far more than words. Then Charn moved on across the close-trimmed turf and Calliope followed.

The fountain was still playing, the sound of it breaking the silence and carrying bizarrely in the quiet. As they passed it, Calliope wondered for the first time in fifteen years how its mechanism worked, then wondered again that such an insignificant thing could occupy her mind at a moment like this. It was a defence, perhaps; something to keep other thoughts at bay. Moving on, they began to skirt the building, and Charn's eyes were constantly alert for any watcher. Once the light of a lamp glimmered briefly inside the building as an angel on night duty made her rounds of the corridors, but the light faded away and no one came near the windows.

Griette's room was on the hospice's eastern side; not daring to speak now for fear of discovery, Calliope signed the way. She could hear the eerie whisper of the willows again, and they seemed to disturb Charn; several times he glanced over his shoulder at them, and once she thought she saw him shiver. Then they had reached the east wing and, counting carefully, she pointed to her mother's window.

Strange that she had never seen it from the outside before. It gave her a frisson as Charn moved like an insubstantial shadow towards it, for it was so anonymous, just one in a row of many, all alike and none giving any clue to the identity or disposition of the human souls on the other side. To the hospice, Calliope realised, that was all Griette was or had ever been. Not someone's mother, someone's beloved, someone with a story to tell; only a name, a case, a living but barely cognisant entity which, like the rest, must pass through their hands and be detachedly cared for until her span ended.

She stopped so quickly that her feet scraped on the gravel. Charn turned in time to see her put the back of one hand to her mouth as she choked back a sob; his eyes questioned, then he saw what had affected her and came back to her side. 'Calli.' His voice was soft, and so gentle that it made the hurt worse. 'If you want me to withdraw from this, I will. Only say. You have the right to decide.'

She hesitated, then shook her head. 'No.' Her whisper was as quiet as his. 'We must go on.'

She knew he wanted to kiss her, a gesture of thanks and something more, but he did not do it, only stepped towards the window. Like all the others it was curtained; but unlike them, the curtain was not drawn. Calliope's heart lurched as she saw him reach it and delicately, carefully stretch out a hand to explore its contours, searching for the slightest gap that would allow him to ease it open and find the inner catch. His fingers were an inch from the glass when the window quivered faintly. Calliope saw it, stifled a warning cry – then with the faintest of creaks the casement was pushed open by an arm that gleamed pale and naked in the moon's glare. As Charn and Calliope froze in shock there was soft movement within the darkened room. Then a voice – Griette's voice, quiet and calm and lucid as it had not been for fifteen years past – said serenely:

'I knew that another of your kind would come. One night. I knew.'

'I made a grave for him.' Griette smiled up at Charn, so sweetly and gently that Calliope had to look away in distress. 'They have never found it, and I shall never tell them where it is. But if you wish to know, and to see, I will tell you.'

Charn's fingers touched her face, as though he were stroking the wing of a butterfly. 'Thank you,' he said to her. 'I am grateful.'

She turned, ghostlike in the white nightgown she wore, and moved to the window, gazing out across the gardens. 'Three willow trees,' she said. 'It seemed right. The willow decays from the heart, you see. The bark, the outer shell, remains, and so to the eye all seems well. But the heart decays, until there is nothing left.'

She heard the muffled sound that Calliope made and could not stem, and looked over her shoulder at her daughter. 'No tears, Calli. Not for me. I have shed too many over all the years, and now I want no more.'

'Mother . . .' But Calliope couldn't articulate what she wanted to say. She felt numb, stupefied, and could hardly take in what was happening. Griette, coherent and calm, her mind her own again . . . she could barely assimilate, barely *believe*. But Charn had known from the first. Calliope had watched as he climbed over the window-sill and into the room, and when she followed she had found him and Griette standing face to face, not speaking but sharing another kind of communion that went far beyond words. Then her mother had looked at her, and the quiet clarity in her eyes plunged Calliope's memory back to childhood, to the days long before the madness began. This was the mother she had known when she was little, and to whom she had been so close, and all she could say, in a husky, stunned whisper was, '*How . . .?*'

She had had no answer to her question, and doubted that it would ever be revealed. But something – perhaps Charn's presence, or perhaps a catalyst more arcane than that – had taken the burden of insanity from Griette's mind and allowed her to be whole again. With unerring intuition she had sensed their coming and had taken up a station at the window, sitting with quiet patience to await them. Was it just an interlude, a lull, like passing through the eye of a storm? Calliope did not know. But here, tonight, her mother was healed – and a moment for which she had been waiting and yearning for fifteen years had finally come. Through Charn, her world and Malorn's had met once more, and Griette could at last make her peace.

She moved then, walking to the table where Calliope had so often seen her sit with her clay and her wooden tools. There was a new carving there. Like all the others it was unfinished, but this time Griette had not crushed and ruined it; instead, she had used the crayons to colour it carefully and meticulously. Blue and grey and black. It was a model of a head, but the face was blank, unsculpted, and the clay had been allowed to dry so that the features could never be formed.

'I think,' Griette said, touching the figurine lightly, 'that I will make no more. There is no need.' She withdrew her hand, then turned to look at Charn again. 'I would like you to know my story. Is that too unkind of me?'

Charn shook his head. 'No. It's not unkind.'

'Then . . .' She moved nearer to him, suddenly hesitant. Charn's gaze flicked beyond her to Calliope; their eyes met and she saw his tacit appeal to her to say nothing, do nothing, not to intervene in any way. She nodded once, just perceptibly, and cast her gaze down as he and Griette faced each other. Charn raised his hands, laid them on Griette's temples, then bowed his head until their brows touched. Griette uttered an odd, truncated little laugh and said, 'Cold . . . I had forgotten how *cold* he was . . . It used to fascinate and frighten me.'

'Tell me,' Charn's voice was very gentle. 'Tell me everything.'

They stood, unmoving, for some minutes. To Calliope, who felt like an intruder yet could not stop herself from watching, it seemed that the temperature in the room dropped as though the air around them had turned from summer to winter. Now and then Griette made some small sound; a sigh, or another faint laugh, or, once, a sob. Charn was silent, his eyes closed, his face inscrutable. Then at last there was a change, a thawing and an ebbing of tension. Charn raised his head, opened his eyes and his hands withdrew. As he began to drop them to his sides Griette caught hold of one wrist.

'At the foot of the willows,' she said. 'Look there – that is where you'll find what you're seeking. No one ever goes there, you see, so it was a safe hiding place. But . . .' Her grip on Charn's wrist tightened convulsively, and suddenly her voice was urgent, beseeching. 'But when you find it . . . oh please, please, don't let my daughter make the mistake I made! The Sacrament – if you love her, if you *truly* love her, *don't let her turn away as I did!*'

An ice-cold shock tingled through Calliope. She started forward, saying desperately, 'Mother, how can—' but Charn cut across her.

'No.' He stepped into her path, barring the way as she tried to reach out to Griette. 'She won't tell you anything more. She can't.'

'He is right.' Griette gave Calliope a sad yet intensely

307

penetrating look. 'Say nothing, Calli. Not yet. When – and if – the time comes for you, Charn will know, and he will explain.' She faced Charn once more, and set her shoulders as though preparing for something momentous. 'Say goodbye to me. Please.'

Charn paused. Suddenly he looked uncertain, and he started to say, 'Are you—'

She interrupted him. 'I am sure. I am very sure. *Please*.'

He looked at Calliope, a look she could not begin to comprehend. Then he drew Griette into his arms and embraced her tightly and powerfully, as a loving and devoted son might embrace his mother. Calliope felt the charge of psychic energy, saw Griette flinch in shock and then smile as her muscles relaxed, and realised, belatedly, the nature of the plea she had made. A panic-stricken protest rose in her – then collapsed as sudden insight came. She had no right to interfere; no right to deny Griette the dignity of her own choice. This was what she wanted, and Charn understood and had granted her the boon.

Then it was done, and Griette stepped back. She was trembling violently, but her face was radiant. Charn helped her to the neat, narrow bed, and when she was comfortable Calliope tentatively approached. Griette smiled up at her and whispered, 'Are you angry with me, Calli?'

Her skin was turning a translucent silver-grey. Calliope said, 'No. How could I be?'

She kissed her mother's brow. Griette touched her chin with one forefinger, tilting her head so that she might see her better in the moonlight. It was a gesture she had often made when Calliope was little, usually to see if her face was clean, and Calliope shut her eyes tightly as she remembered it. Griette said to Charn, 'Take care of her.' She smiled at them both, then turned on her side and nestled her face contentedly into the pillow. She looked like a child herself, settling peacefully for a night's sound sleep. Calliope knew that she would never wake again.

At her side Charn moved. She felt his glove touch her arm and he spoke quietly and without obvious emotion. 'We should leave her now.'

Calliope nodded. The angels would do what was right, and they would do it kindly. She went with Charn to the window, let him help her over the sill. The world outside felt unreal, and for a few moments she stood still, staring up at the moon. She could almost see a face in its contours, and the face seemed to gaze back at her, languid and impersonal. Then the fancy faded, and she let Charn lead her away from the window and the silent room beyond.

Close to, the willow trees had an eerie semblance of sentient life. The rustling of their leaves sounded like voices murmuring to one another in an obscure language, and the limpid movements of their boughs in the faint breeze was like the stirring of alien limbs. Calliope could not rid herself of the feeling that the trees were watching them, and when they ventured under their canopy, so like a grey-green cave, she looked up in quick unease, half expecting to see some spirit guardian sitting high above her.

If Charn felt the strangeness he showed no sign of it but only pressed forward to where the willows' old, gnarled trunks rose from the tangle of undergrowth. There were three, as Griette had said; so close together and so long neglected that they had all but fused into one. At their feet was a small patch of ground where nothing but grass grew. Charn stopped there, gazing down, and as Calliope moved to join him she saw what he had seen.

A small mound, no bigger than a molehill, had been made at the foot of the trees. That someone *had* made it was clear; though long compacted, the soil had been deliberately heaped and firmed and patted into shape. Pale, etiolated grass had encroached over it, but when Charn crouched down and pushed the drooping strands back, something else was revealed.

'Calliope . . .' He beckoned her to him. At the head of the mound was set a small, clay mask of a man's face. It was beautifully and lovingly sculpted, every detail given the finest attention. Calliope gazed at it, at the high cheekbones, the broad, slightly flattened nose above a narrow, graceful mouth, the wide-set eyes, half-lidded and with a composed yet faintly sorrowful look in them. She had never seen the face before, but she knew who it could only be.

Charn said, very quietly, 'It's perfect. Such a complete likeness.'

Griette must have fashioned it during her earliest days at the hospice, Calliope thought. Since then she had tried time and again to recreate it, but had never, ever quite succeeded. That was why she had worked so obsessively, and why every figure she made had been crushed and pulverised back into nothing before

309

the disappointment of it could overwhelm her.

Her throat was tight with emotion as she whispered, 'She said it was a grave.' Yet this mound was so small; far too small to contain the body of a man.

'In one sense, it is.' Charn reached out and carefully lifted the mask from its resting place. 'But only in one sense. Malorn isn't here. I don't know what became of his body; she couldn't tell me, and I don't know what happens to our kind if they die undiscovered in this world. Perhaps it simply . . . faded away. But something else is here. Something that was very precious to Griette.'

'The key . . .?' she asked.

He didn't answer, but began to scrape away the soil that covered the mound. For several seconds Calliope hesitated, trying not to acknowledge the feelings that were assailing her. She didn't want to find the key. She didn't want the gateway to be opened again . . .

With an ache inside her that went deeper than she would ever let herself acknowledge, she too began to dig.

The earth was dry and powdery, and so impoverished here under the trees that it was little more than dust. The box had not been buried deeply, and came free with ease. It was made of silver, and far smaller than the one in which Griette had placed her legacy to Calliope; she could hold it in one cupped hand, and she did so, wondering at the plainness of it. Time and entombment had tarnished the metal and stained it with a black patina, like the stigma of some dreadful illness. On one side was a simple catch.

Charn took the box from her and his fingers touched the fastening. It sprang back; the lid opened. Inside the box were two objects. One was a tiny phial that looked like crystal but, Calliope believed, was a substance more alien, not of this world. It was half filled with a dark, viscous liquid in which flecks of silver gleamed, and, dreading Charn's answer, Calliope asked, 'Is this it, Charn? Is this the key?'

Charn said: 'No.' He was staring into the box again, at the second artefact it contained. Something soft, almost shapeless and no larger than her forefinger, wrapped in black oilcloth . . . She watched him reach in, take hold of it, draw it out. 'This,' he said, 'is the key . . .'

How it happened, then, Calliope would never truly know. Perhaps it was sheer misfortune, a moment's carelessness that gave fate a sudden, capricious twist. Or perhaps, unconsciously, the faltering movement of Charn's hand was a deliberate act. The tiny bundle on his palm slipped suddenly; as he tried to grasp it the oilcloth unrolled, and the object it protected was exposed. The air around them filled instantly with a giddying, narcotic perfume – and Calliope saw the white flower, fragile as the ghost of a moth's wing, lying against the cloth's last fold. The dappled moonlight fell on it, illuminating it for a brief flicker of time and seeming to awaken in it an answering shimmer. Then it withered, crumbled, turned to a smudge of white dust; and the dust in its turn vanished . . . and the key to the gateway between worlds was gone for ever.

Chapter XXV

Charn leaned against the trunk of the willow, motionless, one hand covering his face. Calliope could see the convulsive rise and fall of his shoulders as he breathed, but he showed no other outward sign of the emotions that were moving in him. She could not approach him; nothing she might do or say at this moment could be of any conceivable help.

Charn knew she was there but could not trust himself even to acknowledge her presence. To have come so close; to have found the key only to see it shrivel and disintegrate before his eyes, and all for the sake of a moment's negligence . . . he thought that he might start to laugh, and knew that if he did he would not be able to make himself stop. The goal, the prize, the culmination of fifteen years' searching. Dust. No; less than dust. *Nothing.* He had been betrayed by a single shaft of light, for he had known – as had Griette – that the white flower, the key Malorn had entrusted to her, must always be preserved in total darkness. One glimmer of the moon had been enough to destroy it, and with its loss had gone his only hope of survival, for the gateway was sealed and now he could never, ever return to his own world.

This was not the first time that Charn had faced the prospect of death. As Foss's captive he had believed for a while that he would die, and had learned, at least in part, to come to terms with the expectation of it and with the fear that any rational soul might be pardoned for feeling. But there had been hope then, however slender. This time, there was none.

He had one consolation, remote though it seemed at present. He had fulfilled his promise to Selethe, and in doing so had given the twilight world the security it so desperately needed. Just as he could not open the doorway again, so no human hand would ever unlock it. His own kind were safe; a chapter in their history was ended, and the ending would be a happy one. Even for Griette . . . yes, he had killed her; it was what she had wanted, and she had asked it of him as a final gesture in memory of his old friend whom she had loved. For Malorn, for Griette and possibly even for himself in a convoluted way, it had been the honourable thing to do.

A sound impinged, a noise that was almost but not quite metallic. It was so slight and so incongruous that it snapped Charn out of his grim thoughts. Opening his eyes, he looked at Calliope.

She had picked up the box where he had let it fall on the mound, and now she stood holding the tiny phial with its dark contents in her hand. She did not know what it was, but nonetheless Charn felt a sharp stab of foreboding.

She seemed to sense his scrutiny suddenly, and turned her head. What she saw in his face must have alerted her, for she slowly extended her upturned hand with the phial displayed on it.

'Charn . . . what is this? Why did my mother bury it here with the— the—'

The sentence faded, unfinished, as his look confirmed the thing she had suspected. A strange and very intent light kindled in her eyes and her voice changed utterly as she said, 'This is the Sacrament of Night. Isn't it?'

Charn stared back at her. His expression had frozen. 'How do . . .'

'How do I know of the Sacrament? Queen Selethe told me, Charn. Before she died, she told me. It was the one thing that could have allowed my mother and Malorn to be together, she

312

said; but my mother's courage failed at the last. That was why Malorn died. The Sacrament could have saved his life. And the queen said . . .' Her voice caught; she brought it under control with a fierce effort. 'She said that we have the chance to succeed where they failed.'

Charn continued to stare. He couldn't answer her, couldn't speak, and at last Calliope said quietly, 'Is it true, Charn? Does the Sacrament have the power to allow us to be together?'

Charn couldn't lie. Less than an hour ago he had learned Griette's story; learned the sad and bitter truth behind her years of torment. She had pleaded with him not to let Calliope do as she had done, and that plea had echoed Selethe's entreaties. Against them both, Charn's defences could no longer stand, and suddenly he knew that all his high-minded protestations had been a contemptible sham. Calliope had a right to know the truth and to make her own decision. Selethe had known it, Griette had known it; they had both wanted him to give Calliope the chance and the hope she deserved, and to give himself that same hope, too.

Perhaps, he thought, that had been at the heart of his reluctance all along. The fear of selfishness, of using Calliope to gain something that he himself yearned for. He loved her. How he *loved* her . . . He wanted to be with her, and he wanted to live; wanted it so much that it was like a sickness devouring his soul. If the Sacrament offered him a chance of life, then whatever the risks, whatever the unknown pitfalls, he didn't have the strength to spurn it.

He said, so softly that she could barely hear him, 'Yes.'

Her eyes lit. 'Then we must—'

'No. Wait.' This came hard, but it had to be said. 'You don't know all of it, Calli. You don't know what the Sacrament means, what it demands.'

'I don't *care* what it demands. I want to take it, Charn. I want to be with you!' She was standing very still now, and her voice was not steady. 'Besides, this is the only chance you have, isn't it? Without the key you can't go back to your own world, and the key is gone beyond recall. You're trapped here, and without the Sacrament you will die.'

'That's not reason enough in itself for you to take this step!'

'Oh, it is.'

313

'*No*. Not without knowing what you ask of yourself.'

Calliope looked down at the phial in her hand. A peculiar, light-headed feeling was growing in her; on a detached level she knew it must be the onset of the fever, the price of her contact with Charn and of the sustaining energy she had given him. But another kind of fever was awake in her, and that had a very different cause.

'Then give me the knowledge,' she said. 'Tell me the truth about the Sacrament, and let me judge for myself.' Her eyes met his, and he saw that the colour was fading from them, as it was fading, too, from her hair and cheeks. '*Please*.'

Not knowing whether he was facing salvation or damnation, Charn looked up at the sky. Eastwards, the horizon was beginning to pale from charcoal darkness to an insubstantial grey-blue. The moon had set and the stars were fading; day would break soon. The first rays of the sun, he realised, would shine in at Griette's window.

'Come with me.' He reached out and took Calliope's hand. 'Under the leaves, where the cover's deeper.'

Calliope, too, glanced upwards. 'It's nearly dawn—'

'I know. It doesn't matter; not now.'

She let him lead her into the gloomier shadows where bushes crowded in on the willows. They sat down, shrouded by the leaves, and Charn gazed for a long, silent moment at the phial which she still clutched as though it were a talisman. Calliope could hear the steady sound of his breathing; feel the breath like midwinter air on her face. Then, quietly, Charn said,

'Griette told me her story. It isn't complete – there's much that she has forgotten, or perhaps chosen not to remember. But I think you should know it, Calli. I think I must show you what she showed to me. And through that, you'll learn what the Sacrament truly is.'

Calliope recalled his silent, poignant communication with her mother, and felt a prickling sensation in her throat. 'Yes,' she said. 'Tell me, Charn. *Tell* me.'

Charn nodded. He reached out, drew her closer, then laid his hands on her temples as he had done with Griette. When their brows touched, a shiver went through her. 'Look at me,' he said.

She did. Their gazes met, fused, and, like a dream softly overlaying reality, images came. They were not mind-pictures as

314

such but rather symbols and impressions; yet they told their tale as clearly as any painter or narrator could have done. This was the story that Griette had shown to Charn during their silent communication in her room, and now, for the first time, Calliope understood what truly had happened to her mother, and to Malorn.

In the early days of their marriage Griette and Foss had worked together, seeking to unravel the secrets of the twilight world. For years their efforts were fruitless – until late one night, working alone and with her mind beginning to wander from tiredness, Griette stumbled upon the elusive doorway.

She did not break through, for the darkness in the room was not absolute, and without that the way could not be opened. But she felt the first, telltale shift as the barrier between dimensions started to distort and weaken ... and then, filling her senses with its heady narcosis, came the perfume of unearthly flowers.

But even as Griette's mind reached eagerly out, the perfume was gone, the barrier closed again and the prize was snatched away. She strove to call it back, to recreate the dreamlike semi-trance that had brought her so close to success; her efforts failed and at last she was too weary to continue. But she knew that she would have no peace of mind until she found that intangible key once again and, this time, opened the door.

Her first thought then was to tell Foss of her discovery; but something – and through all the ensuing years Griette had never known the nature of what moved her then – stayed her. She did not *want* Foss to know of this. It was her secret, hers alone, and she would not share it.

So she began her search for the gateway in earnest, but still it eluded her. Then, three quartermoons after that first momentous night, chance struck a second time. Walking home in darkness from the Institute's library, where Foss was engrossed and would remain so for some hours to come, Griette had had her first, fateful encounter with Malorn.

Malorn had been in the human world for three days, and it had taken a dire toll on him. Weak, half-blinded and racked with ague, he was desperate enough to approach Griette in a quiet street, hoping to distract her with some inquiry and subtly feed from her life-energy. Griette, though, knew immediately what he was – and she could hardly believe her good fortune, for this

315

was no ordinary twilight-dweller but a creature as intelligent as any human, and capable of communicating in her own tongue. Such a being *must* know the secret of the gateway; and if she should help him, might he not aid her in return? So she talked to Malorn, and when she learned of his plight she willingly gave him enough of her life's essence to allow him the strength to return to his own kind.

And in the hour that they spent together, in the dark and deserted street, the seeds of their love began to grow.

Malorn returned to Griette. Time after time he came back, drawn by a bond that neither of them could break, nor wished to. No one in Griette's world knew or even suspected what was afoot; their meetings were secret, intense and all too brief. But at home Griette became withdrawn, preoccupied. She began to see Foss in a detached and very different light; as a cold and selfish man who demanded her love and loyalty as his rightful due but conceded little in return. Griette loved her children; she loved her home. But she loved Malorn far more.

Yet Griette and Malorn could never become lovers in any true sense. Like Charn and Calliope, they could not so much as touch each other without inflicting harm; if they tried to draw close together, one or both of them would die. Malorn begged Griette to come with him to his own world; Griette, though, knew better than to try. How could she hope to survive in his world, she asked, when he could not survive in hers? It was an impossible dream, and there was no choice for them but to part. She would meet him one last time, she said, and then they must go their separate ways for ever.

It was then that Malorn had told her about the Sacrament of Night. For centuries past the Sacrament had been enshrined in the twilight-dwellers' history like a dark, alluring but dangerous treasure. Its origins were long forgotten – if they had ever been known – but in a past age it had been the focus of the highest ceremony practised by their kind. A rite that defied the power of death. For the Sacrament was a transformation; not merely of the mind, but also of the body and, it was believed, the soul.

It was said that what the Sacrament demanded would break all but the strongest. The reward for those who could endure was – Malorn had had no better word – metamorphosis; a kind of rebirth into another form of being which knew no boundaries or barriers and transcended the limitations of their own or any other world. But those who failed suffered a savage and agonising death. And once the first step had been taken, there could be no turning back.

In that past age, many of the twilight world's higher beings had dared to take the Sacrament when the natural span of their lives had run its course. The fate of those who failed was known only too well; but the truth about those who succeeded, or appeared to, was obscure. There were tales in plenty, but they had the timbre of legend, and legend could not be tested. How could the twilight-dwellers know what lay beyond the Sacrament's portal, when those who stepped through were never seen again? There might be bliss; there might be torment; there might be, simply, nothing. They could not even say with certainty that the Sacrament's powers were any more than a myth. So as time passed, doubt began to replace the twilight-beings' faith and hope in the ancient ritual. More and more chose to face a natural death rather than brave the terrors of the unknown, and gradually the great rite lapsed into disuse. Its legend persisted, but it was merely a fireside story now. All that remained of the Sacrament of Night was the source itself; a small and perfectly formed pool, like a chalice, set into the rock of the court's deepest foundations far down beneath the hall of remembrance. The pool could not be drained, nor could it ever overflow, and its dark content, whether miraculous life-giver or deadly poison, was the libation that set the feet of those who drank it on a road of no return. It was this libation that Malorn had brought to Griette.

In a few stark words he had told her that his decision was made. He would not, *could* not, live without her; and if he could not survive in her world, nor she in his, then the Sacrament was their only hope. He did not know what it would do; what would become of them. But he clung fiercely to his belief that the ancient tales of its powers were not myth but truth. All it needed was the courage, the will, and they could break free from the imprisonment of their inimical natures and, together, be transformed. Malorn was resolved to go through the portal, and he wanted Griette to come with him.

As she drew the knowledge from Charn's mind Calliope felt an echo of the awful war between hope and terror that had raged in Griette when she understood what Malorn was asking of her.

To take the Sacrament would be to risk everything, for neither he nor any other soul alive could tell her what the Sacrament would do. All Malorn knew – or believed – was that the drinking of the libation would open the gateway to a life unlike anything they had ever encountered or dreamed possible. What they would become, where they would go, could not be known until and unless that first, irrevocable step was taken. But they would be together.

A huge stab of emotion gripped Calliope as she sensed, through Charn, the dreadful confusion that had filled Griette then. She loved Malorn; loved him so much that it was a burning physical ache within her. But fighting that love was a desperate dread. One drop, just one, of that dark, alien liquid on her tongue, and the die would be cast. No chance to recant, no margin for second thoughts. And if, at the last, she could not face what the Sacrament demanded of her, then its power would destroy her.

She begged Malorn for time. Time to think, time to prepare, time to be *sure*. Malorn could only comply, but he was reluctant and Griette knew that he would not be able to contain his desperate impatience for long. At last he extracted a promise from her: one quartermoon, no more, and she would give him her decision. Griette agreed. And throughout the following nights, while Foss and her children slept unaware, she began to pour out her emotions on to page after desperate page, as she wrestled with her longings and her fears.

That, Calliope realised now, had been the beginning of the madness. For Griette had known even then that she would not be able to do what Malorn asked of her. '*I do not have the courage. I must fail . . . And in failing, I will end all.*' A dire prophecy . . . and on the following quartermoon night, it came true.

Malorn returned and they met in the starlit darkness and empty silence of a deserted Public Garden. This had become their refuge and their secret, joyous haven, but there was no joy in Griette as she told Malorn of her decision. Malorn, though, would not accept. He cajoled her, he pleaded with her – and Griette, who found it so hard to deny him anything, began to waver. She wanted him so *much* . . . yet she was still afraid. Then, before she could make a move to stop him, Malorn took matters into his own hands.

Time slipped back, and with awful clarity Calliope saw the scene unfolding before her inner vision. She saw Malorn take the phial – the same phial that she clasped now in her hand. She saw him put it to his lips. Saw him drink; and then, with a sweet, sad smile, he held the phial out to Griette.

She could not take it. Her mind and body were frozen, and all she could do was stare at him in dawning misery and horror. Malorn pleaded. He begged. It was too late to turn back, he said; he had taken the Sacrament, and the Sacrament was irrevocable. The portal to a new way would open for him . . . but unless his human love came with him, he would not step through. If she refused, then he would spurn the Sacrament and die; for death was better than any life without her.

From Calliope's throat came a thin, agonised wail as through the twisted corridors of time she glimpsed Griette's worst memory of all. In dreamlike allegory the Sacrament's door opened, and it was a black, incredible vortex on to a universe of possibilities, summoning Malorn with a power and an urgency that he dared not defy. Yet Malorn did not answer the call. He turned to Griette; he made a final, desperate plea. And Griette turned away from him and fell to her knees, hands covering her face, sobbing a desperate plea for forgiveness as the portal closed again with its command unanswered.

The rest, little as it was, was stark and unembellished. Perhaps Griette had been unable to bare her soul any further; or perhaps over the years she had found the only relief she could by making herself forget the details of that final episode. Malorn died as the sun rose on the following morning. She had kept vigil with him all night, holding him in her arms, striving to ease the agony that racked him as the Sacrament, uncompleted, turned on him and tore him apart. When it was over, and there was nothing left to show that he had ever existed, she rose to her feet, walked to her house, where she sat down and wrote one single word on a sheet of paper. She sealed the paper, and many others, in the box which, with an awful foresight, she had already entrusted to the future care of her elder daughter. Then, as her skin and hair began to turn to grey, the screaming had begun.

Calliope drew back from Charn, breaking the physical contact, breaking the meld of minds that had at last shown her the truth.

She was silent for a long time. The phial in her hand was cold, as if she were holding an icicle that would not melt, and she thought that by rights she ought to be crying. But there were no tears in her. Only a strange, sad aching, as though the story that had been revealed to her belonged to another world that had never truly existed. Yet it had existed. *Did* exist. And now, the circle of that old tragedy was coming full turn again.

You are your mother's daughter. Wasn't that what her father had said, the savage accusation and condemnation he had thrown at her in the moments before her final flight from his mastery of her life? Calliope felt perspiration slicking her palm. What would have become of Griette if she had dared to take that step into the unknown? What would become of her, Calliope, if she should break the circle and find in herself the courage that had failed her mother? The Sacrament of Night offered no certainty of attainment. Charn had shown her that; had made no attempt to hide it. She might die as Malorn had died, in monstrous agony, screaming for release. Or the forces unleashed might twist her mind beyond hope of repair. Or transform her, warp her into something unimaginable and uncontainable that would destroy far more than mind and body together. Or—

She broke the chain of her thoughts with a furious inward jolt. *Your mother's daughter.* No. In that sense, she was *not* Griette's child – and Griette knew it. Griette had known the hideous consequences of regret and remorse which nothing could relieve and which ate into the soul like a wasting disease. She wasn't insane; never truly had been . . . and at the last, she had tried to make Calliope understand that it was better to take the risk of dying than to follow where she had led.

Calliope raised her head and looked at Charn. He had turned away and was staring out across the hospice gardens, not wanting to intrude on her, and afraid of speaking any word or making any move that might sway her thoughts. Following the direction of his gaze she saw that colour was beginning to seep out of the greyness as dawn became day. The tall chimneys of the hospice were touched with sunlight; minutes more and that light would spread over the grass, over the fountain and the flowers to their hideaway here among the willows. It would burn Charn's eyes, sear his skin, drain the strength and the life from him, and this time she could not restore him, for she hadn't the resources left in her. He might, perhaps, survive a day or two more. But after that . . .

He didn't see her turn the phial in her hand, touch the stopper, slowly and carefully draw it out. She half expected to catch a scent from the phial – perhaps the scent of the white flowers – but there was nothing. One instant, and it would be done. Death, or a future; and no means of knowing which way the die would fall.

But without it, there could be no future for Charn.

The sudden, quick movement of Calliope's hand alerted Charn and snapped him from his reverie. His head turned – and he was in time to see her put the phial to her lips, tilt her head back—

'*Calli!*' It was a hiss of shock, almost of horror. 'Calli, no— not yet, you can't—' Then the words snapped off as he realised that his protest had come too late.

Calliope lowered her hand again. Her gaze met his, and in it was a bizarre blend of defiance, terror and elation. 'The decision was mine to make,' she said. 'I didn't want to wait, Charn. I didn't want to risk making the same mistake as my mother.' She smiled at him, tremulously, feverishly. 'I'm sorry . . .'

Charn could hardly believe that this was happening. 'Do you know what you've done? Do you *know*?'

'Yes.'

Something akin to panic was clawing at his mind. 'You can't turn back. There's no cure, no antidote, no chance to change your mind—'

'I know that, too.'

'*You might die!*'

'*Yes!*' She didn't want him to tell her, for suddenly the enormity of her act had come home to her and a panic to outstrip his own was rising in her like a slowly forming tidal wave. *It's too late, I've taken the step, the Sacrament has begun and I've gone beyond the point of no return – I shouldn't have done it, I shouldn't, I shouldn't, oh living spirits, I'm so frightened . . .*

'I did it . . .' Her mouth felt like charred parchment; so *dry*, and there was a taint of copper and sulphur on her lips, though the liquid in the phial had had no taste at all. 'I did it because . . .' *Because you wouldn't have let yourself be first, you wouldn't have forced the choice on me as Malorn tried to force it on my mother; and because unless you take the Sacrament you'll die, and I don't want you to die, and this is a chance for us, a hope for us* ... The words, the garbled explanations, were crowding into her head, but though her mouth worked convulsively with the struggle to say them, all that would come was a choking, gagging sound.

'Calli!' Charn started towards her in alarm. As he did so, Calliope saw – *but she didn't know what she saw; it was a delusion, a mirage, a moment's nightmare* – and with an inarticulate cry she jerked away from him and sprawled on her side on the ground.

Someone was wailing and she didn't realise that the noise came from her own throat. Dragging at the shredded tatters that something had made of her mind she rallied enough self-control to gasp out Charn's name in a terrified plea for help. *But Charn wasn't there. Where he had been was something else, a great doorway, black on black; so alien that she knew she had to flee from it before it overwhelmed and devoured and absorbed her, because if she was human it would kill her, and if she was not human then the terror of it, the terror was too great to be borne—*

'*Calli!*' Charn lunged towards her, catching her arms as she tried to twist away. He pinned her and she writhed like a trapped snake, exerting a strength that should have been far beyond her ability. Her eyes were bulging in their sockets and the whites were turning scarlet as blood vessels broke; she didn't know who or what he was, didn't even know he was here; all she could think of was escape from the dementia exploding through her. The Sacrament – or its genesis, for this was only the very beginning – had erupted into life so fast that there had been no time to prepare. Charn hadn't bargained for that, hadn't even known what would happen to her, let alone how devastatingly and violently it would come, but now it was happening, and he couldn't get through to her, couldn't drag her back and protect her from the unleashed power rioting through her body and mind and soul. Yet without his help, the power would smash her – the rite had to be completed, the full force of it confronted and the transformation undergone, and she could never, ever face such an ordeal alone and survive.

There was only one hope left, and Charn's rioting mind snatched at it. The phial – Calliope had been clutching it, and he wrestled to unclench her flailing, beating fists, as she struggled under him. For all her unnatural energy his strength was still greater; he forced her fingers apart, thrusting, grasping—

Her hands were empty. Whether she had dropped the phial or thrown it from her he didn't know and it made no difference; it was gone. He *had* to find it again!

'Calliope – Calliope, listen to me, hear me!' His hands pressed down on her shoulders and he knelt astride her, holding her spreadeagled in the undergrowth. Her eyes locked with his, and suddenly beneath their wildness he saw a flare of recognition. Then with startling abruptness she stopped struggling and her body slumped under him like a child's rag doll.

'Ch . . .' Her first attempt was choking and inchoate, but she fought it, tried again. 'Ch-Charn . . . c . . . c . . . cold . . . so c-c-cold . . . it hurts me so . . . please . . . oh please, Charn, help me . . . I'm *f-f-frightened* . . .'

'Calli, the phial!' He wanted desperately to comfort and help her but there was no time, not if either of them was to be saved. 'Where's the *phial*? I have to find it!'

She moaned and shook her head from side to side. 'I don't know . . . don't know . . . oh, it hurts so much, I can't *bear* it . . .'

Biting back an oath, Charn scrambled away from her and began to forage frantically through the greenery around them. Something there – no; it was only a stone – the gloves were blunting his fingers' sensitivity and he tore them off and plunged bare hands back into the tangle. Two more stones – he forced back his frustration, resisting the urge to hurl the pebbles at the nearest tree – then suddenly he felt something else, small, regular—

It was the phial. By sheer, miraculous chance Calliope had replaced the stopper, and he could see the sheen of the dark liquid inside. There was enough left; just enough.

'I've found it!' He started to turn back to her. 'Calli, try to hold on, try to keep—' The words broke off.

Calliope had vanished.

For perhaps five seconds Charn stared dazedly at the flattened grass where she had been lying. A turmoil of thoughts raced through his mind, among them the hideous possibility that the power of the awakening Sacrament had somehow snatched her away, out of this world and into another, unimaginable dimension. He started to shake, felt a strangling, asphyxiating sensation taking hold of his chest and lungs—

A cry, distorted by distance to eerie, birdlike shrillness, rang out from the direction of the hospice. Charn's head jerked up – and he saw Calliope.

She was tottering like a drunkard across the lawn, her feet leaving a veering trail of footprints on the dew-soaked sward in her wake. From the main door of the hospice two angels were hurrying towards her. They called an anxious query; one was holding out her arms, proffering help, while the other urgently signalled to someone out of Charn's sight in the building. Calliope was oblivious; she careened on, her own arms now outspread as though she had some mad notion of taking to the air. Through a flowerbed, trampling blooms that were just starting to open in the first sunlight; then suddenly she swung towards the pool and the fountain. Charn, on his feet but paralysed, tried to impel his voice into life to shout a warning, but it jammed in his throat and he could make no sound. Like a sleeper trapped in a nightmare he saw Calliope and the angels reach the pool's edge together. Calliope stumbled against the low wall, lost her balance, pitched forward; one angel made a grab for her and they both fell clumsily across the stones, half in and half out of the water.

Calliope might have succeeded in fighting off the first angel, but the second got a grip on her arm and started to pull her back from the pool. Between them they would overpower her . . .

Charn's paralysis snapped, and he broke cover and ran. The sunlight hit him – it had a savage impact, weak though it was at this early hour – but he ignored it, had to ignore it, as he raced across the lawn towards the struggling trio. He didn't know what he intended; there was no time to think and he could only react blindly, viscerally. Anything, anything to save Calliope; he would fight, he would maim, he would kill anyone who tried to stand in his way—

The angels saw Charn, and screamed. An answering shout came from the building; three men emerged and came pelting across the grass, then another cry rang out from behind Charn. He slewed to a halt, spun round – two gardeners were coming at him from the far side of the lawn, one wielding a spade and the other a rake. They were cutting off his retreat; they would be on him before he reached Calliope, and for an instant Charn's mind froze as terror for her safety clashed violently with his own survival instinct. Then reason slammed back – he couldn't fight so many, and if they overpowered him, as they must, both he and Calliope would be beyond help.

Despairing, and loathing himself, Charn twisted about and fled. He heard the men's yells of consternation as they swerved after him, but he was fleeter than they were; with this start they had no hope of catching him. Into the bushes, in among the trees, *oh, the blessed relief of shadow,* and ahead was the denser cover that divided the hospice from the outside world—

His pursuers gave up the chase when they realised that their quarry had got clear of the grounds and away. By the pool four angels were crouched over Calliope, who in the midst of her fit had suddenly collapsed and now lay motionless, eyes open but seeing nothing. They shook her, they called to her, they rubbed her hands and slapped her cheeks, but there was no response whatever. She breathed steadily and evenly; she had no obvious physical injury. But her senses had shut down, and nothing the angels did could rouse her.

The Hospice Master met them as they carried Calliope in at the front door. He had not yet heard about the disturbance, for minutes ago the alarm had been raised inside the hospice by another shocked and distressed angel. An inmate dead in her room. Dead, and grey. The Hospice Master had just come from the east wing, where he had seen Griette for himself, and when he looked at Calliope's blank, waxen face he felt cold dread move through him like ice in his blood.

He turned to the most senior of his attendant angels. 'Send a runner to Physician Foss Agate's house,' he said sombrely. 'The address is in the book in my office. Tell him his daughter Calliope is here, and . . .' But the rest of it, he thought, could not be explained by a mere messenger. 'And ask him to come at once!'

Charn saw the runner leave. He had returned to the garden as soon as he judged that his pursuers had turned back; a gamble, but his judgement had proved sound. Now he was among the bushes where Calliope had first found him the previous night, hidden from any probing eye but with a clear view of the hospice frontage and the sweep of the drive. It took little imagination to guess the nature of the runner's errand, and Foss was sure to waste no time in responding. An hour, possibly less, and he would be here. While somewhere in the hospice, the Sacrament of Night was working its relentless transformation on Calliope . . .

The phial was still in Charn's hand, and unconsciously he clenched the hand so hard that the crystal-like facets dug their imprint deep into his palm. In the hospice they would try to help Calliope, but their efforts would inevitably fail, for they did not know what had happened to her and they did not know what must be done to complete the rite and cross the gulf and accept what the Sacrament's power would bring. Calliope could still be saved – but time was running out.

He felt his fingers uncurl, loosing their grip on the phial. Don't think, he told himself; don't pause. *I didn't want to wait*, Calliope had said. For fear her courage should fail . . .

Charn pulled the stopper from the phial.

Chapter XXVI

My name is Calliope Agate. I am twenty-five years old. I am an Associate of the Institute of—

But the pain flooded her again then, and though she couldn't cry out – she had no lungs and no voice because the physical body that once had been hers was removed from her, severed from her – within some hideous, internal dimension that might or might not be herself she howled wordlessly for release. The howling and the pain went on for an age, a lifetime; then suddenly both were gone, as though someone had slammed a shutter down on them. Darkness. Silence. Respite.

There was a door. She could see it in her mind's eye, a portal of absolute blackness, and it called to her with a lure of such promise that the summons was like chains dragging at her soul. Yet there was terror in the promise; terror that she had never known and could not face. That way lay salvation or destruction. She couldn't do it. She couldn't *do* it.

My name is Calliope Agate. I am twenty-five years—

But she wasn't. She wasn't Calliope Agate, or anything else that made any sense, because there *was* no sense, not anywhere within or without. *I don't exist. I. I. Who? No one. Nothing. The pain is gone, and yet it hurts, it hurts, it hurts. Something is dissecting*

326

me, piece by piece. Unpicking the seams to see what's underneath. Calliope Agate. I am Calliope. I was Calliope. I—

The door in her mind pulsed violently, and this time she thought that something physical did shriek aloud, for the endless noise of it beat against her mind in wave after wave of sound. Yet when it finally stopped (*it had to stop, of course it had to; there is no such thing as endless, it can't be, it isn't possible*) she knew by the feel of the darkness that she had been wrong. No sound. Too still. Another delusion. So *many* delusions; everything and everything and everything, and she was deranged now, she knew it; deranged by the pain and by the fear and by the knowledge that the person – thing – she had been was breaking apart and fragmenting into half-*people* and partial-*things* and if she didn't pull the splinters together, *now* and *here* and *quickly*, then it would be too late because they would scatter away out of her reach and she would be a formless, moaning spectre, searching forever for a self that wasn't there—

No. Nonono, fight it, fight back, don't go down that road. My name is Calliope. Twenty-five years old. Calliope. Associate. Human. Alive. Though Malorn is dead and Selethe is dead and Griette is dead and Charn is—

Charn. Not here, he was not here, she knew because she couldn't feel him. Couldn't reach out and touch him with the hands that did not belong to her any more. '*All grey*', *my little brother said.* '*Grey man, all grey, all cold*'. *Must never, ever touch him. But I did, and I would again, and I want to again because I want his cold to freeze me and numb me and take away this feeling that someone is cutting my flesh with blunt knives and ripping into me with broken nails and flaying me to get at my soul and it hurts it hurts it HURTS, OH, HELP ME, HELP ME, CHARN, CHARN—*

The shriek that burst from Calliope's throat stunned the hospice physician and sent him reeling back from the infirmary couch. His assistant, a senior angel, spun round from the nearby table in time to see the patient fling herself bolt upright, then as the scream intensified Calliope clamped both hands on her own throat, squeezing and crushing as she tried to *stop it, stop it, the noise, I can't bear it, and the only way to escape is through the black door and I can't, can't, can't—*

The physician gathered his wits and grabbed Calliope's hands, prising her fingers away from her neck. At a barked order the

327

angel snatched up a bottle and a wooden spatula, and between them they struggled to open her mouth and force her to swallow some of the bottle's contents, but Calliope gargled and choked and spat the draught out, *no, no, I can't take your sustenance, it will kill me, it will destroy everything, and I must get free, get*

'—AWAY!' The screech rose to an ear-splitting pitch and with explosive force Calliope jackknifed from the couch, flinging the physician and the angel aside. The angel fell backwards against the table, scattering its contents with a clamour of breaking glass and clattering metal; the physician made a despairing grab for Calliope's sleeve but missed, and Calliope hurled herself towards the infirmary door. She couldn't see and didn't know where she was going; the force rampaging in her was beyond control and there was only the desperate imperative to escape from it, try to outrun the alchemical thunderstorm that was tearing through the core of her existence. Somewhere in another dimension a thing that wasn't human and wasn't animal and wasn't anything that she could ever hope to recognise was wailing on a long, ululating note like unearthly music, and underneath it was a rumble and a roar, giants' footfalls and giants' booming voices, and a background choir of screaming—

The running steps and anxious voices from the passage outside reached the door an instant before Calliope did. The door jolted back on its hinges, suddenly amplifying the noise of agitated inmates from rooms along the corridor, and in a headlong rush Calliope cannoned into the Hospice Master, with Foss a pace behind him.

The Hospice Master staggered back, and Calliope rebounded. '*Nnnnh . . .*' She was struggling to express the pain of the volcanic pressure building up inside her, but no words would come, only an ugly, inchoate moaning. She saw the two men staring at her in horrified disbelief, but their faces meant nothing, for no reference point in the world made any sense now. She sidestepped, a skipping motion like a dancer. Then stopped. Then backed away. *Still there, still there; the black portal in my mind, but I'm too afraid, I'm too afraid* – Her mouth jerked. Her hands, clenched, started to rise slowly to her own face.

'Lorimer!' The Hospice Master flung a frantic glance towards the physician, not daring to look away from Calliope for more than an instant. '*Explain!*'

Foss, his eyes bulging with shock as he stared at his daughter, could hardly take in Physician Lorimer's attempt to reply. He had arrived minutes ago in his carriage but had been too impatient to listen to the Hospice Master's inarticulate tale; his sole interest was in finding Calliope and taking her under his charge. Now though, he realised that he was dealing with something the like of which he had never encountered before. Calliope was possessed – and this possession was of an order far, far removed from the earlier aberration.

Calliope took another pace backwards. Her mouth was contorted in a grimace which might have been pain or might have been an abominable smile. She returned Foss's stare, but what she saw did not register on her brain. He was no one. A thing, meaningless. All she knew was the hurt in her. And the portal, salvation or destruction, still calling and calling.

Foss was breathing hectically. That creature . . . this was his work, he would take any wager on it. He should have killed the monstrosity, cut its throat and thrown its corpse on the city dumps to be eaten by scavenging dogs. And Calliope was in league with it, consorting with it; just as Griette had consorted with that other living obscenity fifteen years ago. Like mother, like daughter, he thought, feeling his fury rise cholerically. But this time he would not be made a mockery of. Never, ever, would he allow *that* to happen again.

He snapped his fingers in the angel's direction. 'Give me an insensator pad!'

The angel looked nervously at Lorimer, who said, 'Sir, that may not be wise. We don't know the cause of your daughter's—'

'*I* know the cause of it full well!' Foss interrupted savagely. 'Do as I say – give me the pad, then restrain her and hold her still.'

Calliope said, 'Nnn . . . *no. Not.*'

'What?' Foss's head came up sharply. Calliope's smile, or grimace, had gone, and she was glaring madly at him. A thin rope of saliva drooled slowly down her chin, and his eyes narrowed. So she understood more than she pretended . . . 'Daughter,' he said ominously, 'do you know me? Do you know who I am?'

'*You . . .' Oh, I know you, I know you. You stand between me and*

329

*the black portal. I see it opening behind you, yawning wide, a chasm,
an abyss. Salvation or destruction. Is it because of you that I'm so
frightened?*

'Calliope . . .' she said. 'Twenty-five . . . Calliope . . . Hhh . . .'
*But no. Not human. Not any more. Never again. Destruction. The
portal . . . Charn . . . and my mother, my . . .*

'*Calli.*'

The voice came softly into her mind, and the sound of it
smoothed away the pain in her. Calliope blinked. Someone was
calling to her, from inside the portal, just beyond the threshold.
She couldn't see who it was, but . . .

'*Calli, my dearest child, don't be afraid.*'

The figure of Foss, overlaid on the inner vision of the doorway,
began to fade. Not knowing that she did so, Calliope put her
hands to her mouth and bit the fingers, *because if I don't, if I don't
stop myself, I'll reach out to that darkness and step through, and I
daren't, no, no, no—*

'*Don't do as I did, Calli. Don't let your fear betray you.*'

'Mother . . .?' Her hands dropped away and she said it aloud,
in a wondering, childlike voice. Foss, now only a pace from her
and with the insensator pad in his hand, tensed and hissed to
Lorimer, 'Damn it, man, get hold of her! Get her arms!'

They poised. Calliope was oblivious, for all awareness of the
room had ebbed away and there was only the black void before
her. Slowly, unsteadily, she started to reach out towards it. One
foot slid forward.

Foss cried, 'Now!' and he, Lorimer and the angel closed in on
her together.

'*Calli! CALLI, RUN!*'

The warning in her mind struck home like a lightning bolt,
and the black doorway shattered and disintegrated as reality
smashed back and Calliope realised what was happening. She
screamed a shrill, piercing scream of fury, and with it came the
pain in a shrieking, blinding tidal wave. There was a rush of
energy so huge that it ripped through every muscle and nerve in
her, then her arms came up with a force that slammed into her
would-be captors and sent them spinning backwards. Somewhere
beyond sanity she heard Foss's bellow of outrage, but the agony
in her was a blazing inferno, and she launched herself at him,
past him, *through* him, and plunged towards the door, *not the*

330

*right door, not the black door, but the black door was gone and she had
to run, run—*

'*Great powers!*' Foss staggered to the threshold in her wake.
His face was bloodless with shock and disbelief, because what
had happened was impossible, inconceivable. Shaking, he gripped
the door-jamb and tried desperately to articulate. 'She – she
went – through me . . . *Through* me . . .'

The Hospice Master stumbled to his side. His skin, too, was
ashen and sickly and he clasped at Foss's upper arm as though to
convince himself that they were both made of solid flesh and
bone. 'I saw it!' Behind him the angel had fainted and Lorimer
stood staring as though his wits had been pulverised. 'Living
spirits . . . is this some deranged dream?'

From somewhere along the corridor came a squeal of fright
and the crash of a laden tray falling to the floor. The sheer
mundanity of the noise snapped both Foss and the Hospice
Master out of their stupor, and Foss said harshly, 'It's no dream!
Quickly – we must catch her!'

Calliope had vanished, but there was chaos in her wake; a trail
of broken china, overturned chairs, bewildered angels striving to
calm excited and disorderly inmates and prevent them from
joining in the chase. Foss ran lumberingly past it all, quickly
outdistancing the Hospice Master whose progress was hampered
by his staff's agitated queries. A rising hubbub of noise ahead
told him the direction Calliope had taken – she was heading for
the east wing, and that could mean only one thing: she was going
to Griette's room. Bitter rage filled him at that thought, though
he could not have begun to explain why, and he shouted her
name with a fury to which desperation lent an extra edge.

But for all his efforts he did not catch up with her in time, for
he rounded the turn of the last corridor as she reached Griette's
door.

Foss slithered to a halt, his lungs working like a blacksmith's
bellows. Calliope turned, looked back at him, and for one awful
moment in the slanting light from a nearby window it seemed to
him that she had no face. He recoiled – and the illusion vanished;
in its place a weird, cold aura seemed to flicker briefly around
Calliope's form, then she thrust the door open and disappeared
into the room. For a heartbeat there was silence. Then Foss
heard her voice, muffled, distant, tormented.

331

'*Mother-er-er—*'

'Calliope!' Foss started forward, but hesitated as he was hailed and the Hospice Master came pounding up behind him, as dishevelled and breathless as he.

'Foss, wait! There's something—'

'Damn waiting!' Foss interrupted. 'She's gone to her mother!' He started off again, but the Hospice Master grasped his arm.

'There's something you don't yet know!' he persisted. 'When you arrived there was no time to tell you – it's Griette; she—'

He got no further, for Foss threw off his restraining hand and ran towards the open door of Griette's room.

Too late. It was too late, for she was gone, far away, far, far away to a place from which she could never return, and the gulf was too great, and the pain which she could have soothed away was too vast, and the black portal had vanished, and Charn was not here, and there was nothing, nothing, nothing—

Foss burst into the room and almost fell headlong over Calliope where she huddled in a shuddering, foetal crouch on the floor. Arms flailing, he tottered, stumbled, regained balance and swung round to swoop on her.

Then froze as he saw what she had seen.

Lit by a mellow shaft of sunlight, Griette lay in her neat bed. She was embracing her pillow as though in dreams she embraced a lover, and on her face was a sweet smile of secret and private joy. Everything about her was grey. Grey face. Grey arms. Grey hair. No subtle shade or hint of anything else; just a complete and absolute absence of colour.

Foss felt himself starting to shake. With ferocious self-control he quelled it and walked slowly to the bedside. Then – it took a greater effort still – he reached out and touched his wife's face.

She was cold. It wasn't merely the coldness of death, though with his physician's knowledge he registered the presence of that, too; this was something deep, unnatural, as though her body had been carved from ice. Mechanically, with the conditioned reflex of his training, Foss moved his hand from her cheek and lifted back one eyelid. The eye beneath looked back – the last look she would ever give him, and it was like the mindless stare of a fish on a market-trader's slab. The iris was grey, and Foss felt his gorge rise. Even *that* paltry token of humanity could not have been left unsullied but had been changed and taken and *stolen*, so that nothing remained of her that had ever been his own to possess.

From behind him a voice said, 'Foss?'

He turned. The Hospice Master was in the doorway, Lorimer and two angels at his shoulder. 'I'm sorry,' the Hospice Master added quietly.

Foss made a gesture that was almost dismissive. 'When?' The question was curt.

'She was found shortly after dawn.' A pause. 'She was as you see her now; the room undisturbed. I think her passing must have been . . . quite peaceful.'

Foss turned away. At this moment he didn't care whether Griette had died peacefully or in shrieking mayhem. All that mattered was that something or someone had taken her life, and in doing so had robbed him irreparably of the secrets that she had kept for fifteen years. The secrets which she should have shared with him, her husband and her partner in scientific study, but which instead she had concealed from him, deceiving and cheating and *lying* as she pursued her illicit and unnatural liaison.

Like mother, like daughter. He turned and stared down at Calliope. She had not moved; she crouched still in that grotesque posture, staring fixedly at the bed. Her lips were moving, mumbling something, but he could not hear what it was. Guilt, he thought. Guilt and remorse, and little wonder, for she had abetted her deviant lover in an act of murder.

But if Griette could no longer tell her secrets, Calliope could. She knew; Foss was certain of it. She knew, and she would tell him. One way or another he would have the truth from her, and there need be no bar and no limit to his methods. Strange that it should be possible to feel so much hatred for one whom in the past he had loved. But the daughter he had loved was as dead as Griette; what remained was no longer his child. He probably did not even hate her. He was merely indifferent.

He realised then that while his thoughts were elsewhere the Hospice Master had still been talking, haltingly trying to explain and excuse and proffer sympathy. Foss neither knew nor cared what had been said, and without any ceremony he cut across the earnest monologue.

'Take Calliope to my carriage,' he said tersely.

The Hospice Master stopped and looked uneasily at the girl

crouching on the floor. 'I'm not sure if that's the wisest course, Foss. If she were to suffer another fit—'

'I'll take that chance. I want her under my own roof, where I can deal with this condition properly.'

The Hospice Master acquiesced, knowing that while Foss was in this frame of mind there was nothing to be gained from arguing with him. Cautiously, he and Physician Lorimer moved towards Calliope. They half expected her to erupt into a new rage, but to their surprise and relief she hardly seemed to notice when they took hold of her arms and lifted her to her feet. Mutely, passively, she went with them, not even looking back, and the small procession left the room and headed slowly for the hospice's main door.

In the corridor Foss paused to pick up the insensator pad, which he had dropped as he ran. He pocketed it in case it should be needed on the journey – easy enough to return or replace it at some later stage – then paused for a moment, watching the others' slow progress before he followed in their wake. All strength and defiance had drained from Calliope; she looked like a rag doll that had been left out in a rainstorm, and Foss felt a spark of pity kindle in him. Then he remembered the magnitude of her betrayal, and the spark dwindled and went out. Griette, dead. Hard to believe. But Calliope would tell him everything; he'd see to that. Philome must be coped with, because she would doubtless have sympathy for the girl and might think his treatment harsh. But Philome, unlike Griette, knew where her first duty and loyalty lay. He could make her understand and accept, for she was what a wife should be.

Suddenly Foss was filled with a very great need to see Philome, and it almost eclipsed the immediacy of his present concerns. There was Calliope to deal with, of course, and then the matter of tracking down the twilight monstrosity; and Nempson would be anxious for news. But an hour or two's respite, an hour or two's *normality*, would restore some measure of equilibrium. Briefly the memory of Calliope's flight from the infirmary flicked through his mind, and he suppressed a shudder as he recalled how she had seemed to rush not past him but through him as he tried to bar her way. Ridiculous, for such a thing was against all the laws of science. He had been overwrought, imagined it. Hardly surprising. An hour or two's quiet normality . . .

With an odd movement that suggested he was shaking off a clammy, invisible cloak, Foss hurried after Calliope and her escort.

It might have been the sunlight that triggered it, for it happened in the moment that the party emerged from the front entrance of the hospice. Calliope, blank-eyed and docile, had been aware of nothing beyond the sheer absence of pain, and the relief was so vast that she clung to it to the exclusion of all else. She had a vague, apathetic notion that she was walking and that there were shapes around her, but they had no meaning. *She* had no meaning; she was nobody, and there was no purpose in anything, and if somewhere deep down in her mind a memory of a black portal and her mother's voice calling to her was trying to stir, she buried it carefully and would not let it be resurrected. She thought that perhaps she was dying. If so, then it was not an unpleasant sensation. Just walking. No need to think. Nothing to fear. Let it happen; let it go as it would.

Then suddenly, in the space of a single step, there was brightness – and it was as if someone had taken hold of twin knives and plunged them into her eyes. Calliope's muscles locked rigid; her mouth dropped open; and an instant later agony hit her like a sledgehammer. It filled her head, it drove into her brain, it exploded through her and detonated every nerve in her body to a height of howling torture. Wildly through the mayhem of it came realisation – *the Sacrament, it was the Sacrament, and she had forgotten and the portal was gone and she couldn't call it back and she had failed and the power of the Sacrament of Night was going to destroy her*—

She broke screaming from the grip of her stunned captors and staggered two paces before pitching forward and collapsing to the ground. Writhing, kicking, rolling; foam flecked her mouth and the foam turned scarlet as her teeth bit savagely into her tongue and through the streaming blood she babbled a plea. '*Make it stop, make it stop, oh, please, I can't bear any more, someone help me, someone HELP me!*'

'*Calli!*' Foss's bitter indifference disintegrated and he flung himself down, grabbing for her arms, wrestling frantically with her as her body heaved and struggled. 'Do something!' he yelled to the Hospice Master. 'This isn't madness, it's *pain* – get help, get a medical pack – damn your soul, you benighted fool, *MOVE!*'

335

The Hospice Master, white-faced, raced back into the building, but Lorimer was beside Foss now, and he shouted, 'Sir, the pad – you picked it up, I saw you—'

Foss swore the filthiest oath he had ever used and dived for his pocket, scrabbling to find the insensator which in the shock of this emergency he had forgotten. Sweat covered Calliope now; saturating her hair, streaming on her skin – and her skin was blistering as though she were burning. *What in the name of every spirit ever created—*

'Hold her!' Foss bawled, brandishing the pad. 'Don't let her – *aaah!*'

The shadow and what it contained came at him out of nowhere, and his cry turned to an inarticulate yell as two powerful, ice-cold hands took hold of him and flung him aside, away from Calliope. Foss sprawled on the gravel, started to right himself with a convulsive movement—

And as Calliope's voice quavered up in a renewed moan of anguish he found himself staring into Charn's demented eyes.

Chapter XVII

He was wreathed in a smoking, sourceless haze that dimmed the sunlight and cast its own eerie penumbra over the drive. His face was haggard, streaked with sweat like Calliope's, and black blood ran from an open wound in one forearm. For what seemed to Foss like a small eternity they gazed at each other. Calliope lay between them, momentarily forgotten, and though Foss was dimly aware of Lorimer behind him and others, angels and inmates alike, drawn to the scene by the commotion, they had no more significance than flies buzzing on a wall.

At last, chokingly, he found his voice, though it cracked as he forced it out between clenched teeth.

'*You* . . .' Nothing better would come, but in the single word was all the loathing and venom that had been festering in Foss's soul since the day of Charn's escape from his house. The insensator pad was still in his hand, and a wild impulse gripped him: *one movement, one strike, before the creature can react*— But it died. Charn was more than a match for him; faster and stronger. And something else had happened. A deeper change, that Foss sensed on a primal level. He could see the creature's face more clearly now, and it was in pain – pain like Calliope's, and the sweating, and the unnatural energy that had enabled it to hurl him aside as though he weighed nothing . . .

'What have you done to my daughter?' he snarled.

Charn continued to stare down at him. His breathing was ragged, savage, but the crazed stare had modified to something quieter, steadier and with an awful sanity behind it. 'I have done nothing,' he said. 'The choice was her own.' His gaze flicked briefly, rapidly to Calliope, and Foss saw something in the look that brought suffocating fury swelling to his throat.

'You lying, murdering abomination!' Then the fury flared out into a surge of ferocious contempt for the ineffectual spectators around him – sheep they were, all of them, gaping and goggling like dumbwits at a rabble-show, but doing nothing!

'*Damn all of you for useless fools!*' Foss's hand tightened on the pad, and his eyes burned a challenge as he looked at Charn again. 'You'll not have her, you filth. These dullards may fear your kind, but I don't – I'll see you destroyed and your remains ground to dust!'

Someone hissed urgently, '*Foss!*' and something was pushed into his free hand. He grasped at it but at first didn't realise what it was, for Calliope was moaning again, an awful, desolate sound, and Charn was taking a step towards her.

'*Don't dare to touch her!*' Foss was on his feet with one movement – and then he saw what he had been given. A surgeon's knife. The Hospice Master had returned with a medical pack and, seeing what was to do, had snatched out the first thing he could find to serve for a weapon. Metal. Anathema to these creatures. Slowly Foss's hand came up, displaying the knife, and he smiled a chill, relentless smile. 'As I said. Don't *dare*.'

Charn stopped. On a cold, detached level that still survived – if only just – under the mayhem the Sacrament was making of his mind, he sensed that this was no empty threat. Struggling to keep hold of his reason, he forced his mind to focus on his injured arm. When the agony and the wildness began he had slashed his flesh with a sharp-edged stone, countering the Sacrament with another and more physical pain that earthed him and might, for a while, keep him sane. But it couldn't last. Time was running out – and suddenly Foss had snatched the advantage.

Between them, Calliope writhed like a serpent and her voice bubbled from between her blood-streaked lips. '*Please, oh, please . . .*'

'Get back.' Foss made a threatening motion with the knife and had the satisfaction of seeing Charn recoil. Use the pad, put Calliope out of reach of her pain, and then he would deal with *this*. He made to kneel, held the pad towards Calliope's face—

'No!' Charn cried out. 'In the name of pity, *don't do that!*'

The change in his voice was so extraordinary and so unexpected that it sent a jolt of shock through Foss. He looked up, and saw to his astonishment that Charn's face was contorted with terror.

'If you use it,' he said, 'you'll kill her.'

As though to add her own dire emphasis to the warning, Calliope started to sob; huge, deep, racking sobs that shook her entire frame. She was convulsing like a woman in childbirth, and amid the sobbing the pleas were flooding from her again to *take it away, make it stop, oh, please, please, somebody help me* . . .

'What she has done,' Charn said urgently, unsteadily, 'can't be reversed, and can't be cured by any power known to your race or mine. You can't ease her pain. You can't help her.'

For a moment Foss almost believed him. But then the tide of memory flowed again. He had been duped before.

'Liar!' He spat the word contemptuously, and lunged towards Calliope.

The speed and ease with which it happened was horrifying. As Foss tried to clamp the insensator pad on Calliope's mouth, Charn uttered a frenzied shout and sprang at him. Foss reeled back; the two of them collided, swayed, and an appalling sense of cold struck through Foss's body. Panic overtook him; he lashed out with the hand that held the knife, and the blade plunged into Charn's stomach and ripped upwards.

Charn gave a choking gasp and staggered backwards, doubling over. The knife was pulled from Foss's hand – he could see the hilt of it protruding from the wound he had made – and as Charn collapsed to his knees with blood streaming black and viscous through his clutching fingers, the shock of what he had done came home to Foss like a hammerblow. The bravado of all his vengeful and murderous visions shattered before the ugliness of reality, and he felt bile rising in his throat and with it horror. To stab, to strike, to take a life so lightly and effortlessly – it wasn't like science, not like the experiments of the workroom and the Institute – this was brutal and bloody slaughter, and it shouldn't have happened like this, he hadn't intended it to be like this, he wasn't a cold-blooded murderer . . .

Around him was a stunned silence. No one moved; even the Hospice Master was frozen into immobility. They were all staring at him, staring. As if he had committed some monstrous atrocity. He hadn't. He *hadn't*. Charn was on all fours now, coughing rackingly, and streams of blood were running from his mouth. *Internal injuries . . . the creature was dying. Killer. Slayer. Criminal . . .*

Charn's throat and mouth were filling with blood and he knew that the knife had made a lethal wound. It didn't matter. None of it mattered, because something far more lethal was working inside him, and inside Calliope, and there was only one chance, only one thing that could save them both. If she would. If she *could*. If he could reach her . . .

Pain. Yes, yes; there was pain, for the knife-blade was still in him and it was doing far worse to him than it would do to a human body. Eating, burning, dissolving him from within. *Pull it out* – but no, for if he did it might bring back the other agony, the agony of the Sacrament, and that could not be controlled. He could withstand this. *Had* to, at least for the minutes he needed. Before it killed him. Before the Sacrament killed him and Calliope.

Calli . . . It was a desperate, silent projection. *The portal. The darkness. We must find it . . .* Oh it was there, in his mind, occluded at this moment but waiting, calling. Go through, through, and there would be hope . . . *Calli. Calli, help me. There's still time. Come to me. Join with me. If you ever loved me . . .*

Something gripped Foss's ankle, and he gave a startled shout. It was Calliope. She had managed to grasp hold of him, and now she stared up at him with recognition and a desperate entreaty behind her pain-racked gaze.

'Fa . . . father . . .'

'Calli – oh sweet spirits, I—I—'

'Help me . . . it hurts, Father, it hurts so, and I want . . . I want . . .'

'What? What do you want?' Foss was floundering, lost. 'I'll take the pain away from you, Calli! Tell me how, only tell me, and I'll take the pain away!'

'*Nnnh*.' She was trying to say *no*, trying to shake her head, but it was almost beyond her. *Charn. She could hear Charn's voice, he was calling to her, urgently, urgently. Why could she not touch him?*

'Want . . . Charn . . .'

Foss felt sick. 'No. Ah, *no*—'

'Puh . . . uh . . . lease . . . please . . . let me . . . touch . . .'

Lorimer was there suddenly, dropping to a crouch at Calliope's side, taking her wrist, pressing his hand to her heart. 'Sir, we're losing her!' he said in alarm. 'There's almost no pulse; she's slipping away from us!'

'No,' Foss said again. 'No. She *isn't*.'

But she was, and he knew it, and no amount of denial could turn the truth into a lie. He didn't want her to die. He had never wanted that. She *was* his daughter . . .

'Calli, don't!' he pleaded. 'Don't do this to me!'

She tried to laugh, as though he had unwittingly made some great joke. *The portal. She could see it now, and it was calling and Charn was calling. Only one step. But she wouldn't go alone. She wouldn't.*

'Father . . .' Yes, yes; she could form the words, enough to make herself understood. 'Please, Father . . . let me . . . touch Charn. Just once . . . just once . . .'

'You can't deny her, Foss,' the Hospice Master said softly at Foss's ear. 'Not now . . . surely not now?'

Feeling that the world was falling away under him, Foss took hold of Calliope's hand. Charn lay silent and still. He might be dead; there was no way of knowing. *That was what you wanted*, Foss told himself savagely. *Be thankful. You've had your revenge; be thankful.*

Almost roughly, he put his other arm under and around Calliope and lifted her. Just a few handsbreadths, that was all it needed. Not enough to hurt her. Just one touch. What difference could it possibly make?

He laid her down again and, with an inward shrinking that he tried hard to ignore, placed her hand over Charn's motionless fingers.

The shouts of alarm that went up echoed Foss's own cry of

shock as a ball of silver fire erupted out of the air. Foss felt colossal, bone-freezing force slam into him; he was thrown backwards into the arms of Lorimer, and together they fell in a tangle of limbs as the cold fire flared skywards, hurling spears of livid brilliance over the scene. People were calling out, figures running, faces at windows, and as the huge, silent conflagration towered up, the voices of the hospice inmates rang agitatedly from the depths of the building in a distant, ragged chorus. Foss knew nothing of the uproar around him, for he and Lorimer and the Hospice Master were transfixed by the sight of the flames and by the vision that was materialising at their heart. It was a place of darkness, complete and absolute, like a door into a world beyond imagining. Across its threshold Calliope's hand lay over Charn's – but their faces and bodies were changing, the contours flowing and shifting and transmuting into something strange and incredible, something less and yet far more than human. Foss's mouth opened and he made a sound like a lonely dog's whimpering. No one heard him. And the darkness in the portal was deepening – *though how could an absolute become greater still?* – and something else was happening to Calliope and Charn, because the distinctions between them were blurring and he was Calliope and she was Charn and something was merging, merging . . .

He watched in a still, strangely calm hiatus of awe and bewilderment and grief as the vision of the portal began to fade. How long it took, he would never be able to say. It seemed a long, long time. But the moment came at last when it was gone, and the silver fire was gone, the last flicker of it vanishing with a faint, gentle hiss like an etherea lamp quietly extinguished. There was sunlight again, bright and strong and somehow unnatural-looking. There were people, standing like statues, not yet able to move or speak or even think. The fountain sparkled in the distance. On the gravel of the drive there was a smear of black blood and, nearer, a few scattered drops of red. But nothing else.

Later, Foss had no memory of sitting in the Hospice Master's office, nor of the brandy he was given, nor of anything but the view of the garden, framed in the rectangle of a window and vivid with the summer morning. Shock, of course, Lorimer and the Hospice Master said. They had all suffered it, and could expect no less; and it was natural that Foss should be worst affected. No, no; of course they could not explain what had happened. Not to themselves, not to Foss, not to anyone. Better to find a rational explanation; there would be one, there was sure to be. Anything else was out of the question, and with time and a little help from medical science they would all succeed in making themselves believe that. Or blot the memory out, which perhaps would be the wisest course of all.

Lorimer, whose hands were still shaking violently, prepared a draught that would give Foss some immediate relief, then went to distract himself in overseeing the settling of the inmates and attending to any other witnesses who might need a calmative. The Hospice Master, more pragmatically, poured Foss and himself more brandy, thought briefly of trying to engage in some harmless discussion, then decided against it. Foss would recover in his own way and his own time, and in truth at this moment the Hospice Master had no more desire than he for conversation.

He shifted uncomfortably in his chair, folded his hands around his glass, and waited for Philome to arrive in the carriage he had sent for her.

No more pain and no more terror. They were passing, fading into a past time and a past existence whose meaning was losing coherence and becoming no more than a half-remembered echo. Threads unravelling, warp and weft cleaving apart as the loom of her life began to weave a new pattern and a new form . . .

And in the silent stillness, which was neither dark nor light but something else that her human eyes could never have perceived, there was Charn and there was understanding and there was a horizon that stretched away into a shifting, turning mosaic of possibility. The dark portal lay behind them and it no longer had its petrifying power, for she had held his hand and together they had made the choice and crossed the threshold and given themselves up to the unknown. Salvation or destruction. They had taken the gamble, and the Sacrament had kept faith.

Her hand still clasped his. No wounds now; such things were irrelevant, for what they were, what they had become, was not confined by the weaknesses of flesh and blood and bone. Yet she could still touch, and feel; and by silent, mutual consent they joined their other hands, raising them together as though in supplication. Brightness formed and sparked from the lattice of their fingers; at first, with her new and strange way of seeing, it seemed that they held the moon between them, but then there came a change and a flow and a touch like glass, and in their hands was a chalice that shone with a soft, milky aura. The chalice was filled, and in its unearthly wine was every colour and yet none, swirling, surging, a tiny maelstrom with a point of utter stillness at its heart.

'*This is the final pledge, my love. The last challenge and the last demand.*' Her words, his words; no longer possible to distinguish between them, for their minds and thoughts were melding into an eerie union. She looked into the chalice's depths. Memories . . . a bright world and a world of twilight. So many left behind who would never take this step and would never understand and whom she could never know again; and suddenly the terror swept back like a rip-tide, for all that she had ever been was spinning away out of reach and from now, always, always, there could only be Charn and nothing more. The past was lost and the future unknown, and she could feel it closing on her, dragging her into its vortex. *A tall house in an elegant square, bright-lit and warm, and alive with kinship. A birthday party. Kisses and laughter. A little boy, building a tower from his bread-sippets. All lost. All gone . . .*

Yet there were other memories. A sad queen upon her throne, with cobweb curtains billowing and the sweet music of a stately dance playing on the air. That same queen tormented, bewildered, dying for no reason and to no purpose, in cruelty and ugliness . . .

In the chalice a face was forming and, for a moment that lasted no longer than a breath, Griette gazed back at her as the perfume of white flowers touched the air.

She could no longer cry, but it seemed to her that a single tear fell into the still heart of the chalice, and as the ripples of it spread, the maelstrom quieted and she gazed into a sky filled with stars. So vast; so empty. There was nothing there.

Yet everything . . .

She bowed her head, and felt Charn's hair touch her face as her lips touched the surface of the wine. They sipped; a taste; enough. She did not see the chalice fading but she felt it, a quiet dissolution as the star-filled sky spread out around her and became her only universe. Nothing, and everything . . . Then their hands were linked once more, and their mouths and their bodies touched and there was no distinction and there could be no distinction, *for his blood is my blood and my soul is his soul, and we are one, and all that we have left behind will be remembered but never, ever regretted.*

She said, without words (for words were the human way and no longer had any meaning), 'I love you.' She knew his reply, felt it as surely as she felt his touch, and as a smile echoed between them she gazed, with the memory of vision, at the great bowl of the firmament. So *many* stars. So many worlds. So many possibilities . . .

Where shall we go?

Anywhere. Everywhere. How can we tell?

Perhaps we'll be guided. Or not. What are we?

We don't know . . . maybe we never will. But . . .

But . . .?

It hardly seems to matter. Not now. This is right. Somehow, it is right.

It was. There might be sadness for all that was left behind, but the recollection of it was a dream now, and slipping behind them in the way that dreams always did when the dreamer awoke. This was an awakening, a beginning, a sacrament completed. They were one. And this flawless night would never end.